THE HOUSE
AT EVELYN'S
POND

WENDY ORR

ALLEN&UNWIN

Allen & Unwin
83 Alexander Street
Crows Nest NSW 2065
Australia
Phone: (61 2) 8425 0100
Fax: (61 2) 9906 2218
Email: info@allenandunwin.com
Web: www.allenandunwin.com

National Library of Australia
Cataloguing-in-Publication entry:

Orr, Wendy
  The house at Evelyn's Pond.

  ISBN 1 86508 544 8.

  I. Title.

A823.3

Set in 12.5/15 pt Granjon by Bookhouse, Sydney
Printed by Griffin Press, South Australia

10 9 8 7 6 5 4 3 2 1

For Tom, always and forever

ACKNOWLEDGEMENTS

Thanks to:

My parents for five years of answering countless questions, interviewing friends and checking references, and a lifetime of believing in me.

Bert Miechel, Murray Pullar, Jack Ritchie, Ian Waterlow and Jack Wellington, who so generously shared their time and stories to create Bill, Ruth and Fred's war experiences.

David Colwell and the Remembering Project, who helped steer me through selecting Bill and Ruth's war services; the elders of Tom Holloway's WWII memories site and the women of the Air Transport Auxiliary who wrote about their experiences in print or cyberspace.

Alan Bailey, Myrtle Balzer, Ed Coleman, Frances Guinchard, Howard Hardy, Evelyn Pond and Della Stanley for their stories of the Annapolis Valley, from childhood memories to Teachers College training, and to Irene Griffin for sharing her arrival there as a war bride.

The many friends who shared a story or information to create Jane's life after leaving Canada: Lyn Armstrong,

Veronique Froelich, Lyn and Andrew McClelland, Rosalind Price, Jenny Reid, Chris Sutton, Raynor Thomas, Anne Witney and Shirley Woelfell.

For Ruth's last trip, thanks to Tom McCormack of the White Waltham Airfield, who not only answered questions but offered to take me flying; Pat Smith, Mary Backhouse and Bob Draper for Ruth's Literary Tour, and John Tempest for explaining the funeral and legal details.

Samantha Coker-Godson, for allowing me to appropriate her acupuncture dream.

Roy Vickers for permission to describe his gallery.

The interlibrary loan officer of the Murray Valley Regional Library and the Cobram staff for their patience and help, and the many friends and strangers who answered questions, loaned books and let me discuss my characters with them.

And especially: my trusted first readers, who loved and criticised: Pamela Freeman, Debbie Golvan, Kathy Harris and Kerry Millard, and my editor Julia Stiles, whose skill and perception made the cuts almost bloodless and the additions a delight.

Chapter
ONE

$\mathcal{E}$mergency or not, it seems poor planning to embark on a thirty-six hour trip—she's added it up, counting the waits—without a book. By most people's terms, if not her own, Jane is a reader: four from the library as well as the book group selection every month, with extras at Christmas and birthdays. Books from her mother, who will want to know what she has read on the plane; once she's asked about the flight itself, Ruth will say, 'What did you read?'

Would have said.

Their last phone call, the Sunday before her mother left Halifax on her charter flight—a 'blue-rinse tour,' she'd described it, a literary tour of England—Ruth had discussed, not how she felt about returning to her birthplace after fifty-two years in Canada, but what she was reading: '...new author, absolutely brilliant—I'll mail it to you when I get back.'

'I thought you'd be getting into the mood, *Pride and Prejudice* and all that.'

'In fact I did read *Wives and Daughters* again the other day—I'm more fond of Elizabeth Gaskell than I used to be—but I don't think one needs to swot for a holiday!'

'And you're looking forward to seeing Mary?' ('The one person in England whom I have any real desire to see again,' Ruth had described her.)

'Very much. Some trepidation about the tour, I admit.'

'I wish…'

'I know, my dear, so do I. Never mind—enforced sociability will be good for me, might curb my crabbit old woman tendencies. As for the reading, I'm taking a few old favourites, one for each region. Oxford is the difficulty—selecting something relevant without absolutely wallowing in nostalgia.'

Nostalgia is precisely what Jane can't risk now. It's not so much the shame of breaking down amongst strangers, it's the fear of the unknown. She simply doesn't know whether, when the news has finished percolating through to her brain, she's going to be strong enough, smart enough, to do what has to be done. How can anyone know until it happens? There are no rehearsals for the end of a mother's life.

On a hazy Chelsea morning, Rupert Bear is ready to embark on another bold flying adventure. He loads his friends into the balloon basket, but the teddy playing Edward Trunk takes too much room and is unceremoniously plunked onto the windowsill. 'You can watch us in the sky,' says Rupert, 'and wave.' He drags a chair over to reach the catch and open the window; then, balancing the basket on the ledge with one hand, scrambles up beside it.

Nanny, who's only left the nursery for a moment, opens the door to see Ruth framed in the second-floor window. A precarious basket of toys balances beside her.

With great presence of mind Nanny does not shriek the

child's name. Her traitorous heart is the only noise as she tip-toes across the floor and, with a quiet movement that feels like a lunging dive, slips her arms around the small body.

Edward Trunk, aka Bear, lurches headfirst into the garden bed below, flattening two yellow and one pink antirrhinums. Nanny, with her struggling charge clutched tight against her, collapses into the chair as she kisses, smacks, and kisses again. Ruth goes on screaming for Bear.

'That's where you'd have ended up in another moment!' snaps Nanny. 'Then you'd have been sorry!'

'Wouldn't!' shouts the four year old, who till the end of her life will have difficulty admitting being wrong. 'We were going flying!'

'I should have gone to live with my sister like I was going to,' Nanny mutters. 'Your father was never this much trouble when he was young!'

Ruth stops bellowing. 'Tell me a story about when Papa was a little boy,' she begs. She doesn't believe these stories but is fascinated by the unlikely thought that Papa, his sisters and brother were once children and Nanny a girl, 'pretty though I say it myself—I could have married when I left your grandfather's house, but it wasn't to be; I went to Mrs Bartholomew when she had her first and was there ten years...'

Ruth fades out until she hears the magic words, 'Then your Papa asked me to come and look after you, and you know the rest.'

'I was born and I was a tiny little baby and you came to be my Nanny.' Though there is a satisfying feeling that this is not necessarily the end of the story. It could also be a beginning.

'That's enough stories,' Nanny says briskly. 'Now, if you can be a good girl, we'll go and rescue Bear.'

She doesn't think it necessary to mention the escapade to the child's parents, but is relieved a few weeks later when *The Times* returns to favour and the *Daily Express*—and Rupert Bear with it—are banished from the Townsend household.

Although that's the last time Ruth attempts to fly off a window-sill, her childhood is always lived from one story to another. Thin armed and gangly legged, dark and sprite-lively, she is Peter challenging Hook, Kim waiting for the Great Game, Lorna Doone watching for John Ridd. Anyone except a cherished only child of elderly parents: father in the City; mother in the house and garden organising the daily, the cook and the gardener; Nanny, too much of a fixture to leave when her charge goes to school, pottering about as needed. But Ruth is waiting for her true life of adventure and romance to whisk her away from the staidly pretty streets of Chelsea.

However, not everyone is content to wait for adventure to come to them, and one May morning when Ruth is eleven, a twenty-seven year old typist from Hull flies out of Croydon Airport and across the world to Australia. Her twenty days doesn't beat the record, but Amy Johnson is the first woman to fly the route alone, and the world's press sees her as an antidote to the grim years of depression: a flash of light and hope. She becomes a heroine.

It's the first current event Ruth becomes aware of and she throws herself into it with passion, following the reports in her father's *Times*, spending pocket money on the *Daily Express* to start an Amy Johnson scrapbook with pictures of Amy as a child, Amy as an aviatrix, the green Gipsy Moth *Jason*. Nightmares of gaping whale jaws follow the 'GIRL FLIER'S FIGHT FOR LIFE' headline: 'SIX FEET ABOVE SHARK-INFESTED SEAS', and ecstasy four days later at the 'poor little typist's' victorious landing. On the August night that 'Our Amy' arrives in London, waving royally to rapturous crowds from Croydon to Park Lane, Nanny sits up late with her knitting, casually barring the door against girls who intend to run away to see their idols face to face.

The scrapbook continues, and though she begins to cheat, adding pictures of other aviators and aircraft, the Gipsy Moth and its young pilot remain her favourite. (For some time, however, Ruth believes that being a typist is a prerequisite for learning to fly, and studies anything to do with typewriters as assiduously as the article in her mother's *Woman's Magazine* on the practicalities of garaging an aeroplane at home.)

Life nonetheless continues on its normal course. Her mother does not rush out and buy a little plane with folding wings; Ruth takes a train to boarding school instead of a plane to Australia. She also grows taller, grows breasts and surprising urges, and is sent to Switzerland to finishing school. It is 1935. The school is not especially posh; there are no princesses or duke's daughters, though it's as dull and regimented as her parents could wish and the girls do learn a little stilted French in spite of the forbidden whispered English. But Madame has a problem: due to unforeseen circumstances she has accepted three more girls than the dormitories can hold. Ruth will be boarding in the village—although Madame assures that the Le Blancs' Calvinist eye will be just as watchful as her own. Ruth can take the toboggan down the hill in the evening and walk up again next morning after petit déjeuner.

This is Ruth's first snow, not melting London sleet but real snow heaped on the ground, fresh and glowing in the moonlight. 'Sit—*comme ça*,' says Madame, bundling her onto the sled. 'Remember you are a young lady. The path will take you straight to the village.'

The dour instructions don't breathe a hint of the exhilaration of adrenalin and fear, of the extraordinary flying freedom, cheeks burning, eyes watering, breath catching in the cold. Around a bend the toboggan skids sideways, tumbling her into the deep and untouched whiteness—virgin in virgin snow, thinks Ruth, reading aloud from the book of her life. Sprawled on her back, she's alone in this new world of mountains, dark trees and cloudless spangled sky—stars as they are meant to be seen, undimmed by the dull glow that is London at night; she can almost feel the world turning. Snow to cool her burning face, snow on her tongue, snow to taste, to drink, to roll in...She is Artemis, goddess of mountains, her life finally a little closer to the story she weaves of it.

∽

At Sydney airport, pacing the endless blue-carpeted corridors, Jane chooses the comfort of calculations. Ian would not have stood sentimentally at the window to watch her plane leave Melbourne: give him fifteen minutes between departure lounge and carpark, two and a half hours' drive...by the time she's finished a rather stale glass of fresh orange juice in the cheerless lounge, he will be home.

If she could be sure of his exact moment of arrival she'd call. Already it seems another era since she left, as if she's been floating in time as well as space; she needs the grounding of his voice. But standing at a pay phone to hear her own answer message is more likely to bring visions of twisted freeway wrecks than comfort—she knows the way her mind works. Better to imagine the more likely truth. He'll have changed into overalls and gumboots, not trusting nineteen year old Jason, Sue's son next door, to check the cows as they should be checked. By now, with the first boarding call to Jakarta and Singapore, he'll be walking around chilly paddocks with the susurrus of chewing cuds and bovine breath, quietly peering at hindquarters or investigating signs of suspicious restlessness. August, the height of calving, is not a good time to be away.

All being well, no calves to pull or the vet to phone for a caesar, no cows paralysed from pressure of a too-large head, he'll return to the house, make a cup of tea, maybe a sandwich for early lunch, and go back to sleep. It was midnight before they'd gone to bed, two-thirty when they got up—more than enough excuse for a nap.

Then his own tea to get when he comes in tonight—no preparing dishes for the freezer as she had last time, no stocking the shelves. His mother will have him over for meals, make a casserole or two and a cake, and Sue, busy as she is herself, will help out in the same way. Neighbours always cosset a man left on his own. Women left temporarily alone are presumed, and often truly, to enjoy the solitude and temporary relief from routines of caring and so are rarely invited out. However, at this time of year Ian is likely to be too tired to accept invitations, preferring to make himself a steak sandwich—his only culinary endeavour—at whatever time he makes it in for the night.

'He's fifty-six,' she reminds herself, 'old enough to look after himself for a couple of weeks!'

It's difficult not to worry. Twenty cows are in milk already, standing lonely in that big dairy twice a day, the five heifers amongst them twitchy and nervous at the unaccustomed liberties taken with their bodies. Ian is good with animals and careful of being kicked, but the best stockman can get in the way of a crazed heifer's hoof. In the next three weeks thirty more heifers and one hundred and forty older cows will join the herd. Pray for small-headed calves, nose down for easy delivery and no cold southern winds to shiver the babies and fever the mothers. Most years she'd add a wish against cold rain, but the irrigation farmers in south-eastern Australia are now entering the second year of drought and getting wet is the least of their problems.

Child and adult, Jane has spent most of her life on farms— latitude and topography aside, there's not that much difference between the Annapolis and Goulburn valleys—but she feels a spurt of anger now, anger so violent it leaves her momentarily nauseated, at lives held constantly to ransom by the sheer caprice of the weather.

'If we'd just had rain I could have met Mom in London.' Pointless to think, impossible not to. They'd planned it for nearly two years, since the demise of Ruth's last dachshund. 'I'm too old to replace him,' she'd said, 'it wouldn't be fair, and it will leave me freer for travel.' As well as visiting cousin Mary, they'd have rented a car for an itinerary of missed historic sites, a little nostalgia, a touch of laying ghosts to rest. Then El Niño had intervened, terrifying Ian into thoughts of barren land and bankruptcy, and Ruth had gone with her busful of genteel Nova Scotian ladies.

The irony, of course, being that now Jane will meet her in London after all, though meet isn't quite the right word; with a trip home thrown in for bonus, though home isn't quite the right word now either. The money that had been inaccessible for fun is suddenly available and acceptable for misery.

On a rainy September day in 1936 Ruth goes up to Oxford to read English, and Beryl Markham, carrying a sprig of Scottish heather and Amy Johnson's husband's lucky watch, sets off on the first solo flight from England to New York. For Ruth it adds a further frisson to the drama of her own journey—women, it seems, can do anything men can and sometimes do it first. The later news that the aviatrix, while successfully navigating the North Atlantic, has ended her flight ignominiously in the mud of a Cape Breton bog seems less significant. Nova Scotia does not seem likely ever to cross Ruth's horizons; flying remains a dream.

But a rapidly approaching dream in the person of Miles Ashby.

Miles, standing on the steps of the Bodleian Library in an instant that remains forever framed in Ruth's memory, is dark and wiry with a thin, intense face, an inexhaustible, restless energy and an air of natural leadership. He is on his way to the Flying Club. It is inevitable that she will fall in love with him.

He takes her up for the first time one absurdly springlike November morning—typical of Miles, Ruth thinks, that he can coerce even nature into stage-managing his performance—but grey skies would have made no difference. Flying is noisier, colder, smellier than she's imagined, but when she steps out onto the field at the end of it she's determined to return as often as she can, and preferably as the pilot.

Suspecting that flying is not quite what her parents had in mind as a university hobby and seeing no reason to upset them unnecessarily, her weekly letters neglect to mention that most of her allowance is now devoted to flying lessons. Once, when they visit her rooms at St Hilda's, she has to borrow a dress because her own would have shocked by its shabbiness; after that she saves enough to have a presentable outfit when she returns home for Christmas and the summer holidays. Working out the flying time she can buy for the price of a new hat and gloves, she quickly adopts a bohemian, hatless image.

By the time Miles leaves Oxford to join the air force in the June of 1938, Ruth is the proud possessor of a Class A flying permit—she can fly solo. She's dreamed of the airy freedom, of being at one with her machine and the skies, of being in complete control of that power and speed. It's one of the few things in life that surpasses expectation. Her final university year is dominated by adding hours, and by September 1939 when civilian aircraft are grounded by the declaration of war, she has sixty-one hours of solo flying in her logbook. Torn between guilt and excitement, she wonders whether this is the moment she's been waiting for all her life.

Germany's invasion of Poland is overshadowed for the Townsends by the presentation of this logbook and the licence behind it: 'I'm joining the air force,' their only daughter announces.

Mama bursts into tears.

'I very much doubt,' Papa says weightily, 'whether even Mr Hitler can induce the RAF to commit the folly of allowing young women inside aircraft.'

'If I already know how—'

'You know nothing whatsoever about fighting. That's what counts in war: killing the other chap before he kills you, and it doesn't matter whether you're using an aeroplane or a bayonet. Women simply don't have that sort of courage; if you must do something useful, be a nurse. There'll be plenty of wounded young men to comfort.'

'I imagine that flying would be most unhealthy for women,' Mama says anxiously. Childbearing, Ruth guesses, although she is no more likely to ask for clarification than her mother is to volunteer it.

The evening is uncomfortably silent. Only Nanny, remembering the moonlight vigil and scrapbook, is unsurprised.

In the end, Papa is right—the RAF doesn't want women pilots. Amy Johnson, Amelia Earhart, Beryl Markham and other pioneers of the air notwithstanding, it is decreed that women are too highly strung, too weak both physically and mentally, to fly military aircraft. Join the Women's Auxiliary air force, Ruth is told; a fighting force is kept in the air by the strength of its ground support and women can be a useful part of that, in anything from ops rooms and offices to maintaining the floating silver whales of barrage balloons (Flossie and Blossom, Chelsea residents call theirs) or as drivers for the men who will do the flying and the leaders who organise them. Out of principle and pique Ruth refuses; from lassitude and some desire to make her mother happy, she instead joins the Women's Voluntary Services. It is ladylike but worthwhile work and fills the days through the strained calm of that autumn, when the country is at war but nothing seems to happen. There are new rules and officious notices but no invasion, rationing but no bombing, many rumours but little news.

Christmas brings an invitation from Miles to a party at his parents' home in St John's Wood. The emotion Ruth had felt for him at Oxford had been a mixture of romance and hero-worship, and because Miles had been seeing several other women at the same time and sleeping with three of them, he hadn't been whole-hearted in his efforts to seduce her. It's over a year since she's seen him, now a handsome uniformed flying officer explaining the intricacies of aeronautics and aerial combat. Hero-worship flares into passion; they spend two nights together before he leaves for France in April 1940. He is not a gentle or a patient lover but Ruth, having nothing to compare him with, is infatuated enough not to mind. Poetry might overstate the sensation, she decides, but sex is not unpleasant—and there is something patriotically thrilling about giving a man his heart's desire before he flies off into mortal combat. It will be the last time the thought of mortal combat rings with echoes of chivalric gallantry; she will recognise courage in the future but little romance.

On 9 May she receives an enthusiastic letter full of the wonders of the new improved Hurricane fighter plane and schoolboy glee at having shot down his first Messerchmidt: *flying out of Longuyon when I spotted him—chased him low over a valley and got off a telling shot as he tried to crest the hill. The kite was on fire by the time he hit the ground.*

It strikes her simultaneously that this is another man's death Miles is glorying in and that identical letters are being written in German about the killing of some of his own comrades. For the first time she understands that the only luck these young men can hope for is to continue killing other men, day after day until the war ends, and she wonders how they will pick up normal lives and loves again when that day comes.

For Miles the problem is irrelevant: the day after his letter arrives, the Luftwaffe begin their blitzkrieg over France, pouring wave after wave of bombers, dive-bombers and fighters across the sky. The Ashbys tell her that he'd reached a score of six by 14 May, the day he was shot down over the bridgehead at Sedan. Is that supposed to assuage the grief? The most horrifying thing is that, ever so slightly, it does. It doesn't change her loss; it hasn't even affected the humiliating defeat of the French and the British Expeditionary Force supporting them—Miles's Hurricane is merely one of five hundred lost before retreat is complete—but there is still a fierce satisfaction in knowing that he accounted for a few of the enemy before he died.

Two weeks later the WVS is called on to serve refreshments to the troop trains coming home from Dunkirk. Ruth sees men who set out for France as a disciplined army and were driven back to the Channel's edge, strafed on beaches, boats and water with apparent impunity by the German Luftwaffe. They have been rescued piecemeal off those beaches by troopship, fishing boat and private yacht, and although tales of courage, of extraordinary resourcefulness and determination will soon circulate to become a legend of English grit, at the moment there is little to see but defeat. These are men with shocked, blank faces; men who've seen friends blown into fragments of flesh and muck, seen them die messily, obscenely, in the stench of blood and fear; men who've lost their helmets, their weapons and most of all their pride. Ruth sees for the first time that England might lose this war, and although she isn't arrogant enough to think that she can singlehandedly do much to change that, she does know that she has to do something more active towards it.

She is still determined not to enlist in one of the regular services, although her reasons have now altered: she needs to be able to leave the instant the Air Transport Auxiliary accepts her application.

The ATA, unlike the WAAF, is not a female branch of a male service. Originally designed as an alternative air system in case air raids or invasion destroy the roads and communications systems, it has quickly been directed into the ferrying of aircraft from factory to airfield, from airfield to factory for repairs, or airfield to airfield—any routine flying which does not need the specialised skills of a fighter pilot or bomber captain. Many of its first pilots are men determined to keep flying when age or disability has rendered them unfit for the RAF, but a female commissioner of the Civil Air Guard can see no reason why women pilots should not join them. Pauline Gower, a small, indomitable woman who took up flying after being told she was not strong enough for any active sport, and who in a tragic twist of fate will die in childbirth shortly after the end of the war, has over 2000 hours of flying time, earned in an aerial circus and her own air-taxi service. Begrudgingly, the ministry allows her to establish a female contingent of eight elite pilots.

There is a predictably enraged outcry at the temerity of women 'without wit enough to scrub floors' stealing men's jobs by attemping to pilot planes. 'The hand that rocks the cradle wrecks the kite,' someone quips and is quoted around dinner tables across Britain. However, the women prove so capable of safely ferrying Tiger Moths to the airfields of southern England that they are soon allowed to deliver these small open trainers to northern Scotland, frozen-faced flying that the men are probably quite happy to relegate to their female couterparts.

And, as the phoney war ends and more pilots and more aircraft are needed—perhaps as the country realises that winning this war will take every bit of effort from every available person—aptitude begins to outweigh genitalia. Both the number of female pilots and the types of planes they're allowed to fly are increased, giving Ruth some hope that one day her offering of sixty-one hours' experience will be smiled upon. In the meantime she will drive ambulances.

She passes her test on the second attempt in a brute of a van with grinding gears and faulty clutch, though most of her driving will be in the family's more amenable Austin Seven. The war, briefly glimpsed on that train from Dunkirk, seems contained to the battle in the skies overhead and, despite the loss of Miles and two other Oxford friends, on the clear bright days of that summer it is difficult to believe that the pretty silver planes trailing white tails across the blue enclose flesh-and-blood young men duelling to the death. Children evacuated to the safety of the country are returning to their parents in London, which shows no sign of being bombed or invaded; Ruth's most dramatic moment so far has been delivering a pregnant woman to a nursing home in Hertfordshire and wondering whether she'll have to deliver the baby as well. Despite the sure knowledge that a roadside birth would be a terrible experience for mother, baby and probably herself, she can't help a flicker of disappointment when the trip ends without the slightest twinge of labour pain or gasping.

That is July. On 23 August the Luftwaffe carries out its first all-night bombing raid on London: the Blitz has begun. The Townsends' whippet doesn't recover from its hysterics and has to be put to sleep.

Two weeks later, at the height of the fiercest raid yet and in the midst of arguing that Mr Hitler is not going to force her to spend one more minute in 'that mole's burrow in the garden' ('the safety of the Anderson shelter,' Papa retorts), Nanny collapses and dies. No one is comforted by the thought that, at eighty-seven, her heart would not have ticked on much longer even without Hitler's interference—and Ruth, who'd left only moments earlier for night duty at the ambulance station, is particularly bitter. If she'd been out saving someone's life, she thinks, she wouldn't feel so frustrated, but the bombs that night had once again concentrated on the slums of the East End, so that she had done nothing but play cards and wait for something to happen in Chelsea, while Nanny died of fright.

However, as autumn slides into long and bitter winter, Ruth sees enough horror and drama to make up for a lifetime of whist. The war has long since lost any glamour: Mama spends her days in endless queues for food and her evenings knitting balaclavas for the troops; Papa, the war having providentially delayed his retirement, leaves for the City every morning with bowler hat and umbrella but spends his nights patrolling for black-out infringements (he prefers to stay out of the air-raid warden's post since the council decided that it would be cheaper to contribute to funeral expenses than strengthen the shelter). Nights are the scream of sirens, the thunder of heavy aircraft, the tympani of guns trying to bring them down, the crashing of bombs and the flare of fires; mornings are the tinkle of broken glass being swept in the street, children searching for trophy shrapnel, and a sense of thankfulness at seeing familiar landmarks intact. Despite the determination to carry on with life as usual, everyone is grey-faced with lack of sleep; nearly a third of the Townsends' neighbours have very sensibly fled to the country, increasing the sense of beleaguerment of those who remain.

Driving through the horrors of an often unrecognisable city, dodging craters that have swallowed buses, burning gas mains, piles of rubble and blood-stained debris, losing her way around unexpected detours and torn-up streets, Ruth feels some sense of adventure and considerable frustration. She has little knowledge and less equipment, carrying her own bottle of brandy for shock and scissors for bandages, but quite unable to supply the comforting touch and jollying manner that a bombing victim might respond to.

'Oh, I am vexed!' an old woman tells her, one arm limp in her lap and blood streaming down her face as Ruth attempts to work out the best way to reach the hospital around the blockades. 'It's taken me six months to finish a layette for my grandson's baby and now it's gone with the house. Where ever will I find the wool now?'

Vexed! Ruth thinks, intrigued at the understatement as well as the focus.

However, despite tragedy and sleeplessness, there are still concerts, cinemas, bookshops and dances; London is full of young men in uniforms from around the world determined to enjoy life while they can and Ruth occasionally enjoys it with them.

Going straight from a dance to the ambulance station on the clear, full-moon night of 10 May, Ruth tries to remember what London looked like when nights were lit by streetlamps and house windows instead of bomb flares and fires. The siren starts as she reaches the door; by morning over three thousand people are dead or seriously injured; the House of Commons is gutted, the British Museum, Westminster Abbey and the Tower are all damaged. On Monday Papa leaves for work unshaven, a symbol of the city's shocked exhaustion and a forcible reminder for Ruth of her parents' humanity and corollary mortality.

The next night there is no raid, nor the one after that; it will be a long time before the end of the war and London is not yet through with horror, but the worst of the Blitz is over. Ruth continues to transport patients with minor injuries in her little green Austin, drives the occasional dignitary in an ambulance service vehicle and spends the rest of her time washing teacups and floors. Nothing that she does couldn't be done just as well by anyone with rudimentary driving skills or a mop. She writes to Pauline Gower at the ATA and receives a refusal that is so encouraging she continues to apply every three months until finally she receives the letter requesting her to present herself for a flying test.

It's over two years since she's flown; at the back of her mind she thinks that even if she doesn't get in, the chance to be up in the air again will be worth the disappointment.

It was Mary who'd phoned. 'My dear,' she began, which was close enough to a blow to the midriff to knock Jane into the old chair by the hall phone.

Twenty-nine years ago, in that most significant summer of her life, Jane had stayed with Ruth's cousin, before Ian and with him, but there'd been nothing but brief Christmas notes since and she could not remember Mary ever calling her dear. The best she could hope for, in that split second before the sentence was pronounced, was that the story had not yet ended and there was still a chance to say goodbye.

But even as she hung up, as she told Ian and tried to believe it herself, even before—responsible big sister—she picked up the phone again and began to dial the long sequences of numbers that would wake Mike in Yellowknife, Rick in Toronto, she knew that if it wasn't the best she could hope for, it was also not the worst she'd dreaded. The worst would have been the scenario that had been at the back of her mind for years, certainly since her father died and maybe before: a call from the hospital—Ruth incapacitated, unable to live on her own. For two years now, before Jane goes to bed, when she's washed the dishes and made two weak cups of tea, she has switched on the computer to check the email. And for two years, as she waits for the screech of dialling, the password acceptance, she's wondered what she'll do if her mother's message isn't there.

The notes had been caustic at first: *Aged P; miraculous survival* (the message went to all three offspring, after Rick had set up Ruth's machine and talked Ian into the new gadgetry as well, but it was tacitly expected that responsibility for the daily check and reply was Jane's, being the daughter). After the initial resistance, Ruth had begun to enjoy the technology; there were sometimes three or four brief messages waiting in Jane's mail. *Re: Exotic Australians and Canadians. A red cardinal arrived in the orchard today, a beautiful and bright exotic. Exotic seems an infinitely kinder word than alien, migrant or the old dp; unfortunate that in humans the word has come to mean dancers, with the* x *a euphemism for* r.

Which suggested that Ruth and her wit were both alive and well, and the question—just where will Mom go if she can't live on her own?—could be shelved again.

Last November's devastating ice storm had brought it to a head, in Jane's mind if not her mother's. The only television news she'd seen had said, 'New York and Toronto,' accompanied by images of iced and buckling electricity pylons in what looked like rural Quebec, but the same freezing rain and wind had frozen the Valley too, with phones and electricity off intermittently for a week. 'She'll be fine,' Rick had said, from his thermostat-controlled, twelfth-floor apartment with power and phones intact, and Jane could not big-sister bully him into travelling two thousand kilometres to check just how fine their mother actually was. 'If we haven't heard by Sunday,' he'd agreed, but on Saturday morning Ruth had called Mike on Gordon Gillespie's cell phone and the panic was over.

But images of Ruth unconscious on the floor, Ruth freezing to death in a snow-bound house, Ruth breaking a hip on an icy path, had lingered in Jane's mind; briefly, she'd schemed alternatives, which her mother, without exactly consenting, hadn't refused to consider for the future.

The Australian government, however, was not interested in Jane and Ian deciding that they could live quite happily with Ruth in a granny flat off the house, not interested in hearing that Ruth could support herself without burdening social services. And though Jane had tried to describe the impossibility of her mother moving to the Arctic where Mike charted potential-rich maps of underground oil, or to Rick's one-bedroom city apartment, the numbers were what counted, and the numbers said that Ruth, with twice as many offspring in Canada as Australia, had no need to come.

One of the more pointless things she'd thought about as she'd waited online for Qantas to arrange this present, complicated route with the further complications of proof-of-death faxes for a bereaved fare, and again as she'd tried unsuccessfully to call Mary back to confirm the arrival time. Ruth would have died, she reminds herself now, wherever she'd lived.

But immigration officers are easier to hate than a long-neglected God, or death.

She doesn't even know how her mother died—in her sleep, Mary said. But even at eighty, even in their sleep, people die of something. Jane knows the terms, we all do, in these days of statistics in newspapers, telephone appeals and 'ER'—cardiovascular accident, cardiac arrest, cerebral thrombosis—but she thinks, heart or head? and hopes it was the former. Ruth wouldn't have liked not being able to think, especially during something as dramatic as death.

By mid 1942, despite the loss of Amy Johnson into the cold grey waters of the Thames estuary, the ATA has seventy women pilots—and Ruth, at last, is one of them. She has passed her medical, signed the secrecy statement, studied map reading, meteorology, the technical detail of aircraft engines and the position of barrage balloons protecting towns or factories from enemy pilots but equally lethal to friendly. She has a navy blue uniform of tunic and slacks—the latter with strict and often ignored instructions to be worn on duty only—as well as skirt with black silk stockings, and a warm flying suit with boots for cold altitudes.

She tells herself that she's no longer the dreamy girl who could find ecstasy in the smell of a leather flying helmet, secretly sniffing before pulling it on and admiring the goggled looking-glass pilot, but the day she gains her wings that dreamer finds fulfilment.

After her initial training and observation, she's posted to a small all-female base near Southampton, where she fits in easily though never makes close friends. She takes a room at the local yacht club, which seems less confining than digs with a family and less irksome than learning to cook and housekeep with one of her fellow pilots. She has never been so happy. Between the base and the various servicemen at the yacht club, there is plenty of companionship, and the flying is all she could ask. Although most flights are short local deliveries, no more than half an hour in the air, over the next three years she will deliver up to five aircraft a day, flying thirteen days out of fifteen, fifty weeks a year, whenever the weather permits and often when it's doubtful.

Starting on the simplest single-engined craft, she works her way through the trickier or heavier ones, eventually flying over sixty different types of planes, some of them, to the astonishment of watching RAF pilots, with no more introduction than the instruction book taped to her knee. Her favourite, however, will always be the Spitfire. Snug in the cockpit with the Merlin's power at her fingertips and the hum of it in her ears, a rudder so sensitive that the plane seems to sense her commands as it lifts and soars through the skies, she can hardly believe that she should have so much fun and get paid for doing so.

By the time the war ends she will be qualified to fly everything except the big four-engined bombers (her shameful secret regret, matching her secret exhilaration at the beginning, is that she will never join this select band of women). Female pilots, although still too hysterical for combat duty, have by now become stable enough to ferry all types of aircraft from base to base. Only the huge flying boats of Coastal Command are exempt, in case honour is compromised by overnight stops amongst mixed crews—ironic, Ruth thinks later, as if fate had determined not to let her meet Bill until the time was right. But since everything is so exactly right when that time comes, she has no real complaints.

❧

Bill is twenty-one when the war starts. His younger brother Albert joins the merchant marine; he's always leaned more towards the sea than the farm, going out with his fishing uncles, the ruddy-faced, white-haired MacTavishes, from the time he could stand up straight in an oilskin.

Bill has never had Bert's feel for cold water, and his father's stories of the trenches of Givenchy—a battle entwined with their family history; a tragedy without which, ironically, he might never have been born—have left him determined to keep whatever space he can between himself and mud. He decides on the air force.

He has few illusions about life in the services, but flying, he imagines, would be the closest a man could ever come to freedom. About whether or not he should go at all there is no real decision; he knows little of the background politics but recognises evil when he sees it. Canada seems a long way from the newsreels of devastated Poland, but she is nonetheless at war and duty, or fear of not being seen to adhere to it, is a powerful motivator. Barely admitted is the desire to test himself in this ultimate challenge of self-identity: the gruesome question of whether he will be capable of either heroism or self-preservation. Although he suspects that in the end one or the other of those qualities will bring him to it, he has no desire to face killing another human being—even at school he was never much of a fighter—which is another factor in the air force's favour.

Is it in protest at losing two sons to Europe that George Dubois falls off a haystack one bright October day and, fracturing a thigh, keeps the oldest at home for another seven months? If so, it's more effective than he could have planned: by May, when he's fit again and Belgium, Luxembourg, the Netherlands and France have all fallen to the Nazis, the Canadian air force's new training program is badly overcrowded. At the Applevale recruiting station, after enlistment, medical and interview, Bill's name is simply placed on a waiting list. 'A month or two,' they tell him but in the end it's four and he's begun to wonder whether the war will pass him by completely when September rolls around again. His call-up finally comes on the day that Ruth's Nanny dies, although of course Bill is aware only of the ending of this part of his own life. Like most young men, he has no conception that the ending could be final.

The Annapolis Valley in the fall is serene and beautiful; in the small community of Evelyn's Pond the whitewashed houses, grey through winter and spring, stand bright and clean against leaves of scarlet and gold. It is difficult enough to believe that the rest of the world exists, impossible to understand that it's being torn apart. Bill has worked quietly and efficiently through the seasons; has spread the manure from last winter's dung heap and cleaned the barn out fresh for the next; cut, raked and carted hay, oiled harnesses, sharpened ploughs, nailed down stray shingles on roofs of house and barn, and chopped cords of wood for the furnace. Now he sends the last of the apple harvest off for cider and knows that the farm is as ready as it can be for his father to manage on his own.

He takes the train from Halifax in a grey November rain, arriving in Toronto on Remembrance Day. He is overwhelmed by the size and vibrancy of the city. The stench of his barracks, however, is familiar:

> *Air Craftsman 2nd Class W Dubois*
> *RCAF Manning Pool, No 1*
> *Toronto*
> *Ontario*
> *18 November 1940*

Dear Mother, Dad, Grandpère and Louise
This is a pretty fancy address but if you're picturing me in a fancy place to match you'd be wrong. Would you believe it's really the exhibition grounds—and my bedroom is in the bullpen! If you write to Bert before I do, tell him that after sleeping with five hundred other fellows and the smell of about the same number of bulls, I'll never complain about sharing a room with him again.

At least I've got a top bunk—the guy below me asked yesterday how much I weighed. I think he's worried that I'll crash right through one night and crush him! Anyway, I can tell you now exactly what I do weigh: one hundred and sixty-nine pounds. The medical officer found out a lot more than that but it would make everyone blush if I told you the rest of it. We also got some shots that might have been left over from when the bulls were in here; I didn't get sick from them but a couple of guys passed out cold.

I had the idea we were going to learn to fly, but instead they keep us busy with marching, standing at attention, saluting the flag, saluting anyone who looks like an officer, more marching, lots of PT, polishing buttons and boots, making our bunks, and then in case we've forgotten since the last time, a bit more marching. It doesn't look as if we'll see an aeroplane till we get to the Initial Training School in a few weeks time, and that's when they'll decide which of us can try to be pilots, or navigators or air gunners or whatever, or if they think you're not fit to go into the air at all and get stuck in ground crew.

The streetcars come right into the exhibition ground, so I went into town with some of the other guys on Saturday. You can use the one ticket all day and I felt quite the city fellow by the end of it. You wouldn't believe the city at night! Yonge Street is just full of lights and noise; even the fellows from Halifax thought it was something.

I trust that you are all managing fine without me. I miss you all but so far I am having a very pleasant time.

In fact he's having the time of his life. Despite the regulations, the marching, the enforced communal life, Bill is a young man away from home for the first time. Away from the farm that has been not only his past but the whole of his future, he is overwhelmed by an extraordinary sense of freedom. He's never before realised the weight of the land he loves, the burden of knowing that his father, a townsman at heart, has always felt himself to be husbanding it only until his son is ready take over. Now, as Bill moves on from the Manning Pool to initial training, pitting himself against the ignominy of airsickness or the treachery of the Link flight simulator—a terrifying bubble designed to destroy the aspirations of pilot hopefuls—there is no one depending on him but himself. Perhaps that's why he performs so well. 'You'll be doing pilot training, for sure!' his friend Bob insists, desperately practising standing on one foot with his eyes closed for next day's medical.

However, the powers that be decree that Bill, who has joined the air force to be a fighter pilot—a dashing and daring flying machine—will become a navigator, destined to fly heavy bombers. It's still aircrew; he's too relieved to be disappointed. Anything is better than joining the small band of white-faced young men blinking back tears as they are posted back for ground-crew training.

'You should have flubbed the math like I told you!' says Bob, who will die soon after on his first solo flight. 'You know the real math brains always end up navigators.'

Bill doesn't believe this, but it wouldn't have made any difference if he had. He can never quite comprehend that the men studying in the bathrooms long after lights out, coming to him desperate for explanation of a complicated calculation, truly don't understand what seems simple and logical to him. Quite a few of them have been to university. They're smarter than me, he thinks, just not looking at these problems the right way. They'll do fine when it comes to exams. And he continues to tutor without any real awareness of his own ability. He's not too honest to make a deliberate mistake, simply too modest.

His navigators' training is in Manitoba; he writes home of the immensity of the treeless prairies, still deep in snow in March and frostbite cold for students taking astro shots through the open hatch of an unheated Anson. It is more difficult to describe his fascination with the craft itself, not simply the study of winds and weather or the identification of the stars in their constellations, understandable extensions of his inherent farmer's lore, but the intense satisfaction of successfully locating an exact ground position from the intricate calculations of sextant and astrotables. He does not even attempt to share the despair of the early flight when he confused port and starboard and would have never found his way home if the long-suffering staff pilot, conveyor of novice navigators, hadn't skimmed low past a grain elevator with the town's name clear and large on the side. But by August, when the rest of his class are being packed into convoys of converted liners and on their way across the Atlantic, Bill is back in Nova Scotia on further special navigational training. He is also, to his own astonishment and his family's pride, Pilot Officer Dubois. An officer.

It's a convenient time to be posted near home; the hay's been stooked but he helps get the last of it into the loft; brings in bushels of apples, butchers two pigs, is feted by aunts and uncles, fed by his mother and teaches Louise to smoke. But the base at Debert is also too close to gloss over the risks and casualties of flight training; when three crashes kill eleven aircrew in two days, the party line network has Bill dead before he has time to phone home.

Those crashes are the one blight on this period. For the rest of his life Bill will be able to picture his native province from the air; the topography of the North and South Mountains bounding the Valley; the darkness of spruce forests and the lakes of Cape Breton. Cruising too high to make out the wartime bustle of Halifax itself, they watch the convoys build up in Bedford Basin: troopships, merchant marine, destroyers and aircraft carriers; so many that it takes another hour's flying out over the ocean to understand the loneliness of those ships once they leave the harbour.

Finally, on Christmas Eve, they become another crew of 'kids flying the Atlantic', as the head of Ferry Command terms them: young men whose first operational duty is to deliver a heavy aeroplane from the Canadian factory to the British Royal Air Force, which is using them up at a prodigious rate. Aircraft have improved since Lindbergh's acclaimed flight, but the North Atlantic is no less unsafe. It is still twenty-five years and another era from the day when Bill's daughter will board a routine flight from Halifax to London, with no thoughts of icing windshields, oxygen masks or the dark water below.

They pick up their brand-new Hudson from the factory in Montreal, so virginally untouched that the navigator's table is still covered with a protective paper which Bill folds carefully, wondering whether he ought to replace it at the other end. It's late afternoon when they land in Newfoundland.

'We're finally out of Canada, boys,' says Hank McBain, wireless operator and crew comedian, 'but it don't look much different so far.'

Next evening, under an icy, low-lying cloud, they load a few cartons of cigarettes 'to trade with the natives,' quips Hank, fill thermoses and collect sandwiches from the mess. Bill's stomach knots as he sets up his table, checks his sextant and charts. After thirteen months of training, he is finally about to go to work.

The pilot's feeling the same way; Bill notices that his voice is a tone higher than usual. 'We've flown distance before,' he tells them. 'We'll just do our jobs and there's not much that can go wrong.'

It's the oxygen that does. Leaving the cold loneliness of Newfoundland, they climb high over the cloud to head out across the lonelier, colder wastes of the North Atlantic. High enough that they are already feeling dreamy when they put on their oxygen masks. The masks, with a valve to regulate the flow, are fed by a long tube from the mother supply controlled by the pilot. He doesn't mention that he's set the supply at minimum and Bill, who's switched his valve to the same setting, doesn't realise that he's receiving virtually no oxygen at all.

In the windowless nose he feels very alone. Alone and sleepy. There is no sense of time; time stretches infinitely; he has been here in this enclosed fug of fuel and fumes forever and can't imagine that the journey will end: he'll be here till the end of his life, till the end of the universe, frozen in this throbbing shell of noise and steel. The times he must calculate—the ETA over ten hours from take-off, the adjustments as winds shift, as the course changes—are abstract figures with as little relationship to reality as meridians have to the earth's surface. He pours a cup of coffee from his thermos, struggling now to remember exactly what the calculations are. The phrase 'triangle of velocities' appears and he repeats it several times, which gives it a pleasing authority though no further clues as to relevance or procedure. Eventually he decides it must be time for a star shot. Staggering down the length of the aircraft, his umbilical oxygen hose trailing, nothing is right: further than he thought and harder to walk, the hatch stiff to remove, the stars won't stay still and worst of all, the sextant doesn't work—the glass is opaque and quite unreadable. He stops himself just short of throwing it through the open hatch in disgust.

'Can you give me the point of no return, Bill?' Ray calls as he stumbles back to his desk.

'Point of no return,' Bill repeats, adding, 'I feel woozy. Woozier and woozier.' He staggers again, which Hank finds amusing; but Ray, who is not suffering from oxygen deprivation, adjusts the main valve until the oxygen starts to flow through their masks and on to their brains.

Bill still feels alone. His world is the table in front of him—charts, graphs, circular slide rule—and sextant, not faulty at all, just frosted over from his own breath. He cleans its glass gently as his headache clears, supremely grateful that he didn't jettison it, and makes his way back to the hatch to take his star shots. The stars, as always, reassure him—they are constant and known—but it is not until he begins the complex series of calculations that will fulfil the pilot's request that he truly understands what it means to be a navigator. The point of no return, worked out on a hot July afternoon in a stuffy classroom, had seemed an abstract equation, its object simply to take him one step further to passing the course. Now the finality of the words and the responsibility of their meaning settle heavily on his shoulders.

He calculates it twice more in the next few hours, until the point has been passed. No matter what the emergency, their only option is to go on. If his calculations are correct, the headwind has added the equivalent of an extra two hundred miles to the flight; they will land safely but there is little margin for error. If his calculations are wrong, if they have strayed off course…It does not bear thinking about.

Next morning Ray descends low enough through the clearing cloud that they can shed the unwieldy, rank rubber masks and Bill, lying on his belly, can see the whitecaps of the waves through the eyepiece of the drift recorder and calculate the wind's direction. Drift, dead reckoning, air plot… Ireland appears exactly when and where he expects it and he takes a triumphant photograph to send home to his parents. It is followed quickly by Scotland, and the triumph by fear as their fuel gauges read empty. They land at Prestwick's grass airfield without circuiting or permission, with less than fifteen gallons of fuel to spare.

Jane's worst moment so far has been the immigration forms handed out at the Qantas desk, green cards to tick and fill in. Purpose of trip? *Visiting relatives*, Jane chooses, because it isn't business and certainly doesn't feel like a holiday, and the form doesn't inquire whether the family to be listed is alive or dead.

It's the type of dilemma that would have intrigued Ruth, and for a fraction of a second before she remembers, Jane sees herself offering, her mother considering.

The habits of a lifetime die hard; the habits of love, it seems, can outlive their recipients.

❧

Albert's memorial service is held on his twenty-second birthday in the tiny Presbyterian church at Evelyn's Pond. It's a grey November morning in 1942, a biting norwesterly blowing in over the Bay of Fundy, but there's no reason to spend time in the churchyard as there's no body to commit to a grave. Bert's body is in the North Atlantic, testimony of another U-Boat success against the merchant marine.

The irony, the bitter irony, is that on arriving in England, Bill had been posted straight to Coastal Command. Daily, in foul weather or very occasionally fair, he's navigated an enormous clumsy tank of a flying boat out of Oban in an invisible grid across the North Atlantic to search for enemy submarines. In ten months of flying over waters so hopelessly cold and lonely that the crews are not even issued with parachutes, they have survived two battles with the Luftwaffe and rescued a dinghy full of torpedoed sailors but have never seen a submarine.

❧

Bill reads the letter in a comfortable chair by the fire in the mess. There'd been no premonition as he picked up the envelope and the news sinks in reluctantly against the tide of shock and bewilderment—surely there's been a mistake, Bert's been picked up and is still at sea, captive or amnesic. But it's the angry guilt of failure that overwhelms all other emotion, and the dark shadow of betraying his brother's safety will linger for the rest of his life.

It's Louise who's written; Mother and Dad are too distressed to write. They barely speak, she adds, frozen in their grief; she doesn't describe her own but it leaks through on every blotched page, the haphazard memories mingling with painstaking repetition of official detail. Underlying it, on a later rereading, Bill thinks he sees the fear, too selfish not only to say but even to admit to herself: 'Take care, my only surviving brother, come home to set me free. I don't want to die an old maid looking after invalid parents.'

Bill doesn't see it as selfish. It's all part of the shock that a torpedo can thoughtlessly tear its way through steel and wood to finish the world that is one man, his own unique range of laughter, of wit and dedication, and the hopes and stories woven round him by the others in his life. It's the ending of innocence and the firm conviction despite all evidence to the contrary that this can't happen to me and mine. It's the realisation that their lives are not and may never be the way they thought life was supposed to be.

Chapter
TWO

$\mathcal{F}$irmly rooted in the security of real parents, solid grandparents and lineage stretching firm and documented
through the ages, Ruth never expects her private dreams of
mysterious adventurous forebears to touch reality: a child's
suspicion is not a woman's knowledge.

Reality arrives abruptly on a mild June evening of 1944.
Its appearance is more than brutal; it is negating, annihilat-
ing, shearing past from present. Her mother's shriek of
rage—rage at nothing, or at everything, at fifty-seven months
that have changed the world, at the whippet's death and
Nanny's, at a way of life disappeared with the daily, the cook
and the gardener, all swallowed up by the demands of factories and the machinery of death—but worse than all that is
the fear for her daughter, doing a man's work, taking a man's
risks, and when it's over, how will this clever, elegant girl
ever be a lady again and settle down to a normal life?

Tonight, when she's presumed Ruth will spend the last
night of her leave cosily in the drawing room—wireless,

reading and attempt at normality—the girl appears in evening wear, bare shoulders, silver gown and a glow of excitement. The explosion point is reached: *'You'll end up like your mother!'*

The world stops.

A wall of glass surrounds Ruth, distancing sounds and images: her father turning white, freezing in a half-kneel with a scoop of coal in his hand; her mother—*her not mother?*—draining from red to grey, sinking into a chair with hand to forehead and what would be melodrama if it were not so horribly real.

Herself understanding nothing, except that if this is a slip, it is a slip of truth not of the tongue. No one appears about to laugh and explain that it was her aunt, her grandmother, her second cousin twice removed whom Ruth will end up like.

So many questions, and she doesn't ask them. Why and who and when? But now a blank, a white void, and her parents part of it, and she puts on her wrap because the night will be cool by the time she comes back and she will have to come back because where else can she go, and sometime, somehow, when she can find the words, she'll have to ask those questions, but the immediate question is escape.

Detached, icily calm and not recognising this as shock, she watches herself step carefully along the street. It's barely twilight in the long June evening and yet she seems to be walking in the dark, skirting newly familiar obstacles—crumpled concrete where number 40's fence was pulled up for its iron railings; the lilac four doors further, untrimmed since the grief of Dunkirk, drooping over the pavement. At the corner she crashes heavily into a man, also newly familiar—the scratch of uniform against her cheek, the smell of wool, of soap and him as his arms go around her.

'Ruth!' he exclaims. 'You wouldn't be running away from me, would you?'

As she doesn't answer, as he realises that she is crying and can't guess why, he tightens his grip and rocks, slightly, comfortingly. 'Are you okay there?' he asks, attempting humour. 'Because I'm never going to let you go.'

Later, Jane and her brothers will laugh and roll their eyes at this story. 'Mom!' they'll shriek. 'You married a man you bumped into because he said *he'd never let you go!*'

'He was coming to meet me,' Ruth will say primly, eyes laughing, because it's not the time for remembering that maelstrom of emotions, or even the earlier dilemma of allowing him to come to the house, knowing already that this man will be part of her life and preferring to delay her parents' inevitably caustic judgement. 'It was our first date—but we'd met months before.'

When they are quite small the first story, the story of how their parents met, strikes them as even more ludicrous. In fact much of their mother's previous life is as magical to them as *Peter Pan* or *Mary Poppins,* stories that they frequently muddle with the anecdotes she tells them. Ruth herself, from her vantage point of Nova Scotian farm wife, sometimes wonders if her own early memories can be accurate: did her father really take his favourite umbrella back to the umbrella shop to be washed and ironed, or was that one of Nanny's threats when Ruth had been caught playing with its silky blackness, tracing the knot in the curved wooden handle with a moistened index finger? No wonder that her children find it difficult to believe in her growing up in a city bigger than they can imagine, bigger than Halifax and Dartmouth put together, playing in a park that locked with a key and usually with a nanny (no, not her grandmother and not a goat or a dog, but a lady whose job was to look after that one little girl), going to a school in the mountains to learn how to pour tea and have polite conversation (a rash of ribald tea parties follow this particular revelation) and then, hardly more wonderfully, had become an aeroplane pilot.

But it's their father who tells this part of the story. In June

1943 he'd been lucky enough, he says, omitting his bitterness at the loss of a chance to avenge his brother, to be transferred to a base in Oxfordshire, navigating heavy land planes to deliver vital supplies or sometimes passengers to where they were urgently needed.

'Crossing the aerodrome with a little Cockney wireless operator and we saw a Spitfire coming in. Of course we stopped to watch, since we didn't have much use for fighter planes on a transport base, and this looked like some show-off fighter ace—he swooped down, beat up the aerodrome and then taxied down the runway in as neat a landing as I've seen.

'No ground crew around so I jumped up to open the canopy—and looked straight into a beautiful face with soft brown hair poking out from under the flying helmet. "You're a girl!" I said, being a bright young man in those days.

'"Where will I park?" she asked.

'"Anywhere you bloody well please, love," the Cockney shouted, since I didn't seem to be able to say anything much at all. "So long as the CO don't see you. It ain't for us."'

'When my mother met my father,' Jane will tell enthralled school friends, 'she beat up a whole airport!'

'That's not *quite* the way it happened,' Ruth objects. 'The cold front came in faster and lower than the Met Office predicted, leaving me stuck up above the clouds looking for a hole to see my way through to land. I couldn't believe my luck when I poked my nose through right above an aerodrome! I came in low over the runway, hoping it was the base that was waiting for my Spittie. By the time I realised it wasn't the visibility was so bad I had to land anyway.'

'And it stayed bad,' Bill continues, because he knows her story is truer, although he prefers his because he'd realised that day how very close she'd been to being stuck above that thick cloud, becoming more and more desperate and closer to the chance of trying a gap that would turn out to be a hill; even now he hates thinking about the conditions Ruth flew in without radio or instruments. 'Nothing could take off for the next four hours, not even your mom!

'By this time I'd got my wits together, so I took her off to the mess to get warm—her lips were as blue as her eyes, she was that cold. Got her hot coffee and a horrible spam sandwich and tried to keep her out of sight of the other fellows because they'd have been swarming all over making a nuisance of themselves.'

And they'd talked. That's what they don't share with the children: they'd simply talked for those hours, casual flirting leaping quite suddenly to the intimate conversation of strangers on trains. Then at about three the unkind clouds had lifted and she'd rushed back to her charge to deliver it before dark.

'So I found out where she wanted to go, which of course was the big Fighter Command base ten miles south-east of us. Drew her a little map so she wouldn't be mistaken again; down went the hatch and off she went down the runway, straight out of my life, or so I thought. She was in the air before I realised I'd never even got her name.'

Jane, however, even when she understands the whole story, is stuck with that first image: a beautiful girl with soft brown hair and flying fists, taking on the world.

Fifty-three years later Jane and Ian were invited to dinner by the neighbours whose boundary ran along the river's State forest, bordering the Gundanna Lagoon. The couple had inherited the remnant of a huge grazing property bought up by the government for the soldiers-settlers of the Second World War. They still felt a certain sense of superiority over those hundred-acre dairy farmers and their descendants, and Jane and Ian were unsure what they had done to have suddenly attained dinner-party status. However, the wife, a forceful woman with a bust like the prow of a battleship, explained that she was in charge of finding this month's guest speaker for Ladies Probus. It was not an easy task in this community, she added bluntly, but perhaps Jane would consider a speech on how she had come to set up a local branch of EcoFarm, a community-based government-supported organisation devoted to combating salinity and re-establishing indigenous plants.

Jane consented, though her stomach churned at the thought—it would still be some time before she became a confident, though never flamboyant, public speaker. Flushing, but slightly disappointed to find that this commitment was the extent of the woman's interest in her work, she shrank back into her chair. The two men on either side of her immediately resumed the conversation their hostess had interrupted. They were Ian's age, maybe a little younger, undoubtedly considerably wealthier, and both amateur pilots. The one on her left had just bought a scale model of a Spitfire.

'You're mad,' the other insisted. 'They were terrible things to fly.'

'Fighter pilots loved them: you read any of the books…'

'Once they got used to them—the visibility was terrible and it was completely impossible to do a three-point landing.'

'My mother always did three-point landings,' said Jane. 'It was an ATA rule. She flew mostly Spitfires.'

The silence was brief but deafening: she felt like a child who'd shouted 'Bum!' at her mother's tea guests. The conversation reverted quickly to farming.

'Did I make that up?' she emailed the next morning. 'I was sure I remembered you and Dad discussing three-point landings, but the more I think about it the less sure I am. And since our family mythology seems to be based around Dad's Spitfire story, I don't think I even want to know if I'm wrong about that!'

She was right, Ruth replied, about both.

Jane vowed that one day she'd ask what a three-point landing actually was.

Ruth remembers the big blond navigator with a rich Canadian voice and, though she says she's not looking for romance, saves the quickly sketched map in her hatbox of letters. There's nothing that's not on the usual charts, except a story of competence and her own sudden fierce determination that this young man must not die—not a premonition of any disaster that she can somehow avert, but simply a feeling that, despite the horrors of the war, all will not be quite lost if a man like this survives.

Sometimes, knitting in the mess waiting for clouds to lift, or daydreaming in the taxi plane home from the last delivery of the day, she remembers the instant he leaned towards her to light her cigarette. A kiss had hovered in the air between them, unacknowledged, unthinkable, and as tangible as if he'd actually touched her lips. Sometimes, lying in bed in her room at the yacht club, she wishes he had.

Four months later, on a forty-eight hour leave in London, she walks into the Covent Garden Ballroom with a friend. Bill is the first person she sees. Ruth knows him instantly, but it takes him longer to reconcile this elegant, bare-shouldered young woman with the girl in bulky flying suit and helmet.

They are both tired and overdue for leave. In the weeks leading up to D-day Ruth has delivered a steady stream of aircraft and, like everyone else in southern England, waited tensely for what is so obviously imminent. The best military intelligence can't hide the huge weight of men, tanks and other weapons of destruction assembled near Southampton; so huge, the saying goes, that only the barrage balloons are keeping Britain afloat. On her last delivery the day before, Ruth saw her Spitfire's wings painted with distinctive invasion stripes before she'd even left the airfield, and later, from her Hamble riverside room, watched the men in open landing craft sailing out, hour after hour, into the darkness. It had been a sombre, unsettling sight, and even as the first optimistic reports were read the next day, impossible not to wonder how many of the men she'd watched were still alive.

Bill, like many other men, is beginning the task of trying to forget what he's seen. He tells Ruth of flying in formation through the stormy night of 5 June, a Dakota loaded with paratroopers, and of the conscientious objector medics they'd dropped into Normandy the following day: 'The bravest men I've ever seen: trained just like the paratroopers, but no weapons, just their first-aid kits.' Much later he'll tell her about the flight he's just returned from, the same aircraft converted now into a flying ambulance for the boys whose war is over, and the half-crazed paratrooper who met each incoming crew, searching for the bastards who dropped him in the wrong place: 'It wasn't us,' he'll add hastily. But he never tells her of the smell that engulfed them as they stepped out onto that Norman landing strip, because that's what he most wants to forget and never does, and although he's a farmer and has smelled his fair share of dead animals and rotting meat, his mind never allows him to identify this par-ticular stink.

They're ready to pretend that this is not the world they live in.

'We danced,' is all Ruth will tell her children. 'Your father won't tell me where he learned to waltz, but he swept me off my feet that night.' And the children will laugh, trying to imagine their parents in this disguise, waltzing to the Hungarian Rhapsody under the shining ball and high ceil-ings of the ballroom.

Which is, in fact, the exact truth. But as Jane and her broth-ers will discover in their own time, superficially honest answers about human contact are often the least truthful.

Bill does dance well; hands and step are light and sure, and he's considerably taller than she is; Ruth, at nearly five foot ten, finds this novelty attractive in itself. Their bodies fit well together, move well together; impossible not to notice how right it feels. Fair, thick hair; straight nose and square jaw; she's met men who were more attractive but is sure, tonight, that she's never been so attracted. Voices through the tangle of music and crowded conversation, the peculiar pitch and rhythm of their own speech, the subtleties of scent amidst the fumes of alcohol, tobacco and other dancers. An air of quiet strength—does she truly notice this as they dance, or is it added in later?—as if one would be safe with him, find peace in crisis. But no safer than she would want to be: his eyes, hazel green, are lit with laughter and desire, with something deeper; and she feels herself reflected: desirable, beautiful. Seductive.

It's the next night that she walks into his arms in front of number 40.

Jane is an adult before she begins to understand that Ruth, safe in that clasp, hears the words as a sign from the fates and knows that if her past has been a lie, this man is the truth of her future.

They don't go to the West End after all. They walk through the misty evening, Ruth in her unsuitable shoes and Bill in air force boots; they huddle on a hard park bench and share a cigarette and warmth and secrets.

'Just ask them,' says Bill, secure in his own rich history of family feuds and saga, 'and if they won't say, there'll be a cousin or an aunt who'll be dying to tell you. There's always someone.'

But Ruth isn't sure yet that she even wants to know.

Instead she drinks in his life: the big whitewashed farmhouse at Evelyn's Pond. 'On the North Mountain—only it's not so much a mountain,' he admits, having now seen mountains that are, 'as a ridge.' The red barn of haylofts, of feather-fetlocked Clydesdales, warm cow breath and the stink of pigs; woods and fields and apple orchards. And to add to the romance, he covers the land with a blanket of snow, deep and soft, straps on snow shoes 'like tennis rackets,' he says and jumps up from the bench to demonstrate the gait, wide-legged and rolling, 'easy once you learn,' to walk her through woods of frozen maple and frosted spruce. To spare her feelings he avoids peopling the land, but she is greedy for details of that interlocked web of kin—siblings and ancestors holding tight in a proof of existence.

His story is interrupted by the wailing of an air-raid siren. They look up briefly and decide to ignore it. The night is cloudy, nearly moonless, and the risk of an enemy aircraft actually getting through is certainly not worth abandoning their privacy for a smelly, crowded bomb shelter.

An unfamiliar, rasping thrum approaches overhead. Searchlights wave, and in the instant before the beams focus on their target, they see that the aircraft's running lights are on.

'How very odd!' Ruth exclaims.

'Pilot must be dead,' says Bill, 'he's not trying to evade at all…but what the hell is it?'

It's very fast, very low, flying absolutely straight, and now that its odd cigar shape and the flame shooting from it are trapped in the great white light, they realise it's unlike anything they've seen before. The ack-ack guns are thundering, blobs of red tracer shooting up at this strange, defiant raider, and in one move they realise their exposed position and tumble together under their park bench.

His body is straddling hers and she can feel him trying to protect her from his weight but their bodies touch anyway, the bony points of her hips and the softness of her breasts, and she doesn't want to be protected from his weight, or from the feel of him growing and hardening against her or from her own ache of longing to take him deep inside herself. She pulls him closer till she feels his tense shoulders relax, stroking his hair, his neck, his back. So this is it, she thinks. What a funny way to start our lives together. The thought is so bizarre that she shoves it quickly to the corner of her mind.

The silence as the engine cuts out is more shocking than the noise. The strange craft plummets straight down, not spiralling out of control as a stalled kite should, and when the explosion comes Bill lifts his face from the curve of her neck. 'His bombs were still on board,' he says. 'That's a hell of a bang.'

They stay where they are as they hear the wail of ambulance and fire engine. And as they are, impossible not to kiss, to hold and touch, but this is not kissing, not holding or touching as Ruth has ever known it, as if everything before has been felt through a veil and only now is she experiencing pure, naked sense. Naked is how she wants her body to be as well, clothes have never seemed so restricting, with this scent of summer grass, a pebble pressing sharply into her shoulder... 'We should have gone to a hotel,' she says.

Bill has kept lust at bay all night, in deference to her distraught state and a fear that she might hate him when she recovers. He has also never had sex with a woman he thinks he could love. His sense of virtue evaporates—he feels cheated and confused, aching with cold, desire and fatigue.

Her dark hair is rumpled and face pale in the grey of first dawn; her shoulders are bare, the wrap lost in the scramble for shelter. Narrow shoulders, very straight, with prominent, fragile collarbones. The fantasies that have flicked occasionally into his mind during the past four months and constantly in the last twenty-four hours are without warning transformed to a vision of waking with that face, this body, in a bed beside him. 'Marry me,' he says.

His face is serious.

'Oh, yes,' says Ruth. 'What a good idea.'

They kiss with a new seriousness, hands straying possessively. Not to spite Mama and Papa, she thinks. Not because I need to belong somewhere and it's no longer here. This is something that would have happened whenever we met. She is suddenly urgent with fear of a fate that might never have let them come together or could now casually remove him with a quick rake of anti-aircraft fire or faulty landing. (Or her, but Ruth has long since decided that her emulation of Amy Johnson stops well short of dying in the same way.)

But the other reasons help. That, and the strong hands and blond-moustached lip, and the feeling that perhaps the poets weren't wrong about sex after all and that there isn't anything quite so urgent in life as finding out for sure. Except perhaps, with dawn definitely arriving, the sound of traffic and the realisation that there are some limits to the loss of dignity—and this morning, she's got to face her parents.

'One thing at a time,' she says, stretching long legs, wriggling her toes in the flimsy shoes and doing nothing whatsoever for Bill's self-control. 'Surely we can organise another leave together soon, and next time we'll find a better place to stay.'

Bill is still in shock at hearing his own question and finds it harder still to believe her answer. 'You'll marry me—truly?'

'I'll marry you truly.'

'You don't really know me.'

She drops the teasing tone. 'I know I love you. I don't see how I can know that any more than I do now.'

'I'd better find out what we have to do about it—permission and all that. It's not something I'd thought about.'

'I'd never thought about emigrating!' And at his worried face—'I didn't say I didn't want to, it's just something one doesn't normally consider.'

'But you won't be an immigrant,' he says. 'You'll be my wife.'

Ruth begins to giggle, helplessly, uncharacteristically. In less than eight hours she's been unquestioningly Ruth Townsend, had no name at all, and is now anticipating Mrs William Dubois. The whole question has become surreal.

'Will I meet your parents this morning?'

'After we've spent the night out together?'

'I'll tell them I intend to make an honest woman of you. They can't be worse than my wing co.'

'I wouldn't be too sure.' She's stiff and lightheaded, has gone right past sleep, and has no idea at all what she wants to say to her parents.

'Tell them,' Bill suggests, 'that we'll be spending many, many more nights together, but never again on a park bench. Or under it,' and the kiss this time has such urgency that Ruth restrains herself only with the suspicion that he's fallen in love partly with the image of her as an English lady, one whom he might expect to be rather more inhibited than she feels at the moment. (She is in fact wrong in this, not yet understanding the complex web of English-aristocrat-loathing history that has raised this man. He has fallen in love purely and simply with Ruth herself; her passion for reading the stories of people's lives sometimes leads her to forget that, occasionally, a cigar is just a cigar.)

They catch the first bus past, which has to detour around its regular route where emergency services are working feverishly in a blocked-off road. A three or four house gap is obvious in the line of roofs.

Bill feels Ruth growing remote as Savernake Street comes closer. 'Are you sure you don't want me to come with you?'

'One thing at a time,' she repeats. 'First I've got to find out exactly what they meant last night.'

'You don't think it was just a mistake—saying things in an argument they don't really mean?'

Ruth sees again the frozen parental tableau. 'I don't think so.'

Bill can do nothing but walk her to the gate, belatedly exchange addresses and catch the tube back to his train station and base. It was easier when she was crying; he has no idea what to do for this self-possessed young woman who is looking so coolly at her loss of identity.

'Just ask them,' Bill said, but it's not so simple.

'Papa is sleeping,' her mother whispers as Ruth enters the

house. 'Try not to wake him; there was a raid last night and he's not long back.'

'I heard it.'

So that's it, she thinks. Yesterday evening didn't happen.

This is her family's usual response to emotion, but the emotions this time are too huge to be ignored. Mama had screamed that Ruth wasn't her daughter; Ruth had spent the night out with a strange man... The man she was created for, she thinks, and for an instant glows again with that certainty before misery overtakes her. This is not the way life is supposed to be: she's met the man she intends to marry—she ought to be able to tell her parents and they ought to be happy for her. But she can't imagine telling them any of this, because she won't be able to open her mouth without asking who she is.

And it's so impossible I'm not me, she decides, against a rising tide of nausea, that I can't understand anything else.

In her room she changes quickly into uniform for the trip back, mechanically shaking the grass from her evening dress, dusting off shoes, packing them quickly with nightdress and underwear into the holdall, *The Screwtape Letters* into her handbag for the train—CS Lewis's devils would be shrieking for joy at this particular misery, she thinks, better than anything the *Letters* have devised. It's too early to leave but she can't face going downstairs. Maybe Mama will come up, she thinks, because cynical as she can be when cynicism is wittier than trust, Ruth will remain an optimist for the rest of her life.

Mama doesn't come up. Ruth continues to sit on the edge of the bed, her optimism deserting her, with a despairing feeling that this might be the last time she'll ever sit here, in the room where she grew up. Ruth Townsend's room. Yellow floral wallpaper, chintz curtains, Queen Anne dressing table and wardrobe, the two bookcases with wing-backed chair between, the two paintings that have always been here, and the *Daily Mail*'s print of Amy Johnson in front of her *Jason*, framed with Ruth's own pocket money. She's had this bed, as far she knows, since she grew out of a cot. As far as she knows—there's the rub, as Shakespeare would say. How far does she know?

❧

Taking off from Jakarta, the Pavlovian association of excitement with the acceleration is for just an instant stronger than grief: Jane tries to imagine that she's going on a holiday instead. ('Visualisation,' Megan often says, 'is the first step to doing what you want.' As Megan, since birth, has been rather good at doing what she wants, there may be something in it.) Not a trip to Canada, because Canada is family and what she doesn't want to think about, but a proper luxurious, sight-seeing holiday. Difficult to imagine why she's going without Ian; maybe he's too busy. Maybe it's a working holiday, EcoFarm sending her on a European study tour; Australia is not the only country in the world battling the problems of salinity and erosion with tree planting and improved farm management.

Funny how problems run through your mind, periodically lying low but refusing to die away. The whether-or-not-to-take-the-job dilemma, dormant since Mary's phone call, has just sneakily resurfaced under the guise of a fantasy holiday. Not that EcoFarm is likely to send her to Europe, but if she takes—if she applies and is appointed to—this new Coordinator's position, there will be occasional trips to Canberra, maybe even to Queensland and Western Australia as well as the closer States.

To research and report, the job description said, *on the land degradation problems in each region, the effect of EcoFarm on the ecology of these regions and the impact of change on the lives of farmers participating in the programs.*

'They need a sociologist for that,' Ian had said, but Jane had been invited to apply, on the strength, she presumes, of the history she'd prepared of the Gundanna Lagoon, a similar project, though smaller in scale.

Ian worries that this will be taking on more than she can cope with; he doesn't want to see her hurt, by which he means fail. She is a primary school teacher, not a trained researcher or university lecturer; a room full of bureaucrats or hostile farmers is not, he'd pointed out, the same as a class of eight year olds.

'Not as different as you think,' retorted Jane, who's seen more of both.

And was she really going to be happy, he'd wanted to know, turning herself into a supercharged businesswoman, bustling off to Melbourne conferences or interstate flights? Which was more difficult to argue with. She suspects that a power suit and briefcase would simply make her look pretentious, like a child dressing up in her mother's clothes: she's just a woman who started planting trees because she was homesick on the flat bare lands, and happened to learn a little along the way.

Too hard to think about now. Go back to the fantasy holiday. Why couldn't it be Canada? She can't cut herself off completely just because her parents are dead; it simply gives her the freedom to see more of the country, as Megan's doing now, to visit scattered relatives and friends. Not that she has contact with many of the latter: Gail's in Vancouver, sending a yearly chatty newsletter, but she lost touch with Patsy years ago. Winston, naturally, she's never heard from at all.

'My first lover was black.'

Jane's offering to the reunion of teachers' college friends in the cheap wine induced haze of sisterhood, loss of virginity the theme this last night of summer school 1968, before they all go back to being prim young teachers.

She said *first* as if others had followed; *lover* as if sex was something they'd been in the habit of. But it was black that was the betrayal.

Her friends saw themselves as liberal, liberated young women who, while not burning their bras, had occasionally gone without, who believed in love not war, in racial equality, and—absolutely and implicitly—in their own freedom from the shadow of prejudice.

The one word freed them to write their own versions of her story—radical heroine; free-loving hippie ahead of her time; lucky bitch coupling with a big black stud. It was in what they didn't ask as much as what they did. They didn't need to know what he was like, his thoughts or what he wanted out of life, because they knew all that mattered: gleaming skin and rippling pectorals, feline grace and sinuous rhythm. But what they most wanted to know they didn't dare ask, and Jane never told them.

She wasn't sure that she could. They'd only made love once, and it hadn't been very successful.

His father was a blacksmith (Jane was an adolescent before she realised that the word didn't refer to his skin). They must have been about eight when they first met, because it was Grandpa's old horse being shod and he'd died the following winter, and difficult as it would be to believe it later, Winston had needed to be coaxed out of the pick-up while his father unloaded anvil and tools. Ruth set up a milk and cookies picnic on the bales in the barn, and Winston had explained the procedure to Jane (a memory that was easier to imagine) while Mike climbed on the hay.

It was grade 10 before they spoke again, the first day at Applevale Regional High, when the commercial stream and tech school had syphoned off aspiring typists and mechanics, leaving a smaller group than had jostled through the various elementary schools and junior high. Winston sat behind her in Latin. She could not believe he was the same solemn boy she'd played with in the sweet smelling, prickly hay.

'Why are you here?' he challenged. 'Don't you know it's a dead language?'

Jane panicked. She was never good at this. She would watch the girls who could throw little balls of conversation into the air, juggling words that meant nothing, that meant everything, teasing, promising, denying. And because life is unfair and laughs at losers, this gift of sparkling was given to the girls with curves—curves of waved hair, curves of Playtex breasts, curves of waist and hip—girls who didn't need to juggle words to feel a boy's hot hungry eyes follow her or hear his breathless whisper on the phone begging for a date.

'Why're you?' she snapped.

'You need it for law,' said Winston, leaning back in his chair as if the answer should have been obvious even to a numbskull like herself. 'I'm going to be a lawyer.'

Jane had never had a proper boyfriend, but she knew what he would look like: tall, tanned, lean and athletic, a strongly chiselled face and several years older than she would have been allowed to date. Winston was short and stocky, the same body shape as her grandfather and herself, the tight curls of his hair cropped short to his skull. (If we ever have children, she thought once, when the possibility did not seem remote, they'll come out square! At the same time realising this would be the least of the children's problems.)

The six grade 10 students who hadn't realised that Latin was a dead language quickly developed a clique of their own. A Latin word in the middle of a sentence—in the halls, the lunch room, in other subjects—would convulse the six of them into peals of only slightly artificial laughter. For the first time Jane was part of an exclusive group and it didn't matter that no one else particularly wanted to be included.

But she remained nervous of Winston. She'd always thought of herself as bright enough; some people were smarter and many stupider, but Winston's brain moved on another level, not simply gathering information with an inexorable logic and formidable memory, but leaping from concept to concept, across chasms she couldn't imagine bridging. It was pointless to argue with him and difficult not to. Listening to him debate, she told her mother, was the best entertainment the school offered: building up arguments against himself only to scatter them all at the last moment with one telling deathblow, so that his opponent, bemused at appearing to be bettering the formidable Winston, hadn't the slightest hope of picking up the pieces. She didn't describe her own vacillation between fascination and fear of that wounding wit; he had a knack for picking out her secrets and showing them to the world and herself. ('How do you know me so well?' she asked one night the following summer, when she was lying in his arms out of sight of a campfire, out of earshot of friends, but he'd had half a bottle of Southern Comfort and what he wanted of her that night was not intellectual.)

That was later. All through grade 10 they continued to spar, the yearning for physical contact sublimated into verbal dancing and feinting. Then came summer, vacation time, the North Mountain suddenly a long way from town, the farm an outpost where Jane burned restless energy making hay, mucking out the winter barn, and riding. Riding bony Bold Brennon bareback till their sweat mingled and the dark patches on the bay's back left the girl's inner thighs coated with dark hair, sticky and suggestively obscene.

The evening before the exhibition fair Patsy phoned—'Talk your parents into letting you go, I'll meet you at the gate. What are you going to wear?' Jane chose her new summer dress, white to show off her tan, and they met and exclaimed over one another, but Patsy's eyes were restless. It was Randy McLeod she wanted to see and be seen by, and when she found him, she ensnared him in her chatter and drifted him off into the crowd, losing Jane as if by accident.

Jane hardly noticed. She'd spotted Winston coming towards her, also as if by chance, and was busy studying the strung-up prizes above the floating ducklings until she could turn in surprise: 'I didn't see you!'

'I was practising merging into the crowd. In case I decide to be a private investigator instead of a lawyer.'

He was so obviously the only black face in sight that she didn't know what to say; she never would when he joked about his colour. Without further discussion they drifted away from the ducklings and found themselves in line for the Ferris wheel.

Jane's mind whirled. If they each bought their own tickets they were friends; if he paid for both it was a date.

Winston stepped ahead to the booth. 'Two adults.'

Two adults—now the possibilities were endless. If she could just get the first step right (How do you learn this? Who teaches the rules?).

'I love the Ferris wheel,' she said.

They sat carefully separate as the bar was locked in place, but when the ride jammed on its second circle Winston stretched his arm over the back and she relaxed slightly against his side.

The seat rocked gently, triumphant over the summer crowd, above the hot sweet smell of candy floss and hot dogs, a tiny child in a frilled dress leading a pair of enormous oxen, barns crowded with champion heifers and squealing piglets. Impossible not to feel a certain smugness that fate had been so kind.

'I'd hate to be in one of the bottom seats,' Winston said. 'You'd feel too stupid—you'd have to jump out.'

Jane felt surprised and ridiculously honoured at learning that Winston could feel stupid. It was something she'd never considered. 'I like being up here anyway,' she said gratefully. She smiled, and he lowered his arm to her shoulders. Jane moved imperceptibly closer.

They sat, and rocked, and stared out over the exhibition ground with sudden exclamations of excitement, as if determined to ignore the way that their bodies had wiggled to the centre of the seat, glued side by side while Winston's arm tightened around her bare shoulders.

The rest of the fair passed in a blur. They rode over and over on the Scrambler, in thrall to the centrifugal force that pressed their bodies together, and the thrill of joyful terror that made it equally impossible not to scream. Couples in the other cars blurred past: Patsy, her mouth an O as she clung to Randy's side, quiet Heather O'Neill screaming into Jim Lightfoot's shoulder. And us, Jane thought. Winston and Jane. Jane and Winston.

That was the beginning. It built up quickly once school went back, through conventions of school dances and movie dates, waiting for the long-short-long ring of the phone. Dreaming of a phone of her own, like the privileged girls of American TV, whose phone calls didn't have to be whispered against a backdrop of teasing brothers or Mrs MacLeod's asthmatic breathing over the party line.

Another summer, another fair, filled now with memory and romance, and on to grade 12. The future loomed closer; as they clung to each other in the back seat of his parents' car, in the woods behind the house, on the beach, once in the hayloft of the old barn, the sweetness of his weight on hers, hay prickling her bare legs, Jane would have given whatever he wanted. 'All the way,' the girls whispered on Monday mornings. 'Do you think they go all the way? I won't go all the way till I'm married. Guys don't respect you if you go all the way.'

Winston had decided they wouldn't go all the way. Not yet. Not in school. Not unprotected. Touching, stroking, nibbling, yes, pressing, moaning, please, tongues and fingers, another button, another inch of bare flesh...Not fair that she should be the one to stop, to stay in control, saying no while his body pleaded to hers, while she melted and swirled, drunk with longing and exultation.

'Be careful,' her mother warned, 'this is getting serious. You've got your whole lives ahead of you, don't cut off your options.'

'Racist!' Jane flared, turning gladly from the frustration of saying no, the wondering if there was a way of getting to Halifax and finding a doctor who'd give her the pill, that wonderful, liberating pill, read of and never seen. 'You're only saying that because he's black.'

'You're quite right,' Ruth smiled, sarcasm heightening her accent, or accent sharpening sarcasm, Jane was never sure. 'Find a nice pimply boy with pink skin and I won't mind at all if you get pregnant and drop out of school.'

Jane skated carefully around the dangerously rounded word. 'College isn't the only thing in the world—Dad never went.'

'And neither did Winston's parents, nor millions of other people who have nothing to do with this argument, which is that you both intend to, and that it would be a sin against nature if that young man didn't get to where he wants to go. Besides which, my dear, I don't think he'd ever forgive you.'

'So if we go to college, if one day...' She couldn't say it, switched back to triteness and challenge, 'You'd let a Negro marry your daughter?'

'Ah, the fear of decent white folk, the big black penis— Is it black? Or pink like palms?—but you know what I mean. Big black man in my little white girl.'

I will never, Jane vowed, argue with my mother again. She's insane. To actually say it, big black penis; for crying out loud she's my mother, she's not supposed to talk like that. Jane scrunched her knees to her chest, hiding her face.

'That part, my dear, doesn't bother me at all, not if you wait till the right time—which, by the way, is not grade 12 and was all I was talking about in the first place. Though I can tell you that any mixed marriage is hard—'

But a mixed marriage like her own, she said (a clash of culture rather than race, and Jane's own eventual destiny), was difficult only for the people concerned, the children seaming invisibly into the society in which they were born. Which would not be true for Winston's black children born of white Jane.

Easier to call her mother racist. Uncomfortable to hear a parent's fears of pain for her, for her and unborn, unthought-of grandchildren.

'If the world was kinder...I would hope that your children's generation will find it easier, surely they will, but it's not easy to be the pioneers. And a shotgun wedding is no way to start.'

'No chance,' Jane mumbled, still against her knees.

'You know what took me by surprise?' Ruth went on, as if she hadn't heard. 'No one ever told me that it would be so hard to say no. I was taught that nice girls didn't, but no one told me that nice girls wanted to.'

She loved him for his wit, his humour, his wry view of the world, and of course whatever invisible chemistry breeds love's insanity, and if the dark gleam of his skin was part of that, it was in the same way that features of a beloved always become part of the lover's mythology. But when shadows of his blackness and its blacker history intruded, she felt herself rubbed raw and open to wounds, as if layers of her own skin had been peeled back in recompense for its pallidity.

'When did your family come to Nova Scotia?' her mother, ever avid for family stories, asked, and Jane waited for Winston to explode—she'd heard his views on anyone who suggested that he must be newly arrived in this bastion of Anglo–Celtic society.

'My father's family claims it was in the American Revolution when the British offered freedom to slaves who made it up here. My mother's family doesn't know; probably the same way unless they'd been brought here as slaves before that. I can't see it matters much either way now.'

'It has to matter!' Ruth protested. 'What we know of our history is what makes us who we are!'

'*I* make who I am.'

'Spoken as someone with history behind them. Without ancestors and their stories, there are no guidelines, no solidity to the past. One's own history begins with one's first memory—a rather fluid base at best.'

'So knowing my great-grandparents' story makes everything that happened to them okay?'

'"He was in logic a great critic,

Profoundly skilled in analytic,"' Ruth quoted.

'"He could distinguish, and divide

A hair 'twixt south and south-west side..." Naturally it doesn't make it *okay*! Of course you should be filled with horror, grief, rage at what they went through. But if you know it, you can know that it shaped you; it's part of you. You can choose what you look at and be proud of them—after all, they all must have survived, at least to childbearing age—and that strength has shaped you too. It seems to me that even people who have well-documented family histories *choose* their ancestors.'

'Ancestors must mean something different in England. In Canada they're the people who lived *before* you, which makes it tough to choose them.'

'Rubbish! You know perfectly well what I mean. Think about it—all those hundreds, thousands of ancestors bearing down on each individual. People choose the one or two who are interesting; nobody remembers the ninety-nine great-grandmothers who were scullery maids; it's the one who kissed Bonnie Prince Charlie who's claimed by her descendants.'

'I can guarantee that none of my great-grandmothers kissed Bonnie Prince Charlie!'

'And there,' Ruth said with a fluid leap of logic, 'you have the advantage of me. You can choose whether or not to be proud of your ancestors, but at least knowing who they are gives you that choice, whereas the only certainty for someone like me is the guess that their parents are unlikely to have had any stories to boast of.'

'What was wrong with our Townsend grandparents?' Jane asked.

'Nothing, except that they weren't my parents and wouldn't tell me who were.'

'We don't have English grandparents?'

'Probably—I just don't know who they were.'

'You should have told us!' Properly, she meant; calmly. Not to score a point in an argument.

'I was just waiting,' said Ruth, with a bizarre expression that Jane later realised was shame, 'for the right moment.'

Inappropriate timing in revealing family secrets, it seems, is not entirely dependent on heredity.

Jane couldn't share her mother's selective view of history. Loving Winston meant being excluded from parties at some homes that she used to go to; meant suffering the poisoned, genuine kindness of the economics teacher as he double-checked that Winston's sharp brain had understood what the dullest member of the class had easily followed; meant hating the careers teacher for her obvious shock that this black boy hadn't waited for her advice on a suitable trade and had already applied to university. Not, however, for law. In one of his interminable debates with Ruth he had been suddenly struck with the full realisation of the ephemeral nature of the spoken word. (Why are they arguing? Jane wondered. They both believe in the same thing. She had never been competitive enough to enjoy argument for the sake of it and, watching the fire in her boyfriend's and her mother's eyes, was unable to control a small pang of jealousy.) The only way to share his ideals and ensure that they were remembered, Winston decided now, was to write. 'Journalism isn't just reporting,' he proclaimed, as if he were talking to a wider audience than one adoring girl and her mother, 'it's a chance to say things that will change the way people see their world, which is the only way to change the world.'

Because there was no doubt that the world still did need changing. Occasional news reports crossed the border—the sheet-draped evil, the burning parody of Christianity, hangings, castrations. If they drove far enough south on their own continent, they'd be banned from entering a restaurant to eat together, from sitting side by side on a bus. If they crossed the water back to the southern tip of his forebears' original land, their still-chaste love exploded from immoral to illegal. She would wake with nightmares of hanged men with Winston's face.

He'd had years to accustom himself to these stories, to channel and control his rage, but touching her life for the first time, it rolled over her like an avalanche.

'How can people think like that?' she demanded.

'They think the way they're trained to,' Winston said. 'If we lived in one of the souths, we wouldn't even want to be together. We'd just go along the way we were told to—you'd go out with a nice blond boy and I'd be a blacksmith like my dad or, since I hate horses, I could try something different, like a janitor. Who says we'd be the ones smart enough and brave enough to see what's wrong with the way we'd been taught?'

She didn't believe him. His gift of seeing the world had nothing to do with accidents of birth; whereas she—no, to think that in another place, another time, she could have accepted him as a servant, a nonbeing...it was unthinkable. She would have always seen him as he was, would have always loved him.

And did love him, finally, at the party after graduation. A bonfire on the rocky beach, the bottles of Southern Comfort and rye passed around the circle, but Jane and Winston were barely drinking that night, they were drunk on the end of school and exams and the unreality of the future spread dazzlingly and immediately before them. Surreptitious fingers in the dark, languorous, teasing kisses becoming urgent until the longing became overwhelming and the shelter of the driftwood log was no longer enough. Without a word they picked their way across the rocks, stumbling in their haste and inability to let each other go, tumbling to the softer, pine-needled ground in the privacy of the woods. The culmination of two year's kissing, necking, making out and petting, feeling up and feeling down, the clumsy adolescent words a mockery of the glories of sensation, the tentative beauty of each new surrender, lips to lips, a touch of tongues, fingers on a well-clothed breast, a bare nipple, searching under jeans... It was over, the mystery gone, an instant of bare flesh on flesh, a quick, sharp pain and warmth, and Winston pulling wetly out, saying, 'Shit, I'm sorry. Oh shit, why'd you let me do that?' when she wanted to hold him and cry and lie in his arms forever.

She didn't get pregnant; there was no drama, no abortion or adoption, just a week of tension and a period that was so regular, so on-time and normal that it was as if her body hadn't even noticed that her life had changed forever. Winston stood by her all week; he was a good man, a responsible boy, a person who would do the right thing and he loved her. But he was also going to be the first person in his family to go to university, to be a famous writer, to be known for what he said rather than the colour of his skin, and he was not going to risk that for a postponable ecstasy.

'I think,' he said, and his eyes were full of so much love and compassion that her mind whirled with confusion, because she'd known what he was going to say before he began to speak, 'I think it'd be better to start university single. We don't want to make...'

...love? thought Jane, but 'mistakes,' said Winston.

Babies, he meant, though it might have been more than that. He undoubtedly wanted freedom to explore and become the new person he was in the process of evolving into—but in the instant that he spoke, he still loved Jane and it was only the fear of fatherhood that made him desperate to leave her.

℗

The baby in the seat in front begins crying as the plane leaves Jakarta and shows no sign of stopping as they begin the descent into Singapore. Jane envies the total lack of inhibition and ability to bellow troubles aloud but does not know how it feels, not really; the gap is too great. Her memory of travelling with a baby, however, is still so clear that she can recreate the exact mixture of frustration, embarrassment and sheer exhaustion that the young parents are demonstrating. Funny to think that while she doesn't feel much different from the woman she was then, the only trace of the two year old Megan is the innate optimism and ready smile. Crying had not been the problem on that trip, or at least not until the wait in the grimly stuffy Los Angeles holding area, enough to make anyone howl. The main risk to sanity when travelling with Megan had been ceaseless chirpy questions.

Megan is now travelling on her own, no mother to hold her hand on the trip of a lifetime, the Grand Tour Australian-style; but Megan being Megan, daughter of Jane, grand-daughter of Ruth, is not in Europe or Asia, another Aussie abroad, but is the child of a migrant discovering her roots, just as Jane had done—different country, same exploration—twenty-nine years earlier.

A got-here-safely phone call from Vancouver. No roots there, but Megan's determined to see it all, from westernmost meridian to the east: her first and only pre-booked organis-ation for the entire trip a seaplane flight to the wild west coast of Vancouver Island. Words blurring with excitement, she'd called not from the gleaming new airport but the sea-plane's small wooden terminal, a brief and disconcertingly seatbeltless ride away but redolent with the scents of cedar and sea.

'The plane's coming in now. It looks like a toy. I wish you could see it!'

The little-studied gene for love of aircraft can apparently skip a generation.

The first letter ten days later is bursting with exuberance and descriptive supelatives, though the highlight so far, Megan says, has been almost spiritual.

She'd spent a morning in a cedar gallery built in the style of a First Nations longhouse; an artist who had also come back to his roots, digging deep into his Tsimshian father's culture. It was the first day of a two-month budget, not the time to spend significant money on a painting; she bought a calendar, a dozen cards. The art was stylised, stark and vibrant, always with a hidden legend, a story in the clouds—Raven in the new moon, Thunderbird, Orca. Megan wandered dreamily through the semi-darkness, focussed on the stories of the backlit lithographs: she did not know why they touched her so deeply, she said, and the artist smiled.

The Visa card smiled too; she knew the one she wanted; there was no other purchase she could want as badly as this. It was, she decided, an auspicious beginning.

Jane is not so sure. It's sometimes difficult to remember that a daughter is an adult, to understand that it is no longer your responsibility to ensure that she can balance a budget or be trusted not to become stranded halfway across the country. Still a shock to find that she is not only living in Melbourne but has become a Melburnian; not even a student but a businesswoman, surprisingly successful—surprising to Jane and Ian not because of doubts about their daughter's ability but sincere reservations about whether even in inner-city Carlton sufficient people would be willing to pay for the privilege of having the meridians of their bodies punctured by needles—small, disposable, but still needles and not always painless.

❧

Jane's response to Winston's desertion (she will cringe at this later; alter history with half-truths) was not to go to university at all. There was no point, she argued to her bitterly disappointed mother, if all she was going to do was teach at the end of it. She could do the same thing much more easily and quickly by going to teachers' college. And it was ridiculous to say that she should be teaching high-school math or geography; how on earth could she ever control a class of grade 12s? Little children she could learn to manage, but she'd never be tall enough to have authority over senior students.

Jane has no idea, Ruth wrote to Mary, *how strong she is. She thinks that she wouldn't be able to cope with the chance of seeing this boy on campus or in the town. I don't scoff at this as puppy love; it was real and intense and perhaps I should be pleased, in view of her age, that it's over. I don't know how I feel about that, to be honest, not just because of the complications but because I've developed such a great respect for this young man's mind and am genuinely fond of him. However my interest in him hardly compares to how I care for Jane, and one thing I do know is that her life is not about to end with the close of this affair. I told her the story of my romance with Miles and of my extraordinary luck in meeting her father, but as I suppose one should have predicted, she was not impressed—whether because of her mother's fickleness or what she sees as the minuscule chance of her having the same luck, I'm not sure.*

Second chances in love are not the most tactful thing one could discuss with a spinster cousin, but this does not strike Ruth until after the letter is mailed. Mary's line is that the advantage of being an old maid is that no one interferes with one's pets, and Ruth has never probed more deeply.

So Winston went to Halifax and St Anne's; Jane went to
Truro and the college on Bible Hill, kilometres from where
her father had also studied, although there's not much in
common between a classroom of elementary school children
and a North Atlantic crossing—apart from the disadvantages
of losing control, though Jane didn't find this amusing when
Bill suggested it. In fact, for most of that summer Jane was
positively Queen Victoria-ish about any form of humour.

She saw Winston in Zellers at Christmas, and they both
froze so guiltily that if Applevale had run to store detectives
they'd have been arrested immediately. Winston was the first
to say hello and she thought that he would have chatted if
she could have borne it. She couldn't. For long after, even
when accidents of distance made it impossible that it could
be him, a glimpse of the back of a close-shorn black skull or
the scent of starched cotton on young male sweat would twist
a small dart inside her.

Some first love stories could be shared, laid out and admired
without losing their brilliance; some were best locked away
to be trickled through fingers in private. One betrayal was
too much, and she never again—no matter how many shared
confidences or bottles—thrilled her sisters with that particular jewel.

✐

A real sister would be nice in times like this, Jane thinks
now; not that there are many times like this. Her brothers
are strangers, last seen at twenty-one and nineteen but younger
still in her mind, stuck in the childhood when she covered
up for Mike and cared for Rick. On rare phone calls, when
she hears a middle-aged male voice saying, 'Mom said,' or
'Dad did,' she feels a sense of shock that they're referring to
the same Mom and Dad that she is. She might have kept in
closer contact with a female sibling, but the closest she's had
is Sue. Neighbours for fifteen years, friends for not much

less, there's very little they don't know about each other. You can't hide much on dairy farms anyway, not in this soldier-settlement area where the farms are laid out neatly side by side, dairies and houses close to the road and the trees still too small for privacy. When Col and Sue's cows trampled a fence to get to a newly sown paddock, Ian was the first to see them and leap to his motorbike to chase them off; Col has jumped the boundary fence to stick a knife into a greedy cow's bloated belly and save her life. On mornings when the shouting from next door's dairy is particularly prolonged or obscene, Jane knows that the phone is likely to ring during the morning: 'You probably heard that dummy-spit... Is your kettle on?'

'I don't know how Sue puts up with it,' she often confides to Ian, grateful that he isn't abusive in the dairy, to her or the cows, although she knows that Sue is equally relieved at Col's acquiescence about anything she wants to do outside it.

'Just tell Ian you're taking that job!' says Sue. 'What's he got against your doing well?'

'Nothing,' Jane defends. 'He's just afraid I'm taking on more than I can handle.'

'Bull! He's afraid you'll find out how strong you are and start standing up for yourself. You know that's why he talked you out of the principal's job, and now he's doing it all over again, and you really want to do this EcoFarm thing.'

Jane could as easily suggest that Sue order Col to stop screaming at nervous heifers, but thinks it would be rude to say so.

'What are the rules?' she'd ask Sue now, if Qantas had a phone for their morning chat. Maybe there's some kind of Emily Post on the etiquette for the loss of a parent. Does she feel too much or too little? How much of the grief is for Ruth and how much for herself?

Then there's the relief: relief that brings guilt, though a part of her can stand back further still and know that it shouldn't because most of it is for Ruth, who at one stroke (Is that a dreadful pun? Is there something wrong with her if it is?) has been spared the worst indignities of old age. Relief born of love, knowing that her mother would have hated—as who wouldn't, but Ruth more than most—to lose faculties, to feel her sharp mind dim, would have much rather died than suffer being jollied in an institution or long-term hospital bed.

'But you could have let me say goodbye!' she tells God. 'You could have let her live till I got there.'

'With pain? With confusion?' answers—probably not God, more likely the other part of her mind. 'You'd put your mother through a few days of hell for your own satisfaction?'

'That's not what I mean!' she snarls, because she and God both know perfectly well that what she'd wanted was a simple, classical deathbed scene without pain, confusion or bodily fluids.

Except that she's not completely sure Ruth would have wanted to die holding someone's, even her daughter's, hand. Given the choice she probably would have chosen privacy.

Maybe she did choose. If so, Jane's grief is for herself, the abandoned child: now no one stands between her and her own mortality. 'I'm an orphan,' she tries, but it doesn't work: at some age one becomes too old to be an orphan.

*A*lone in Singapore airport, Jane wanders. Six hours: the length of a school day—with planning she could have taken a city-sights bus tour, but the thought of asking and arranging drains her with unutterable weariness. She has to remind herself of her continuing ticket, a destination, and feels too lost to believe in it. This, she thinks, is how a refugee must feel—and is immediately ashamed, because there is no similarity whatsoever and no reason, in this affluent gleam of duty-free, for refugees to come to mind at all.

Except that, midway in this spiderweb of adopted and birthplaces (from her adopted country to that of her mother's birth, from mother's birthplace to adopted—refuge?—which is of course Jane's own home and native land) tangible assets seem suddenly less important. Like any refugee, she is not sure which home is hers.

Tangible assets—the great tourist shopping spree—are, however, much in evidence. A more glamorous woman, or a woman who loved glamour more, might have been distracted even from grief by the arrays of jewellery, make-up, leather goods and perfume. She does nearly buy a book, fingering Anne Tyler's *Ladder of Years* until the voice of logic points out that she has not only spent a vast amount of money on this journey, but that she is so exhausted anything she reads now will be utterly wasted.

You'll have worked out by now, Bill writes, wondering exactly what to say to the stranger who's agreed to marry him, because he certainly can't put into words the thoughts that have obsessed him since that night, *that the plane we heard crash was Hitler's new surprise—and I'd have to say a plane without a pilot is some surprise. I thought it was a joke at first. A guy from Chicago says they're nonunion planes—'trying to put us all out of a job.'*

PS, he adds next morning, *I'm sorry I joked about those buzz bombs. I just heard that one of our ground crew, a bright young kid from Rhodesia, was killed last night in London. Doesn't seem right, somehow, to come all this way and be killed on a week's leave.*

'If there's anything you'd like to discuss, Ruth,' the CO says quietly.

Ruth thinks quickly over her last few days' work: a broken Oxford, which she'd limped with some difficulty to its final role of target practice for student bomb-aimers. She'd been quite proud of the fact that despite its official Essentially Non Airworthy status she'd managed to land without adding to its long list of damage—there couldn't have been any complaints there. A beautiful factory-fresh Spitfire to a fighter base, and a return trip with one to the factory for servicing; a horrible Walrus seaplane which had given her a bump on the forehead when climbing in but no other problems; two more Spitfires and a Mosquito. Nothing had bounced or broken and she'd been too overwhelmed by the rollercoaster of her personal life to attempt any unauthorised aeronautics.

'You haven't looked well the last few weeks,' the CO prompts.

'Oh, I'm perfectly well, thank you,' but she can feel herself flushing, she hasn't blushed like this since—no, never like this, not this burning heat of throat, even ears, but then she's never before felt shame like this. It's bad enough that she should wake at night wondering who she is and where she's come from, worse that the doubts intrude on her dreams of Bill and the future, but worst of all would be to discuss this humiliation in public.

'Perhaps a little tired, as we all are.'

'That's true. Well, just let me know in good time if you're going to need...if there's anything you need to discuss.'

Pity, that's the expression, concern. But how could Margot have guessed the truth? Compared to the strained waiting of those with husbands fighting or missing in action, her own drama is petty, sordid and hardly the most likely thing to come to mind. Ruth Townsend looking a little under the weather? It's only natural, she's a bastard, an abandoned baby, no one knows who her parents are. For a person as private as she, it's a bitter twist simply to know that she's been unguarded enough to leave someone else contemplating what her problem could be. Sometimes she is still amazed that she told Bill, sobbing in his arms—she is neither a sobber nor a blurter of secrets, which leads her back to the beginning: perhaps she's not any of the things she'd always thought she was. *How do I know I love you?* she'd written last night, after a day in which falling in love seemed just another impossible thing to believe. *Because some atavistic part of me believes that in handing my story to you I've delivered my soul to your keeping. I've never been sure what I believe about the soul, but the joining, the recognition of ours, seems the only way to explain what has happened between us.*

One of the many letters that she doesn't send, crumpled into a tight ball, it sits in the rubbish basket as she begins today's.

Dearest Bill
I had the strangest talk with our CO tonight, and laughs aloud as she finally recalls the recent notice about pregnancy, pilots and the forbidding of. Margot's worrying about offspring, not ancestors.

The letter joins last night's and instead she constructs a funny story about her trials in taking the Oxford to its final resting-place—*It's a shame they couldn't have just bombed the silly thing where it was!* She doesn't know Bill well enough to joke about conception.

⟡

A letter a day, a testament of faith, the beginning of the web of letters that will over Ruth's lifetime stretch across continents. He replies almost as often: scraps of words, an alien medium for a man whose life has been lived with other men for four years now, his own world seen in the lines of charts, the meridians of the earth's body.

His letters to her are at first indistinguishable from those to his parents, following the army as it clears its way across France: details of rolled metal landing strips, red wine in a village cafe, the carefully imprecise geography—*somewhere in Europe*—belying his constant knowledge of the exact coordinates of wherever he is.

But inexorably, letter by letter, defences are stripped away.

12 July 1944

Dearest Bill
I had breakfast in a Bomber Command mess, and if I weren't a bit thin at the moment—She hesitates over this admission—does he like bony women?—*I think next time I'd prefer to*

wait and hope for a chance of lunch. It's not simply the way everyone avoids looking at those empty places—and there were so many of them this morning—or that all ears are straining for the sound of another aircraft coming in long after time. It's those haunted, hunted faces themselves; one wonders how they'll ever return to a normal life when this nightmare is over. Yet I know that if one saw them a few hours later the look would tell an entirely different story, and they'll be ready to go again by the time it's dark tonight.

What particularly wrung my heart, however, was a young WAAF who literally collapsed, sobbing at her table. A friend went to her and I presume took her back to the Waaferie where she could grieve in private, but as I left I heard a pilot say, 'She's a regular chop girl, that one—that's her third. If I see anyone in my crew with her...'

So now this poor girl, who has obviously just lost her lover, will be ostracised by the rest of the squadron.

The very worst of it is that as superstitious and illogical as it is, I know exactly how they feel. This war is not making any of us better people.

I don't think it's making me a better person, Bill agrees. *The more I see of France and what's been done to the people, the angrier I get.* Does he hesitate here, too, wondering if he's describing a desirable husband? *We took a bit of flak as we landed the ambulance Dakota this morning, so I had a look at the town while we were waiting for emergency repairs. The people are so grateful; two girls gave me flowers as if I'd been one of their liberators instead of just doing the tidying up afterwards, and one woman gave me a glass of wine with some bread and sausage. I didn't feel good taking it, she looked right skinny herself (Are you truly getting thin? Please take care of yourself.) but it seemed awfully important to her, so I felt like it would be better if I ate. Then she told me that the Germans had shot her husband as they left, no particular reason as far as I could understand except I guess he was there, and maybe when you're retreating from a place you thought you'd won, that's all the excuse you need.*

The funny thing was she called the snack a 'gouter', and I always thought that was a word my Grandpère made up, a sort of baby talk, because I never heard anyone else say it. So hearing it now, it did make me think of him, and how if history had been different maybe he would have been living here now in one of these villages that I've just seen. But then I wouldn't have been born, and I wouldn't have met you, so I'm glad that history turned out the way it did.

You'll like him, and I know he'll like you—he likes beautiful women.

Because of course they know what an audacious thing they've done, tying themselves to the phantom of love at first sight, with fate determined to thwart all their attempts at meeting—leaves rearranged, aircraft stuck out in distant places for a night, a motorbike bought in high hopes then borrowed and broken. Now the intensity of the letters fills the gaps, the tentative getting-to-know of a more leisurely romance.

Do I tell you too much? Ruth asks. *I write to you each day as a schoolgirl confides in her diary, or a nun in her prayer. Do you feel overwhelmed?*

I feel honoured, says Bill, *though I don't much like the thought of you as a nun.*

❧

Letters to Bill are not the only ones Ruth writes. Finally, she has written to her parents. *I must know what Mama meant, and understand who my parents are, if you are not.* Determined not to pollute her new life with the messiness of the past, she decides not to mention Bill until this is cleared up.

16 August 1944

My dear Ruth

I read your letter with some surprise. I am pleased to say that your mother was not in the house when the post came, and I do not intend to inform her of its contents.

You remain, as you always have been, our daughter. Your Mama made a slip of the tongue, which she sincerely regrets, in referring to your, let us say, Darwinian forebears. Biology, while a fascinating science, is surely the least interesting component of what makes up an individual; although we use the term breeding, what we in fact mean is upbringing and your upbringing, my dear, is pure Townsend. I cannot conceive of what possible good it could do to bring to light any earlier sordid history.

I do not think there needs to be any further reference to this subject.

I trust that you will be able to return home for another leave soon, as your Mama would very much like to see you. The flying bombs are proving a trial for her nerves, having been quite constant since early June. At least in the Blitz one knew that a cloudy night would bring some respite, but now one never knows when the next bomb will arrive. One must also admit that the peculiarity of the noise, and the interminable silence between the engine cutting out and the bomb landing, is rather unnerving.

Your Mama watches the post anxiously for a letter, so I would ask you to be so good as to send her one soon, but I repeat, without reference to the questions in your latest.

With best wishes,
Papa

And because duty is a habit, Ruth writes to her mother the following day and continues to do so regularly—and if the letters give away nothing of herself, at least they don't contain any embarrassing questions.

But questions are all that fill her mind.

I have to know, she tells Bill. *I want it all sorted out before I tell them we're getting married.*

❧

Digging through the haze of scrambled memories, Ruth arrives at one that is distinct amongst early recollections by not being attached to a family story or photograph. True or not, it is her own.

She is standing, holding a woman's hand, at the front gate of an unfamiliar grey stone house with small windows. It is cold but not raining; it could be autumn. This is where her new Mummy and Daddy live. The woman has told her this, although Ruth can never hear the voice.

The woman's coat is heavy, rough, a muddy brown that the adult Ruth has always hated; perhaps this explains it. Or perhaps it's simply aesthetic. She can't see the face—she is, after all, very small. The hand, the coat, are at her own level. But she can't picture the hand either.

Her mother? Someone from an orphanage? An image she's conjured up to fill a gap?

❧

Tomorrow, if there are no disasters on the farm, no sudden fusions of tractor motors or cows, awkward in pregnancy, cast on channel banks, Ian will go to the river. In times of need or reflection he's always found himself at the Murray's side, and tomorrow, having woken alone, he'll feel the weight of their separation and the need to replenish himself for the coming season. And because he is human, with the usual burdens of thinking and feeling, he might reflect on the impermanence of life.

The river, home of ancient and more recent tales, is a fitting place for it. It's peaceful now, biding its time over the winter months to digest its prey; last summer it took more than its ordinary share of sacrifice. As in war there is occasional collateral damage: the oncoming drivers wiped out by a broadsiding ute in the dust; the parents caught in the current of rescue when children step into sudden depths. But in further imitation of war, the river's favourites are the boys, youths on the verge of adulthood; some years it takes more of the region's young men than Vietnam did in seven. Filled with alcohol or bravado or plain bad luck, they swim too far, are caught in unseen currents or unsuspected snags, dive onto shifted sandbars or drifted logs, plunge cars down perilous embankments.

Such a fine line between good luck and bad, between a moment's adrenalin rush and irrevocable change: a brain rewired after concussion, a body unwired by snap of spine. Fragile creatures, humans, and nature hasn't heard of the end of corporal—or capital—punishment.

Nevertheless, even for Jane, who hasn't grown up camping every summer along the crowded banks, who hasn't built her first sandcastles on the white beaches or learned to water-ski behind spraying speedboats, the river's solace outweighs it random tragedies. In the early days, when the ugliness of flat treeless paddocks pressed heavily on her soul, she could find beauty in the river's grassy slopes and white sand, gazing up at the gums' topmost branches till she was dizzy and calmed. It was there that she first heard a kookaburra and saw a koala, initiations as special to her as Ian's childhood and less savoury adolescent memories. She had realised that if this sort of natural beauty existed on the river banks less than a kilometre from the house, there must be a means of recreating it, to some extent, on the farm, and specifically, on the domestic dam just down the laneway from her garden.

She had started all wrong, of course, but in 1970 one didn't have to be a recently introduced specimen oneself to miss the significance of indigenous vegetation. Willow cuttings from the trees on the main channel were set to fringe

the edges of the dam, and in a few short years, willows growing as they do, appeared in the twilight as elegant as a Japanese
print. Ducks landed on the dam's surface, and one year a pair
of black swans stayed for most of the winter. When Ian
installed a bore to pump cleaner water for the house and dairy,
he'd agreed to leave the dam as it was instead of bulldozing
it in as their neighbours were doing.

Within another ten years, when it could no longer be denied
that, contrary to popular wisdom, willow roots in the long
run caused more damage to waterways than they solved, as
well as offering nothing to the birds Jane wanted to tempt,
Ian agreed to chop down the willows and drag them off for
a winter bonfire. Jane had already begun to plant the first of
her rows of native trees along fence lines: 'You'll appreciate
this one day,' she would tell the cows as she dug, mulching
around the tiny sprigs, juice-carton tree guards against rabbits and a fence against cattle, but the cows rarely listened.
The bulls especially seemed to view each tree guard as
a challenge, smashing their way through double rows of
electric fencing to charge any sapling poking its head above
the long grass.

Despite the hazards of bulls and frosts, the majority of her
plantings had survived and the proportions increased each year
with her learning. By the time she replanted the dam she had
read widely, talked to the Department of Conservation and
knew exactly what she wanted. For trees and shrubs she used
*Eucalyptus camaldulensis, Callistemon sieberi, Acacia retinoides,
Melaleuca parvistaminea,* the sonorous names suddenly as familiar as maple and spruce, and underplanted them with the
delightfully named billy buttons and native bluebell. Later
still, she added native grasses and water plants at the dam's
edge, water ribbons and yellow rush lilies. The birds came,
from tiny blue wrens to gaudy rosellas, more species than she'd
known the region supported. Nothing in her life had ever
come to fruition so exactly as she'd dreamed.

'Jane's oasis,' Ian teased with perhaps a deeper truth than he realised, because it was as much an oasis of Jane's soul as a physical haven for the birds. And if she rarely sat there for the quiet times that she had imagined, usually finding some new task to occupy her, there was a gift of tranquillity in simply knowing it was there.

It was the beginning, too, of the path that led her to EcoFarm and the study of the Gundanna Lagoon.

☙

The Lyons teashop outside Paddington Station is crowded and Ruth is seated with strangers, a dejected-looking woman in the seat where she'd hoped Bill would be. Her hands are clammy as she orders a third pot of tea; the train from Oxford is late.

The men at the next table are having a vociferous discussion about a gas main that exploded earlier that morning. 'I'm telling you, there's something going on here we're not being told. That's the third in two days.'

'One in Chiswick the day before that. It took out four houses and made a bloody big hole in the street, my daughter said. Worse than a buzz bomb.'

'The one I passed yesterday was being guarded by American soldiers. That's what put the wind up me—why would a squad of Yanks be guarding an exploded gasometer? The government must think we're idiots to believe that—I tell you, we're looking at Hitler's new surprise!'

Ruth has other things to think about than the likelihood of exploding gas mains. It's nearly three months since she's seen Bill, and she's beginning to wonder if she'll recognise him. Beginning to wonder if those intimate, intense letters have led them into a terrible mistake; whether the written word is all that binds them and face to face the magic will die. It seems impossible that they could recapture that feeling of certainty and delight from those two fleeting nights;

her stomach is churning with the fear that nothing exists out-side her own imagination.

Then her heart skips, as if it recognises him before her eyes have time to do so: taller than the crowd and quite oblivious to it because he's seen her now and is intent on nothing but reaching her. Holding her.

'Excuse me, sir,' says the waitress, 'but people need to get past.'

I should feel embarrassed, Ruth thinks, but I can't be bothered.

Bill doesn't want tea, doesn't want to stay in this stuffy, clammy shop; he propels her out and down the street, she takes his arm, they're decorous, respectable, but shoulders touch and sometimes hips and the warmth of his body is singing to her.

'I've booked into my hotel,' he says, gazing across from the bus stop as if fascinated by the peculiar shape of the bomb hole in the pavement there, 'for two nights.'

'My parents are only expecting me for one.'

'But your leave is for two.'

'Have you got a suggestion?'

'Well...I did mention, when I was booking in, that my wife might be able to join me at some stage.'

'Wise man,' she says lightly, as though emotion is not threat-ening to choke her, as though her eyes are not dancing with laughter and fire. 'I like wise men.'

Bill thinks that as he should probably try not to be more than three hours late to meet his future in-laws, he would be wiser still not to dwell on this promise in public. Especially squashed into this crowded bus, Ruth against his chest, reaching for the overhead strap. Think of her parents, that'll cool him down—'What have you told them?'

'That I'm bringing home a very dear friend whom I want them to meet.'

'Did you mention that the dear friend was a man?'

She's laughing again; she can't help it, she should be nervous but it's such an extraordinary relief, Bill's here in flesh and blood, oh very much in flesh, one flesh is what they'll be and it can't be too soon, because the man from the letters, the man in her dreams and the man beside her are all the same, all gloriously true, and she loves them all. 'I think they'll realise.'

Bill decides it's silly to worry if she's not. Although he's still not looking forward to it—she's said nothing to make him think that they'll welcome a colonial son-in-law, or have anything in common. Her father imports lumber (timber Ruth calls it), maybe they can talk about wood or trees; he does at least know a little about that, though snigging a few logs out of the woods isn't quite the end of the business that her father will be interested in.

I'm glad I'm an officer, he thinks suddenly, and for the first time. He suspects that it will make it infinitely easier to face the Townsends.

Not that he's good at making it easy. Faced with the subtle condescension of protective middle-class parents, he knows he'll become the colonial, making mistakes with grammar and cups of tea. The more he feels he is being patronised, the more he'll play country hick. (Add a hint of Anglo-Canadian snobbery and he'll be speaking with Grandpère's accent which, given the scattered childhood phrases and nursery rhymes that is all his French consists of, endears him to neither French nor English Canadians.)

'How about I just drop to my knees on the doorstep and say, "Please, sir, I want to marry your daughter."?'—a bit louder than he'd intended. The woman across the aisle is too polite to turn, but her mouth twitches.

'Perhaps you could wait till we get inside.'

He can see the tension beginning behind the teasing smile, and his arm tightens around her. 'If it's too bad,' he whispers, 'you can come straight back to the hotel with me. And if they don't like it you'll soon be on the other side of the world and you won't ever have to see them again.'

Ruth doesn't hear the words so never knows that he regrets them for the rest of his life. The bus stops around the corner from Savernake Street, but they're aware of something wrong even before they see the blockade and the queue of emergency vehicles leaving from the other end. A pall of brick dust and smoke hangs low in the sky; the smell is choking. There are guards, not American this time, but Ruth sprints past them and leaves Bill to explain it's her home, her parents, and the guards let him follow. The windows in every house from the corner are cracked and broken; shards of glass, vegetation, bricks and unimaginable debris litter the road. Her run slows to a scramble as the litter turns to mounds; she is kicking her way through glass, climbing over chunks of masonry and timber. Now whole windows, doors, walls, are missing; half of number 44, the front wall of 39. Shattered rooms inside are humiliatingly nude and instantly sordid, family intimacy on display.

A yawning crater, filling with filth and water, is all that remains of numbers 40 and 42.

Ruth registers the scene as a series of disconnected snapshots, as if she's observing from somewhere outside herself; there are almost titles on these cliched scenes of tragedy.

The house is as completely demolished as if it has never existed; as if Ruth has imagined it, along with her childhood, her parents; herself. 'Ruins of a Chelsea home', although ruin suggests something recognisable, something dignified, and this mound of rubble—bricks shattered and scattered, matchsplinters of wood no longer distinguishable as front door, Queen Anne table or tapestry frame, surreally twisted metal and shards of glass glinting in the afternoon sun, scrap of fabric, unlikely flag in the pattern of her winter nightgown, waving from what once might have been a roof beam—is neither recognisable nor dignified. Rescue workers are picking their way through the rubble, methodically and hopelessly; Ruth is unable to understand what they could be searching for.

The frame switches to a tall, slim young woman, smartly dressed in a pale blue dress from Oxford days, the matching hat—concession to her parents—perched on waving brown hair; silk stockings and black pumps. She leans against the shoulder of a taller, fairer man in RCAF uniform. They're both healthy, young and attractive; it could be a wedding photograph or an advertisement, until you notice the holocaust behind them, the shock written clear across the man's face, his arms supporting and protecting the sagging girl, his head bent to hers as if to whisper. In this sharp-edged image only the girl's face is out of focus.

There is one simply entitled 'Grief': Mr James from number 39, in a statued freeze, crossed arms and a vacant face staring at the missing portion of his house while Mrs Hutchinson, unnoticed, pats him on the shoulder as if he were one of her terriers.

Impressions after that are jumbled: Mrs Hutchinson's face moving slowly towards her, chalky-grey with dust and shock; a thought frozen like a sentence in time: If I leave now, I won't have to hear what she's going to say. The layer of mind below that already knows the truth. A confusion of mumbles—asking about Mrs James, Mrs James who was not badly hurt but in hospital with her injured grandchild, a baby with a leg gone and the daughter-in-law that Ruth has never met, dead. Mrs Hutchinson still talking, more news, of people not suffering, didn't hear anything till it happened, no warning at all, just a crash and a terrible boom, never heard a noise like it before, ears are still ringing, never even time to be afraid, they wouldn't have known what hit them and Ruth really ought to have a cup of tea before she does what has to be done. And she, Ruth, unable, unwilling to understand what has to be done or why, swimming through the words, cold and detached, wishing she could go to sleep, go to some other place so this will all make sense when she returns.

Bill's voice the only clear auditory memory in this jumble, as if her mind has set up a wall that only one specific timbre can breach: 'She's trying to tell you that your parents are dead.'

❧

On a black and white screen a man named Armstrong walks—bounces—leaps—across the moon. He repeats the performance on the evening news, the weekly round-up, countless news clips ever after. Ruth and Bill, earthbound for twenty-four years without ceasing to yearn for the skies, watch them all, including a documentary on the history of rocket flight. The first rockets, the commentator drones in the measured tones peculiar to documentaries, were developed by the Germans during the Second World War and launched as the ultimate terror weapon, although in fact too late to change the course of the war and ineffective anyway, in that only two thousand seven hundred Londoners were killed by the five hundred and seventeen bombs that reached the city. Old footage is shown of an imploding cinema in Antwerp and the splintered ruins of an unspecified London house. *Vergeltunsgwaffen*, they were called: vengeance weapons.

'The terrifying thing about these V2s,' explains an English scientist now working for NASA alongside some of the original developers of the bomb, 'is that because they travelled faster than the speed of sound, there was absolutely no warning—one heard the boom as one realised that the house next door had disappeared.'

❧

There'd been no emergency farewell flight on Bill's death, four years earlier. Jane had spent three weeks with her parents in May of that year and had found her father unexpectedly frail and uncharacteristically removed. He'd had a series of ailments through the winter—chronic bronchitis, prostate problems that were not cancer but irritating, a duodenal ulcer, an

ingrown toenail that had become infected and refused to heal—
and was embarrassed by the misery of what he considered
minor, almost hypochondriacal, complaints. It had struck
Jane that she mightn't see him again; the thought had weighed
down their easygoing relationship. Bill must have thought it
too, but it wasn't something she could talk about.

Still a shock when it happened, so much sooner than she'd
expected: a summer cold tightening its grip, becoming pneu-
monia; he'd died in July, three months after his seventy-sixth
birthday.

'No point in coming again,' Ruth had said, and her daughter
had been secretly, guiltily, relieved. Her redundancy, or
incitement-to-leave-teaching package, so fat and promising
on first view, so full of new houses or extensions and reno-
vated kitchens, had shrunk in the end to a new milk vat and
her trip home. A second fare in the same year seemed pure
indulgence, father's death or not. In the end, so much of her
natural grief had been subsumed by the worry of how her
mother would cope that the death itself had never truly been
faced.

She'd phoned regularly for a few months, until it was
obvious that her mother was managing well and they could
settle back to weekly letters.

Jane had never known of the anger, Ruth's despair at the
desertion. Bill's parents had died in their early eighties, and
his beloved Grandpère, dying suddenly soon after VJ day,
had been ninety-two and anticipating his first great-grand-
child. Despite all evidence to the contrary, Ruth had presumed
her unknown genetic heritage to be inferior to his proven
one. Ideally she would have believed in Baucis and Philemon,
and if she could not be a linden tree to Bill's oak had never
been sure whether she was selfish enough to wish to leave
him alone or brave enough to be the one left—for Ruth was
clear-eyed about the silent strength she'd leaned on for forty-
four years: 'My ebb is come, his life was my spring tide.' She

was still unsure which fate she'd have chosen if death had let her vote.

One never thought of him as proud, she wrote to Mary, *because he had no arrogance. But there's a certain reverse arrogance in refusing to bother a doctor when one is genuinely ill!*

Of course the problem was that he didn't believe he was genuinely ill, and he was sick to death, the last three words had been crossed out, and then, since it was presumably the most accurate phrase possible, written again, *of the doctor's visits, tests and hospital stays he'd had with all his problems last winter. The toenail demoralised him more than anything; he seemed to find it shameful that a foot that had survived a bullet should be crippled up by its own toenail. (And there was no point whatsoever in pointing out that it's a common complaint, which might happen to anyone of any age!)*

I don't know if it was part of the old guilt about having had a comparatively safe and injury-free war—as if he'd chosen that bit of luck! I thought he'd left that behind, but maybe one never completely leaves anything behind, because I think at the end he was back to feeling that since so many of his friends had been denied the privilege of ageing, he had no right to complain about the inconveniences that go along with it.

How do you manage, Mary, waking every day with no one to speak to? How am I going to learn it now?

However, in letters to her children, Ruth was quickly her usual independent, acerbic self. Jane was left once again with the unreality of distant death, as she had been for her grandparents, several great-aunts and uncles, even Aunt Louise of lung cancer at only fifty-seven; all dead in that nineteen years between her first visit and second. Nineteen years—a lifetime, a death time—is too long between visits, but it can't be changed by worrying about it now, and when it came to realities, the three-month gap between seeing her father and it being too late to see him again hadn't done much to make

her understand that he was gone. There was simply no con-
clusive proof. Her mother was the letter writer, his news
came second-hand. On the phone she would hear the surge
of pleasure in his voice: 'I'll call your mother,' he'd say, enjoying Ruth's excitement more than his own, his birthday the
only time she could convince him to stay and chat. She'd always
known that in some ways she'd never quite believe he was
dead until she'd been home and seen his absence for herself.

But she hadn't expected not to see her mother again and
can't help feeling that losing both was unfair. Careless, as Lady
Bracknell said to Algernon. (Jane, who believes she never
uses literary quotations, finds them leaping into any contem-
plation of Ruth.)

This time there will be no denial, no semiacceptance of
reality. This time she is the one who must cope, who must
do...whatever it is that must be done. Her ideas are hazy on
exactly what that is. She and Ian had helped his mother
when his father died: buried in the Narling Cemetery, the
United Church ladies organising sandwiches and cake afterwards. There really hadn't been much to decide. This was
not going to be so simple.

Is this one of those things, like esoteric housekeeping lore,
that other people simply know and she's somehow missed
out on?

Her mind flits, from Fred's funeral to Princess Diana's, to
the Belgian undertaker who had once tried to pick her up,
strolling uninvited at her side past the Sunday art on Bayswater
Road with earnest explanations, also uninvited, of his fu-
nereal studies in London. Before she met Ian. She should
have paid attention.

❧

When Jane had travelled through Europe and eventually to
Australia, she'd sent home letters with neatly sketched maps
of wherever she was. Although they were all marked 'Mom

and Dad', everyone knew the letters were for her mother, the maps for her father. The shapes and forms of land, the directions of roads and rivers, were indispensable to the tale of her travels and as obvious to her as if marked with compass and surveyor's pegs. Which was how she and her father seemed to picture topography, whereas her mother, that airier spirit, saw maps simply as a means to an end, preferring to find her own images in the surrounding words.

Megan's letters, on the other hand, are more concerned with the tenuous threads of synchronicity and fate than hard details of time and place, although she tries to include facts that she thinks will entertain.

Dear Mum and Dad
Vancouver is great; it reminds me a little of Sydney—but I try not to let that prejudice me. Is the universe sending me a message to broaden my horizons from Melbourne? In fact the longer I spend here the more it seems a city you could live in, like Melbourne.

A warning bell jangled in Jane's mind.

After my last (first) letter I spent a little longer on Vancouver Island. I skipped some of the tourist things that seemed as if you had to be sixty-five and on a 'see all of North America on a three-week bus trip' to qualify, but there truly is something about the region that is awesome. Sitting on the beach that first morning, on the west coast of Vancouver Island, I knew that if I projected my mind far enough, I'd be able to see all the way to St Kilda. Nature's gods seem very close to the surface.
Now I can hear Dad laughing! But I've fallen in love with this place.
Did I tell you about this tremendous carving, the first thing you see when you get into Vancouver airport? It was so powerful, like nothing I've ever seen, so I asked the Customs guy about it. He said if I was interested I should go to the anthropology

museum at the University of British Columbia, where another of the artist's works is featured (and a few other things too of course!).

Well, you can imagine my reaction to starting off my holiday with a university museum! But you know what happens when fate decides something. (You DO know, Dad! You just deny it.)

So I had a day exploring the city—would you believe I even found a Tai Chi class to join in a Chinese garden? And then at the Y that night I was talking to an English girl. She's been here nearly a month and the one place she thought I should definitely see was—you guessed it.

Anyway, you'd be proud of me because I got a bus map and worked out what buses I had to take and got out there the next day without getting lost once. And it was worth it.

Didn't Nan say once that Grandad had a, was it Mi'kmaq ancestor? I stood in front of the huge carving of the story of creation for an hour. All the creatures are about to burst out of a clam shell, and though I couldn't have identified them all without the legend, I could feel the energy flowing from it and I felt such an affinity that I thought I must have some First People's blood somewhere in me.

Anyway, I'd been staring so long that I was the last person to leave, and a man who works there gave me a lift back to the Y when he saw me waiting for the bus. He wasn't doing anything for the evening so we had dinner together. I thought he must be part of the anthropology department, but it turns out he's actually in admin and was just at the museum for something else. But he's very interested in things, not a business-type nerd.

I told him how much I'd loved Vancouver Island and especially the west coast, and he's going hiking there next week, in the Pacific Rim National Park. You have to book a place so that the trail doesn't get too crowded, but he was going with a friend who's just changed jobs and can't get leave after all.

I know I've just been there, but I didn't walk much. I'm starting to wonder if I should do that instead of the trip from Banff I was thinking about. Apparently Banff is quite touristy and I do want to experience this country properly—you know how Nan's always going on about understanding your heritage! I'll never do that from behind a train window.

I'm meeting him for dinner tonight so I'll find out a bit more then, but all this synchronicity suggests that it's something I need to do.

Jane's warning bells escalated to full-scale air-raid siren.

ᔕ

Bill takes Ruth to her aunt in St John's Wood to deal with the grim formalities of tragedy. Ruth is white-faced, moves like an automaton but doesn't cry; by the end of the day she's swaying as she stands, close to collapse. There's no question now of hotels; in the evening, the aunt puts her to bed in her daughter Mary's empty room and Bill is left to talk to another cousin, a pukka RAF type with an unfortunate resemblance to Bill's wing commander. He has an almost overwhelming desire to rush into Ruth's room and carry her away to safety—from whom or what he isn't sure. Briefly, he considers announcing that they have already married. But this is Ruth's family, he tells himself. She needs to be with them, not a man she barely knows who can't be trusted to keep his hands to himself.

'I wanted you so badly,' Ruth will tell him later, when these things can be said. 'I lay there in Mary's bed just aching for you to come and hold me, to lie with your arms around me so I could feel that you were real.'

Bill returns the next morning, meets more relatives and attends the funeral with her before returning to base. Ruth stays with her aunt for a few more days of compassionate leave.

She has been left with the few possessions in her yacht club room: clothing and uniforms, the evening dress and wrap, handbag and shoes, a silver framed photograph of the people who said they were her parents in formal evening dress—it will be years before she can look at it again, but she will be grateful that she'd stopped herself from destroying it in that first agony of impotent rage and grief—and of course the books, ten, from the impulsively packed *Peter Pan* of childhood (she seems to have become one of the Lost Boys rather than Peter), to the Henry James bought the week before. There is also a will that endows her with a considerable sum of money when she turns thirty and no provision against destitution in the four intervening years, a block of unsaleable land and an abiding sense of rage.

The Townsends might not have been able to will the V2's flight path directly onto their home, but it had nonetheless been an answer to their prayers. She is convinced that her parents, the people who acted as her parents, would have chosen death in preference to answering her questions.

They have their way; the questions remain unanswered; the trails are all dead ends. At the funeral she shocks the minister by asking to see the baptismal records, abandoning a last grain of hope when she finds she is not on them. Her grandparents had died when she was tiny; she asks aunts and uncles, both sides of the family, but the answer is always the same. In 1920, when her parents were in their forties, they announced to the family that after years of childlessness they now had a two year old daughter. They were not prepared to discuss it. 'You know your father,' says her mother's brother; 'You know your mother,' echoes her father's sister, 'when she said "no discussion" she meant none at all. Father asked a simple question and they didn't return to the house again until he was dying.'

They'd been living in Hampstead then, an uncle volunteers, a house right across from the Heath, had moved to the present, now nonexistent house shortly after. He remembers meeting Ruth for the first time at the family gathering in Chelsea on Christmas Eve: a solemn little girl looking slightly lost in the welter of middle-class childhood, grey dappled rocking horse, fragile dolls and the first of her life's abiding passion—books: John Gilpin, Kate Greenaway's *A Apple Pie*, a brightly coloured Jack and Jill, Jack's brown-paper-wrapped head the only thing that made her smile.

'Which reminds me,' the uncle adds, 'your father loaned me a book last time I saw him; I suppose you'd better have it,' and Ruth adds Nevil Shute's *Pastoral* to her meagre library.

She goes next day to the address in Hampstead, a two-storey grey stone house with a *Garden flat to let* card in the basement window. Standing outside on the steeply sloping street she cannot tell whether it was the house of her memory, but in the Hampstead Church records she finds 'Ruth Elizabeth Townsend', christened 21 November 1920, and for the first time, she cries. She does at least exist.

Born on Armistice Day, christened two years and ten days later...but now even her birthday seems doubtful, like a date chosen—a child of about twenty-four months, give it a birthday with some significance, as one might a puppy, perhaps the date it arrived (ten days an appropriate amount of time to arrange a christening?). And if the anniversary of the ending of war seems an unlikely day to give away a child, the chances improve if one looks at it as a public holiday, her father home from the City to take possession.

The child is taken in, christened and transformed into a Townsend, a Ruth—she feels instinctively that any previous name would have been stamped out—the ready-made family move to a new home, new neighbours...a unit intact and unquestioned.

That is as far as Ruth can go. Adoption, a clerk at the Registry of Births, Deaths and Marriages tells her, hadn't become a legal procedure until several years later. Short of tracing every female child born in south-east England in November 1918, there is no way of discovering the woman who bore her, or the reasons for abandonment. Still less the man who'd contributed that strong-swimming sperm, a casual gift, an act of love or drunkenness. An advertisement in the papers would be a possibility, but what exactly would one say: *Lost, November 1920, two parents?* She can't picture the steps required: the taking of a post office box; walking into newspaper offices to place the advertisement; facing the strangers who might result from it...

What did her father mean by sordid?

She studies herself in the mirror for traces of family resemblance. It is not impossible that she is her own father's daughter, an act of indiscretion forgiven when the marriage's barren state could no longer be endured or ignored. But there is little to match her to Townsend bloodlines and in the end she returns to the suddenly bleak fantasies of childhood: a changeling child, a gipsy orphan, though she's not swarthy enough for Romany and can't imagine her parents accepting a child with a heritage too distant from their own.

The family are distressed by her questions; it is not, they think, good form to dig up the muck her parents had so tastefully covered. Their voices become distant; the invitations to stay shrivel to nothing: best, they suggest, to get back to work as quickly as possible, as if life is a bolting horse that must be remounted before fear can set in. Cousin Mary will continue to write weekly chatty notes from a farm in Sussex, humorising her life as a land girl, and though at nineteen there is little else she can offer in the way of comfort or advice, Ruth finds this correspondence oddly comforting. They would both, however, have been surprised to know the length and depth it will attain over the succeeding decades.

On an Evelyn's Pond church stall, Ruth finds a copy of *A Apple Pie*. She turns the pages, almost expecting to find the corner of 'R ran for it' missing, but this book has been less loved than hers and its pages are intact. Her face softens; she holds it to her breast and strokes it like a puppy.

Jane is mortified. At nearly thirteen, her parents are a constant source of embarrassment, but soppiness over a picture book is truly sickening.

'That's too young for Rick,' she bosses—Rick is now nine, Mike eleven.

'It's for me,' says Ruth, 'not my children. If my grandchildren are very good, I'll let them look at it.' In fact the book will be given to Megan when she turns five, because her grandmother, having owned it for a while, can pass it on as she would have if it had truly been her childhood book.

Jane, a more fortunate migrant with a whole trunk full of childhood, will watch her daughter open the parcel and regret the adolescent sarcasm.

Chapter
FOUR

$\mathcal{H}$eathrow is the most vast, the most mind-numbing, of the airports Jane has sampled on this farewell tour, although that could be simply because fatigue has increased exponentially since Singapore.

It almost seems the most depressing part of the trip, coming through the gate with people holding welcome flowers and waving, some of them jumping to see and be seen above the crowd, and not one of those watching faces or hug-waiting arms can be for her.

But: 'Jane!' calls a voice, proper and British, and suddenly Mary appears in front of her, whiter and stouter but essentially unchanged from the woman who'd waved goodbye to Jane and Ian from this same airport twenty-nine years ago.

Jane's not sure why she hasn't expected Mary to meet her, as if her mother's dying has made the rest of that generation too frail to drive, as if no communication has been possible while she herself has been in the air.

'Ian phoned with your flight number,' Mary confirms. 'I couldn't possibly have let you take a train after all this.' All this including the noise, the crowds, the waiting for luggage, as much as death.

In the privacy of the car Jane asks for details. Mary sits quietly and makes no attempt to start the engine.

'She'd been so well; I was amazed at her stamina. We had a quiet Sunday after the busy week; took the dogs for a good walk in Burnham Beeches and sat out in the garden after lunch—it was a lovely day. She spent a good part of the afternoon writing letters.'

Jane so badly wants one of the letters to be to her that she can't speak. She didn't know they were the last letters she'd write, she reminds herself. There's no significance in who they're to. But of course there is.

'We had a light supper,' Mary continues, clearing herself of overburdening an ageing circulatory system, 'poached eggs on toast: nursery tea. We finished a game of Scrabble—she won, naturally, but said she was rather tired and went to bed early.

'Next morning, as I said on the phone, I let her sleep, but she'd been getting up at seven every morning, so at nine I thought I'd just see that she was all right.'

For the first time Mary dabs at her eyes. 'It's funny, I thought I ought to check, and yet I didn't really imagine that anything would be wrong. It was such a shock.

'I suppose I should have waited for the doctor before I phoned you, but I knew she was dead and felt as if you ought to know first. Silly, when you come to think of it, though it's not really something one can mistake. The doctor said she'd probably died quite early in the night, around midnight.'

'Did he say how?' Jane asks hoarsely.

'Stroke.'

You couldn't even get that right, God!

'He says she'd have barely had time to feel anything before it was over. I have to believe that's true, because I didn't hear anything. I don't sleep particularly soundly—surely I'd have heard her cry out!'

Guilt, Jane realises, spreads its wings far. She pats Mary's hand and wonders if she could hug her, though is prevented by the physical awkwardness of gearsticks and handbrakes.

'So where...?'

'She's still at the hospital mortuary. You can see her there if you want to, but it might be pleasanter to wait till she's at the funeral home.'

Jane pictures the mortuary scenes on 'Taggart' and 'Morse'. Funeral homes have never sounded more appealing. 'When does she go there?'

'When you arrange it. It has to be next of kin.'

Looking as disorientated as she feels, Jane is unable to imagine a first step: are funeral directors listed in the Yellow Pages?

Mary adds quickly, 'A friend recommended one who was very helpful when she lost her husband.' Mary's friends being at the age when husbands are lost, but Jane's tired brain pictures her checking under beds and behind the couch.

'There's another thing, dear,' Mary adds, still making no attempt to start the car. 'I'm afraid you have to go and see the coroner this afternoon.' Coroner, with its further connotations of murder and mystery, is not a comforting word.

'It was an unexpected death,' Mary explains, as if reciting a lesson. 'The doctor was legally bound to report it to the coroner.'

Jane hadn't considered exactly how a doctor would know what had killed her mother. 'So they did a—?'

'Post-mortem,' Mary says, trying for brisk and not quite succeeding. 'But that's all over with. All the coroner will want now is personal details, date of birth and that sort of thing. Just routine.'

'Poor Mom.' Though Jane is not sure that she doesn't mean *Poor me*. 'And then I contact the funeral director and start organising?'

'He'll help you with the details. You know your mother wanted to be cremated?'

Jane nods: Ruth had never shirked from discussing her own death or disposal. Jane suspects that she would have handled this situation much better than Jane herself is doing.

'And you'll take the ashes...' Mary stops. 'Are you going straight back to Australia?'

'I haven't sorted anything out yet,' says Jane. 'But I'll have to take her back to Evelyn's Pond. If Mike and Rick can come out, we can sort out the farm and...the ashes. Mom and Dad wanted to be scattered together, in the woods.'

Like Hansel and Gretel, says an irreverent voice in her mind, the part of her that finds cremation too bizarre to fully believe; except that Hansel and Gretel scattered crumbs of bread, not themselves.

Returning to Hamble after losing her parents for the second time in three months, it's only in the air that Ruth knows who she is. The drill of pre-take-off checks—hydraulics and gauges, flaps and tail wheels—is a lifeline: I know this, she says to herself, this is what I do. Take-off itself, even in the midst of grief, is a heady mix of independence, power and an initial rush of adrenalin, and when that flash of elation dies down, the importance of safely delivering the plane steadies her; responsibility and concentration crowd out brooding thoughts.

Now, on a hazy September afternoon, in sidcot suit and helmet, her Blue Bible of flying instructions taped to her knee, she taxis down the runway in a refitted Wellington bomber. If not the size of the big Lancasters dominating the continuing massive raids over Germany, it's still a big, heavy crate, the largest she's qualified to fly and the one on which she has the least experience. On this last delivery of the day, it takes all her concentration and strength to keep the nose up for successful take-off; she levels out over the trees and heads towards the Midlands. She has no philosophical problems with delivering bombers, seeing the situation simply and fiercely—the more Allied bombers that go out, the sooner the war will be over. Of all the complex mess of emotions whirling inside her, hatred of the enemy is the only simple one. If she could load this with bombs she would fly happily to Europe herself, to flatten all resistance wherever Bill might be on his supplies-for-wounded exchange. She thinks of them only as the enemy—Nazis, the Luftwaffe, antiaircraft gunners who would kill Bill if they could—cannot let herself think of the people facing ruins like the ones in Savernake Street.

Cannot think of Savernake Street at all.

Spotting the airfield, descending, taxiing down the runway, the handing-over routine; a sigh of relief at no accident report—she's still not worried about her own life but damaging a craft on landing is a constant nagging fear. Little is forgiven a woman pilot, and she can't imagine how she'd exist if flying were taken from her.

The mist closes in; she's glad of the overnight bag stashed in her cockpit and a phone call to home base confirms it: she'll be sleeping in the Waaferie tonight, in some night-duty WAAF's bed. It's never a comfortable situation, but in the mess, in the company of the men she thinks of as the true pilots, she keeps up the front—not even a front, an alternate personality, a truer Ruth Townsend because she is familiar to herself and others. The men are drinking heavily, showing off to each other as much as to her; strain shows on young faces. They never know when they go to bed whether they'll be up that night, waiting for the hand on the shoulder in the middle of sleep, 'You're on, sir.'

It's leaving the mess that she sees one Nissen hut separated from the other barracks. A tin mortuary. In vivid restless dreams that night she sees it stacked with dead airmen, all in RCAF blue. The top layer have Bill's face, but underneath, although she can't see them, are her parents. Birth parents or Mama and Papa, she's not sure; she'll never be sure, and that's the knowledge she wakes with. That she'll never know the things she needs to know.

There is no sense of time. The blackness around her is less total than that within. With absolute clarity she sees that there is no point in life, in love, in being. She may survive or she may not; Bill may survive or he may not, and if they both do and if by some freak of chance Bill still wants to marry her, she won't let him, it wouldn't be fair for him to marry someone who barely exists, someone with no thread of history to anchor her to life. Because this same terrible clarity tells her that if he does, if she lets him and they have children, there will be no point in that either. If we have children only for the survival of our genes, then the only reason for our children's lives is for them to have children and on ad infinitum, and where then is life? Who is the one actually destined to live and not just survive?

Bleakness more terrifying than fear, blacker than despair, and she does not recognise that it's born of both. In half-waking dreams she tumbles down pits, a slippery-sloped abyss, endless, bottomless, whirling and dark.

In the morning the mist has turned to fog; the taxi Anson is still grounded. No time for breakfast before the train, and she's reminded of the letter she wrote Bill some lifetime ago. I'm even thinner now, she thinks, but it doesn't seem as important as it once had. Too slow to find a seat, she perches in the corridor on her overnight bag.

An American soldier squats beside her, young, crew cut and curious about the wings on her tunic. Not curious at all, it's just an opener, he's trying to chat her up. She looks at him, amazed that he can't see she doesn't exist.

'How does a girl get to be a pilot?' he asks, allowing the train's movement to rub khaki shoulder against blue tunic.

'I can't talk now,' says Ruth, and closes her eyes.

There is a two-hour diversion for track damage; the journey takes six hours; she has not eaten since the night before and sways when she gets to her feet to step down. The soldier reaches an arm to steady her, 'Take care, ma'am,' and she wishes he were Bill and that it was the morning before her parents died and all she had to grieve over was not knowing who she was and there was still some possibility of finding out.

Back at base, more welcome than tea, she finds the notice confirming her requested transfer to White Waltham, just out of Reading and not far at all from Bill. There's a letter from him too, but she tucks it into her pocket to keep for evening and the solitude of her own room. Simply touching the envelope that his hands have held, his tongue has sealed, makes it less likely that he's changed his mind about loving her, but her equilibrium is too finely balanced to risk emotion in public.

I don't know what you're thinking or how you're feeling as you read this, so you'll have to forgive me if I'm on the wrong track. I can't help worrying about you; your letters are brave and cheery, but I know you're suffering. I know that I can't understand exactly how you're suffering, but I'm doing my best to fathom it. It seems to me that as well as the terrible way you lost your parents and how anyone would feel about that, you feel like you've in some way lost yourself as well with the news they gave you that night.

If I'm wrong, don't even bother reading the end of this letter and remember that I'm a country hick who's got the wrong end of the stick again.

If I bought a horse because it was out of a certain mare and stallion and it was the best horse I'd ever had, I wouldn't sell it if I heard that the breeder had lied about the bloodlines. It's the horse that matters, not the pedigree. Seems to me it's the same thing and it doesn't matter if your parents aren't who you thought they were, you're still the person you thought you were, and the person that I met. (He wants to say, *and fell in love with,* but is afraid the words sound phoney.)

That night in the park you wanted to know about my family

and my childhood and maybe you'll think, 'easy for you to say', but your life is still just as real and belongs to you just as much as mine does to me. Everything that happened, all your memories, are still true.

I know you want more than that. I've been trying to imagine how I would feel if I discovered that not only my mother and father weren't my parents, but that my grandparents, especially my Grandpère, who's lived with us nearly as long as I can remember, and all my aunts and uncles, were not related to me. I know that I would feel as lost as I think you do now—and yet they'd still be the same people. It wouldn't change how they'd treated the child that I used to be, or what they thought of me as a man, and it shouldn't change how I feel about all that.

Probably I'm not saying this very well. I'm not even sure what I'm trying to say, except I believe there's a part of us that's always us, no matter what happens. Maybe that's the soul. My Grandma, my mother's mother, took a stroke a couple of years before she died; her right arm and leg were useless and she couldn't talk. But sometimes she'd watch you and listen to what you were saying so that she looked like Grandma again and you could see Grandad thinking she was the same girl he'd married all those years ago. That little bit of her was still her.

You're still you. You're more yourself than anyone I've ever met.
All my love,
Bill

Tears come to her eyes and keep coming; she is crying now, not delicately sobbing; this is gasping and hiccupping, head under the pillow to muffle shame. Tears of blood is what they feel like—smarting, angry tears; it's a long time before she exhausts herself into some sense of peace. The letter can't retrieve her identity but it pulls her back from the brink of the abyss. He's a good man, a wise man, and he really does seem to be in love with her.

The following Sunday, a clear and cloudless morning, Ruth arrives at White Waltham to find that no aircraft will be delivered or picked up today. The seventeenth of September has been chosen as a day of commemoration for the valiant few of the Battle of Britain, and although it's pleasant to be able to attend the church service, Ruth can't help feeling that they are tempting fate by not being in the air in such perfect weather. There is also still a slight trace of bitterness at Miles's fate— one of the even fewer, killed too soon to be named valiant. She repeats the Lord's Prayer mechanically, wondering how long their love would have survived if he had. There is no doubt in her mind that she would have fallen in love with Bill whenever and however they'd met, but her conscience stirs uneasily at the hint of gratitude for Miles's death. 'Forgive us our trespasses,' she repeats, to Miles as much as God.

The 'Amen' is followed by a drone of heavy aircraft and the reason for the grounding begins to become apparent.

'Pity a sparrow trying to stretch its wings today,' a Cockney flight engineer mutters, and then the planes are overhead, drowning speech, hymns and organ. Ruth is impatient for the service to finish, but the formations are still passing, wave after wave, long after the congregation finally files outside and is free to watch.

It's like D-day without the ships, Ruth thinks as the hours pass and the aircraft continue—bombers, troop transporters, gliders swaying behind their tow planes, fighters flanking them. Bill is up there, there mustn't be a crew left in England, and fear for him combines with the overwhelming, the unencompassable thought that the war is about to end. Nothing could stand up to what she guesses correctly is the biggest airborne invasion in history. In the silenced crowd outside the church, she is praying soundlessly, wordlessly, with every fibre of her being as she had not been able to inside.

Fifteen hundred feet above, Bill feels her prayer. His logical, mathematical mind tells him that this is no more than the awareness of flying over her base, knowing she'll guess that he's up here. Adding one and one and getting three, he tells himself, but it doesn't change the feeling that their thoughts have touched.

It adds to his buoyant mood. At the briefing yesterday they'd been told that this invasion of occupied Holland would secure the crucial bridges across the Lower Rhine and take the Allies right to the threshold of Germany. One of the most immediate effects of success will mean the end of the V2 bombs terrorising the women and children (not the men? Bill wonders) of south-east England. If he's never been able to avenge his brother's death by submarine, he's all the more keen to participate in revenge for Ruth's parents.

And, the whisper adds, this will mean the end of the war by Christmas. The Germans are already defeated; their few troops in the Netherlands the dregs and the untrained, invalids and children. Against them, in this one morning, the Allies will drop 16500 paratroopers and 3500 troops in swaying ply-wood gliders, with more men and equipment to follow over the next two days. In three days this airborne army will have met up with the thousands of troops and tanks of General Horrock's XXX Corps, waiting in Belgium and poised to sweep through the country like a liberating dose of salts.

But first the men need to be landed, and it's only a small part of Bill's mind that is playing with the thoughts of Ruth and what the end of the war will mean. The rest of him is sharply aware that he is near the head of a long—a hundred miles long, he learns later—column of aircraft, with another column the same size on either side; and, just to make sure everyone is paying attention, a great clumsy glider, nearly the size of their Dakota, bouncing along behind on a three hundred foot towrope.

After rendezvousing just north of London, they are heading north-east towards Aldeburgh and their route across the Channel.

'Skipper, look out!' he shouts into the intercom but Dusty has seen it in time: the glider ahead of them has broken loose and is hurtling towards the earth, tow rope whipping wildly beside it. Bill imagines certain death for the thirty prisoners of this fragile tomb, but at the last minute it levels out and bounces across the ground in a relatively normal landing. The infantry passengers will be shaken and disappointed but alive to follow in the next day's armada. No one wants to be left out of something this big.

As they leave England, the navigation is embarrassingly simple, a child's dot-to-dot game following the launches strung neatly across the North Sea—though they're not just direction aids, he realises, spotting the first white glider bobbing perilously on the waves and the ship darting towards it. Their own charge continues its faithful following, but by the time the Dutch coast and the less welcome smoky puffs of flak come into view, several more have ditched and are awaiting rescue.

Over the flat green of Holland, Bill is reassured to recognise the expected landmarks, rivers and canals, and finally the vital rail and road bridges of Arnhem. Smoke billows up from the devastation of the dawn bombing raid, but Bill doesn't have time to consider the irony of bombing a town to near-extinction in order to liberate it—as they approach their target, he's simply grateful that the raid has apparently accomplished its aim of blowing the antiaircraft guns out of existence.

The gliders ahead of them are casting loose and their tugs heading for home, still flanked by the fighter planes who've been guiding them all the way. The sky is thick with aircraft— 'Like Piccadilly Circus!' the pilot's voice says in his ear.

Their turn is next. They watch as the glider casts off its

towrope and floats neatly into the orange-marked square on the green field; the men begin to scramble out, waving and thumbs-upping. A white dot that is Willie the parachuting ferret, cause of jocularity and respect as the men boarded, is held triumphantly aloft. The scene looks like some strange kind of holiday camp: the glider parking lot, the waving men in the peaceful fields—a perfect picnic day.

Dusty detours briefly to drop the vicious snake of a towrope onto a large hotel, obvious candidate for German officers' quarters, and they turn for home.

The next morning they're heading out again. Like migrating geese, the gaggle has gathered strength and their Dakota is now one of 4000 aircraft.

This time, however, there are no illusions of picnics or holiday camps. Red tracer bullets and grey flak thunder up from all around the target areas; the landing zones themselves pitted and muddied from mortar shells, machine gun sprays, blood and wreckage. The remains of a glider are burning below them; Bill feels a sense of betrayal for the men they are about to jettison.

They're well back in the column today, and in the distance they can already see the freed tug planes heading for home. Bill is anxious to join them. He can see the landing zone clearly now. Four to go, he thinks, counting the plane-and-glider combinations ahead of them, the first glider just about to land. Its tow plane turns; Bill pictures their sigh of relief and counts, 'Three.'

'Christ!' but he isn't sure whether the scream is his own or Dusty's. Where the first tow plane should be is a ball of flames.

'Jump!' he wills the crew. 'Bail out now!' But no parachutes appear, and as the stricken plane hits the ground, an obscene inferno of molten metal, he sees flames coming out of the Stirling behind.

Its glider releases and lands, followed by the plane. The

crew should live, Bill thinks, but they won't be getting home tonight. And it'll be some wait, here in the middle of a battlefield, service revolvers against mortars and machine guns. Most of the poor bastards can't shoot anyway; it's not a skill aircrew expect to need much.

'Two more ahead of us, Skip,' he calls mechanically, though as the wing tip is shot off the third plane, and the one directly ahead of them shudders with a hit he's unable to determine, he's not sure whether he's commenting on the landing zone or their own imminent deaths.

Miraculously, both the gliders land safely and when theirs joins it they are somehow still unhit and in the air, and 'Bloody glad to see England,' Dusty says as they head towards the mess several hours later.

There is a feeling of dread as they set out again the next day. The Met Office has promised three clear days for this operation, but the clouds haven't listened to the weather reports and come in thick and heavy on the nineteenth. The Polish Brigade, waiting anxiously in the midlands, will wait another twenty-four hours before their drop into what becomes a suicide mission. Of the planes and gliders leaving southern England, many will have to turn back when the glider pilots are unable to see their tug in front of them. Bill's crew, dropping relief supplies instead of more troops, is one that makes it through the fog to reach the hell that is Arnhem.

That it's a disaster is now obvious, though it's another six days before it's over, and longer before they learn the full extent of it: more than 17 000 men killed, wounded or missing; another 6000 captured. The war will not be over by Christmas, least of all for the Dutch starving in retribution for the Allied attempt at liberation. What Bill never knows is that none of the supplies his crew nearly died to deliver were dropped to their own men. Their painstaking accuracy had delivered them all to the enemy.

My dearest Ruth

If you've been worrying about me, you can stop now because I'm here, all in one piece, and so is everyone else on the crew.

One of the unexciting bits of news I probably didn't mention in a letter is that I got my boots resoled last month. The result was right heavy and clumsy; I was none too happy but the shoe-maker said I'd 'wear them out fast enough anyway'. If he only knew how right he was!

You'll have guessed where I've been the last few days, and yesterday we dropped supplies, medicine and blankets and such, to some friends of ours by parachute in those big wicker baskets, you've probably seen them. You can imagine how low and slow we had to come in, and I'd have to say that it was about the unhealthiest place I've ever seen for that kind of flying. I was some proud of our skipper, he just stuck to the directions I gave him, cool as anything, like it was a training exercise, but now it's over I can tell you it was like driving through sleet, except this sleet was hot and coming up from the ground. There were a few fighters too, but it was the ground stuff that gave us the problems.

So finally we were circling the field and pushing out the baskets. I went back to help because the way Dusty had to hold her nose down, the rollers were rolling the baskets back into the cock-pit instead of out the doors, and by the time we'd gone around once we still had two of them on board. When I told Dusty he just swung around again to get back to the target. I had the doors open, pushing out this basket of blankets, with our new wireless operator behind me (a young American guy, Steve Crocket so we call him Davy; it was the first time he'd crewed with us and very nearly the last). All of a sudden my leg was thrown up in the air; I landed flat on my back and figured I'd probably lost a toe at least; the bullet had gone straight through my shoe and it stung like blazes. A second later a cannon shell tore a huge hole in the port wing, but Dusty finished his circle and we got both the bas-kets safely out. I guess we all knew how desperate those fellows were, and however bad it was up here, it was a lot worse for them down there.

I took the controls, which wasn't easy as it took me a while to allow for the extra drag from the wing, and Dusty checked the damage. It looked fairly grim, I don't mind telling you; we'd lost our trim tabs, brakes and hydraulics, and even you, my darling Spitfire, probably prefer to land with some combination of the above. However, Dusty was just as determined as I was to get back to his girl and keep out of a POW camp, and apparently he'd read something in an RAF magazine the other night that he figured might be useful. I think we ought to send a bottle of whisky to whoever wrote that article. Though after this, we might want to keep a spare bottle of whisky on board ourselves.

The theory was we had to collect every drop of fluid we could find, so when we came to land we could pump it manually onto the wheels, a kind of do-it-yourself hydraulics. We had half a tin of oil, three quarters of a thermos of coffee, and my dear, I won't offend you by describing what the other fluid was, so let's just say that every man contributed what he could and we filled two more thermoses. Young Steve was ready to man the emergency pump, so I sorted through my maps (for paper thickness rather than topographical accuracy) and made a funnel.

We radioed ahead and they had ambulances and fire trucks waiting, but in the end we disappointed them and sent them home unused. Dusty went into a dive and pulled up sharply to make the wheels drop; he didn't know if they were locked, but there was nothing we could do about it by then except trust in God and our home-made hydraulics, which now went into action: I funnelled fluid straight into the pump and Steve pumped away for all he was worth. Dusty came in low over the fields, lined up the runway; we ran off the end of it and into a ploughed field—and stopped.

I'd forgotten all about my foot by then, and it wasn't till we were in the mess later and Wing Co asked if any of us had been hurt, that Dusty reminded me I'd taken a bullet. I took off my *shoe and the bullet rolled out; my toe's turning a lovely colour yellow, but it hadn't even drawn blood. The shoe will have to be resoled again, but I won't mind the chance to thank that cobbler!*

The other thing I didn't tell you is that the way young Steve was standing behind me, the bullet would have got his face if it hadn't hit my foot.

So I was feeling pretty lucky when we were in the mess, but now I don't know. What's so special about me? You know, of the guys I was buddies with going through the training program, only two of us are left alive, and the other one's in prison in Germany. Maybe I just didn't know the lucky ones.

I guess I'm just feeling this way because I can't stop thinking about the guys we dropped three days ago, the ones who were laughing and joking, and now I don't know how many of them are dead. Probably I shouldn't be telling you all this, but we've made that commitment to know each other as well as one person can know another and maybe now you know me a little better.

The postscript came the next day:

I think I wrote you a strange letter last night when I was feeling low. I talked about our commitment, but sometimes I wonder if I pushed you into it when you were vulnerable. I'll understand if you don't want to continue.

The only thing he's right about, Ruth thinks, is that they don't know each other very well. She'd definitely fail a 'How well do you know your hubby?' quiz: How does he like his tea? No idea. Don't North Americans prefer coffee? Favourite food? Definitely not powdered eggs, but that's as close as she can get.

She'd have better luck guessing what most of the Hamble groundcrew take in their tea or preferred for dinner, than the man she wants to spend her life with. Selected snippets of family life and history; his looks, his feel and smell; the sound of his laugh, his voice, the way she feels when she holds his unopened letter in her hand. In this uncertain life, those things are more than enough.

Cursing wars, distance and censors, she writes immediately.

My dear, my dearest dear, I want you to see inside my mind so that you will never again doubt how much I love you.

The simple truth is that I am happy when I am with you, and miserable away from you. I know that you are the best, the truest and most honest man I've ever met.

No, not just my mind; you need to see inside my soul, for although I love you with my mind, it's my soul that cries out for you. And my body emulates it; our bodies have a wisdom of their own and mine knows that it belongs to yours.

Can you know how, in these bleak lonely nights, I comfort myself with your image? When I feel so lost that I don't know who I am, when in spite of my rage I could pray that Mama and Papa were still alive, not just to ask them the questions I need to know, but simply to have them there a little longer; then my soul lets me rest with you. You open the dark wings of your soul as I lie against you, letting me sink into your chest, into your body; I am encircled, encompassed; absorbed by you and your love. So how could you ever think that I could exist away from you? Without you, I cease to exist.

My body weaves its own dreams. It remembers the look in your eyes as they discovered my breasts in the silver dress, and it knows what that look meant. It wants to wear that dress again for you, and shed that dress for you, it wants to stand naked in the moonlight before you and give itself utterly up to you. And my body's stories of our lying together are the complement of my soul's, for it sees your face above my own and feels your body over me, and it dreams of your body entering mine, till you in your turn are encircled, encompassed, absorbed, by me and my love.

And my heart? Well, my dear, that's the strongest of all, because my heart doesn't need reasons, it simply loves you.

I love you, Bill: heart and mind, body and soul; I'm yours, and nothing in the world can ever change that.

Of course she doesn't send it. Honesty about true passion carries the risk of convincing the reader that the writer is insane or wanton, or both. The fifth attempt, careful breathless spontaneity, seems to capture a balance between the veracity of love and terrifying the lover, and that's the one he receives.

Idiot! My dear, dearest idiot. I fell in love with you the first time I saw you; I would have married you then if you'd asked. If I could rewrite history and erase the night of Mama's admission, I wouldn't do it, because the discovery of our love outweighs that misery by far. Your being there for the terrible day of their deaths was simply proof, if proof were needed, that this was right. I don't believe that I would have been strong enough to survive it without you—but you must never think that gratitude had any part in my decision. Even well-brought-up English girls don't carry gratitude to that extent.

You say that we don't know each other very well, and I can hardly deny that truth. I don't know what you like for breakfast or if you'll ever be able to face spam again at the end of the war. We haven't even discussed religion, and it strikes me now that you may be Catholic while I am C of E, and perhaps we have been remiss in not discussing such an important point, but I can't believe even that will be a problem. Sometimes I think that although it's the last way one would choose to conduct a romance, these letters have given us an extraordinary gift, of following up that coup de foudre *with enforced platonicism, while our minds have become so intimate that I wonder if many long-married couples can say they know each other so well as we do.*

So the answer, if I haven't made myself clear, is that I want to marry you, not to honour 'our commitment' but because I love you and want to spend the rest of my life with you. I want to be close to you, my love, in every way, and while the only way now is through these letters, sharing our thoughts and hearts, the rest will follow when we meet again in the flesh.

There is no more talk of releasing her. Daily, he reveals more of himself, his desire sometimes so lightly veiled—*when I lie awake at night I see again your bare shoulders in that silver dress, the beauty of your body beneath it*—that she smiles at how nearly he's echoed the unsent letter, and refuses to let herself think beyond that until she too is lying awake in the dark. The need for privacy, never outgrown in years of school, has taught her to lie absolutely still, breathing gently and regularly as she retreats ever deeper into herself, until her body feels as if it is floating slightly above the bed's surface and her mind roams free. Now she lingers over the words in Bill's letter, her weightless body touched with heat, sometimes with a feathering of kisses so real that she feels they must truly be his and longs to ask if he's dreamed of her at the same time. But she never quite dares—as he said, they really don't know each other very well.

Leaving the car park, Mary drives quickly and competently around enormous roundabouts and down the motorway, past the council flats and dreary industry of Slough, on to narrow winding back roads that make Jane realise with a twinge of excitement she's in England again. Glimpses of mansions through gateways, and then they're in the village and pulling into the short driveway of Mary's white house.

The child Jane, seeing the address 'White Cottage, Cherry Tree Lane' on Christmas letters, had realised instantly that Mary was in fact Mary Poppins in disguise. This also very satisfyingly explained the extraordinary coincidence of the two older Banks children being named Jane and Michael, though she was never sure who had been named after whom.

'I never told anyone. I always hoped that if I kept your

secret you'd give me a magic reward one day—a picnic on the ceiling, something like that.'

'Tea on the terrace might be the best I can do at the moment,' but they are interrupted by a burst of aggrieved barking as the front half of a large black head thrusts itself through a cat flap on the side door. 'Barney,' Mary explains. 'You haven't gone so Australian that you won't have dogs inside the house?'

Jane, long married to an Australian who believes exactly that, can't think of anything more comforting at this moment than the warm fur and companionship of a dog. Although this does sound a particularly noisy one.

'Daisy's quieter,' Mary promises.

Daisy is white and fluffy with beseeching brown eyes. 'Poodle Pekinese, I think. I'm sure she would have gone to a good home, but something about that face...and I hoped she might calm Barney down.'

Barney is dancing on hind legs, aiming kisses at faces. Mary bellows 'Down!' with the force of a sergeant major twice her size and half her age, and fills the kettle. The kitchen is clean and bright, so it must have been repainted and updated since she last saw it, but to Jane it looks exactly the same.

'I'll show you your room,' says Mary, 'and then you can have a cup of tea and a nap; your bed's ready.'

'Is it...?' She can't finish the question.

'I've put you in the double room,' Mary continues tactfully, understanding that even after forty-one hours of travelling there are limits to where one wants to sleep, 'where you and Ian stayed before you went to Australia. Your mother was in the other one—I thought she'd prefer the garden view.'

Jane climbs the stairs; her suitcase, unladen with the usual gifts of international visiting, is not heavy. Kneeling to open it, she shakes out and hangs up her good dress, her three shirts and other pair of slacks, changes into a short-sleeved shirt and leaves the rest in the case; she won't be here long enough to settle in. Should have pulled the curtains to change, living so long on the farm she's forgotten the house across the street, upstairs windows facing directly into hers. She wonders if it's still the same people there and hopes not, remembering the girl undressing for her new husband–lover, that afternoon when Mary was out, teasing, Ian reaching for her, caressing, tumbling onto the bed and only later, languidly redressing, seeing the shocked face staring out the window opposite.

They wouldn't recognise her anyway, a lifetime later. She can barely recognise herself, or remember that overwhelming urgency of youthful sex, the gut-twisting delirium that once dominated their lives. Sex is still good, she decides, but life is easier now that desire isn't quite as imperative as it used to be.

Daisy appears politely on the threshold, like a maid sent to tell her that tea is waiting, and Jane follows the shaggy white bottom back to the kitchen.

'Would you like to phone Ian?' asks Mary.

At the fourth ring Jane hears her own voice requesting her to leave a message and even in her numbness has time to wonder if she really sounds like that. And then to wonder at her own shallowness.

Ian calls back before the tea is drunk; all is well. One cow calved successfully while he was at the airport, another last night, and he is just in from helping a heifer deliver her first.

'Three heifer calves!' he says proudly, because in calving as in any other birth, the outcome of healthy mother and infant quickly obliterates the rest of the story: the straining and swearing, muck and blood, the wondering if it's time to interfere.

But in dairy cows as in other dynasties, the infant's gender determines the extent of celebration. It just happens that as cows are valued for milk rather than aggression, it's the females who are feted. Heifer calves are a return on investment, on

money and time spent poring over bull catalogues and inject-
ing expensive semen, and three together are a good omen for
the season.

Jane, remembering this as if it's something she's read,
makes suitable noises to disguise her sense of dissociation.
The noises are not entirely effective: Ian tells her to get
some sleep; she says she has to see the coroner first and he
says she won't manage it without sleep. As she hangs up it
strikes her that this is the epitome of middle age—bicker-
ing on a transatlantic line in the midst of funeral
arrangements.

Mary asks brightly if Ian is having any problems with snakes,
a non sequitur that does nothing for Jane's sense of reality.
Ruth's death must have affected Mary more than she'd realised.
She explains that it's the wrong time of year, or at least the
right time of year for not meeting snakes. In midwinter, paddocks and long grass can be walked without fear.

'I could never get over,' says Mary, 'your having venomous
snakes in the house, although I suppose one becomes accustomed to anything with time.'

Jane has never met anyone who's become accustomed to
the presence of snakes: brown, black and tiger, all common,
all deadly. Red-bellied black snakes the most timid, tigers
outright aggressive—though there's a theory that the mild-
mannered red-bellies will drive tigers away from their territory
and so should be encouraged, if one only knew how. And
could bear it. It's a matter of discussion amongst neighbours
every spring, the first time one is seen coiled on a verandah,
the first slim track across a driveway or dead body on the
road, sinister even in death so that the children riding bikes
home from buses swerve and fall and beg their mothers for
a lift till the end of summer. The cats that survive with
antivenene, the dogs that invariably die, the farm where a
king brown took up residence in a round bale of hay one night
and kissed twelve soft cow noses with the swipe of a deadly

tongue. The fear always for babies and curious children...
and she realises what Mary's referring to.

'Megan was two and still in a cot—she was supposed to
be having an afternoon nap. Ian had killed a snake on the
doorstep a few days before, and had shown her, telling her it
was a *bad bad* thing and she must never touch it, but we had
no idea what she'd take in.

'I thought she was singing at first—she often sang to herself—and then I realised the chant was "make, make, make"
and there she was, lying down with her arm through the
bars, a few inches above a big brown snake. They can stand
up, you know, when they want to strike—if it had noticed
her and felt threatened, a few inches would have been nothing. I'd always thought I'd be terrified if I met a snake on
my own, but there wasn't room for emotion. I don't even
know how I crossed the room, but I grabbed her from the
back of the crib.'

Mary is intrigued by the switch to the Canadian word but
doesn't comment. Jane is flushed as if her heart is racing, reliv-
ing her story.

'I shut the door behind me to trap him, locked Megan in
our room and grabbed the shovel from the dairy. I remember shouting for Ian, but I didn't know where he was and
didn't even slow down to see if he'd heard. Megan was bellowing by the time I got back, and I was terrified she'd find
something to drag to the door and reach the handle before
I'd got rid of the snake. He was still under the crib when I
got there, and I chopped his head off—and then I chopped
him into little pieces.'

She's half laughing, half crying, as she hasn't, not yet, for
her mother. 'When Ian came in I was still standing in the
bedroom in my gumboots in a big mess of chopped-up snake
and linoleum. Completely wrecked the floor; we had to put
carpet down.'

'"The female of the species is more deadly than the male!"'

quotes Mary, clearing away the teacups. 'I'm glad it's not a regular occurrence. Somehow, ever since your mother told me about it, I'd pictured it as a part of your daily life: milk the cows, kill the snakes...'

Jane remembers something Ruth had said in the letter that arrived the morning before she died, describing incidents on the tour and peculiarities of her fellow literary tourists.

Jane Austen was, as usual, exactly right when Mr Bennet told Lizzie that we are here purely for our neighbours' entertainment. In the end we're nothing but the stories that other people remember. I suppose the sad thing is that people often remember things we've forgotten ourselves, or at least would not have chosen as our memorial.

A more appropriate word than Jane had realised on first reading.

ℭ

Compensating for the grinding boredom of grief, Ruth's mind begins to invent further tragedies. Sometimes she is so sure that disaster is coming it seems only a matter of time before she's notified, before a phone call comes from someone in the squadron—she's not official next of kin, but Bill's made arrangements, she knows, for her to be told. (As she has, but she is not yet able to see enough significance in her own life to believe that she could die.) Some days certainty is so absolute that the only way she can go on is to attack each chore with a combination of magic ritual and pragmatism: 'If I've combed my hair and brushed my teeth it'll be easier to bear.' 'If I get to the duty office—check the met report—get to my plane—get back to base—before I find out.' And by the end of the day: 'If I can sleep all night then it's another day he's been alive.'

It's been such a long time since she was in love, although that hectic hero-worship she felt for Miles is so different from the aching longing, the deep surety and sense of home-coming she shares with Bill, that it's difficult to call them by the same name. The men she dated in between were good friends or good fun but nothing more. Just once, with a scared young rear gunner, she'd agreed to sex from pity; although in the end, since he was either more drunk or his nerves more shot than she'd realised, the evening was no more comforting than it was romantic.

The following night his crew made it back to England for an emergency landing after the rear turret with the young gunner inside had been shot right off. Ruth had already vowed that if she never fell in love again, she'd never have sex again—the former seemed likely, and the latter not much of a hardship. On hearing the news she amended the decision—she would simply not care for anyone until the war was over. It was an easy enough vow to keep until she met Bill.

Now she's starting to wonder if breaking it has been a wise decision, if love for her, whether romantic or parental, may carry a curse. She cares too much for Bill not to be supersti-tious: love is such a tenuous, inexplicable miracle, not far removed from magic. And if white magic exists, why not black?

Certainly black magic seems to be dogging their plans. With her annual fortnight's leave not due till May, and forty-eight hour passes consistently knocked out of kilter, she is begin-ning to despair that they may never get closer than their midnight longings and increasingly urgent letters.

I know that I'm the luckiest man in the world, his latest note finishes, *or will be when we can finally have some time together. Ruth darling, there are some things a man can't say to a woman in a letter, no matter how much he loves her. I need to hold you in my arms to know this is real.*

The next day, unexpectedly off duty, he manages to track down the last missing part of his damaged motorcycle, scrounges petrol and arrives at White Waltham just as she steps out of the taxi Anson from the afternoon's last delivery. She puts her hand to his cold face: she can't hold him, not yet; it's too much to believe that he's here and if she puts her arms around him she will never let him go.

'Twenty-four hours,' he whispers. 'I've found a hotel.'

Pillion on the bike, no choice now but to hold him, her face against his shoulder, chest against his back and arms around the firmness of his stomach. Her legs are shaking when they dismount. He's chosen the hotel carefully, a location away from likely acquaintances, without bomb damage or sordidness, but alone in the room she is suddenly paralysed by fear. Too much emotion, built up for too long.

'I can't do this,' she whispers, white-faced, and his questing hands drop from her shoulders. If he'd been more sophisticated, more worldly, she might have left it there: better the hurt of rejection than death—and Jane's story and therefore Megan's story would never have happened—but Bill's face, which in the transition from country boy to battleworn man has learned to guard against betraying fear and cold despair, cannot hope to disguise a wound dealt by the woman he loves.

'I'm so afraid of bringing you bad luck!'

Bill begins to unbutton her tunic. 'And I thought you were smart! I'll tell you what would be bad luck—to love each other and be too afraid to do anything about it!' He works as slowly, as gently, as the most experienced seducer, or perhaps more accurately, as a stockman gentling a nervous horse, and by the time Ruth helps him peel off the regulation black stockings—ugly things, she thinks, but they nearly bring Bill undone—she feels herself melting into his hands. For the first time she understands that making love is not simply a favour from a woman to a man.

When Ruth tells Jane this story, slightly edited and not till the visit just before Bill died, she adds, 'It was the only time in my life I've ever been paralysed by an irrational fear. But you'll be pleased to know your father wasn't.'

Jane, slightly shocked to discover that her generation had
not invented sex before marriage and not quite ready even at
nearly fifty to hear about her parents' participation in it, is
glad to be spared further details.

⌖

The night together reasserts Ruth's natural optimism. Her
sense of smell, mysteriously absent since her parents' death,
returns with the fresh smell of linen in their room, the faint
scent of Bill's sweat as she rolls into his arms in the morning
and the peculiar heady smell of aviation fuel and engines when
she arrives on base. She begins to believe that the shock of
her mother's revelation and her grief over their deaths will
ease with time, and although she thought she'd been sure
before, she now knows with absolute certainty that just given
the chance of survival, she and Bill can share a life. The
shape and context of that life is less clear: it's difficult to visualise Nova Scotia as a real place where real people, let alone
Ruth Townsend, live.

Tell me more, her letters beg, *about your family, your farm,
your country.* Canada floats constantly on the periphery of her
vision; from books and scraps of conversation she constructs
it, like the elephant described by three blind men. There's
Beryl Markham's crashlanding in a Cape Breton marsh and
Bill's stories of maple trees in spring, the warming snow soft-
balling and time to tap for syrup. Canadian airmen, from
Red Deer and Saskatoon, Victoria and St Johns, from Niagara
to Cold Lake; men from the prairies, the mountains, the Arctic,
the southern cities, have their stories drawn out like threads
from a spider to weave a picture of Ruth's future, a tax on
the delivery of their freshly serviced plane.

Canada is big, they brag, you English can't understand how
big it is. You can see forever across the prairies, drive fifty, a
hundred miles before you hit another town—a man can
make something of himself, it's what you do with your life,

not what you're born into. Bears can be a problem in Prince Rupert; hang a deer in your garage overnight and find a black bear in there as well next morning. They're okay though, not like the grizzlies, you want to be careful of them. The cabin by the lake where I learned to canoe in the summer— that's Canada, those Ontario lakes. At Portage-La-Prairie, an Australian adds, the snow was so deep that we skied right over the top of the hangar.

'Not many bears in Nova Scotia,' Bill replies. 'No prairies or rattlesnakes; it's gentler country. Settlers from the lowlands of Scotland thought it looked like home, and before that it was Acadia—Paradise.'

Ruth narrows her search, quizzing men who've learned about the province in elementary school history and geography and not thought of it again until it hit their lives as the end of a troop train and the start of an Atlantic convoy. 'Fish and fog,' they tell her. 'Halifax harbour; never seen so many men loading onto so many ships; and of course there was the explosion in the last war, munition ship blew up and took half the town with it—a hell of a bang that must have been, you can still see where a man was blown through the stained-glass window in the church. Some places around there speak Gaelic, I heard, and French too.'

A kaleidoscope of impressions, few of the fragments coinciding with Bill's images of apple orchards and oxen. In the library she finds *Barometer Rising* and Longfellow's *Evangeline*: Nova Scotia the home of explosions and expelled lovers. A bookshop in Reading produces the slim *Autobiography* of Oliver Goldsmith's eponymous grandnephew, but his life in the capital a hundred years ago yields little insight into what hers will be in the country now. City girl, she writes to Cousin Mary: *How will I ever learn to be a farmer's wife?*

Mary sends back vivid tales of gassing rats, killing pigs, and the WAAFs refusal to share a table with land girls in the mess. *They say it's because we stink,* she boasts gleefully, *which is true. But the real reason is that they're jealous because we can wear dresses instead of uniform to go out at night and the men remember we're women.* Which is amusing, but not much help.

Living on a farm is the same as living anywhere else, Bill writes naively, *except for more fresh air and freedom. There's nothing to learn. The only thing that matters is that we'll be together; I love you and you'll be my wife. One night, my dear, is not enough; I want to spend every night of a million nights with you. I want you to have my children and I want our children to grow up in peace and never have to understand what we've been through. The Germans must realise soon that they've lost the war and when they do, everything else will be simple.*

Ruth agrees about the nights, but is less confident about the simple. She has never cooked a meal, cleaned a house or done any of the myriad jobs she suspects farmers' wives around the world carry out daily: feeding hens, milking cows and most daunting of all, the whole sequence of food preparation: peeling, coring, preserving, boiling, stewing, baking, roasting, icing, whipping; pastry, bread, cakes, jam, jellies, conserves— solid food for hard-working men and hordes of hungry children.

❧

The coroner is politely sympathetic and human enough to be intrigued at a daughter arriving from Australia to take an English-born mother's ashes back to Canada.

'She had an interesting life,' Jane says wryly, and hears herself prattling her mother's birth history: the date can't be confirmed, the place is a guess, the maiden name assumed.

Shortly before Jane left Canada on the holiday that became emigration, Ruth had discovered that she was not, as she'd always presumed, a citizen. She'd been as furious as if threatened with deportation. It was nothing to do with keeping her previous identity—Jane's reason for having stuck so obstinately to her first nationality—Ruth had long believed herself to be Canadian. The rage had been at the insult of proving it and the difficulty of doing so, although it's only now that Jane, as she recounts her mother's humiliatingly scant details to officialdom, understands what she had not even attempted to empathise with at the time.

The coroner has heard worse tales; his face does not register surprise until he comes to 'Occupation when employed?' and Jane answers, 'Pilot.'

'Just during the war,' she adds quickly. 'She was a housewife after that.' Although aware that her mother would have shuddered at the term.

The coroner is Jane's age or a few years younger; he has obviously not heard of the Air Transport Auxiliary and equally obviously is beginning to wonder if the woman in front of him is deluded as well as jet-lagged. 'The Royal Air Force,' he says gently, 'did not use female pilots in World War II, which I presume is the war you're referring to.'

Jane's case is not helped by her brain's refusal to remember either the Falklands or Gulf Wars, which might have clarified the last remark, or any details about the ATA. It takes a few moments to persuade him and he offers, by way of apology, the comment that it's a shame to wait too long to discover one's parents' history, and that she should be pleased to know so much of her mother's—which he admits is ironic, given that so much of it is a mystery.

Jane suspects that he has waited until too late himself, but does not like to ask.

❧

Home from arranging for Ruth's body to be released into the care of the recommended-by-Mary's-friend funeral director, Jane sits on her bed to change clothes and goes to sleep. Eighteen hours later, still fully clothed but blanketed, she wakes to the sound of kitchen clattering and thinks she ought to appear before Mary wonders if history has repeated itself—though is rather shocked at her mind's flippancy.

'I thought you might like a proper breakfast this morning,' Mary says, shooing dogs and ushering Jane to a chair like an invalid. 'You didn't have supper last night and you'll need your strength today.'

Jane sits obediently for eggs and sausages; between Megan's lectures about additives and the bathroom scales' reminder of fat, she hasn't eaten sausages for years but is hungry enough now to wonder why. She finishes with toast and marmalade, and is glad that Ian isn't here to see the dogs cleaning up the frying pan.

After a second cup of tea she's ready to think about why she'll need her strength. Looming like a vulture over the straightforward though grim bureaucracy of phone calls and appointments—the Registrar for deaths with the Coroner's pink form—is the approaching afternoon. She doesn't want to see her dead mother, to see her mother dead, but she's flown more than halfway around the world to do so and it would be cowardly not to now she's here. It's reluctance to invade her mother's privacy, she tells herself, not a fear of death— which is more than half true for although Ruth is trapped in the greatest privacy of all, she is unable to enjoy or guard it.

Chapter
FIVE

$\mathcal{R}$uth's Canada rises out of the ocean on 22 December 1945. At eight months pregnant she feels roughly the same size and shape as the boat that has carried her from the last sight of Southampton's graveyard of masts, across the grey Atlantic to the fogs of Halifax harbour. A ship full of war brides, many pregnant, some with babies, a few with children; most feel bridelike only in the sense of facing the unknown, and perhaps, despite seasickness, in the honeymoon atmosphere of luxury and leisure: real eggs and bacon, orange juice and bananas, with nothing to do except look after themselves. And wait, and wonder.

For ten days Ruth has shared a cabin with three other women and two tiny babies. Gladys is Welsh, the other two from northern England; their accents are thick, their backgrounds poor and in prewar England Ruth would have been unlikely to have exchanged more than a request for services with any of them. They are shy of Ruth, her accent, her bearing, her history. Ruth is wary of their banter, their quick

understanding; their ease with handling the tiny fragile creatures. She watches surreptitiously.

'Come on then, you're dying to hold him, aren't you?'

The three of them watch Ruth juggle the baby tensely on
her arm.

'He's not a puppet, love; tuck him up against your
shoulder!'

The baby, an amenable child, settles. Ruth smiles nervously.

'Have you never held a baby before?'

'No,' she admits.

'And you've got how long to go? Three months?'

'Two,' says Ruth, feeling as ashamed as if she'd landed a
Walrus at a Spitfire base.

'Tall ones always carry well,' one confides to another.

But the baby's mother has realised the crux of the matter.
'Are there nannies in Canada?'

If there are, Ruth's baby will not be having one.

One of the most terrible things, Bill wrote after an ambulance
flight from Cherbourg, *was hearing a young officer crying out
for his nanny. I guess it doesn't make any difference what they
say in that terrible time when no one can help them and they no
longer know who or where they are, but it somehow seemed even
worse to me that when another boy would have called out for his
mother, this poor guy wanted someone who wasn't even his own
flesh and blood.*

It had been too early, and too unlucky given the context,
to discuss their own possible future children but Ruth, who
if moved to call on anyone in extremity would never have
chosen her parents, understood what Bill hadn't even realised
he was discussing. She hadn't really considered children before,
hadn't considered having to live up to someone else's ideals
of motherhood. She had never told him how terrifying she
found the prospect.

'We won't have a nanny,' she says now, and the bond is

formed, close and instant. The women's fears and doubts are much the same, but Ruth's inadequacies have presented them with an immediate challenge. Before the first whalespout is spotted through the portholes, Ruth is fully competent to pick up a baby, feed it a bottle, pat its back afterwards and change its nappy, which none of them have yet learned to call a diaper.

Now they are pulling in to the docks, all straining for the first sight of their new country, although the two with babies, once through customs, will be boarding a train and heading into the endless west. But for Ruth and Glad, this is the capital and the entrance to the province.

There are husbands waving from the quay but Bill is not one of them. He is in India, repatriating other ex-soldiers, having perhaps helped return some of those very men swaying now with grins on faces and wives in arms. But Ruth has no need of the helpful Red Cross ladies or the immigration officer with cups of tea and Fig Newton cookies, which nourish Glad till she can be put on the train to wherever she is going. Ruth has been recognised from the wedding photograph, exclaimed over and hugged—taken to the bosom, she thinks as she stiffens slightly from it, of her new family.

She can see Bill in his mother. Myrtle is strong and nearly as tall as Ruth, her ruddy blondness only just beginning to grey. Louise, who Jane will resemble, is more like her father and his Breton ancestors: stocky, small and dark—uncanny because, apart from the accent, George's voice could be Bill's. Like Bill, he seems a quiet man with a glint of humour, but shyer and more awkward; he shakes hands diffidently, although that may have been partly because of missing digits and mangled palm.

They have all got up early, organised the farm for a day's absence and driven the long road to Halifax, just to meet her. They are her new family; her future is now entwined with theirs; the baby bulging the front of her coat carries their history.

'Did you think we'd let you take the train all that way on your own?' Myrtle demands. 'Bad enough that the air force hasn't sent Bill home yet—the least we can do is welcome you properly!'

She has tears in her eyes. So does Ruth. This has been, for her, the most surprising effect of pregnancy—tears glistening at the least emotion. She has already cried twice this morning—once at the sight of land and again at saying goodbye to Glad and the other women. She hopes it's not a permanent change.

Adding to what would later be called culture shock as Ruth is thrown into this new life, is the feeling that bulky as she is, she is still an empty vessel into which her mother-in-law is determined to pour not just wisdom of farm life, because much of that is so basic that Myrtle never does understand how little Ruth knows, but all the background lore of family: who speaks to whom or why not. There'll be no formal family gathering, not with Ruth the shape she is and Bill not yet home, but closer uncles and more curious aunts come in for afternoon tea or invite them all for Sunday dinner. Patchwork history, scraps hurriedly shaped as an unannounced cousin appears at the door, or more leisurely formed as vegetables are peeled in the kitchen, to be reconciled and stitched together with the snippets Bill has told her already.

Myrtle's own story is one that fills a long hour of potato peeling and chopping for rappie pie. 'We're a big family,' she begins, 'and we've been farming here since the first Leighton came up after the Revolution. I don't know much about that but my oldest sister has some interest in it, if you want to know. In my family we were the three older girls, then the two boys, Donald and William, and then me. By the time the Great War began the other girls were all married, and the boys were all fired up to go for the adventure.

'That's not quite true,' she interrupts herself, 'and since you're family you might as well know it all. Donald wanted to go; he was the oldest but he'd never been as fond of the farm as William. William was a born farmer, had the gentlest hand with animals and a way with oxen like you'd never see again; they'd haul anything for him and with never a blow.

'Well, the farm needed him, our father was getting older and farming was tough then, without the machinery and electricity and all we have now, and he'd have been happy enough to stay. It was a long time before we knew what changed his mind, and you have to understand that in that war it was even worse than this one as far as the young men thinking it was glory and adventure and a chance to see the world. They were afraid of nothing except that it would all be over before they got there, poor fools. So everyone thought that William had just got swallowed up by this too. I could never quite fathom it because we were close, us two, and I'd never known him to want to leave the farm at all, but I didn't guess at the truth.

'He'd been seeing a girl from further down the mountain, towards the springs—Ada Black, she was then—but she'd dropped him when he didn't join up. He was a quiet boy, didn't say much, and it hurt him worse than we knew. Well, she wasn't content with breaking his heart, and it seems that she sent him a white feather. No note, just the feather, but he knew who it was from and so he joined up, not long after Donald in the end. They both left for England at the start of October '14.

'They didn't like England much, either of them,' she adds apologetically. 'They were camped on a field at a place called Salisbury, if you've heard of it; they said it was the bleakest, muddiest winter they'd ever lived through.'

Ruth visualises Salisbury Plain from the air, the way that she will see most English landscapes for the rest of her life: the spire of the cathedral, the shadow of the old Roman

roads still visible below the grass and the more ancient dol-
mens of Stonehenge.

'Donald took an interest in the place; he went off to see a
big circle of stones that people said were there before Christ,
whether that's true or not...But William, I think he was homesick and George thinks he knew he was going to die. At any
rate, he and George met up at the camp; George is from the
French shore, and it was the opposite story for him—he'd
been wild to join up and his parents were against it so he'd
gone off without their blessing, which hurt him some. So I
think the two boys were a bit miserable and homesick together,
and in a funny way that cheered them up and mattered more
than the language, because George's English wasn't so good
back then.

'It seems William showed George the feather, and the
story behind it. He'd carried it with him, all that time, and
an envelope with Ada's address. He said if he was killed,
before he died he'd dip that feather in his own blood and
stick it back in the envelope to go right back to her. George
tried to tell him he wouldn't be killed but he just said maybe
not, but if he was, that's what he was going to do.'

Myrtle hasn't told this story many times before; she stumbles a little over the difficult parts and although she smiles
now, her eyes well with tears. So do Ruth's.

'He was a quiet man, William, but a good hater when he
set his mind to it. Well, they left England in February, and
I guess they must have soon wished they were back there if
not home. All George has ever said about Ypres was the
mud, and watching the yellow gas roll over the land like a
fog...But with all you've been through, my dear, and in your
condition, you don't want to think about it, it won't bring all
those men back to life now. But the three of them survived,
right through till summer.

'William used to get spring fever worse than any of us—
not real crazy, just silly-happy; he loved the spring. Any road,

that was the last one; he died at a place in France called Givenchy, in June '15.

'George says he died fast, without feeling any pain, and I've always tried to believe him. Anyway, George gathered up his things because they'd made a pact to do that and Donald was at some other end of the place, and there was the feather in its envelope. George says he was that mad, he did what William wanted: dipped the feather in blood and stuck it into the envelope. And the next day he had his hand blown off—you might have noticed there's a couple of fingers missing—and so they decided to send him home, but the envelope went off first, from the field hospital.

'We got the telegram here in June and then about six months later George came to see us. He brought the little things that William had wanted saved, and it was such a comfort to talk to someone who had known him over there. It's hard to imagine that it could be true, when they're killed so far away and you can't even imagine the place at all. So it was hard, because it made it truer, and it was better too.

'You know, the French shore seemed further away those days than it does now, with cars and all, and it seemed only right that he should stay for a few days when he'd brought us this news. By the end of that time I knew he was the man I was going to marry.

'My family could nearly overlook his being French on account of being William's friend and wounded in the war, but he didn't have a cent to his name. They were always proud that we had the biggest farm and the best house in Evelyn's Pond. I guess it's natural that they wanted me to marry someone who could give me an easier life. And his family wasn't going to forgive him for marrying outside the faith, so there was no help there! In the end it was decided that he would stay and work on the farm until Donald came back, because it was more work than a girl and an old man could manage. I have an idea that my father thought I wouldn't marry George once he was the hired man, but seeing him every day only made me more determined—and they never actually said no, so we got married. Then poor Donald was killed in Belgium, right at the very end of the war. It was a terrible shock; he'd made it through all those battles that you hear about and then when they'd just about won, he died.

'Well, by then my father was used to George and he could see George was used to the farm, so when he died the farm went to us. My sisters had a bit to say about it, but by then George had worked it for eight years, mostly on his own... Father just seemed to lose heart when Donald died, and after my mother took a stroke he hardly left the house at all.

'You can see that we had to name our first son William,' she adds, 'but I always wanted him called Bill. I worried that it might bring him bad luck when this war started, but in the end the name didn't matter.'

Ruth has to ask. 'What about the feather?'

'Well, George worried about that for years. He said once he stopped being angry he felt right sick to think how that girl would feel, and he couldn't believe he'd done such a thing. But it never seemed to bother her. She married after the war. Ada White she is now, would you believe it? It was years before I could bring myself to speak to her, and now, well, it's not something you can ask, is it?'

The baby is due on 12 February and Bill three days later. 'But he'll be here well before it's born,' Myrtle assures her. 'It's a rare first baby that isn't late.'

Ruth has visited the family doctor, seen the hospital and is still healthy, though uncomfortable and occasionally breathless in these last weeks of pregnancy. She is aware that both mother-in-law and doctor are anxious about her narrow hips and general leanness, but thankfully unaware that they have also factored in her temperament: what they see as nerviness and the unwomanly behaviour of having done a man's job. Myrtle is secretly proud of this oddity, but does not feel it bodes well for the ordeal of childbirth. She tries to prepare Ruth, gently but honestly, for what lies ahead, having always wished that someone had done the same for her twenty-eight years earlier.

So when Ruth's indigestion, which had lessened during the past fortnight as the baby removed its head from her diaphragm and settled into her groin, starts sharply on the morning of the second, she does not think it worth complaining about. And when the snow begins later that day, whiteness whirling soft against the windows, frosting the fir trees in the woods like painted Christmas cards, she remembers Switzerland, a lifetime ago, and is entranced. Just before noon the pain becomes stronger and more regular, and she has just decided to mention it to Myrtle when it disappears.

They spent much of yesterday afternoon making tourtiere: 'Bill's favourite,' said Myrtle, 'no reason just to have it at New Year,' and Ruth was keen to learn. She ground the meat in the big grinder clamped to the kitchen table, a fat pork shoulder that had given her a cramplike stitch as it was transformed into a pile of greasy mince.

'You'd think that after all those years of cranking down an Anson undercarriage I could grind up a bit of meat!' she laughed, and Myrtle, who had no idea what either an undercarriage or an Anson was, looked at her sharply. She didn't need to imagine a world where women in slacks or flying suits, en route from airport to airport, took turns winding down the wheels of their taxi-plane, one hundred and fifty heavy revolutions; it was enough to understand that Ruth was breathless. She ordered her onto the day bed in the corner; Ruth refused and was allowed to stay at the table on condition that she content herself with watching and not helping.

The kitchen was warm and became fuggy with steam as the well-spiced pork, a chopped onion and a handful of raisins for sweetness simmered on the wood stove. Ruth's nausea at the sight of the meat and stitch from grinding it subsided and she was left with a sense of wellbeing and lassitude which in the end sent her up to her own bed, that big empty bed waiting for Bill, to doze for an hour or two. She was too uncomfortable to sleep well at the moment, and perhaps because of the nap, slept worse than usual that night.

This morning she has tried her hand at pastry, using fingertips to rub the lard into the flour, mixing a little too much cold water so that more flour has to be added, having to add still more to roll it out, and suspecting that she will never learn the quick flip Myrtle demonstrates to lift the pie-sized circle over the rolling pin.

'Just practice,' Myrtle says encouragingly, although she can't remember a time when she couldn't make a pie herself and is beginning to share Ruth's suspicion that it may be something her daughter-in-law will never learn.

The pie is ready for dinner, which they eat at what Ruth would call luncheon. 'I can see why this is Bill's favourite,' she says after the first mouthful, and everyone, even Louise, smiles as if they've been waiting for this verdict.

It's rich, though. For a stomach used to five years of rationing, excessively rich.

'A sliver more?' Myrtle tempts, worried about the more obvious effects of those lean years. 'Don't forget you're eating for two!'

Ruth feels that she's eaten for six. When the dishes have been washed and tidied she goes back to her own room. The euphoria of the day before is replaced by a wave of depression and the certainty that she will never fit in here: she not only can't cook, the daily routines of a country household are foreign to her. Every night when Myrtle settles the big porridge pot on the wood stove to be ready for morning, all Ruth can think of is the Starkadders' boiling-over porridge in *Cold Comfort Farm* and as a result still can't remember the correct proportions of water and oatmeal. Now she's discovered that she can't even eat the food Bill is used to.

When Myrtle brings her a cup of tea later that afternoon she is too ashamed to admit the indigestion that has recommenced: spasmodic, increasingly severe attacks which once again disappear just as she is on the point of wondering whether it is in fact baby rather than pork.

Outside, the snowfall has blossomed to blizzard. George and Louise constantly clear a path the few feet from the end door of the shed to the barn; around the other doors the drifts are piling high. Ruth's mood has lifted again and she is excited by the wildness of the wind and isolation. The moon is full; she sleeps little on a full moon at the best of times, and tonight lies in a half dream wishing, as she wishes several times a day and constantly at night, that Bill was beside her and that they were alone in a snowbound house, a cosy private cave. A baby does not intrude on this frigid honeymoon vision.

She must have slept, because she wakes in a wet bed. There is no pain, simply a pool of rapidly cooling water; something that she'd understood happened after a period of labour. She wonders how long she will have to wait for contractions to begin; wonders if she should wake up Myrtle; wonders how she will cope with this and what it will be like, and will she really have a baby at the end of it? Wonders what time it is and sits up to pull the light cord over her bed.

No light. The electricity has gone.

Climbing tentatively out of bed, her wet nightgown clinging stickily, she crosses to the window with clock in hand and pulls the curtains.

The snow has stopped falling; the wind has passed. The world gleams white in moonlit magic and mysterious slopes, and the wonder of it becomes part of the story of her firstborn child. (From next December on, when Ruth reads 'the moon on the breast of the new fallen snow' to her children on the night before Christmas—and forever after that because when the children are too old for it the words have become part of her Christmas habit—she will relive the night of Jane's birth.)

It is probably only seconds before she looks at the clock, because the room is cold and her nightgown chilling quickly around her. Quickly, anticipating the onset of pain, she changes into a clean nightie, strips her bed and feels her way down the hall to the linen closet in the trunk room, taking an armful of sheets from the darkness and making her way back to her room without tripping or stumbling.

She has just managed to flip the mattress, damp side to the springs, when the first pain begins and Myrtle appears, ghostly in long dressing gown and flashlight.

'How long have they been coming?'

Ruth waits for it to ebb before replying. She is slightly humiliated by the wet bed, but Myrtle waves the thought away and begins covering the mattress with an old blanket before tucking in sheets.

'No need to go to the hospital yet,' she says, once her daughter-in-law is settled back into bed, 'you might as well be comfortable.' Her voice is calm, but she can't help a quick, betraying glance out the window.

For the first time Ruth understands the full meaning of snowbound. 'We can't get out, can we?'

'Not right now,' Myrtle admits. 'But that doesn't mean we can't get the doctor here when you're ready.'

'On snowshoes?'—remembering Bill's waddling description with a laugh that is choked by the grip of the next pain.

'George would love the excuse to use the sleigh; he hasn't had it out yet this year. It's a wonder he hasn't carried you off for a ride in it already, baby or not, he's that fond of the thing. And you know, my dear, I had Bill in this house, and Louise—and Albert,' she adds resolutely, with only the slightest quaver. 'Of course I was born here too, and my father too;

now doesn't it seem a wonderful thing that your child should be born here in his turn?'

Ruth, resting between pains again, loves her for this. With one stroke the baby has been given a secure place in family history. She sees generations of women, far longer back than this house, labouring as she is now to produce the next part of the web that is family, and realises that historyless or not, she is part of it too.

'Now, my dear,' Myrtle says briskly, returning from another bustle around in the trunk room with what looks suspiciously like an antique chamber-pot, 'I'm going to go downstairs and poke up that fire. We don't want you getting cold. While I'm gone you might like to use this.'

Ruth blushes scarlet. She had expected childbirth to be painful, not humiliating.

'You can't wait till it's over and we don't want you walking up and down those stairs for no reason. Nothing to be ashamed of, between women.'

Another pain begins, and Ruth realises she wouldn't have time to get down the stairs and back between them. Myrtle waits till it's over, trying not to look as anxious as she feels, then flies downstairs to the basement furnace.

Crouching over the pot in the moonlit room, hanging on to the bedframe for balance, Ruth is overwhelmed with relief that Bill isn't here yet. They don't know each other well enough, she thinks, for him to see her like this. Another pain begins before she's finished and she's suddenly terrified that she'll push the baby out into the pot by mistake, a disastrous beginning to life, though a small voice points out that these pains, unpleasant as they are, are not devastating enough for what she's heard of childbirth.

They are coming closer together, though, and each one is a little stronger. Myrtle reappears with a kerosene lamp but the smell makes Ruth so nauseated that at the next pain she cries out for the first time.

Myrtle runs across the hall to wake George. Louise comes in, tentative and dishevelled. The first time she's been in my room since I've been here, thinks Ruth, feeling at a distinct disadvantage though minding less than she'd expect. 'Sorry to disturb you,' she pants. 'It's just that lamp.'

Thoughts flit across her mind in random patterns, dream-like; is this how it was for her own mother? ... Did her mother die? ... Where is Bill now? ... Why does the smell of kerosene make her sick and sad? ... And here it comes again.

'Get some candles, Louise,' Myrtle orders, 'and then go check that fire. Take the baby blankets down with you and put them in the warming oven.'

'Baby blankets!' repeats Ruth in wonder, as if this particular outcome has never struck her before.

'George is going for the doctor,' says Myrtle, 'but you're doing such a good job, you might be finished before he gets here.'

'Why don't you phone?' demands Louise.

Her mother glances at her sharply. 'It's out.'

Louise takes the offending lamp and heads into the trunk room. George clumps hurriedly down the stairs.

'Myrtle,' says Ruth, 'do you mean I'm going to have a baby now?'

'If you're not, you've eaten far too much tourtiere!'

'How soon?'

'I don't know, dear. They're unpredictable creatures, babies. Like men.'

A longer contraction interrupts the conversation but this time Ruth holds the thought.

'Have you ever delivered a baby before?'

'Goodness! I've seen that many born I couldn't count—more than twenty, certainly.'

Louise returns with candles and goes to dress; it's going to take some shovelling, her father has reported, before he can get into the barn, much less get horse and sleigh out.

The moonlight has dimmed now and the sky is grey, still hours before dawn. The pains rest briefly and reappear with less pattern and renewed intensity. Ruth is glad that the others are out of the house and can't hear the noises she's making.

'You're a brave girl, that's for sure,' Myrtle says. 'But if you can't shout when you're having a baby, I don't know when you can.'

Her voice comes from a distant place. Ruth's pain is no longer controllable; her insides are being torn apart, like the ancient victims sundered by wild horses.

'Oh, God!' she groans as the next pain changes into the most powerful, the most primeval urge she has ever known. 'I'm having a baby!'

'You certainly are.'

'Now!' Ruth shouts, her face contorted with pushing.

Myrtle pulls back the covers and peers between her daughter-in-law's legs to see the crowning head of her first grandchild. Tears spurt to her eyes.

'It's nearly here; take your time. Squeeze my hand when you push.'

'I'll hurt you,' Ruth pants, readying herself for the next wave.

Myrtle would have preferred to be hurt and share the burden, but has to content herself with smoothing hair off the damp forehead between contractions and watching the baby's progress during them. Neither woman has much sense of the passing time, but dawn is barely breaking when the baby shoots out in a sudden rush of blood, its hurry turning it a bright surprising blue, identical in the dim candlelight to the periwinkle blue of the wallpaper flowers.

Its grandmother lifts it gently, unsure what to do with the thick pulsating cord, but Ruth holds out her arms in yearning demand and the baby is placed on her stomach.

'A girl,' Myrtle says as she lifts and the baby pinkens obediently under its layer of protecting grease, becoming within seconds a so obviously healthy, normal newborn that neither woman is quite sure whether she has imagined the blueness.

This is not how Ruth has imagined birth. This is magic, this is euphoria, this is a tiny human being nestled on her bare midriff, mouth gawping blindly as a fish, and she had thought babies were ugly but this one, blotchy and bald, is quite beautiful, and she's done it, she's done it all by herself, made this wonderful baby.

'Hello, Jane,' she whispers, touching the frail head with a finger.

Another contraction, vicious in its unexpectedness. When she can think, Ruth expects to see a twin, but it's simply the afterbirth, something else Myrtle is not sure what to do with, all the mothers she's attended previously having eaten it without comment.

Ruth rests a moment and begins stroking Jane's head again. After some hesitation, Myrtle produces the kitchen scissors, carefully washed in one of her forays downstairs, and cuts the cord. Ruth is astonished not to feel pain, not yet understanding that the baby is now separate from her. With increasing intensity, Jane begins to nuzzle at her mother's stomach, and after a moment of absolute panic at handling so tiny a creature, infinitely smaller than the sturdy babies on the ship, Ruth wiggles her higher until she attaches herself to a breast.

'Well!' says Myrtle and sinks into the chair beside the bed, satisfied but utterly drained. 'Well!'

'Won't Bill be surprised!' Ruth says suddenly, breaking into helpless shaking giggles, which Myrtle has just recognised as shock when Louise appears to say that George is leaving for the doctor.

'You might have told us!' Louise snaps, and Ruth covers herself instinctively against the glare.

'For pity sakes, girl, you can see it's just happened! Go and tell Dad; he'd still best fetch the doctor, but he could have his porridge first.'

Then there are warmed blankets to tuck tightly around mother and babe, and the kettle on for a cup of tea and a hot-water bottle because Ruth is still shaking, and water warmed for the baby, still covered in bloody vernix, to have her first bath. George comes up to say hello from the doorway before he leaves, beaming at this sight of his son's daughter, and Louise stays there too, as if uncertain of her welcome, till Ruth asks if she would like to hold her niece.

Louise's tense face softens. 'Will I bathe her for you?' she asks briskly, and Ruth, feeling as if her heart will break at this first separation, but better that than wash this dearest being in this chilly room, agrees and sees her daughter disappear to the kitchen to be washed and inexpertly wrapped, Louise not having had much more experience than Ruth in the matter.

Jane is returned and tucked into her own cot, where Ruth, sitting up against her pillows, can gaze at her in wonder, tears flowing softly now in gratitude for her daughter, and grief for Bill not being here to share her.

'We'll leave you alone to rest.' Myrtle bends over Ruth as if she would have liked to kiss her, but contents herself with stroking a tear away from her cheek.

Ruth catches her hand. 'Thank you. There ought to be a better word—but thank you.'

'It was a privilege,' says Myrtle sincerely. 'To see my own grand-daughter born; something most people don't get to see these days, with hospitals and all.'

'But the other babies you delivered?'

'All had four legs, my dear, but I didn't think it was the time to say so when you asked.'

◯

In the same room, fifty-three years later, Jane will read Ruth's letter to Mary announcing her birth.

I had intended to write immediately on my arrival in Canada, but have procrastinated long enough to announce the arrival of a brand-new Canadian. Jane Myrtle Dubois was born three days ago, in the house of her ancestors. A true Canadian, she arrived in a blizzard—though to be honest, I am not completely sure at what point snow becomes a blizzard, and it's possible that this was the Nova Scotian equivalent of a London drizzle. It was, however, enough to bring down electricity and phone lines for a day, and block roads until now. From my window the world is still quite white; only the trees in the woods behind the garden are starting to shed their coverings and stand out, green or bare according to species, against the snow. Drifts are piled deep against the front of the house and barn, looking as high as my head, although perhaps I exaggerate. The only route to the outdoors is through the long outbuilding at the end of the house, where a brief path has been shovelled to the barn door. (One wonders why the original builders didn't simply attach the barn to the other end of this shed, so one could go in comfort all the way!)

Needless to say, I haven't attempted this route myself. The baby and I spend our time ensconced in bed where, like royalty, we grant occasional audiences.

I had always thought tiny babies to be rather hideous creatures, and never understood the hypocrisy of calling them beautiful. I now understand that it is simply because there is no other word to express the emotion that fills one's heart on seeing this tiny new creature. Objectively, Jane has a small, slightly squashed-looking red face with a strange little bruise on her forehead as a result of her rush to greet the world, which the doctor assures me will disappear. This will, I think, be a person who will make her way in whatever she chooses to do. However, it is impossible for me to look at her objectively; what I see is simply the most important being in the world and I am tied to her by something like a physical cord. You cannot imagine how one feels when she cries! One's stomach clenches and one could howl oneself. But when she's happy, sleeping or nursing or just lying in my arms with her strange glazed look, I feel the most privileged person on earth, happy and exultant. At some stage during the process of birth I seem to have lost a layer of skin, so that the slightest breeze of this tiny person's desires blows directly across my soul.

This is so unlike the mother she knows that Jane will have to stop at this point and make a cup of coffee before she can go on. It's also a revelation to learn that Ruth and Mary had been so intimate, and she cannot know of the gaping need Ruth had felt, with Bill now on ship and out of letter reach, to explore her feelings on paper.

Today, however, I can't stop wondering about my own mother, the woman who bore me. Did she feel like this when she looked at the infant that was me? How did this cord break, or did it break her heart to give me away? One would prefer to believe that she had died first, because it is simply unbearable to imagine the grief that she would have experienced if she had felt only one tenth—one one-hundredth!—of what I feel for Jane. Or am I descended from some unnatural strain of parent? The very thought of ever having to leave this dearest being in the care of anyone else fills me with despair. Perhaps Papa was correct; perhaps one couldn't bear to know what extremes in life would lead a mother to abandon her child.

Ironically, at the other end of those extremes of poverty (or brutality or madness—but I can't think of those), I'm also unable to imagine surrendering her to a nanny. It may be just as well that I married a colonial with such strong ideas on the subject; if one had married Miles would one have gone on accepting without question that a nanny should rule in the nursery, with parental visits limited to courtesy? (I picture Nanny coming in to me now and lifting Jane away. 'That's quite enough of all this blither,' she'd say at what I've just told you. 'Never did anyone any good to sit around thinking about themselves!' Would one submit? I'd like to think not, but it's never easy to break the habit of a lifetime.)

I'm picturing, of course, life returning to normal in Britain now that the war is over, but I wonder if that's true. Will all those women who've worked as men for six years be willing to hand over even the care of their own children now we're at peace? Did you not have the tiniest bit of regret, not for peace, but for the work and the life you were making for yourself?

This is a very strange letter, Mary, but I don't know what else to do with this tumbling of emotions. Dear as she is, I have not been able to bring myself to tell my mother-in-law my pathetic little history, and although she thinks this baby quite wonderful and is rather proud of her own role in bringing her into the world, I could not describe my feelings as I just have to you, with the benefit of paper and distance.

I do so long for Bill to come home! I'm grateful that he was not around for the indignities of labour, but he's missed three days of his daughter's life already, and more than enough of his wife's. I am so proud of having produced her; I'd like him to share that, and in the hours when I fear that I will never learn to be an adequate mother for her, I long for him still more, because in even the blackest mood I can only picture Bill as a loving father.

It is clear, too, where he came by that solidity and strength. His father is quiet, shyer even than Bill, but with a sense of humour that catches one unaware. I had not expected him to have a French accent! Bill never mentioned it—perhaps he doesn't hear it. It took me by surprise, but adds a certain charm to his speech, as that touch of French always does, even when, as in this case, the accent is markedly different from that of France. He claims that the French of the Acadians is the pure language, uncorrupted by time since its arrival in the seventeenth century. (Are there any parts of the world, I wonder, where people speak the English of Milton?) However, that is the only thing he's told me of his background and he has apparently nothing to do with any of his relatives now that his father, the grandfather Bill adored, has died. What a waste, to have all those lines of family and no communication!

*I want my children to have all the family they can, all the ances-
tors and their stories, and cousins to play with, so they grow up
secure in knowing who they are.*

*The only member of the family I am not completely sure
about is Bill's sister Louise. One feels rather sorry for her,
although she would prickle even more if she knew. She has spent
six years working on the farm—I was going to say working like
a man, but in deference to you I'll not—and now that Bill is
coming home it will be handed over to him. George and Myrtle
have, most graciously—and wisely, I think, for much as I like
them, the thought of living constantly under their supervision is
quite terrifying—decided to retire to the town. Perhaps after the
years of living with first Myrtle's parents and then George's
father, they would also like to have a house unencumbered by in-
laws. George has bought a feed shop (oats and animal feed, not
human) and will take over its management when Bill returns,
when they will also move into the house in Applevale that they
are now in the process of buying. One assumes that we are to pay
an equivalent amount for the farm, but it's obviously not an issue
they feel comfortable discussing with me. It seems to be presumed
that Louise will go with them; I'm not sure what say she's had
in this but am certainly not about to ask!*

*One suspects, though, that it's not the farm itself she would
like, but a little gratitude. It seems that the family's grief for Bill's
brother and anxiety for Bill have overshadowed life until now,
when we have not only the anticipation of his return, but a
grandchild to celebrate. I've often wondered how the hard-working
brother of the prodigal son felt on being asked to kill the fatted
calf—I suspect Louise would be able to tell me.*

*Interestingly enough, her mother had a similar story: working
the farm with her parents while her brothers were away at war.
The difference was that although she lost two brothers, she gained
a husband. I imagine Louise finds me a poor exchange.*

*In case the length of this letter has you picturing me lying
here in complete leisure, I must hasten to add that it has been*

written over two days and interrupted by many sessions of baby-feeding, resultant napkin changes, and a bit of adoration on bended knee from various family members.

We shall have photographs taken very soon, but for now you will have to be satisfied with this word-portrait of my new home and your new—I'm not sure exactly sure, and perhaps given Mama's revelations the exact relationship is quite irrelevant, so shall we just settle for niece?

The funny thing is that Ruth, with her straight hips and restless temperament, has babies as easily and calmly, well, not as a cow in a field, but as easily and calmly as any western woman is likely to: Jane at twenty seven, Michael following twenty months later, and Richard a neat two years after that. A five-hour labour, four then three; the babies all cooperating by greeting the world the right way around, face down and healthy.

It's her placid daughter, grown to generous-hipped woman, who can't get it right. Megan, a child who a few years later will announce that she prefers reading standing on her head because the words look more interesting that way, starts as she means to continue by trying to slide out of the womb feet first. It doesn't work. To be fair to Megan, it appears that Jane's childbearing hips are a sham, as narrow on the inside as they are wide on the outer, and no large-headed child will fit through the gap. In the end, after a twelve-hour trial of labour, sentence is passed and Megan is born like Caesar—so Ruth points out, though Jane does not find this particularly comforting.

Although she'd have been glad, overjoyed, eternally grateful, to have had the next pregnancies by caesarean, if they'd only stayed around long enough for the privilege. The third miscarriage is too much: there's a limit to how much hope and heartbreak you can put yourself through, how much anticipation and despair, when everyone you know is having babies, popping them out effortlessly, big-bellied women every-where in the streets, at playgroup, at the kindergarten and school, flaunting their fortunate fecundity, and haven't you thought of having another one, Megan's a good age now—she's two—she's three—she's five—you don't want to leave it too long. There's a limit to how many times you can fail before the only sensible thing to do is quit. A few months after Jane came out of hospital from the last sad tidy and scrape, she returned for a tubal ligation and, at thirty-one, the end of this particular hope.

This period, with its constantly hovering black cloud of depression, she sees as framed by her first trip back to Canada and her mother's later visit after the surgical confirmation of failure—there is never any doubt in Jane's mind that she has failed an essential test of womanhood. Ruth hadn't seen it that way and neither had Ian. They were both genuinely bewil-dered at why she should feel such despair when the one child she had produced was so demonstrably perfect, and Jane was unable to explain it to them. Because her mother had three babies, forming the standard Jane expected; because she feared that the traces of selfishness she saw in Ian stemmed from never having to share with siblings; because she simply ached for another baby, for the cocoon of contentment that enfolds newborn and mother, the suction of a small grasping mouth on her nipple, the prickle of letting-down milk and miracu-lous knowledge that she could supply all its needs. She would have liked to feel that satisfaction, that success again.

The Christmas that Megan was eighteen months, gleefully waddling through the rustle of wrapping paper, Ruth and Bill's present to Jane had been a small white envelope with a postal order and handwritten voucher: *This entitles the bearer to a return air ticket from Melbourne to Halifax.* If Ian wanted to come, a note added, this could be thought of as a half ticket for each of them; Megan, who would travel virtually free until her second birthday, would be easily covered by the amount. Jane saw a flash of disappointment cross Ian's face but was not sure whether it was because he'd have liked a ticket too, or he wished he could have afforded to give her such a gift himself or because the envelope had engendered hopes of a smaller but stringless cheque. Milk prices were low that season and the outlook worse. (Preparing to leave the following May, Jane was surprised by sharpness from acquaintances: 'Some people are managing alright!' and found herself constantly prefacing her trip with the defensive: 'My parents sent me the ticket,' as if this good fortune was somehow shameful.)

It was nearly six years since she'd left home and the strength of her emotions shouldn't have but did take her by surprise: a snug contentment at the sound of Canadian voices on the flight from Los Angeles, a sense of homecoming in simply standing in the line at Halifax airport with the other Canadian passport-bearers, no longer migrant or alien. Despite photographs demonstrating that there'd been little change in Ruth or Bill, she felt a small undercurrent of fear that she wouldn't at first recognise them, that they would have aged—as they had, in the barely perceptible way of healthy people moving from their early to late fifties. She spotted them a fraction of an instant before they could see her, the anticipation on their faces mirroring hers, and was so overwhelmed by love and relief that all she could do was scoop Megan up to see: 'There's Nana, Megan, and Grandad!' Her daughter, who had been practising these names against the photos for weeks, stared at the strangers and hid her face.

'People kept saying,' Ruth said that evening, when Megan had finally collapsed from the excitement and been put to bed, '"Won't you be pleased to see your grand-daughter!" and I said, "Yes, but I'm more excited about seeing my daughter,"' and Jane was inordinately gratified by this because the same thing had been said to her. 'Your parents will be

THE HOUSE AT EVELYN'S POND

looking forward to seeing Megan!' and she'd been unable to quell the thought, But I'm the one they know!

They'd discussed then the foibles of grandchild-doting neighbours who appeared to believe that the infants had sprung from some other line than their disappointing son and loathed daughter-in-law, direct perhaps from their own forehead like Athene from Zeus.

'That's some little girl you've got there,' said Bill, coming in from the kitchen with cups of tea and unable to understand their laughter when he added, 'and doesn't she look like her grandmother!'

It was true, though; she looked more like Ruth than she did Jane, and Jane was surprised when Ruth denied it, saying that from the pictures she'd seen there was a lot of Ian and a fair bit of Jane too.

❦

May and June are apple blossom time, when the Dubois farm and the Valley generally are sprayed with pinky-white blooms; a season of festivals and Apple Blossom Queens— Patsy the year they were in grade 12, though it was hard to believe it now, her generous curves flabby and her conversation soured with complaints about Randy, his mother and the children. She was curious about what sort of house Jane had and what sort of income Ian made but the old intimacy was gone, as if the girls who'd lain side by side on sleepover nights, whispering delicious wicked secrets, were entirely differently people from the young matrons they found themselves now.

But Patsy was the only homecoming disappointment. Ruth's horse Lochinvar was still spry at twenty, and Jane took him over all the back roads, up to her favourite mountain lookout and through the fields and forests she'd covered on bony Bold Brennan.

'I feel like a kid again,' she told her father, jumping down with her hair tangled and eyes shining.

'Look like one too,' said Bill. 'Why don't you get yourself a horse in Australia? Surely you've got enough land to support one spare pony.'

It wasn't a year for luxuries, Jane explained, and who would mind Megan while she rode? Easier to simply enjoy it while she was here.

The Valley was smaller than she'd remembered and the farms poorer. The countryside, the beaches and ocean, wharves at sunset with the delicate tracery of masts and spars etched black against the pink, all overwhelmed her with remembered belonging. Megan, who knew hills only as something where Jack and Jill tumbled and broke crowns, was frightened by them until her grandfather showed her how to run up a small slope and roll safely down. Introduced to dulse, purple-brown and richly salty, Megan delighted her grandmother who could not abide it, and her mother who had craved it since leaving, by asking for more. There were afternoons with George and Myrtle, not yet frail but definitely old and moved almost to tears by the sight of their great-grand-daughter; visits to other kin from St Mary's Bay to Cape Breton, two days with chain-smoking Aunt Louise, the younger cousins now surprisingly adults, one of them engaged to a girl whose family still spoke Gaelic and busy learning it himself, Louise unsure whether to admire her son's industry or mock a language she couldn't share.

By the end of the three weeks, despite the pure, contented warmth of talking to her father, discussing books with her mother, playing Scrabble in the evening when the news had been watched and the TV turned off, of seeing her daughter explore the house that formed her prototype for the word, she was ready to return. She'd missed Ian from the beginning, in the sense of wishing he could share her pleasure, wanting him to see Megan being read to by her grandmother or riding bedecked in apple blossom through the orchard on her grandfather's shoulders, and always feeling the bed incomplete at night without him beside her. Letters took too long—although she wrote and he answered, it was hardly worthwhile and they'd never had a reason to write before, so there was no habit or history to continue. The longing intensified. The days were incomplete without being shared and at night she missed him so much, so blatantly and in such shameless dreams that she didn't know whether he'd be more flattered or shocked if she told him. It wasn't surprising that she became pregnant in June, the first week she was home.

She felt surprisingly well, in contrast to the nausea she'd experienced with Megan, which made it all the more devastating when her body gushed sad bright blood in August. Spontaneous abortion, the doctor called it, an ugly word which did not improve the verdict. 'But don't worry,' he said, 'one miscarriage is common; you've proved you can carry a healthy baby to term, this one just wasn't meant to be'—and Jane tried to believe him.

That was the year prices slipped so low that calves could not be sold. Stopping on the way to the sale yards, Ian came out to find five extra calves loaded onto his trailer. It would have been funny if he hadn't ended up with a loss after paying the yard fees. Dairy wives who depended on their calf-rearing money for spending throughout the year were distraught; Jane, reminded of life's priorities, risked social isolation by trying to avoid the doomsday conversations. In January she was pregnant again, telling herself that the unremitting morning sickness was a good sign, although within the first trimester that had proved a lie.

By now the state of the industry was desperate. The price of milk continued to plunge as butter factories closed, while between drought and plummeting beef values, cow prices had dropped so low that there was nothing to do with barren beasts but collect the government's two dollars and shoot them into pits. Only in debt and interest bills did farming show rampant, luxurious growth. Financial reward from work seemed to be something reserved for other people, city people on a wage. Ian, feeling cheated by life as well as government, turned his anger to something that could be fought, joining angry rallies in Yarralong and a march, 6000 angry dairy farmers strong, through the streets of Melbourne. Hard times hadn't mattered when it was just the two of them—they could make do, look to the future—but Megan was their future and they didn't want her to grow up deprived of what other children would take for granted—siblings and material goods, lessons for ballet and tennis, Brownies and Guides.

The doctor ordered Jane's body a rest and it was nine months before she became pregnant again, a year almost exactly when she miscarried for the last time. The letter from her mother arrived the day of the tubal ligation, Ian presenting it as a consolation prize when he visited that evening. *Photographs are all very well, but it's time I saw your new home for myself. Your father and I have decided I should fly out in July, in time for Megan's fifth birthday.*

In a *Through the Looking Glass* version of Jane's homecoming trip, Ruth was introduced to her daughter's new life: Ian's parents—she and Dulcie had nothing in common except Megan, but that sufficed—the peaceful winter river where she heard kookaburras and saw kangaroos, and the farm itself, admiring Jane's oasis and Ian's dairy, taking rolls of photographs for Bill. The resemblance between her and her grand-daughter was stronger now, and although she continued to deny this, her delight in the child was palpable.

'Isn't it funny,' said Megan, 'you have three different names and they're all different colours.' And when Ruth did not immediately comprehend: 'Granny calls you Ruth, so that's a blue name. Mummy calls you Mom and that's yellow, and Nana is red, round red like an apple.'

'What about your name?'

'White and red!' Megan laughed, surprised at such an obvious question. 'And Ralston is dark red and brown like a Jersey cow. What's your last name?'

'Dubois. That used to be your mother's last name when she was a little girl.'

'I like that one best of all,' Megan confided. 'Do you?'

'Yes,' said Ruth sincerely, but could not help asking, 'What colour is it?'

'You know! Blue like sky and gold like a sunset.'

More surprising to Jane was Ruth's rapport with Ian. Although she'd badly wanted them to like each other, she could not help anticipating friction between two strong-willed people with no common interests. However, Ian's dry humour suited Ruth exactly, and he enjoyed the way she argued with him. *Why can't I stand up to him like that?* thought Jane, but did not yet feel strong enough to try. And since she also hadn't learned to stand up to her mother, she tended to keep silent while they debated, as she had years ago with Winston.

All the same she felt enveloped by the love that had arranged this visit. And whether it was that, or time or her mother's delight in Megan that made Jane see her anew and wonder how she could have ever wanted to share her love with another child, the black cloud began to dissipate.

Chapter
SIX

Grade 2 was Miss Lake, Eatons catalogues and the Arctic. It might have been for a week, it could have been for two, but in Jane's memory they flew north every morning—thirty-one individual planes standing neatly beside their desks, arms outstretched for take-off and vrooming over the Bay of Fundy and New Brunswick, across the St Lawrence and on over Quebec, the cold waters of Hudson Bay where its eponymous explorer had drifted and died, across the tundra to the Great North, the soul of the country, proud in its snow and cold.

Landing in the Arctic, they switched off engines and stepped out, knees high to show descent. Pretty Miss Lake led them to marvel at roaming herds of caribou, puzzle at lemmings hurling themselves over cliffs, shiver at howling wolves (in 1953, *Never Cry Wolf* still unwritten, wolves were still purely sinister). On sheets of white paper with firmly clenched pencils, they learned to build igloos, drawing bricks carved from ice and stacked round into cosy houses; and although they built their snow caves that year in the usual way, scooped from the snow-ploughed drifts, the rectangles they scratched on the walls felt satisfyingly authentic. In the evenings they did homework, poring over old Eatons catalogues to cut out pictures of provisions and supplies, parkas and boots, to be pasted in place the next morning.

At the end of the year Miss Lake left to marry and move to the north where she would live by the side of her own Arctic lake.

Adult Jane, being aware of the mix of memory with word association, imagination and superimposed knowledge, thinks this unlikely. It is more probable that the newly married teacher moved to Halifax, across the Bay to St John or to the bleakness of coal and steel in Sydney or Glace Bay.

But when faced with the statistics of girls of her era who turned to teaching because they could not see other careers beyond it, Jane objects. It was set firm for her, flying to the Arctic in grade 2.

Although I still believe that Jane chose teachers' college for the wrong reasons, Ruth wrote to Mary, choosing her Christmas words with a fraction more care than July's, *it may have been the right choice for her. She has never been as confident as she deserves to be. Much as I would have loved to see her grow in the more challenging atmosphere of university (and still believe that her mathematical mind will be wasted on tiny children), it isn't doing her any harm to be one of the brightest of her group.*

For her part, Jane would always be grateful that although she must have thought it, Ruth never even suggested 'I told you so,' when her daughter began correspondence studies twenty years later, finishing her Bachelor of Education not long before she left teaching for good.

Moving into the dorm that first anxious, exhilarating day of term, Jane bumped bundles with a tall, slim girl. A few evenings later Gail came giggling into Jane's room, 'Oh God,

I'm so embarrassed! You know those lights in the middle of town?'

'The traffic lights?'

'Mm—Do you have those in your town? I've never seen any before.'

'Applevale's too small, but…haven't you ever been to Halifax?'

Gail shook her head. 'Nowhere. You know, they're pretty neat. When they're red the cars stop and when they're green the cars go again. So I was standing there on the corner watching, for quite a while I guess because all of a sudden that really tall lecturer came up to me. He said someone had phoned him…This is too embarrassing!'

'They didn't think you were…?'

'Trying to be a prostitute!'

'God, that would be scary,' Jane said. 'How would you do it?'

'If we fail teaching we can always find out.'

It became a password after that: 'I can see that red light!' as they came out of a particularly nasty exam or a rioting practice class. They were closer even than Jane had been to Patsy, now happily planning her wedding to Randy McLeod.

Jane's only romantic interest was a pleasant but dull young man from the agricultural college, thus thwarting the founding fathers' intentions of keeping the good girls of teachers' college safe from the attentions of the agricultural men, although they mightn't have felt thwarted if they'd seen how unbearably dull the romance was and how placidly the boy accepted Jane's removal of his hand from the buttons of her blouse. Years later she wondered if he might have been gay, but in 1964 he simply seemed further confirmation of her own lack of sex appeal.

If Winston had enjoyed making love to me, she wrote in a diary which she later burned, *he wouldn't have left, no matter*

*how determined he was not to be tied down at university. If he'd
truly loved me then making love to me would have been more
important than being free.*

She wondered what would happen if she let the young
farmer go further. However, on the next date, without even
kissing her, he took her hand, gazing meaningfully into her
eyes. 'I'd like you to come home and meet my mother next
Sunday.'

Jane jerked her hand back quickly from the weight of an
invisible ring. 'I can't...I don't think we should see each
other any more.'

'But we've had such a good time going out. I thought we
might, you know, in a year or two—'

'No,' said Jane, before he could say it. Staying single
would be infinitely better than dying of boredom. And if
she was going to be free, she might as well make the most
of it: 'Let's go to Europe,' she said to Gail, some time in
second year.

'This afternoon?'

'I'm serious. When we're finished college. Don't you want
to see the world before we get old?' Because she was aware
that her own excursions to the province's landmarks had not
really made her much more sophisticated than Gail with her
traffic-light wonder, and any map made it clear that Nova
Scotia was a very small province, a peninsular footnote to a
vast but young country.

'Okay,' said Gail, but fell in love in their first year of
teaching, which shrank her travel plans to wherever the navy
was going to post her fiancé next, and Jane ended up being
bridesmaid instead of travelling companion.

'I don't mind,' said Jane, having decided that she alone in
this world of coupledom was unlikely to find love and had
better get used to independence. After three years of teaching, living at home for economy's sake and driving across the
Valley to a small school on the South Mountain, not so different

from the one she'd attended a few years earlier on the North, she was ready to go.

Jane was no exception to the rule that grandparents or remoter ancestors hold infinitely more fascination than the direct heritage of parents. All the same, if your mother has grown up in Chelsea where swinging young designers are now setting the world's fashions, if her nanny had taken her to Kensington Gardens to stroke the soft-eared bronze rabbits of Peter Pan's statue, if her bowler-hatted father had worked in the City like Mary Poppins' Mr Banks, it's difficult to differentiate between natural tourist interest and personal mythology.

So there was London and for similar reasons the rest of England, so tantalisingly nearly known: Dartmoor for *The Far Distant Oxus*, the Lakes for *Swallows and Amazons* as much as Coleridge, and Cornwall for *Jamaica Inn*. For someone who doesn't consider herself a reader, Jane's world will always be well peopled by books, although having grown up with the tangible history of Annapolis Royal, she also demanded ruins and historical evidence: Hadrian's Wall and Edinburgh Castle, the archaeology of Rome and Pompeii: *'Oh you hard hearts, you cruel men of Rome, knew you not Pompey?'* quipped her mother, who never minded twisting a quote for her own purposes. Athens and Crete more ancient still; maybe even Egypt. There was Vienna for the Spanish Riding School and Siena for the Palio—'heritage, history and horses', was how Jane planned her trip, Bill claimed, but Jane's longing for the Palio pre-dated her passion for horses. It stemmed from an Easter visit to Aunt Louise in Glace Bay eleven years earlier, and coming round a bend to see icebergs like ghostly ocean liners drifting in from the sea.

Bill told them the story of the *Titanic*. 'Drift ice, just like that, and not so far out there.'

'The unsinkable ship,' Ruth added. 'If it were fiction one would think the dramatic irony overstated.' She placed a comforting hand on Bill's knee. She was thinking that after the last war no one would ever again boast of an unsinkable ship, but knew that Bill was caught in the specifics of Bert in the icy water.

'Look!' shrieked Rick. 'A boy on the iceboat!'

'They're not really boats,' Bill explained. 'Drift ice is very dangerous; you can't ride it.'

'There's another one!'

'With flags!'

'Can we—?'

'No,' said Ruth.

Bill stopped the car. Through the grey water, scattered with smaller floes of drifting ice, floated several substantial white peaks, glowing in the sunlight, the stuff of arctic photography and sailors' nightmares. Perched on the two nearest, indistinct but unmistakable, were brightly snow-suited figures, each with a firmly planted flag waving behind.

'Don't even think about it,' said Bill, pulling back onto the road and into the McBain's driveway.

Their cousins wandered in an hour or two later, snow-suits sodden, damp flags trailing from pockets—samples of the exotic souvenirs collected in their air force childhood in Europe, the flags, Louise explained, came from the banner-waving, riderless-horse mayhem of the Corso del Palio in Siena.

'And isn't that where the Brownings spent the summers before Elizabeth died?' Ruth wondered, running up the stairs for a reference work on English poets.

'It'd be good to see Holland, now it's recovered.'

'You can't miss France—or at least La Rochelle—you'll have to see where your ancestors came from.'

'Why don't you two go?' Jane demanded, but Bill couldn't leave the farm, which was more or less true, though why Rick couldn't have worked it one summer holiday was never explained. Ruth switched tack—the Bras d'Or, after all, was as beautiful as Switzerland; if they wanted theatre the Neptune in Halifax was a lot closer than London and probably as good. Jane would never be sure of the real reasons for her mother's reluctance to return, but suspected that much of it lay in the file of ATA newsletters and invitations to reunions, press clippings of former colleagues: speed records broken by Jacqueline Cochrane and Diana Barnato, a film review of *Those Magnificent Men in their Flying Machines,* with special mention of the female stunt pilot, and lists of books. It sometimes seemed that Ruth was the only woman in the ATA not to have written a book on her experiences. Some were in the bookcases in her library, as were the surprisingly readable scholarly texts on Byron and Burns by her only correspondent from St Hilda's. Surrounded by these mementoes, that surreally philosophical weekend alone, Jane would realise that happiness—and she was convinced that her mother's contentment had been real—doesn't always ensure against feeling a failure in the eyes of the world. Ruth's generation had probably the hardest route of all, Jane would think then, having developed careers when young and been expected to drop them to find complete fulfilment in home and family.

But thirty years earlier she'd been planning the trip of a lifetime: 'You won't be able to see everything in three months,' was Ruth's most useful advice, undermined by her steadily growing pile of books.

Meanwhile Jane and Bill sat huddled over maps and atlas, charting alternative routes through long winter evenings. 'If you got a train from Calais to Paris...'

Letters flew back and forth to Mary. Jane could stay as long as she liked, however she liked, live there for the whole three months or treat it as a hotel to return to for breathing space. Finally the itinerary was complete: on that first June day of summer freedom, Jane would leave Halifax for London. She'd return on the Labour Day weekend, just in time for school, which was the only part of this story that she would feel guilty about later.

On the way home from the registry office, with an hour to spare before meeting the funeral director, Jane thinks to ask when her mother was booked to fly home.

'Oh Lord!' says Mary. 'Four-thirty this afternoon. I should have thought of it sooner if you were going to use the ticket!'

That was exactly what Jane had planned to do, though plan is not a particularly accurate word. It's now eleven o'clock and, 'Impossible,' she realises, with a covert flicker of relief. Airline companies being unlikely to simply take one's word that the ticket-holder, now travelling in a small casket, no longer requires a seat and would prefer it to be given to the casket-carrier, she'd realised that the transferring, if possible at all on a charter flight, would be laborious and draining, requiring death certificates and depositions. It is not the kind of experience to be faced when fragile or frazzled.

She phones Ian, who at nine-thirty is already asleep but in front of the television and glad to be woken; he'd intended to check the cows half an hour ago and go to bed. 'I'm not going to be able to make Mom's flight,' says Jane, guilty at his fatigue.

'Bloody hell.'

'The funeral's tomorrow.' Is it a funeral, with no one else there? There'll have to be another, a memorial service, in the Valley. 'I'll go to Canada after that.'

Ian, feeling that he hasn't been as supportive as he ought, starts to say, 'Give her my love,' and realises it's no longer appropriate. 'She was quite a lady,' he says instead. 'I wish I could be there with you.'

'So do I. Have you heard from Megan?'

'No. She must be on that big hike she was talking about. She'll probably call when she's finished.'

'I hope she's alright.'

'Just pity the poor bloke with her! A few days walking with Megan and he'll be exhausted—which wouldn't be all bad, come to think of it.'

'What if she stays with him?'

'She's just met him! You're imagining things because you're overemotional right now. Anyway,' he adds, 'I thought you'd be happy for her to marry a Canadian.'

Jane's not interested in patriotism. She doesn't want her only child to live at the other end of the world and go through what she is doing now.

❦

Jane's only child is at that moment asleep in a tent at the start of the West Coast Trail, as her father suspected. The waves crashing onto the beach below her have rolled uninhibited from Australian sands to the rocky shore of Vancouver Island, or so Megan likes to believe. She is always more interested in possibilities than facts.

The man her mother suspects is rolled in his own sleeping bag beside her.

They will be together for seven days and nights, days of sweating and stumbling, of demoralising mud and debilitating drizzle; nights on stony beaches with damp wood for fires. They should pass the hikers starting each day from Port Renfrew at the other end of the trail, and they may meet some of the travellers on their own southern way, but apart from these brief encounters will be on their own. In case of real emergencies—'not blisters' the brochure warns—they will be able to summon a ranger for rescue.

It would test the most established relationship.

And so Megan and Adam are cautious. They are careful of privacy and boundaries. Adam is surprised at his own impetuousness in inviting her; Megan is not. Adam becomes reserved on the long bus trip from Victoria to Pahena Bay, wondering if he should say anything about sex, about not presuming. Sharing tents doesn't mean sharing bodies. Seclusion doesn't mean unbridled lust. Will it make it more awkward if he says so? Hiking partners; friends not lovers.

He hasn't felt like this since he was sixteen and his hormones at their explosive peak; physical exhaustion and cold ocean may be his only safeguard. He's brought condoms just in case.

Megan's heart is singing. She sees his struggle and wants to draw him to her and comfort: what will be will be.

Tuesday when they met; Wednesday and Thursday Megan played tourist, explored the shops of Chinatown for ingredients not seen since her acupuncture student practice in Hong Kong; fed the squirrels in Stanley Park, walked the Seawall Promenade and, with a shock of pleasure, recognised Siwash Rock from the lithographs at the Gallery. Then the evenings, meeting after work for dinner, Wednesday at his apartment where he cooked fettuccine and spread brochures and books across the table. This is a seventy-seven kilometre hike, he explained, not a walk; you need boots, experience and ability.

Megan has brought boots; she's hiked the Australian Grampians and Victoria's High Plains; her legs are strong and supple, she flexed calf muscles and he didn't care if they never left his couch. But did not want to frighten her off. He has a tent, sleeping bags, backpacker's stove, has organised dehydrated food and everything else they need, he explained, impersonal as a tour guide and less jolly than most.

Friday Adam had things to do—he did not say what and Megan was content to let him sort whatever needed to be sorted. She is a self-sufficient person, gregarious but rarely lonely and was shocked at the length of a day without him, though not at her Saturday morning excitement. From different sides of the city they travelled separately to meet at the ferry terminal; Adam, more cautious or more pessimistic, showed strain, as if he had not been sure he'd find her there. She kissed him gently, for his worry. 'Trust me!' her heart sang, and her words too, more lightly.

A buffet breakfast on the ferry, leisurely luxury. 'Don't get used to it!' Adam warned. The postcard scenery outside the window, watching the other's face, fingers holding toast, hands cupping coffee, tongues cleaning crumbed lips—all more absorbing than the blue water and islands rising like mountaintops from its depths. Breakfast, even buffet-restaurant breakfast after being up for hours, keeps its early-morning aura of intimacy.

On the bus Megan thought of a line from *The Transit of Venus*, about a bus not being able to throw bodies together that do not want to be so thrown. These bodies wanted: shoulders rubbed companionably; knees bumped from time to time and did not jerk away.

But this first night they are each wrapped politely in their own cocoons.

The drizzle has lifted; they wake to the rare west-coast sunshine and the trail is not just a trial of mud and exhaustion, it is also eagles soaring and sea lions barking, modern-art driftwood and cathedral-ancient firs, soft moss on old logs and the private life of tidal pools. It is triumph and exaltation; it is magic and it is Canada. And Megan, who doesn't have an ancestor from west of Manitoba, has found her roots.

What will be will be.

And if, in this country of jutting rocks and soft yielding moss, of spraying waterfalls and secret silent pools, of ferny crevasses and totemic trees, if, in the cool, cougar-wandering night, after he has bandaged her blisters and she has massaged his cramp, there is only one thing that is right to happen, then it will happen. And if there are lips and tongues and fingers and sighs, if there is discovery and knowing, magic and completeness, then that is what will be, and Megan and Adam in the twining of their love know that is the only way it could ever have been.

❧

The Pacific Rim National Park is not the tropical Pacific and the West Coast Trail is not a honeymoon idyll. Megan and

Adam are lucky with the weather and have nearly five days of sunshine in their week—possibly a record, Adam says, for an area with a three hundred centimetre annual rainfall. The first time he hiked it, as a teenager, it had rained without stop.

'And you're doing it again?'

'I was trying to figure out why people think it's so great.'

It had been thirteen years earlier and the trail not so well established with boardwalks; he shows her places where he'd fallen, slipped, been covered in mud. Though it's hard to be sure. 'We'd lost interest in the scenery by then; we were hoping one of us would sprain an ankle so the ranger would insist on evacuating everyone.'

Like Ruth and Bill through their letters and Jane and Ian on their bus, they weave a tapestry of stories for each other: warp of lives and woof of fact, of interest, of flights of fantasy, of anything that touches them.

Perched high on a gnarled bole of a red cedar—a sapling when white men first landed on the east coast of this land, ancient when they came to stay—they talk of chi. 'Energy,' says Megan, 'like the essence of your life.' Untranslatable, she admits, tracing a meridian from neck to toe, which certainly sparks some sort of energy through his body.

On the salt-sprayed rocks Adam paints a picture of foundering ships and peoples the thundering breakers with dead and dying—the reason, he says, for the trail's beginning: a life-saving path from the Graveyard of the Pacific. They touch hands and imagine climbing this route as battered survivors of a shipwreck, starting in gale and rain without benefit of guidebook or boardwalk, ladders or hope. 'In long skirts,' Megan imagines, feeling sodden draperies twist around her legs. And they are grateful, for life and good hiking boots, and for each other.

By the side of a campfire, damp wood blazed by cedar shavings, resting backs against a moss-covered trunk, they talk of past and dreams, of family and friends, of legends and land rights, black bears and wombats.

Nothing is taboo except the future.

It is skirted around in suddenly polite questions, imposs-ible to look past the ending of this week, when Megan must travel on across the country with uncle-stops along the long road to her grandmother in the east. And cousins, she offers, second cousins or twice removed, but still Christmas-card kin, in Cape Breton, who speak Gaelic.

Though Gaelic-speaking cousins are a poor temptation to move on from the small V'd scar in the hollow of this man's collarbone. 'Ran full tilt into a branch when I was seven,' he tells her tracing fingers. 'My mom had suspected for a while that I needed glasses, but I lied so desperately she let it drop. The branch blew my cover—straight off to the optometrist the next day.'

And they've swung around to the safety of the past, away from the risky future and its promises, because they are too worldly-wise to believe that love could happen like this, and too much in love to doubt it.

The funeral director, a solid man with a comforting presence and deep Midlands accent, is a surprise. In some confusion of Dickensian characters and despite her experience when Ian's father died, Jane pictures undertakers as Uriah Heep charac-ters, oily and hand-rubbing. He anticipates her questions and advises on details of cremation, coffin and casket; and as if she hadn't filled in enough forms with the Coroner, has still more for her to sign. She hadn't known death was so complicated.

Details organised, he takes her to see Ruth.

So long dreaded, and in some ways worse than the dread-ing, it's at the same time somewhat of an anticlimax. The body bears a strong resemblance to Ruth but is so obviously not, because her mother, that most vital of people, is so definitely not home, that she finds it difficult to relate to it as the source of her grief.

'Goodbye, Mom,' she says, because she feels she has to say something, and after some hesitation kisses the forehead, which is just as cold as books have led her to expect. She does not stay long, but the funeral director, who's told her to take whatever time she needs, does not appear surprised to see her reappear so soon.

❦

At the end of a long damp day, six nights into the trail and one to go, Megan is light-headed with exhaustion. Fording a creek in the morning she'd slipped, thrown by the current and tumbled by it with a feeling of what it would be like to drown, only moments but that's all it takes. Her swept-away legs are wooden until evening, when her blisters bleed. Adam feels a primeval urge to spear a bear or a fish for dinner, but cooks dehydrated noodles and tells her to eat before she sleeps. His heart is tight with the image of her slipping and the fear is still sour in his mouth; he knows that, river or not, she'll slip away from him soon. He watches her breathe in sleep, feeling like a protector and an intruder; it's not sex he desires but to be part of her, all of her, without waking or moving a muscle. He curls beside her and is content to breathe in unison.

Later, but still before the August night is fully dark, she wakes them both by sitting up suddenly, tears in her eyes. 'Nana's dead.'

'It was a nightmare,' he says, 'because of the creek.' His own sleep has been full of restless, broken snippets, but Megan says no, it was not a nightmare, it wasn't horrible. She had simply met her grandmother's soul whirling in the void, not troubled but travelling. 'Like stars,' she explains; it's not what she means but as close as she can come: the essence of a person, distilled into light.

'But you were just dreaming,' Adam says, and she could

weep to think he doesn't believe in the truth of what she feels, till he adds, 'she might have been dreaming too.'

Which could be true; which could just as easily be true and she opens her arms to him for comfort and gratitude.

Mary's White Cottage, significant in different stages of Jane's life, had been more full than usual with stray animals in the summer of '69. As well as the three dogs and two cats, there was a broken-winged crow and a baby hedgehog—'Mrs Tiggywinkle, naturally.' That first week of June, Mary had taken a week's holiday from the animal shelter to devote herself to her guest's all-important introduction to England. Into London for the Changing of the Guard the first day, Windsor Castle the next; Oxford and then London again, this time the Tower...Busy days rounded off with energetic walks with the dogs in the long summer evenings.

But however happy Mary was to have her, the village was too far from London for leisurely exploration. After a last quiet day when she returned from busing her way around Britain, north as far as the grey stone and history of Edinburgh—a time of magic with money disappearing before her eyes—Jane went back into London on her own. If she could find somewhere cheap enough to stay, she could explore the city properly before her trip to the Continent.

Chambermaids wanted, said a discreet sign in a Bayswater window. *Eight pounds per week, room and board included*.

It was a pleasant looking hotel, white and Georgian, facing a locked park that she would learn to call a square, but to which she would never be allowed a key. She applied within.

Work started at six, so apart from serving at the occasional evening meal for a school party, virtually the whole afternoon and evenings were free. The interview was a matter of checking name, nationality and whether she could start tomorrow; basic cleaning and waitressing ability were assumed inherent in a female. She phoned Mary, who sounded slightly disappointed that she'd found something so easily.

Her room was a furnished, windowless broom cupboard on the second floor, a long way down the hall to the toilet—which she had just learned not to call the bathroom, after dumbfounded looks or directions to rooms with baths and sinks but not the item she was looking for—and further still to the actual room with a bath. She had a saggy single bed and not quite enough space to open the wardrobe door, which faced the wrong way. It was independence in the greatest city of the world, and she could have danced with excitement at the sight of it.

Some of the other chambermaids were going down to the pub 'about half seven', and Jane was grateful, ready for her initiation into Swinging London. And if the pub itself was nothing like she'd imagined, it was still quite different from anything she'd ever experienced: darker and smokier, the music more deafening, the patrons much drunker and the pick-up attempts infinitely more blatant. Compared to the Canadian taverns she'd visited, where the law insisted on drinkers remaining staidly seated for barmaids to hand them their drinks, as if standing upright with glass in hand was the first step towards total depravity, this was a positive den of iniquity, or a more honest admission that the purpose of the evening for most of the men and a large proportion of the women was to get as drunk as possible and with a bit of luck get laid as well. Jane felt virginally provincial.

She was with two Greek Cypriot girls, a brash Londoner about the same age as herself, and a Liverpudlian who was leaving in the morning. The Greeks stayed demurely sober, but the Cockney sang aggressively all the way home and the Liverpudlian, swaying on her feet, suddenly began to cry.

'Poor old thing,' Jane said sympathetically, uncharacteristically throwing her arm around the other girl's shoulders. She felt supremely happy but blurred around the edges. One more drink, she thought, and I might have been drunk. She couldn't remember how many she'd had, and gave up the effort of working it out.

As well as the girls she met that first night, there was a constantly changing flux of workers using the hotel much as she was, staying a week or month before setting off again on more adventurous travel. Two South African physiotherapists flitted through, annoying Jane equally with their self-righteousness as they handed around bowls of thin soup from the large Jamaican cook, and by their quite legitimate superior activisim, having left the country more quickly than anticipated after an antiapartheid demonstration had turned nasty. And then there was Maggie, a tiny, rather frail looking girl from Newcastle, with an accent so thick that Jane could understand one word in two—occasionally they had to resort to writing down phrases unintelligible to their differently trained ears.

'Will you come shopping with me?' Maggie asked one morning. 'I want to make myself a new dress.' Jane, touched but confused by the misery on the girl's face, put aside her afternoon's plans. Keat's house had waited a long time without seeing Jane; it would still be there tomorrow.

Walking to the big department store on the corner, she thought of shopping expeditions with Patsy and later with Gail; silliness and fun enhancing acquisitive pleasure. Shopping with Maggie didn't appear likely to be long on any of these qualities, but Jane tried valiantly, half best friend, half big sister: with legs like Twiggy's, why not a miniskirt and top, something a little more fitted, 'show yourself off a bit!'

'I'm not that thin,' Maggie muttered, which made Jane, fully conscious of the stodgy hotel food already settling around her own middle, laugh derisively. She stopped when the younger girl, on the verge of tears, smoothed her sloppy top over the neat round bulge.

'Oh God,' Jane groaned, wondering whether knocking her head repeatedly against Whiteley's fabric counter would be adequate apology. No, not even close. The poor kid had presumed that Jane—sensible, educated, older—would have already guessed her shame but instead, Jane had managed to drag every ounce of humiliation out into the open. *A miniskirt, for crying out loud!*

She felt as if she were the one in shock and had to rouse herself to be sensible, finding a pattern for a peasant-style dress gathered loosely under the breast and a small-flowered cotton print to make it from. 'It'll suit you—and it's one anyone could wear; you wouldn't have to be...'

Maggie dragged along like an obedient child, barely speaking except to say yes, she liked the navy better than hot pink. It was hot in the shop and she looked as if she might faint again, as she had last week in the steamy breakfast kitchen (a sign anyone would have recognised in a film or book, but more difficult to read in life). Jane picked up the parcel and steered her towards the door and the coffee shops of Bayswater Road for a cup of tea.

The coffee shop was Turkish, hard glossy tables and smoky air; they were the only women and the only English speakers and though it wasn't quite the comforting atmosphere Jane had been looking for, Maggie began talking as soon as her tea was brought. Maybe, thought Jane as the rush from the sweet muddy coffee hit her brain, it was the best place after all, with no discreetly eavesdropping matrons.

Maggie's story was from another era but it didn't strike Jane that her self-possessed mother might find this story more painful than interesting.

This isn't exactly how I'd imagined London, but working in the hotel I'm seeing the city's subculture rather than the middle-class façade. I'm pretty sure a lot of the girls here are illegal immigrants; heaven knows what they get paid, and they never get days off—after all, who can they complain to? They're sad, exploited creatures, but even the English girls seem to move through life as if they've never heard of ordinary rules and laws. The Cockney I met the first evening is getting married next month. She already has one husband but doesn't know or care where he is...

The pregnant young Geordie girl is the one who really bothers me. The couple who own the hotel are very good to her, cutting her working hours and giving her lighter duties in reception— which surprised me, because their treatment of the illegal immigrants hadn't suggested a particularly philanthropic bent. However the story is, if you haven't guessed, that they're childless and are going to adopt the baby, and apparently without any complicated legal arrangements—because they're not British and can't adopt here? Because they've met the girl and can't bear to let the opportunity pass? I don't know; and I'm not about to ask. As for little Maggie, I think she's just grateful to be able to solve her problem without having to go to a welfare authority—her own family seems to be out of the question. The poor kid. These people will give the baby a good home, they obviously want it so badly that I'm sure they'll love it and the baby won't have to spend any time in limbo in an orphanage. I guess it's an ideal solution if you don't mind about details like birth certificates and other legalities.

☙

Shortly after Bill dies, Patsy McLeod brings Ruth a long scroll of paper. 'I thought you'd be interested, being English and knowing how you like family history stuff.' She's traced her family tree back to an Essex baronet in 1763: the names are captured, pinned to her sheet with dates of deaths and births.

'It's very satisfying to have it done,' she admits with honest smugness. 'You want to do yours before it's too late.'

'Before I join the dates?' Ruth asks and Patsy covers quickly by telling her about the offer that had come in the mail from a company that traces coats of arms and will sell them mounted on a plaque for the hall.

'Tess Durbeyfield's father would have liked that,' Ruth murmurs, and feels mildly contrite at the eager offer of an address. It's not Patsy's fault that after fifty years the thought of searching for guarantees of identity still leaves her with a dry mouth and faint nausea.

❧

The vicar from Mary's village church is a young, bouncy man with a bushy beard who comes to the house when they've returned from the funeral home. He's new and not popular in the village, Mary tells Jane, because of his guitar playing and up-beat theories, but he assures them that the funeral service will be entirely traditional. Jane is relieved; she doesn't like to tell this enthusiastic believer that the words of the King James Bible had been infinitely more important to Ruth than the meaning behind them.

There are some things, like death and the internet, that one can believe in but not comprehend. In church the next morning Jane finds it impossible to imagine that the coffin before the altar contains her mother, at present nearly as life-like as a Madame Tussaud's model and soon to be reduced to a transportable residue in an imeldific shoe-box sized casket. (A new synonym for ostentatious, Ruth had informed her in one email; it was the kind of obscure, esoteric information she'd loved to collect, God only knew from where.)

Is this a sign of grief, Jane wonders, this butterfly flitting of thought? Or a new stage of menopause?

'A courageous woman,' the minister is saying, 'not only in the demanding times of war, but in the demanding times of life, following her new husband to an unknown country in the days when travel was not the simple thing it is now, when international telephone calls were virtually unknown.' He adds that although her death has caused logistical difficulties for her daughter, there was comfort in knowing that she'd died in the land of her birth, with someone who loved her. Jane wonders if he has understood her fears of her mother's body lying undiscovered in the lonely farmhouse and the service loses its incongruity and becomes suddenly intimate.

They don't attempt the hymns, two thin voices in the echoing church, but listen as the organist begins 'Amazing Grace', which Jane thinks now was probably not one of Ruth's favourites, though it is her own. The coffin leaves on its journey to Slough—Jane wishes irrelevantly that the town had a prettier name—and the crematorium, where that body which is still somehow her mother will be reduced to cinders.

Cinderella, Jane thinks, and almost smiles. Ruth would have enjoyed the pun. For just a moment a glimmer of the end of pain shines through the unescapable realities as she sees the way that her mother will live on, separate from sad ashes and memorial stones.

Chapter
SEVEN

*R*uth is feeding Jane in the window seat of her bedroom when Bill arrives home.

The snow plough had finally reached the road to the farm the day before, Valentine's Day, but snow had fallen again in the night and the road is once again impassable, so Bill has taken the train to Applevale, where his father met him in the sleigh. The road in fact has been cleared between the town and Evelyn's Pond, but George couldn't imagine waiting at the corner for some other relative to deliver his son home from the war.

'He's that impatient, I'm surprised he didn't drive the sleigh right to Halifax,' Myrtle had teased, as if she hadn't lain awake with excitement herself, as if she hadn't spent the last two days baking, cleaning and unable to sit still. Only constant movement can contain the welling of both love and grief, can assure that gratitude for one son's deliverance outweighs bitterness for the other.

Ruth has her own mixed feelings. Perspective from the upstairs window alters the driveway scene to a tableau: Son

Welcomed Home from the War; sister hovering, stroking a shoulder in spite of herself; father, replete with the luxury of the last hour's uninterrupted contact, beaming at the sight of a mother in her son's arms. Addition of a third woman would be superfluous. The man is tall and fair, handsome in his air force greatcoat, but the incongruous home-knitted tuque pulled over his ears is a reminder that this will be the last time he'll wear a uniform—she has only ever seen him in uniform or nude, never civvies. It could have been a worrying reminder of how little she knows him, except that she finds it impossible to worry while her milk is flowing as it is now, her daughter's mouth tugging securely on her nipple. Feeding is the only time of her life that Ruth ever feels truly placid, and she can never decide whether or not she enjoys the sensation.

Bill looks up to the window and the scene is a tableau no longer. He sees her framed through the cloudy glass, dark hair and a whiteness of breast obscured by pink-blanketed bundle, and he bolts from his mother's arms to the door. And although Ruth had wanted, planned to meet him in the privacy of their own room, she jumps up now, disturbing Jane mid-suck, tucking leaking breast back into blouse, dropping the astonished baby back into her cradle, picking her up again at the roar of protest and running to the stairs as Bill reaches the top. He has kicked off his snowboots and pulled off the tuque on his way up the stairs but his overcoat is dripping. He holds the two of them wonderingly, longingly, and as Ruth's blouse dampens with mingled milk and snow she understands that the strangeness of the environment is an illusion: this man's familiarity is the only thing that matters.

'Meet your daughter,' she says, and though she's rehearsed this moment for twelve days, the reality is both less dramatic and more moving. She has also forgotten, with the intensity of motherhood training, just how frightening it was to hold the baby for the first time: Bill procrastinates, throwing his coat over the back of a chair, sitting on the side of the bed in preparation.

'She's so tiny—is everything really all right?'

'She's perfect,' says Ruth, and as she lays the baby in his arms she watches his face change as he accepts the truth of this statement. Jane passively submits to his scrutiny for nearly a minute before her face puckers into a grimace that crescendoes alarmingly to a wail. Bill looks panicky and Ruth hides the reflexive twist of pain behind the smugness of experience.

'Just hungry,' she says, and although she wonders what the emotional tumult will do to her milk, she takes the baby and sits on the bed as well, legs outstretched and leaning against the headboard to unbutton her blouse. She is flushing slightly as she inserts the brown nipple into the baby's mouth; the wail ends with a gulp and Ruth strokes the back of the fuzzy blonde head, watching till the sucking settles into its usual soothing rhythm before meeting Bill's eyes. She wonders if she will repulse him in this bovinely milky state.

'I'd forgotten how beautiful you are,' says Bill. 'Like a Christmas painting.'

But he is not thinking of madonnas as she lays the replete and dozing baby back in the cradle, her blouse still open and the blue-veined breasts, swollen like a fertility goddess's, falling free. 'Lie down with me,' he begs, opening his arms, and she tumbles on top of him with the kiss that had been impossible with the baby between them.

'But the doctor…' she murmurs, because much as she longs for him she is raw and sore and and shrinks from the thought of more pain.

'Dad said. Six weeks he said, a month from now.'

'Surely less,' says Ruth and when Bill says, 'Just let me look at you,' she acquiesces, trusting as he undoes the rest of her blouse, her skirt and stockings, till she is naked and he can trace her outlines with eye and finger and tongue, tasting the warm breasts with the sweetness of his daughter's milk, the rounded red-traced belly, long legs and the dark miracle between, still spilling salt traces of blood.

'Is this a good idea?' asks Ruth.

'Probably not,' Bill admits, 'but I need to.' Need to know you're still there, need to understand what's happened to you, what the changes are and how we go from here. And torturing myself like this is infinitely better than imagining the same thing in a bed on my own, especially the last week of a troopship full of men thinking of nothing but what it will be like to be home again, practising being civilised during the day with table manners and fines for swearing, and you know they're all obsessed at night with how it'll be being back with their wives, their girlfriends or whatever fantasy of a hooker they dream of. And all the family's waiting downstairs with tea and cookies but I need to lie here a moment longer between my wife's thighs and know that I'm home.

He doesn't say that, but Ruth strokes his head and wishes that birth wasn't quite such a brutal process, and guesses as much as any human being ever can what another one is thinking.

It's a strange sort of honeymoon–courtship they enter on from here, as far removed from the actual day following their wedding as if in another life. It had been obvious the war would be ending soon when they'd organised leave and set the date of 8 May; a quiet ceremony with friends on both sides, a few relatives on hers but no parents for either—and yet in the end it had been celebrated with delirium throughout the country, bell-ringing, bonfires and dancing in the street, so that Jane was not the only baby conceived that night of relief and joy. And then the tidying-up had begun: Bill transporting wounded, prisoners-of-war, even concentration-camp victims early on, which had left him waking in cold sweats from nightmares; Ruth still relaying planes to bases, the service winding down now but Ruth determined to fly as long she could keep her pregnancy discreet, and had done so until her final day in September, marching in the ATA closing parade as Japan surrendered, the war truly over at last. She had moved into digs near his base then, those last three months before her ship, so that nights together had been easier to arrange, but it was not a married life.

Now, as Bill begins to pick up the work he'd left off five years earlier, and Myrtle tries to distil a lifetime of house-keeping lore into a few brief lessons before moving to Applevale, Ruth continues the more instinctive and important lessons of learning her daughter and her husband. She presumes that she'll be able to grasp what's needed in house and farm and by early March is becoming impatient to try, but this fortnight there's an adolescent sense of holiday, of not yet bearing the final responsibility for anything except these two tasks. At night, with Jane in the cradle beside the bed, they fill in the gaps of life stories, of the times they've spent apart and unshared thoughts, so that Louise, who can hear the mumble of their voices through the wall, complains one break-fast time that they must have said everything there was to be said by now and hadn't they thought of sleeping? Which makes them blush because speech is not the only use for tongues and they have been continuing the leisurely and erotic exploration of each other's bodies long after their other conversation has stopped.

On an afternoon free from work and sad chambermaids, Jane took a bus to the City and began to explore: impressions of dark pubs and Dickens, banking and business; associations of Mary Poppins's ubiquitous employer and Jane's own English grandfather tall and serious in bowler hat and umbrella (adding a mental note to ask Mary if she knew exactly where his office had been). She worked her way back to St Paul's and on to Fleet Street; Fleet Street meant journalists and journalists meant Winston. She waited for the usual stab of misery to accompany his name, but there was nothing but a memory of the habit of pain, like a paler circle of skin where a long-picked scab has finally healed. She wanted to dance a celebration jig on the sidewalk: 'I'm free of you, Winston,' she told him, winging her thoughts towards the west and wishing he could hear, 'and no man is ever going to make me doubt myself again!'

She felt more than buoyant—she was invincible, stronger than she'd ever been. In three weeks of exploration, she'd bused or Tubed and walked her way around London, climbing so many stairs in search of views that a whole new group of muscles had appeared across her abdomen, and laying down a mental map until she could picture herself at any particular point on its grid. From Piccadilly she could work her way across the yellow and green Monopoly Board names: Oxford Street and Bond, Regent Street and Leicester Square. In Chelsea she'd found Savernake Street, the new houses in the middle where numbers 40 and 42 had stood, and windowshopped the length of the King's Road down to World's End, where the trendy boutiques ran out and two Australians in an antique shop invited her in to play with the lion cub lolling in the window. Somehow it had seemed no more surreal than the rest of the day.

She strode on now till Fleet Street became the Strand and the way back to familiar Trafalgar Square and the joy of the National Gallery, the luxury of being able to step inside and study one painting or ten and know that she could come back another day, and the comforts of Canada House with its newspapers and familiar accents to assuage incipient homesickness. Passing Australia House on the way, the grim grey building at odds with her image of open spaces and dry red dust, she watched a man (young, tall, interesting rather than handsome) going up the steps and amused herself by imagining that he could also be searching for news from home, in the *Darwin Herald* or whatever the paper might be, surrounded by the familiarity of that strident accent.

'So you knew!' Megan would interrupt. 'It was fate!'

'It might have been fate,' Jane would answer, 'but I didn't know.' Although it's strange how clearly she could picture him decades later, shaggy brown hair to just above his shoulders, long sideburns, purple T-shirt, flared jeans and shiny leather cowboy boots—'Riding boots!' Ian would say indignantly.

A cavalcade of Volkswagen buses was parked along the next block, for sale signs in their windows and homesick owners, travelling done and restless now to be back in the sun, lounging in the open doors or squatting on the kerb. One man with long blond hair and a purple peace T-shirt leaned forward to catch her eye: 'Never missed a beat, all the way to Morocco and back,' he confided. 'Buy it and you can have me free!'

'Sounds like a bargain!' she called without slowing, and wondered what made her so obviously a tourist, a colonial-type tourist at that, someone who might on a whim buy a van and head off into the wilderness. No one else—the miniskirted dolly-bird secretaries, the pale-faced delivery boys, the grave suits—had been approached and they mightn't have been tempted if they had, but Jane imagined herself at the wheel, driving down French country lanes, exploring the Continent by car as thoroughly as she was doing London by foot. Her steps slowed; she detoured down a side street to play with the idea a moment longer. It was a dark and rather unappealing street, which seemed to have become a headquarters for shabby travel agents.

Magical Mystery Tour, screamed one poster. *London to Turkey return! See it all—travel by bus! Campgrounds selected by our experienced guides! SEE US NOW!*

So she did. Jane Dubois, equivocator extraordinaire over life's most minor dilemmas, walked into the shop, picked up the brochure—which said little more than the screaming poster except to list the countries en route with the added enticement: *Flexible itinerary: you come, you vote*—signed up for the tour and changed her life.

☙

At six a.m. on 15 July, in front of the same little shop where she'd bought her ticket, the other travellers assembled around her, trepidation began to outweigh anticipation.

A few years later there would be a variety of companies running slickly organised camping tours with trained couriers, well-planned routes and age limits in the hope of some sort of compatibility. The Magical Mystery Tour, all flower power, free-thinking, idealistic muddle, would have scoffed at their uptight timetables and routine vehicle maintenance. Part of the experience of travelling, or so their theory went, was the freedom of changing a route when a better idea came up or, more frequently, when a search for a mechanic gave a meaningful insight into the daily life of wherever the bus had happened to break down.

The majority of Jane's fellow travellers were her age or slightly older; she amused herself by guessing nationalities— South African for two girls who reminded her of the physios; three American boys, another lone girl who might be Canadian and two who looked Welsh. She was uniformly wrong. Slightly younger were a group of four English boys, rowdy, crude and at first indistinguishable from each other—'the hooligans' Jane named them, and for the rest of her life their image would spring to mind at the word 'soccer'. The more surprising members were an elderly, rather frail looking Yorkshire couple who turned out to be trainspotters; a New Zealander retired colonel and his strident wife; a Canadian ex-air force pilot with a magnificent waxed handlebar moustache, whom Jane kept well away from in some vague fear that he might want to be her buddy; and an American woman of indeterminate age and indeterminable weight, so vast that the rest of the bus would have to be balanced against her bulk.

It was ridiculous not to have realised there'd be so many people, but if Jane hadn't burned quite so many bridges and spent quite so much money, she might have slipped away from the group and walked on down the street and back to adventure on her own.

'Feels like we're off to school camp!'

It was the young man she'd seen going up the steps to Australia House. She changed her mind about running away, muttered something inane and, in an effort to sound more sensible, asked what they were waiting for.

'The teacher, I reckon!'

'That would be me then.'

Dear Mom and Dad

As promised, here's the first instalment of travelogue through Europe.

A slightly inauspicious beginning, as unfortunately our driver couldn't work out why the bus wouldn't start (there are two fifty-seater buses travelling together, with twenty-five people on each—the theory being that we can all fit if one bus dies en route?) Luckily Ian, an Australian guy who grew up on a farm, figured out that the problem was simply dirty battery terminals and once he'd cleaned them up, we were off, only about an hour behind schedule, and it was such a beautiful morning it was hard to mind about anything—one of those days when you just have to feel happy.

Ian's an electrician, he's always wanted to farm but his parents' place isn't big enough to support two incomes, so he's trying to decide whether he's going to start up his own electrician's business now or go out sharefarming. Apparently instead of buying his own farm right away he could build up a herd of cows while he farmed someone else's land, and then they'd share the income. What's interesting is that his part of Australia is not only known as the Goulburn Valley, but sounds so similar to our Valley, all dairy farms and orchards. I can't quite picture it, because I thought Australia was very hot and dry. He says yes, it is hot, often over 100°F—can you imagine?—and would be dry if it weren't for the irrigation, which comes via channels or canals from the Murray River. It sounds beautiful: wild parrots, koalas and of course kangaroos! Though he says the latter are only down by the river, where there are still lots of trees, as the farms have been heavily cleared.

The crossing from Dover to Calais...

'Travelogue, eh?' Bill commented as Ruth read aloud. Always, over the years, Jane's letters would be shared, and sometimes interrupted, this way. 'I'm glad she noticed the Channel at any rate.'

'Perhaps it's a wartime bus, with blacked-out windows.'

'That would explain it.'

Ruth picked up the letter again. to read descriptions of campgrounds, Jane's Swiss tent-mate, and a comparison of the excitement of Paris with the tranquillity of the Burgundian countryside:

Ian says he's beginning to feel quite sure he wasn't meant to be a city person! I have to say I agree.

'Does this fellow say anything she doesn't agree with?' Bill asked.

'I doubt it,' Ruth said glumly.

○

The Magical Mystery Tour continued on its way; majestic mountains and limpid lakes; covered bridges with painted ceilings. From Switzerland into Italy—'Oh, woman-country, wooed not wed, Loved all the more by earth's male lands Laid to their hearts instead!' quoted Ruth, which Bill suspected might be more apt than they wanted to know—life became a blur of early starts and long bus days, the scenery outside the window a backdrop to the story being lived within.

Jane's map of Europe would always be dotted with these

milestones—the first touch, the first confidences; Venice the first quarrel. They were pooling their food money by then, comfortably enough when it was groceries, less so for restaurant meals, but in the city of romance, where they watched a beflowered gondola bear a white-veiled bride and her groom serenely down the Grand Canal, Ian was so furious at paying double the listed price for a midmorning *Mont Blanc*, eaten standing to avoid the table surcharge ('You used our spoons!' the cafe owner cried in explanation) that they skipped lunch, and that evening, weary from the sightseeing of basilicas and glass blowing, canals and bridges, trudged from cafe to still smaller cafe searching out the best value.

'How many times in our lives are we going to come to Venice?' Jane demanded, though they were both too irritated to notice the significant pronoun. 'Does it matter if we get cheated once?'

It did to Ian. Jane was too proud to tell him that she felt ill with hunger and too shy to explain that menstruating could make her faint, until she proved it in the final cafe and had to be given water and helped onto a chair by kind black-clad women who couldn't believe that a rich tourist would be too stubborn to eat. Escaping into the fresh air—Jane embarrassed, weak and teary as always after fainting, Ian a complex muddle of emotions, angry at himself and at Jane for not standing up to him—they turned a corner into a Communist Party street festival.

'Sit here,' Ian ordered, finding a vacant doorstep, and returned with thick slabs of baked polenta, stodgily nourishing, which Jane would try to duplicate for years in her own kitchen until discovering that the appeal had lain more in context than taste. The most romantic image of a Venice evening remained for Jane, not dark gondolas on star-spangled canals, but her Australian country man returning with Communist bounty and saying, 'Don't ever do that again.' First reconciliation.

Into Yugoslavia, hugging the coast of a country uncharted by calendar pictures or familiar books—'read Rebecca West's *Black Lamb and Grey Falcon*,' Ruth had ordered, but the letter arrived after they'd left and all either of them had was a muddled association with partisans and dark history; the clean white sands of the Dalmatian beaches were a revelation as if to first explorers. In Dubrovnic they walked the ramparts, gazing down at sixteenth century roofs and ocean, and feeling the sense of history Jane had expected and somehow missed in Rome. Years later they would watch its destruction on the nightly news, raging helplessly and guiltily aware of how trivial their link compared to the loss of lives and ancient history.

☙

Historic sites mean different things to different people. For Ian, Gallipoli was a complicated mixture of dutiful nationalism—'I'm an Australian,' he'd said when they'd voted on the route, 'how could I miss Gallipoli?'—and inherited resentment that this site had captured his country's imagination so much more thoroughly than the slimy trenches of Fromelles. Sand and sea are more romantic than mud, though his own father would have been equally bereft if Grandfather Ralston had died on a celebrated beach.

For Jane, Gallipoli was where she first realised she would marry Ian.

Not that her body hadn't been insisting on some kind of union. Not that she hadn't felt tremulous every morning when he appeared from his tent, or wondered at her extraordinary luck in meeting someone amongst this oddly assorted crowd whom she could talk to day after day without boredom or irritation. Not that she hadn't understood, incredible as it seemed, that he not only enjoyed her company, he desired her too, and that unless disasters in the form of death or curvaceous blondes intervened, the questions now were reduced to time and place. Duration she hadn't allowed herself to consider.

Walking hand in hand down from the windswept hill to the beach as Ian related the Anzac history, she had an image of his passing the same story on to children, embellished by this act of walking on the very grains of sand that had soaked up the young warriors' blood. Our children, she thought— and banished the image quickly, flushing with the fear that he might be somehow able to read it.

'You'd like my parents,' she said, 'they're both into history, but Mom especially.' And immediately regretted the implication that she thought history was something relegated to parents, but Ian seemed gratified, and in the tidying of memory for storage, those twin images of Ian with family past and future were crystallised into the decision that this was the man with whom she'd live out her life.

Ian would say that for him there was no blinding light, simply the gradual realisation that he wouldn't be ready to say goodbye when the Magical Mystery Tour came to an end, and that some sort of commitment would have to be made to prevent it. 'It was the only logical thing to do,' he said when Jane asked later, 'if I didn't want to live without you.' Ian is never embarrassed by talking about love, but sees no reason to mystify it.

Nevertheless, as the bus left Gallipoli the almost over-whelming urge to pull Jane down into the sheltering dunes and let the tour explore Istanbul without them had been sub-limated, for the next few hours at least, into explaining the family he came from and his father's obsession with stories of war.

'He says the worst thing about being a POW was that you never knew what was going on in the rest of the world. He felt like a fool at the end of the war when he hadn't heard of D-day or the Kokoda Trail, and he was going to make up for it; same with the first war—never got to meet his father, so he at least wanted to learn something about what he went through.

'That's why I voted for Troy, too, to get some photos for Dad. He didn't get very far in school and he doesn't read much, but what he doesn't know about the *Iliad* and the *Odyssey* wouldn't be worth knowing.' He hurried on in case Jane happened to know more than the names, which was as much as Ian had absorbed himself. 'They wouldn't have had a book in the house when he was a kid; from what he says they did it tough even after his mum married again.'

The bus swayed; his arm tightened around her shoulders and Jane leaned into him. We're comfortable together, she thought, and although she was in that stage of infatuation where diagrams of electrical circuitry would have been fascinating if they were what Ian had wanted to tell her, for a moment *comfortable* seemed more important even than the history Fred had carried into his son's life.

Fred, younger than Ian was now, torn between duty to country and wife, the appearance of valour versus grimmer reality, was determined not to leave a child fatherless as he had been left; if his wife was to be a widow, he'd told adult Ian, she should have a chance to live again. Dulcie—Ian was unsure of his mother's age now or then, but certainly no older than Jane—may have been equally determined that if her husband was killed she'd have something to remember him by. She never told her side of the story, at least not to her son, but what is certain is that Ian was conceived on Fred's last leave. Or it could have been simple unbridled passion, but parents and passion are never easy concepts to put in conjunction.

Ian and Jane's own lives were dwarfed momentarily by the magnitude of these decisions, the dramas of an era normally too close to their own for interest or empathy and quite outside their own experience. By the time conscription started for Vietnam, Ian and his friends had been too old to worry about the lottery no one wanted to win and too distant from the cities and universities to listen to rebellious peaceniks; Ian's support of his government's actions had been untroubled by personal consequence. Unimaginable, the dilemma of going off to face death, of leaving a girl—a wife—either with seed implanted or free to love another, luckier, man. (Ian's mind said *girl*, but the face was Jane's and the body too, and *leaving* was a startlingly clear image of her sated in a rumpled white bed—because of course it was themselves they were discussing, obliquely parrying the question of how their futures would be shaped, and whether those shapes would be entwined.)

Ian dragged his mind back to his father, a safer image for a crowded bus than the texture of Jane's inner thighs, firm and hidden today in yellow jeans—'I'm not wearing a skirt again till we're back in the west,' she'd said yesterday after a particularly forceful grab to the crotch—but creamily bare in his mind's eye, infinitely strokable; there was a pang of envy in his anger at the anonymous, rough-knuckled hand that had thrust between their softness. (Later in the tour, under cover of maps or jackets, he would slide stealthy fingers under a jean's zipper or upwards through the leg of her shorts, stroking till Jane's eyes glazed helplessly and she moaned softly against his shoulder, the thrill of this unexpected power worth his own discomfort.)

'I don't know how long Dad's going to be able to go on dairying. It's hard work, and he has trouble with his ankles and knees; back too, sometimes, from playing football during the war. Cold mornings he can hardly walk.'

Ian was twenty-seven and the story was older than he was, a joke almost, his father coming through the war with nothing but sporting injuries to bother him. It was only now, hearing himself tell it for the first time, that he doubted. Of the myriad football accidents he'd witnessed, he could not think of any combination that would injure two ankles, knees and spine. 'I was three and a half the first time I saw my dad. Went off to meet the ship, excited as anything—and then I chucked a wobbly because Mum was hugging this strange man. Poor bloke—what a welcome after all those years in Changi Prison and the Burma Railway—you know, the film *The Bridge on the River Kwai*. That's the most he's ever said about it all—reckoned the film was a load of bull, with the bloke working to help the Japs. But I don't think he ever saw it.'

'My dad couldn't watch *A Bridge Too Far*, the one about the English losing a big battle in Holland,' said Jane, 'though the only war stories he ever told us were funny, like when he thought he'd had his toe shot off, but when he took his boot off the bullet rolled out and the toe was fine.'

'Dad's story was that he took his boot off and the toe rolled out!'

Jane laughed in shock and felt ashamed.

'He reckoned it was so cold when he was working in the Japanese mines that when he dropped a rock on his foot, the toe broke off, but he didn't notice till he took off his boot that night...Poor bloke must have wondered what was going to drop off next.'

In this first, overwhelming stage of love, they felt no compunction at carving family history into succulent shock-and-share morsels, or at viewing coincidences as omens, as if the universe had been unable to resist these small parallel connections en route to the inevitable entanglement of their lives.

'Do you think he got those other injuries when he was there?' Jane asked. 'But why wouldn't he say?'

'Doesn't want to upset us, I reckon.'

'My mother,' Jane offered, 'never told us, until a few years ago, that she was adopted.' (She didn't add, 'and even then she told my boyfriend first, to win an argument,' because that still hurt.) 'She acts as if she's ashamed of it, which is stupid, because it wasn't anything she did.'

'My dad acts like he's ashamed of being a POW,' Ian said slowly, 'and he didn't have much more say in that than your mum did about being adopted. He said once that his war ended in 1942, as if he'd packed up and gone home for a spell. I didn't know even know about Java and Changi and all that till I was thirteen. Then this car just pulled up in the driveway one day, a bloke he'd been through the war with; drove down from Queensland to see him, didn't think to tell us he was coming—that's one good thing about a dairy farm, you're not going to be far away.'

'Not for long,' Jane agreed. Unlike her mother, she knew what it would mean to fall in love with a farmer.

'Dad cried,' Ian said, still wondering. 'You know what kids are like at that age—my father and this other man hugging each other, tears in their eyes—I couldn't stand it; I took off. All I can remember about the visit is sitting down for tea. Dad asked if rice would do. The bloke looked crook for a second: "Are you dinkum, mate?" Dad said, "Not bloody likely,"—and they both burst out laughing. It was one of those things that sticks in your mind because you haven't got a clue what's going on. Dad saying bloody at the table and talking about rice—we always had meat and three veg; it was like a religion with Mum. I never even tasted rice till I left home. I never thought it might be because of Dad being a POW.'

He stopped, wondering if she thought he was an idiot.

Jane lifted her face from his shoulder and kissed him on the cheek, a gesture of friendship, nothing more. We're too old, she thought, to neck on a bus like a couple of teenagers; but when he reached for her lips—hungrily, a romance novel would have said, and Jane could not think of a better description when she replayed it in her mind—there didn't seem any alternative.

That night, after a bit of bargaining and a sniggering paying-up of bets between the hooligans, the tent placements were rearranged. Four years later, lying in her hospital bed the night after Megan's birth, Jane would realise that this was the first night since Gallipoli she'd spent a night without Ian.

◌

At five and a half, Megan would stand at the end of the driveway, a dangerous intermission between the bull paddock and the channel, to wait for her school bus. Jane was gradually banished from holding-hand position to watching the slight, blue-checked figure from the house.

Was it in year 1 or 2 that she released a piece of paper—something important, a permission slip for an outing perhaps—which flew over the barbed fence and into the small bare paddock. The lesser of two evils, Jane thought later, because Megan, though long schooled in the dangers of both channels and bulls, didn't hesitate. Crawling under the fence, she snatched the precious paper from under the bull's nose, and was promptly thrown by that same ringed nose a good three metres back over the fence to the road.

The whole thing took less than a minute. Jane, sure that she'd barely looked away, noticed that there was something odd about the way Megan was standing as the bus pulled up, and thought no more about it until the principal phoned to say Megan had stepped off the bus saying, 'I was flying!' and then fainted with the pain of her broken arm.

It became the school's favourite 'we breed them tough in the country' story, but although Jane and Ian shared sleepless nights conjecturing about what might have happened had the paper gone into that fast swirling channel or the bull tossed her to his own side of the fence, and Jane never ever lost the guilt of negligence, it was flying that Megan remembered and would return to in dreams.

Dreams to Megan were not easily forgotten night fantasies

or fears; as a young child she described vivid, intense adventures as real to her as her daytime life. It wasn't so much that she didn't understand the difference between dream and reality, she simply saw them as equally significant.

Jane and Ian, lovers of maps and traceable tales, found this uncomfortable. When they lived through incidents, insignificant in themselves, that Megan had described in a dream weeks earlier, they would justify, doubt their memory of her wording, criticise their own perceptions as unduly influenced by their daughter's words.

'And Megan dreams so much,' Jane pointed out, 'that statistically some things she's dreamed of must be bound to happen,' though she was not sure how this statistic would work.

For a brief spell in Megan's early adolescence Jane even transcribed the recounted dreams into a notebook, as if that would prove the victory of coincidence over mystery. It was during this period that Megan had her cat dream, so it was there, recorded and dated in Jane's notebook, and after that Jane and Ian accepted that the stories in their daughter's life came from more amorphous sources than their own.

There was no action, simply the image of a large orange cat with nails sticking out of his head, but Megan insisted that it wasn't a nightmare; the cat was quite happy. When Jane opened the *Weekly Times* three months later she understood why, because there he was, in black and white rather than orange, a cartoon illustrating acupuncture for animals.

To Jane's credit, she showed Megan. Partly in a vain hope that Megan would sigh with full adolescent scorn, 'No, Mum, that's nothing like the cat I told you about!'. Still, she didn't feel as shaken at Megan's recognition as she would have once; after all, her daughter had been training her for thirteen years.

'So that's what I'll be,' Megan announced. 'An acupuncturist!'

It was only a word, vague and oriental, none of them had any real idea what it meant.

'You've got lots of time,' Ian said, as they'd said ever since Megan had decided that she couldn't wait any longer to discover what she was going to be and had begun reading careers handbooks as intently as if she were leaving school in weeks rather than years.

'You'll have to find out more before you make up your mind,' Jane added, because that was the sort of advice a good mother should give. She knew as well as Megan that the decision had been made.

Jane herself had to wait till she was fifty-two to have a dream that could not be explained by either analysis or sifting the day's trivia. It must have been a month or two ago, June or July, because she'd woken cold before putting another blanket on the bed and crawling back in beside Ian's warmth to listen enviously to his steady breathing. Breathing, she thought. Don't think, just breathe; the deep relaxation breathing she'd learned in antenatal classes twenty-five years ago and been nagged by the product of those classes to practise more regularly: 'Meditation would be good for you, Mother!'

Which Jane didn't disbelieve, although as she couldn't quite justify the time she compromised by practising when she woke early, those small hours when she'd had just enough sleep to think of problems and calculate how long left till the five o'clock alarm.

Now she was surprised to find herself dreaming because she hadn't thought she was asleep yet, but she must be because she was flying, moving rapidly and rigidly through the air, face down to study the ground below. She'd never had a flying dream before and the unexpected lack of birdlike freedom was frightening until she thought, I must be in a plane with Mom or Dad. Which seemed logical, and she relaxed.

The view was so clear and precise that she felt she not only ought to be able to identify it, but also, if she'd known more about flying, would have known at exactly what height the plane was travelling. She woke wanting to check an atlas; refused to let herself, but did tell Ian. 'It was over a river or a channel; I was coming in from the left and couldn't see if the channel continued or led into something else. The land was quite flat, very green, and the fields neatly fenced right down to the river—unless the lines were small irrigation channels? It was all very tidy.'

'That rules out Australia,' Ian had said lightly, and she could see him hoping that she wasn't going to continue any weirdness.

It had ruled out Nova Scotia too; far too smooth and flat for a Bay of Fundy shoreline. She wondered about Holland but was unable to think why she could have dreamed of it; she wondered if all her dreams were this clear and were simply not remembered. And finally tucked it away.

Until now, because after the funeral, when she's rambled around the garden with galumphing Barney and prim Daisy, has had another cup of tea and some biscuits with cheese, she finds herself sitting in Mary's other guest room with Ruth's suitcase and collection of purchases. On the top is a book, *Britain By Air*, and she chooses to read it rather than rifle through the pile, sorting and discarding in the dreary finalities of mourning; it seems a gentler, less emotional link to her mother's life. Was there one particular photograph that had meant something, that brought back a clear sky and the exhilaration of a twenty-four year old pilot? Or a general feeling: yes, this is what it was like, this is what I saw?

On the last page Jane's stomach clenches so tightly that her hands snap the book shut in sympathy and she has to open it again to find the landscape of her dream, as clear as Megan's cat in the *Weekly Times*. The banks of the river— for it is a river, the Hamble—are perhaps more natural than she had dreamed them, not quite as smooth, but that is the only quibble; and the unknown ending is the sea, Southampton Water. The town is also called Hamble, and she is quite sure she has not only never been there but never heard of it.

She waits till she can speak about it naturally before taking the book back downstairs; she can't imagine discussing any sort of psychic phenomenon with down-to-earth, practical Mary. 'Did Mom mention this book to you?'

'She showed it to me when she came back from visiting the airfield—she was certainly very pleased to have found it.'

No hope then that it had been brought from home, that Jane has seen and forgotten. But she didn't know about the airfield visit either.

'White Waltham, near Reading. She was based there during the war, and went to see it just the day before. She had a wonderful day! It may be in the letter.'

Because the letter Ruth wrote the afternoon of her death is after all to Jane, who will read it soon she promises herself, though she hasn't managed it yet. She opens the book. 'This is pretty; do you know if she ever went there?'

'Hamble? She was based there too; more than once, I think; the ATA moved them around a fair bit. One would think, with the way that I hero-worshipped her, I'd remember where she lived when her parents were killed. I can still see her face at the funeral, and of course I remember meeting your father... Southampton! I'm sure she took the Southampton train home, so she'd have been at Hamble. Of course it'll be in the letters.'

Either Jane is more jet-lagged than she'd realised, or her dead mother has written to her about sixty year old train timetables. She is beginning to feel like Alice, as that same dead mother would have said.

'Didn't I tell you? I've saved every letter your mother wrote to me from the time I joined the Land Army; I think she knew I might feel rather lost and lonely. She was older than me and always so elegant, but she was the first person in the family to treat me as an adult...you know what that is, when one is eighteen.' For a moment her eyes brim with tears.

'Sherry?' she asks briskly.

Alcohol sounds infinitely appealing. 'We always had sherry on the terrace before dinner when I stayed with you before; it made me feel very adult and sophisticated.'

'A significant time in your life...I always remember that I met Ian before your parents did, and wrote to tell them that he seemed really quite respectable...One heard such terrible things about Australian men then.'

'Good old Barry Mackenzie!'

'They were supposed to treat women badly,' says Mary, who had managed to live through the seventies without encountering the barfing archetype of Australian manhood. 'But Ian didn't strike one as a male chauvinist. I liked him.'

'I still do,' Jane says, with what seems wit to her benumbed brain.

'A bit mean with money, and liked his own way...'

Jane had forgotten about Mary's sometimes uncomfortable honesty.

'...but I've noticed that compromise is something young men take their time in learning. I wasn't worried; I knew that any daughter of Ruth's would be strong enough to work things out.'

Jane is silent, but Mary, lost in her own thoughts, doesn't notice.

'Petty, the things one takes pleasure from at times,' she continues and Jane understands. Husband-and-childless, Mary had enjoyed being able to vet her admired cousin's new son-in-law and is now burdened by shame at this smugness, Ruth being unable to ever vet anything again.

After a generous sherry, the letter—several pages in her mother's rushed copperplate, grown less familiar with the years of email—is not only unavoidable but welcome.

White Cottage
16 August 1998

My dear Jane

I'm sitting under a tree in Mary's lovely garden, on an English summer's day hot enough to seek the shade. I am thoroughly enjoying this time with Mary, and am looking forward to the next few days. I'd been a trifle worried that ten days might be too long a visit for two old women who hadn't met for half a century—and, in fact, who hadn't known each other terribly well then. The age difference seemed considerable when we were children, and even as young women, although perhaps it has appeared again; Mary seems to recuperate more quickly than I. We go out for a walk each morning, and afterwards I'm quite glad to sit and read with a cup of tea, while Mary rushes about doing something or preparing our next excursion. The indulgence of being a guest!

I told myself that I wouldn't mention again my disappointment that you couldn't have met me here; I know it was even more disappointing for you as you haven't had a holiday since the last time you came home. I also suspect that no matter how much I tried to avoid it—because I was also suffering from some guilt, wishing that I could have afforded to simply send you the ticket—you've probably felt a little guilty at sending your aged P off on her own. (If you haven't, please disregard the last sentence!)

Well, my dear, wonderful as it would have been to have travelled with you, I've realised over the last few days that this part of the trip would have been quite different if you'd been here. Not better or worse, but different in what I've enjoyed and what it's meant to me.

By the way, I won't bore you with trip details now but I have kept a journal of the actual tour and will write up some sort of enthralling travelogue when I return to send to each of you. I'm never sure how interested the boys are in doings such as these, but they can read it or not as they choose.

*What has been special about this past week is some discover-
ies I've made about myself and where I come from. No, not the
'sordid Darwinian details' as my Papa once called them—I've long
resigned myself to their remaining a mystery. This is a vaguer
thing, and something that I suspect you have dealt with much
better than I ever have: the realisation that no matter how much
I love my home—and there is absolutely no doubt that the Valley
is my home now; this trip to some extent has defined that even
more clearly—but England, both her 'green and pleasant land'
and 'dark satanic mills', is the place that formed me and will
always, has always, been part of me. I'm not sure now why I've
denied it for so long.*

*Of course the latter is not completely true; I do know that it's
because of my anger at my parents, but prefer to profess igno-
rance rather than admit that any rational, reasonably intelligent
woman could let rage deny her of a significant part of her identity for more than half a century. I'm not saying it wasn't a
justifiable or understandable rage; I just wish I'd dropped it a little
sooner.*

*Looking back, I feel desperately sorry for that young woman
suddenly deprived of identity; loss of identity, for whatever
reason, is I think one of the most fundamental griefs—and a terribly difficult one for anyone else to assist with. When Rick lost
his job, before he moved to Toronto, I felt quite helpless in the
face of his depression, largely because I could do nothing about
it but also because I identified with it so strongly. Your father
managed much better; perhaps because of all the practice I'd
given him! (I'm still quite amazed that he insisted on falling in
love with such a confused young woman, although I'm very
grateful that he did.)*

Perhaps you're not quite old enough, tears are streaming lib-
erally down Jane's face, but she smiles in spite of herself,
muttering, 'I'm fifty-two, Mom!' *to be able to look back at a
younger self and see a separate person from the one you are now.*

However I, as I said, look back and see that young Ruth as so separate from me that I can empathise without any sense of self-pity. The benefit of hindsight, or old age, also lets me feel some compassion for her parents—not for their deaths so much as for the people they were. Whether I am my father's natural child or no relation at all, they loved and cherished me as much as any parents could; it seems a pity that they were not secure enough to let me have the facts which would have given me a story of my own. I mightn't have liked the story—there is, after all, no chance whatsoever that it was a happy one—but I would have liked the chance to decide for myself how I felt about it, and perhaps even embroider it into a more respectable shape, as one does with uncomfortable tales.

Your father used to tell me that since few of us remember the period before our third birthdays, I had my own story just as much as anyone else, but although he meant it sincerely as well as kindly, he was mistaken. You don't remember your babyhood, but you do know the story of your snowstorm birth and all the other details that make up your personal history.

The absence of those early tales has been far worse for me than any query about genetics and family health—although you cannot imagine the relief with which I saw that all my children resembled your father's side of the family and were presumably unlikely to have inherited any congenital weakness from my unknown ancestors.

This is a very rambly letter, my dear, but since this paper comes without cut and paste or delete keys, I'm afraid you'll have to read it as it is.

The converse of accepting my love for my birthplace is the realisation of how my adopted country has become my own. There's no other way to explain my emotion at seeing General Wolfe's house in Bath, where he recuperated—assiduously taking the waters, no doubt—after capturing Louisbourg from the French, and from which he left again to capture Quebec. One can't help wondering how different history might have been if he'd stayed on somewhat longer to enjoy the delights of the Pump Room. After Canada's

history and it must, in the end, affect our own; alter one ances-
tor's fate and Bill—and you children—would never have been.

As you can see, the tour turned out to be much more than lit-
erary pilgrimage, but I must admit it's been a joy to visit quietly
with Mary since it ended: our reminiscent sightseeing has been
well interspersed with peaceful strolls and chats.

The highlight, however, was an outing I did on my own.
Yesterday morning Mary drove me to White Waltham Airfield,
and left me there for a blissful though somewhat emotional day.
This airfield used to be the ATA headquarters and base for ini-
tial flying training and several of the subsequent upgradings, so
I was there for quite some time at different periods—and in fact
finished the war there (which was wonderful as it was much
more convenient to your father in Oxfordshire than Hamble, where
I was based when we met and for a brief period again when we
married, on VE day).

Hamble again, Jane thinks. No wonder it was significant
to her. Except that it was Jane who had the dream, and she
realises that there simply will never be an explanation for
that. It is not an easy thing to accept.

I'd read about the ATA reunion a few years ago, so I knew the
airfield still existed and possibly had some reminder of the service,
a polite plaque or some such. I was sure the flag would still be
in the chapel and would have been content to have seen that, if
nothing else. I'd always felt the ATA, not being officially part of
the air force, was rather discounted after the war, and presumed
it had been completely forgotten.

Even I can sometimes be glad to be wrong.

Returning somewhere after a gap of fifty years, one is braced
for the shock of change, but I wasn't at all prepared for what I
found. Much of the airfield is exactly as it was when I flew from
it; the runways are still grass—I thought there'd probably have
been regulations making all runways tarmac by now! I can't
describe how I felt to see the clubhouse, which is quite unaltered

from its days as the ATA mess, right down to the old wicker RAF chairs.

I'd like to think that the charming man I happened to meet as I arrived had recognised me from my photograph (a subtle way of slipping in your mother's entry in a hall of fame)—one wall is full of pictures of ATA pilots beside their planes, mostly Lancasters and Wellingtons (Very Big Bombers to you). I didn't ever fly one of those, but I'm in one of the pictures anyway, heaven knows why.

Because you were gorgeous! Jane thinks, remembering her father's description and their few wedding photos.

However, it's more likely that eighty year old women don't commonly wander around airfields and no doubt he was worried I'd step in front of a plane and break it, or my hip. At any rate, he was so pleasant that I explained why I'd come, greatly doubting that he would have ever heard of the ATA.

That was the point at which I was taken into the clubroom, shown the photo wall etc, and then (feeling rather like minor royalty by this stage!) one of the hangars, also unchanged since the war, which had several Tiger Moths and other aircraft whose names would mean nothing to you but which brought back floods of memories to me.

By now I was feeling quite sated and would have been more than content to have had a quiet cup of tea and call a taxi to the train. My cup, however, was about to run over. This wonderful man intended, he said, to take his Cessna up for a short flight— would I care to go with him?

My dear, can you imagine how you'd feel if, not having been on a horse for over half your lifetime—and leaving aside the problems of stiff joints and unaccustomed muscles—you were offered a ride on an exquisitely trained, beautifully mannered thoroughbred? Double that joy and you'll have some idea of how I felt at the thought of being in the air again.

The reality surpassed it. I think I'd have been happy in anything that managed to leave the ground, but this was a lovely little machine and, perhaps not surprisingly, considerably more advanced than the last plane I flew. It responded so beautifully— yes, he let me fly for a short spell when we were up, but in fact I was content to simply be there. The luck of it was that it was such a lovely day—we've had many drizzly times since I've been here, but yesterday, as today, was perfect. The clouds appeared to have been placed there purely for scenic value, although even this tiny plane came with enough instruments that clouds would not have been a worry. I would have almost liked to have flown through one simply to experience it without the sheer terror that I associate with being surrounded by white mist. However, I'm certainly not complaining about the wonderful visibility and seeing the countryside in the way that I still always picture it, from a height of two thousand feet.

I'll try not to wax too lyrical, but we soared and swooped with all the freedom of the air that first made me fall in love with flying. Aircraft may change and landmarks alter, but that extraordinary feeling stays the same.

(The difference, by the way, between flying as a passenger on a DC 10 or 747 and flying a small plane solo is that of being a passenger on a school bus and driving a sports car. The former does not, believe me, count as flying.)

This letter has gone on long enough, and there'll be time for another quick one before I leave—in between a look at Blenheim Palace on Wednesday and an expedition to the two Globe Theatres (that is, the new and the remains of the original) on Friday. However, interesting as they will no doubt be, this trip has already fulfilled all that I could ask of it—and far more than I thought I had asked. If it ended tomorrow, it would be enough.

Chapter
EIGHT

On Trojan plains, where Hector slew Patroclus and was in turn vanquished and dishonoured by the grief-maddened Achilles, the second Magical Mystery Tour bus headbutted its leader.

If it hadn't been raining it would have been no more than a jolt: broken headlights on one and dented bumper on the other.

What ifs, as every storyteller knows, are the makings of legend. Rain was the reason the second bus had skidded in the first place, bouncing sideways, sliding crabwise down the road, passengers tumbling off their seats, knocking teeth or foreheads along the way. The first bus, in which Jane and Ian dozed in the sated relaxation following predawn sex, spun in an awkward pirouette, slewed into the ditch and toppled gently into the mud.

Ian grabbed for Jane as her head smashed hard against the window and she slid unconscious to the floor. Nothing in his life had ever been as desperate as the need to get her out of there to safety. He leapt onto the up-ended seat and began kicking out the window.

Jane woke from a dream of a bull tossing their tent across a Venetian canal to a squeal of pain and torrent of abuse from her former tent-mate, who seemed to be accusing Ian of kicking her in the head, although the only word Jane could reliably decipher was 'Merde!'

'You got in the way,' Ian grunted, and knocked the last of the jagged glass free of the frame.

Jane was surprised to discover a window in the roof, though more intrigued by why Ian was so intent on smashing it.

'If you go up first,' said her father, which was another surprise, she was sure he wasn't supposed to be here, 'I'll help from this end.'

Ian pulled himself out of the window onto the bus's side. 'It's alright,' he called, 'seems stable.' The Canadian pilot— Bill had disappeared—pushed the Swiss girl out next, and then Jane. Dreamily fascinated by the shaking of her hands and knees, she sat on the side of the road as her companions scrambled out one by one and stared at the occupants of the other bus, streaming down the road to escape the operatic screams inside.

Dear Mom and Dad

Well, this is going to be a bit of a shock. No, I haven't eloped or anything like that!, but I have just written to the school board and resigned. I've given it a lot of thought and it really is the best thing for me to do.

The main reason is that we're stuck in Turkey for maybe a few more weeks and I'm going to miss my flight home. Please don't worry, but the buses had a minor accident. Nobody was seriously injured, I had a bit of a bump on the head and was a little vague yesterday but feel fine again today. In fact the most dramatic incident was a New Zealander on the other bus who was convinced that someone had stolen his cans of sardines in the confusion and insisted on searching everyone's luggage before they got off the bus, and the fat girl had hysterics because she thought the suspicion must be aimed at her. Ian's just glad she wasn't on our bus because he was in charge of pulling people out the window, since the bus was lying on its right-hand side, which is the side with the door. It was all very heroic.

However, the buses are both in terrible shape; ours doesn't look as if it'll ever go again but everyone thinks we should be able to get some parts from it to fix up the other one, though no one wants to say how long it's going to take. We'll all fit on one bus to get back to London when it's done.

There doesn't seem any point in mentioning that several people, with jobs to go to or planes to catch, have hitchhiked back to Istanbul and the train station.

The other reason is that there's so much to see in Europe and who knows when I'll get back again. It takes so long to save up the airfare that it makes more sense to stay longer. I know Mary would be happy for me to continue using her as a base—I don't think she's just being polite; she seems to quite enjoy a stray who can actually answer when spoken to! I haven't decided yet whether I'll try to get a teaching job or short-term work so I can travel every few weeks. Who knows, I've already made it to Asia, maybe I'll decide to see the whole world while I'm at it!

It evolved gradually from Italy's 'One day I'll get back to Siena at the right time and see the Palio', to sighing over the missed opportunities of Bavaria and the Romantic Road: 'Next time we'll hire a car and go at our own pace.' Jane-and-Ian ('Ian-and-them' his mother Dulcie would say) was a permanent phrase; marriage had become a question of when not if. Equally obvious was that they would settle in Australia, although nothing was discussed until the last week of September, as they drove through the flat canalled Netherlands. 'If you take out the villages and windmills, it looks a lot like home,' said Ian, the latter word presumably the trigger for adding, 'It'd be easiest if we got married in London, as soon as we get back. We don't want any hassles with immigration.'

It wasn't the proposal that Barbara Cartland readers dream of, but the essence of it was that Ian loved her, and Jane told herself that was all the romance she desired. A small wedding, she thought, maybe in Mary's village church; nothing fancy.

A registry office, said Ian, was the only practical thing; no mucking around with flowers and lace or ministers and churches. His best mate's wedding had been endless fuss over cummerbunds, hired dinner suits and the engraving of place-setting cards; he couldn't see what relevance that all had to what should be a private statement between two people in love.

Jane thought of Patsy's wedding and agreed. Despite some severe misgivings about Randy by the time the great day arrived, Patsy had been far too in love with her dress and the gala reception to think of changing her mind. Clean and simple was more honest, and if Ian's idea of simple was more spartan than hers, it must necessarily be more honest as well.

They would return to London, check into a hotel, and from there make the arrangements—registry office first and then Australia House.

They convinced themselves that their parents would enjoy the fait-accompli surprise, which neatly skirted the probability of listening to reasons why one should not get married within seven weeks of meeting. It also ruled out having Mary as a witness, which not only gave them the exquisite pleasure of picturing her face when Jane introduced Ian as, 'my husband', but ensured that Jane couldn't be expected to spend the night away from him before the wedding.

She was weak-kneed at the thought.

Dulcie's letter was waiting at Australia House.

Dad's not feeling the greatest. This calving season's knocked him around a fair bit and you know Dad, the world would end if he didn't check them all every night. At least they're finished now and he's got a breather till the water starts. You'll be glad to hear we had a good lot of heifers, you've had eleven out of yours, but you lost old Popeye. Wasn't she the one you reared when you were still in school, before you started your apprenticeship? She must have been nearly twelve, a good innings and she calved alright (a little bull) but then she cast herself on the channel bank and was dead when Dad found her the next morning. So you've got nineteen cows and heifers, ten yearlings and eleven heifer calves. We got your letter saying you've decided to go farming when you come home, so that will give you a start.

If you could send a telegram to answer this letter it would be good because Dad's thinking of buying Robinsons', you remember the place on the east side of the outpaddock, the one with the dam in front of the house. The old man died and it's too much for her. It's not a very big house but Dad thinks it will do. The toilet is inside the house; I'm not sure I like the idea but it might be good in the winter when we get older. It's good country, three hundred and twenty acres so it'll give him just over five hundred with the outpaddock. He wants to run beef cattle on it, Herefords probably. It's not so far from here so we'll still be able to meet up with all our old cobbers and Dad says when I've driven across the bridge a few times it won't worry me.

So if you want to come home on the farm, you could share-farm and buy the cows or, if you want to buy it Dad could guarantee the loan for you. He says you can work it out when you get home but he needs to know if you want to do it so he can put an offer on Robinsons' before it goes on the market.

There were several things Jane wanted to query, but the more important were difficult to frame. 'What's an outpaddock?'

she asked, and understood little more of her prospective in-laws with the knowledge that it was an unirrigated block of land some distance from the home farm.

◯

The first available seat to Halifax is not till the following Wednesday.

'You can have a bit of a holiday,' says Mary and so does Ian, trying his best to disguise disappointment: 'You've already spent the money, might as well enjoy it.'

The irritation, or the bonus, is that there is absolutely nothing Jane can do about all the chores and decisions that await her once she reaches Evelyn's Pond. She phones Mike and Rick, and then has no choice but to take the advice and relax.

Walking in Burnham Beeches, the leaves still green on the trees, she longs suddenly for a full-blooded Canadian fall, thinking how much more attention she would have paid to the bright dying leaves of '68 if she'd known they were the last she'd see, and then wonders how long it is since she'd simply gone for a walk without checking tree guards or irrigation or calving cows.

'What I'd really like to do,' she tells Mary, 'is some of the things you and Mom did which meant a lot to her.'

She fits in, naturally, the places that mean the most to her: a walk down the Strand past Australia House, though she has no urge to enter; the street where the Magical Mystery Tour met, through Trafalgar Square and into Canada House, where she feels like an impostor—the newspapers are meaningless and she knows that if she speaks she won't be recognised as Canadian. In Bayswater she saunters past the hotel where she'd worked, cleaner now than then, takes Mary for coffee in a cafe that could even be the same one where she'd sat with poor sad Maggie, and strolls in Hyde Park.

She nearly doesn't go to White Waltham. It was the last place Ruth visited, a day she'd described as the pinnacle of her trip, but the aircraft will mean nothing to Jane and she doesn't want to meet the kind man who took her mother flying: 'It's too complicated—he might think I blame him.'

'Why mention your mother at all?' Mary asks. 'There must be other reasons people without planes visit airfields.'

It is not, of course, the first lie Jane has ever told, but it is the first elaborate fiction she's embroidered. 'I'm doing a thesis,' she claims, 'on women in wartime.'

Needless to say, no one questions this story. Jane does not look like any sort of saboteur and it's not a military installation with secrets to hide. She's directed to the clubroom with gift shop and photo wall, where she's able to spot Ruth amongst the assembled crews; it doesn't take long and no one offers to take her flying, but it feels indecent to leave too quickly. Buying a copy of the Blue Book, the ring-backed instruction manual her mother would have taped to her knee each time she flew an unfamiliar aircraft, she orders a drink and, with the alien details of throttle and trim before her, envisages Ruth sitting perhaps in this same chair, writing to Bill as she waits for fog to lift, or squinting into the afternoon sun to watch her friends land just as these small pretty planes are doing now.

It strikes her that this is the first drink she's bought since she met Ian, which is just about forever. She wonders if this gin and tonic is significant in some way, and whether a woman should be able to buy a drink without feeling awkward, and how much easier she would feel if it were tea instead of alcohol—and whether anyone who can waste this much energy worrying about sitting alone in a peaceful club has the right to even consider a responsible public relations kind of job.

The 5 October 1969 dawned a bright autumn morning, or so Jane always remembers, although the photographs showed a

greyer sky, as if some brightness had been lost in the developing. She wore for the first time the heavy cotton dress she'd bought in Yugoslavia (something new and as old as their history went). Shapeless and indecisively midcalf, it was the least flattering dress she owned, but it was white and the silvery discs on the red trim jingled festively. When she used it as a maternity smock a few years later, she would imagine unborn Megan listening to the music of her mother's movements.

Pressed close to Ian's side on the top front seat of the double-decker bus, a heady, contradictory combination of moral certainty, vulnerability, Christmas-morning butterflies and sexual excitement threatened to explode into giggles. The same feelings were reflected in Ian's face—grinning like a Cheshire cat, her mother would have said—and Jane looked up at him, aiming at sexiness and looking, Ian thought, exactly as she must have at twelve, on the way to buy her horse.

Jane imagined the other passengers wondering at their glow of happiness. Would they add it up with Ian's dark purple suit, her jingly white dress? Would they be part of someone's story tonight, 'Never seen two people more in love than that couple on the bus!'? She was torn between fantasies of bursting out with their glorious secret and laughing because no one else knew what an extraordinary day it was.

The remnants of the Magical Mystery Tour were waiting outside the registry office: their driver, the Swiss tent-mate, the Yorkshire trainspotters and one of the hooligans. They filed through the labyrinthine building, past sombre offices to the chilly august room where the registrar waited, a red-faced stout man in a foul temper who seemed convinced that their only conceivable reason for being there was to irritate him.

'Marriage is a solemn sacrament!' he warned, scowling at their overwhelming joy at being so lucky, so clever and blessed, in having found somebody to love. 'This is not something to enter into lightly. What you do here today will affect the rest of your lives.'

The rest of our lives! Jane thought ecstatically. Ian's rather bony face was handsome in profile; a muscle twitched as if he might tell the officer to get on with it, but when he turned to look down at her he was still beaming, as if dazed by his own good fortune. She squeezed his hand and the ceremony began, ending so soon after that she wondered whether something had been left out and how they could really be more married now than they'd been three minutes earlier. However, she was wearing a ring, a plain gold band but wide to make up for the lack of engagement diamond; had signed her new name, Jane Ralston; and marvelled briefly at how Jane Dubois had been wiped from life, as if her entire existence up to this point had been merely preparation for marrying Ian.

The furious registrar shook their hands; the trainspotting wife, despite the absence of overt sentiment or ceremony, wiped her eyes neatly with a hanky; the hooligan gave Jane a smacking kiss on the lips and they trooped back through the dark offices to the street.

Jane and Ian hadn't thought further than this, at least as far as public celebrations were concerned, but the sense of anticlimax was palpable until the driver remembered a pub around the corner.

'The registrar could do his next lecture on timing weddings around opening time!' Jane suggested.

'Oh, he was sour!' the trainspotting wife exclaimed. 'But don't you mind him.'

'Cranky old git,' agreed the hooligan.

Jane and Ian laughed; they couldn't have explained that a cranky old git only highlighted their happiness, as if they had faced their first adversity together and prevailed against the odds.

In the pub ('We should have had champagne!' Ian said later, but at the time Heineken beer, in honour of the tour's

afternoon at the Amsterdam factory, had seemed appropriate) the Swiss girl and the trainspotter both pulled gifts from
their handbags. Jane hadn't considered presents. 'It's your wedding, isn't it!' the older woman scolded, loudly enough that
several other drinkers turned to stare, and one or two to smile.

Reddening self-consciously, they performed the first joint
action of their married life, unwrapping the gold-embossed
leather address book from Florence—either bought with amazing prescience or originally intended for the Swiss girl's
parents—and a small china teapot painted with a steam engine.

'Talyllyn, the world's first preserved steam railway,' the
trainspotting husband explained, which led him to a discussion on the Puffing Billy, Australia's first preserved steam
railway which they hoped one day to ride too.

'Stay with us!' Jane offered, more to practise saying *us* and
picturing a home into which they could invite guests than
any desire to have them visit.

From the pub farewells they went straight to the post office
to send their respective telegrams.

Will buy farm. Stop. Married today. Stop. Home soon. Stop. Ian,
Jane.

Married Ian today. Stop. Very happy. Stop. Letter follows. Stop.
Love, Jane, Ian

❧

'Ian will be just getting up now,' Jane says as she fills the
teapot and Mary butters currant buns for afternoon tea.

'Five o'clock? I wouldn't fancy that.'

'You get used to it.' And, in fact, although she enjoys the
luxury of sleeping till seven as much as anyone, and is beginning to feel that it's about time their days of constant and
heavy work came to an end, she's also aware that at some
level she'll miss that early morning routine. The sleepy stillness of the house as Ian leaves, whistling to his dog to drive

the cows down the lane while he takes the motorbike to open gates and move electric fences for the day's grazing. Jane dresses more slowly, boils the kettle before heading for the dairy with thermos and mugs in hand. In anything except midwinter or driving rain it's the best time of day, magpies carolling their extraordinary liquid joy and mist rising off the grass, a peace rarely repeated even in evening.

'People think kookaburras are the sound of Australia,' she tells Mary, 'but it's the magpies I'd miss if I ever left. Not that I'm planning to.'

In the dairy she opens and shuts gates, installs clean filter liners, puts hoses in place, switches on the vat's cooling system and the radio's Classic FM. By the time Ian locks the yard gate behind the stragglers, Jane has the first thirty-two cows in place, has pulled the lever to deliver their portions of grain, and is slipping the pulsating cups onto the second row of bulging, leaking udders. There is a satisfying tug as each teat is enclosed in its steel mouth, mechanical reproduction of a hungry baby's mouth on a mother's nipple.

It's the crises that are memorable—breakdowns of machinery or animal—but most milkings are busily uneventful: disjointed conversation, a shared look of exasperation or amusement at a particular cow, sips of rapidly cooling coffee. Unlike the heated voices from next door, it's rarely necessary to ask what the other is doing or to explain their own actions, reading body language as much as habit to anticipate needs. There's a sigh of relief as the last row of cows is released to the paddock, and they each swing into their own routines again for cleaning up, Ian finishing off the last of the hosing as Jane starts home to shower and make breakfast, with coffee that has a chance of being finished hot. If she does take this job, they'll have to find some way to replace that morning companionship, the half-finished sentences and shared thoughts as they plan their day.

The immigration interviews were, logically enough, conducted at Australia House, where Jane had first glimpsed her future.

The surprise was that she'd not only be allowed into the country, but the Australian government would pay most of her fare.

'Provided you stay for two full years!' the immigration officer snapped. He was a harassed looking man, sweating unseasonably in an outgrown suit. 'What'll you do if you don't like it?'

'I'm married!' exclaimed Jane, bride of two weeks. 'I'm not going to leave my husband because I don't like the scenery.'

'It's been done.'

'Not by me!' Her face was flushed and there was a set to her jaw that Ian hadn't seen before. 'When I said I'd marry Ian, I meant for life. I'm not going to walk out!'

The officer admitted defeat and changed tack. 'You'll find things are different in Australia. It's not all proper and formal the way it is in England.' Warming to his theme, he wrenched his too-tight jacket off his shoulders. 'Australians are very relaxed!'

Jane suspected that laughing aloud would not improve her chances, but 'I'm Canadian,' she reminded him.

'Right,' he said, nonplussed. The rest of the interview continued more calmly.

And so, after an excursion to Harley Street for a medical and chest X-ray, Jane Ralston, née Dubois, became an assisted passage migrant to Australia. She was allowed extra baggage allowance on the plane as well as a trunk to be sent by sea.

Mary, who had already provided a wedding gift of ten pounds 'for the theatre or a weekend away; nothing practical', as well as a Royal Doulton milk jug, crazed with age and chosen from pride of place on her own mantelpiece, threw herself into the task of filling the newlyweds' trunk. Subtlety was not Mary's strong point and she thought that the family had not treated Ruth as well as they ought; revenge was implied in the afternoon tea party, a wedding reception in all but name, to which all living relatives were invited. Jane and Ian weren't sure whether this was also some form of vengeance on them for not having had a proper wedding: Mary's reaction, when they'd arrived on her doorstep the afternoon of their marriage, had been more shock than delight.

'Good Lord!' she'd exclaimed. 'Are you sure?'

Jane extended her left hand in reply.

'Good Lord!' Mary repeated. 'Does your mother know?'

'I hinted in the last letter. They won't be surprised.'

Mary, shooing the dogs away from Ian, suspected differently. 'Sherry?' she asked brightly, and they were sipping Harvey's Bristol Cream and recounting their story—laughing, words and hands entwining—when the telegram arrived.

Congratulations. Stop. Wish had known. Stop. Much love and happiness. Stop. Mom, Dad.

Jane was twenty-three, in love, and had been married for six hours. She had taken the wording at face value, and it was not until the morning of the Great Afternoon Tea, as she and Ian referred to it, that it struck her just how much *'wish had known'* might cover. Maybe even a wish that they'd been given a chance to see their daughter's wedding.

'Mary,' she asked, 'may I use your phone?'

There was more to say than three minutes could hold. 'I can't believe you told Mary before your own parents!' Ruth exclaimed, all the last weeks' hurt spilling over in that one cry.

The fun and surprise were suddenly a feeble excuse, although she added the expediency, the happiness and: 'I wish you and Dad could have been here,' allowing herself to realise it for the first time.

'So do we,' said Ruth. 'How soon do you leave for Australia?'

But Jane didn't know, Ruth was too hurt and proud to rush to England on the gamble of meeting her son-in-law and saying goodbye to her daughter—and their time was up. Jane hung up, tearful with the first complicated intimations of being an immigrant wife and emigrant daughter.

Ian was more concerned with her using Mary's phone for a transatlantic call. 'But I'll pay for it!' Jane insisted, and their guests arrived before she could discover whether he was worried about an abuse of hospitality or expenditure from their now joint finances.

The guests' arrival was in fact more than enough to put petty irritations out of mind. Jane had no idea that her mother had so many relatives, but there were elderly aunts and younger cousins, twice and thrice removed, a smaller clan than the Dubois, but an ample gathering in Mary's small house and a confusing whirl to meet at once.

'I remember meeting your father, the day your grandparents died—terrible thing, that,' said one elderly but still pukka great-uncle. 'Good chap, I thought.'

'And your mother, such a spirited girl, and so clever. I wouldn't have ever imagined her living in the country,' added a great-aunt. 'Does she get up to town often?'

'Is Ruth still alive?' asked an even older aunt. 'Didn't they all die in a buzz bomb?'

'It was a rocket,' said her daughter, 'and remember, Ruth was away flying.' She made it sound vaguely disreputable, but it could have been the accent, so similar to Ruth's irritated voice.

Afterwards, however, Jane and Ian were equally bemused by their horde of gifts. 'So that's why people have weddings!' Jane cried flippantly, confirming her husband's prejudice against the ceremony as they sorted through fondue pots, antique vases, fragile glassware and practical sheets. 'Look at these pillowslips, Ian—aren't they pretty?'

Ian was studying a framed print of *The Rape of the Sabine Women* and wondering whether Great-uncle Adrian had intended some obscure warning or could simply no longer bear it on his own wall. 'Where do you suppose we go to buy a trunk?'

❧

The streets of Chelsea are still pleasant to stroll through, and it does not take a great stretch of the imagination to picture a nanny and pinafored child in the locked gardens or behind the upstairs windows. The distance her mother had travelled in life is more obvious to Jane than ever before; the time, however, is now so remote that it does not do a great deal to bring her closer.

On the high street, not far from where the younger Jane had met the lion-owning Australians in a bizarre presentiment of her future, she and Mary pass an antique shop and are irresistibly drawn to gaze in the window.

'Your mother saw a tea service here that reminded her of your grandmother's. It gave her quite a jolt, she said, and she asked to see it just so that she could handle it again. Of course she had no intention of buying it...not very materialistic, was she, your mother?'

'Only with books. I sometimes wonder if the way her parents died made possessions seem irrelevant—sort of got things into proportion?'

'Perhaps...although even when she went away to school she gave me her favourite doll because she thought it would be better off with someone younger.' It strikes them both that Ruth had sprung from a mother who was the very epitome of nonmaterialism, having given her own child away.

Jane, however, has not been given away, has not seen her family or home bombed, and she knows herself to be extremely materialistic. This is quite plainly a shop which will have absolutely nothing that would suit her, as she'd been told once long ago, but she wants to see what had captivated her mother.

It captivates her too. Not replaced in the window since Ruth handled it, it reposes on a gate-legged mahogany table as if simply waiting for tea and the ladies to drink it, deep blue Royal Worcester cups and plates, achingly beautiful. Maybe it's Mary's mention of a doll that makes her think she hasn't wanted an inanimate object this badly since the golden-haired bride doll with blue blinking eyes in the 1957 Eatons Christmas catalogue.

She realises suddenly that both Mary and the shop assistant think purchase is a serious possibility, an idea that would normally make her panic but today, as if imbued with her mother's spirit, lets her enter into the game of being a woman of independent means and inclination, a woman who could decide to spend hundreds of pounds on an item that was not necessary and would rarely be used. Better yet, this mythical woman *would* use her china, for book group and similar ladies' gatherings, would nonchalantly pass precious cups or cake plates without wincing. Jane's friends, after all, had not yet broken Woolworths' own; they were unlikely to mistake the Worcester for frisbees.

She doesn't see until later that the main attraction of this alternative universe Jane is in the decision, not the china or use of.

'We ship anywhere in the world,' the sales assistant is saying, which means that it's time to end the story, but it's not easy, it's surprisingly difficult, to get out of it before the Visa card flies from her wallet. But credit cards, says Ian, are for emergencies and it's probably an exaggeration to say, as she might have at sixteen, that she will die without this china. (Ruth had died without it, but Jane has to admit that it was probably not a causal link.)

'You might as well,' says Mary.

'I'd have to ask Ian,' says Jane, which raises Mary's eyebrows ever so slightly. They both know that Jane will not ask

Ian because she knows what he's going to say and doesn't want to hear it. The only difference of opinion is on how much what he says should matter.

❧

Jane celebrated her twenty-fourth birthday by arriving in Australia. Not even the Qantas welcome of greasy rewarmed sausages and meat that Ian identified as lamb chops or the ritual spraying of insecticide before disembarkation were enough to darken the omen.

Sydney airport a sealed, air-conditioned daze of confusion and frustration, her new country so near behind the glass; the flight to Melbourne passing not far from the farm, Ian said, but too high to see more than a blur of greens and browns. Gently rolling hills as they descended to Melbourne's new airport, summer-dry and barren; another airport maze but this time real with the urgency of arrival; suitcases and knapsacks safely off the carousel, through customs and immigration, the red spot on her jacket bringing her a welcome from an immigration officer—'I can see you're alright,' the woman said, nodding at Ian, and disappeared to search for more forlorn migrants.

Jane recognised Fred and Dulcie on the other side of the barriers not so much from their photograph but the intensity of their gaze and Ian's own look of strained expectancy on his father's face. Ruth's story of meeting Bill's parents floated through her head like déjà vu as she was hugged and exclaimed over; the main difference apart from her not being about to give birth being that Ian was with her to share it: 'You're so pale!' his mother complained. And so was Jane. Had they been crook?

'It's just from winter,' Jane explained, and stepped out into summer.

It was hot, even by Australian standards, a hundred and two in the scale they were used to, but like Ruth facing her first snowstorm, Jane had no means of knowing whether this was the norm. The heat hit as if she'd bent into an open oven; it rolled shimmering off tarmac and car roofs, and when they got inside the car the oven simile became still more uncomfortably apt.

Dear Mom and Dad
The first day in my new home! It's all a bit hard to believe.

Ian's parents met us at the airport, and they do seem very nice. They want me to call them Mum and Dad, but it doesn't seem natural for people I hadn't met till yesterday. So far I've just avoided calling them anything, but I guess I can't do that forever. (Although in the end that was precisely what she did until she could begin calling them Gran and Poppy on her daughter's behalf, and continued on her own.)

Fred is quiet, a bit shorter than Ian or Dad, wiry and balding; Dulcie chatters a lot and I get the feeling that her life revolves totally around her husband and son, though it might be just the way she talks—'I'd better get their dinner now,' or 'They'll need their morning tea,' as if she wasn't going to eat too. The language is surprisingly different. Lucky I've got Ian to translate for me or I might never have figured out what happened when his 'two cobbers had a bit of a barney', though apparently it wasn't a 'real blue', which would have been worse (ie his friends had a fight)!

The countryside is very flat with the irrigation channels branching through the district and smaller ditches through the farms. There's hardly a tree in sight except for a few weeping willows along the channel banks, branches all evenly trimmed, which I thought was an amazing effort till Ian explained that it was the cows, not the farmers, who'd shaped them so neatly. The other funny sight as we came onto their (their crossed out and replaced by *our*) *farm, was that one field, or paddock, was full of black and white Friesian cows, and the next one with black and white ibis, looking equally domesticated and fenced in! Apparently Fred*

floods the paddocks one by one, so each in turn becomes a smorgas-
bord for wading birds.

The house was built just after the war when this area was divided
into farms for returned servicemen. The bathroom—or at least the
toilet—is in the garden, but I guess we won't ever have to shovel
snow to make a path to it! Ian warned me about red-back spiders,
which sound like black widows; he says they like to live under the
toilet seat but I'm not sure whether he was joking or not.

The stove is wood and the hot water runs off it, so you can't
decide not to light it just because it's a hundred degrees outside.
(When Ian came in from the dairy this morning, I was certainly
in favour of his having a hot soapy shower!) It must be easier to
use than our old one, though, because when we got here yester-
day, Dulcie bustled around and made scones for afternoon tea
before milking.

There does seem a lot to learn! (crossed out)

I had a 'lie-in' this morning while the two men milked, but
I'll start helping tomorrow so I can learn how. The women here
do a lot more of the active farming work than they do in the
Valley, but I'm looking forward to it. Fred and Dulcie will move
to their new place, about twelve miles away, over the next few
days, and then the farm will be ours. I don't know the financial
details but I guess it'll be sorted out eventually.

The letters over the next few months follow the same
pattern. The weekly news is interspersed with snippets that
had caught her eye or ear: the old ladies of Yarralong strolling
in the sun with their umbrellas, the first time she heard
someone say, 'Fair dinkum!'

Ruth is intrigued by the novelties but fascinated by this
mirroring of mother's and daughter's stories. She is thrown
back into her own days of discovery: the wooden houses, the
big barrels of salt pork and dill pickles in the grocery store;
the fishing boats tied to a wharf forty feet above, waiting for
the great Fundy tide.

Bill finds himself acutely aware of the repeated *Ian says*, and wonders what lies behind Jane's bright and breezy tone. When they read, *Ian says that women in Australia don't work after they're married. Teachers have been allowed to for the last few years, but it's not really done*, half a world's distance is not enough to fool either of them. Bill shovels out the barn's manure stack three months early and Ruth, who hasn't cried for ten years, not since she found her dog dying in a porcupine trap, weeps angry, despairing tears.

๑

The battle had dominated the first few weeks of her Australian life.

Babies were what Jane had pictured terminating her career, angelic bundles in the distant future, but this was the man she loved handing down an arbitrary edict: from now on she would be a dependent housewife, married to home and farm as much as man. She'd been alternately furious and devastated, and overwhelmingly betrayed that he hadn't brought up something so important until now. Ian had been equally angry that she was so determined to work and equally hurt that *she*'d never mentioned it. Neither had completely understood the other's assumptions, which was why it had been so terrifying: Ian was more than her husband, he was the only person she knew in this whole vast country, and if she couldn't communicate with him she would be as lonely as any explorer in an uncharted desert. The immigration officer's words and her own self-confident retort returned to haunt her—what if this marriage was a terrible mistake, and no matter how much she loved Ian she never fitted in to his country and his way of thinking?

The first major rift in their understanding and it had seemed irreconcilable.

Maybe that's when her interest in reforestation had begun. In all their hundred and four acres, there wasn't one tree to hide behind, not a single private place to cry. She remembers keeping away from the house in case Dulcie popped in—'But who'd get Ian's dinner if you were at school?' her mother-in-law had asked. (Jane had wanted to scream, wondering if she was expected to tear her hair, rend her clothes in contrition: *Why didn't I realise the man would starve if I left him alone for the day?*) Striding across paddocks to burn off her anger, she was painfully aware that both neighbours and husband could see any aberrant behaviour such as throwing herself on the ground to weep. It wouldn't have been so bad if she'd had a dog to walk with her but dogs were another source of contention—'Working dogs can't be pets,' said Ian, still in shock from their stay at Mary's, where the dogs not only slept on the couch but licked out the roast pan after dinner.

Then one lunchtime, as she stood at the sink filling the kettle for tea, he announced that if she really thought working would make her happy, she should do it. She'd been too grateful to question this sudden understanding, and it could have been coincidence, she tells herself now, that he and Fred had visited the accountant that morning and the full scale of the debt they'd taken on had been made apparent.

It must have been at much the same time, because she either hadn't started working or was still just doing infrequent emergency teaching, that she had gone in to Yarralong, armed with the fat total of wedding cheques, to buy a set of china. Something classic—they'd already bought orange and yellow stoneware for every day, but fine china lasted a lifetime and she wanted to love it still when she set the table for their golden wedding anniversary. The thought made her glow and she dressed carefully, a brown maxi skirt she'd bought in London and a soft, slightly clingy shirt from Sears that always made her feel good—the last time she'd worn it they'd had to go back to bed before she got out the door.

It was the first time she'd planned a major shopping day

in Yarralong: the dinner service, two blue bath towels, some pump belts Ian hadn't been able to get locally, and then a bulk grocery in the supermarket, so much cheaper than Narling. Narling, though fractionally larger than Applevale, was very similar: small stores and personal contact, shopkeepers fascinated by her accent, where was she from and how long was she staying; the perennial question of what was the difference between Canadians and Americans, wasn't it all one country now and was it true they ate doughnuts for breakfast? It was friendly but sometimes wearing and much of the attraction of Yarralong was that it seemed large enough for a difference in vowels to be unlikely to mark her as particularly foreign.

She was smiling as she walked into the jeweller's on the corner, past the diamond solitaires and strings of pearls to their array of china, Royal Albert plates, Wedgwood and Noritake. She pictured placing them in front of Ian, for dinner parties, for Christmases.

'Can I help you?' the saleswoman asked.

And Jane answered. 'I'm looking for a set of good china,' she must have said, or something like it, because what else was there to say, but she saw the woman's face freeze as the words came out, freeze and harden with something like contempt, though surely there was nothing contemptible in spending this gift, the thoughtful, unbreakable sum of Jane's assorted aunts and uncles.

'We don't have anything in this shop,' the woman said, and now the contempt was no less confusing but it was not a mistake, it was real and as blunt and heavy as a baseball bat, 'that would suit you.'

'Unbelievable,' Sue would say years later, when Jane had recovered enough to see that the shame was not hers and could tell it as an amusingly pointed anecdote. 'I know people hated Americans during the war, but 1970, and in Yarralong… I can't believe someone could treat you like that!' Sue would hug her then, in anger and apology, because someone had, and no matter how often Jane rewound and replayed—was there a tear in her skirt, was a shirt button undone?—the woman continued to advance with a smile until she heard Jane's words.

'Thank you,' Jane replied, or maybe even 'Sorry,' because habit was stronger than thought and she was obviously in the wrong. Then she must have turned and walked out into the street and past the department store where the bath towels would also remain unbought, although those moments were as blocked from her mind as the instants surrounding an accident, which was how she felt, physically winded, her breath taken from her by scorn. How can I live here, she thought, if I can't even get served in a store? Then, So this is prejudice. This is what life's like for Winston, except I'm invisible until I talk. And knew that this was simultaneously gross overreaction and truth.

She felt shrivelled, diminished in body and soul, and wished she were home with Ian without the interruption of a forty-minute drive. Ian would be angry on her behalf, his outrage would comfort her—there was nothing wrong with her, Ian would say, this was not how things should be.

The day had taken longer than she'd realised; as she pulled in the gate Ian was already on his motorbike, driving the cows home for milking. Jane hurriedly stowed perishables, changed into jeans and rushed to the dairy to clean the milk vat, dumping in the first bucket of boiling water as Ian returned.

'Did you get the belts?'

She produced the bag. 'But I couldn't buy the china!'

Ian was already squatting at the pump, threading on the new belt as she told him the story. 'She wouldn't have expected you to buy something so expensive on your own,' he said. 'You shouldn't have gone without me.'

☙

When you have only one guide to a foreign land, you don't question whether these are the rules of the country or the rules of the guide; you forget that in any culture, norms vary from individual to individual, family to family. You only know that to be different is to be wrong, and that conformity will bring peace. And then you store away your mistakes, your obvious alienage, in the part of your soul labelled shame.

Or maybe you're more likely to react that way if you've always doubted your ability to live up to expectations; if you've always felt that life is a race run on an ever-accelerating treadmill of unachievable standards. If when you were five what you wanted to be when you grew up was tall like Mommy, and when you grew up you found that small was how you were going to stay.

At any rate, that's how Jane felt.

With the benefit of hindsight, it seems that she'd gone to Europe to finish growing up but had married Ian instead, and somehow along the way she'd exchanged living up to her mother for living up to her husband. She remembers thinking that thirty, her generation's definition of age and untrustworthiness, must be grown up, but when thirty arrived she was the mother of a demanding toddler and cast down by the repeated failures of miscarriage, and the self-confidence of adulthood had passed her by. Maybe it was one of those pivotal developmental stages, like encouraging a two year old's innate sense of tidiness before you condemn them to a life of disorder—if you don't become an adult at thirty, you've missed the boat, doomed to a permanent, insecure adolescence.

Now here she is in a London antique shop, coveting a fragile, frivolous set of china, and realising that the wedding present money had never been spent.

Chapter
NINE

The joy of Bill's homecoming, the delirium of reunion with his wife and introduction to their new daughter, is tempered by the fresh realisation of the absence of his brother and grandfather. Although it is not the same sharp grief he feels for Bert, he wishes Grandpère could have waited to meet Ruth and Jane, and so on the soft June morning that is the first anniversary of the old man's death, the three of them visit the grave.

'You know,' Bill says, his hand on Jane's bonneted head, shielding it from the cold wind of hatred, 'once he left the French shore, Grandpère never saw any of the rest of his family again—not even his children. Dad says no one even came to the funeral. You wonder what went wrong.'

With a satisfying sense of theatre, Ruth watches a short, stocky woman, bright eyed and brisk stepped, carry a generous bunch of lilac across the cemetery towards them. 'We might be about to find out.'

Tante Isabelle is the youngest of Grandpère's six children; never married, she's been brought here today by a nephew

THE HOUSE AT EVELYN'S POND

with business to do in Applevale. She begins in French but switches easily to English at the look of incomprehension on Bill's face. Ruth does not fare much better—school-girl Swiss French bears little resemblance to rapid colloquial Acadian.

'So you are William?' she demands. 'Or Albert?'

'Bert's dead,' Bill says gruffly.

Her face softens. 'Too many nephews dead; Raymond and Robert, and now you say Albert as well, and we didn't even know it. That's long enough for this nonsense, don't you think?'

Bill nods, but Ruth adds, 'We were just wondering what… the nonsense was.'

'That takes some time to tell!' says Isabelle with the gleeful expression of a storyteller with a captive audience. 'And this is perhaps not the place for it, you standing with that little one.'

Jane blows a raspberry, waiting for the usual expression of delight, but Isabelle's aching for a baby is too long outgrown for her to find this clever. 'She is how old?'

'Nearly five months.'

'She will not be tall like her father, I think. I never thought I'd see a Dubois so big as this one! But there is something of Georges around the eyes. And Georges?' she adds quickly. 'He is well? It's an eternity since I've seen him, since the war, and now there's been another war and still I haven't seen him. Such stupidity!'

They find a bench in the warming sun. Tante Isabelle, to hear the story as she tells it, has always been the peacemaker, wanting Maman to forgive her son for marrying outside the faith, but who would listen to her? And then when Maman died and Papa wanted to make the peace, the others were so strong against it, saying Maman had died of a broken heart and it was all Georges' fault, so that there was no peace at all and Papa went off to live with Georges. She, Isabelle, had tried again to make peace, but they couldn't be reasonable.

Then the letter about Papa's death had gone to the wrong address and arrived the week after the funeral, and they said that Georges had done it on purpose, but she had said to them, is he a magician, to know Louis had built a new house?

She has not drawn breath by the time nephew Bernard, oldest son of Louis of the new house, the bad back, and six other features that Ruth and Bill have already forgotten, arrives. Bernard is stoic and silent—perhaps in self-defence, thinks Ruth, if this is a sample of the women in the family—but he shakes hands warmly and is content to wait. If there is bad blood between the families, it doesn't seem to have bled on to the cousins.

'Do you have children, Bernard?' Ruth asks, already plotting, already greedy for Jane and a net of kinship to anchor her so that she will never ever wonder who she is and how she came to be born where she was.

Bernard grins shyly. 'Three of them, and my wife waits for another in July.'

'Jane,' says Ruth, 'you have cousins!'

'Twenty-seven cousins to Bill,' says Isabelle, counting briefly. 'And the children of cousins—I don't know how you say that in English—that I will need to think, because it changes.'

'A plethora of cousins', Ruth murmurs in Jane's ear, adding in Myrtle's ten nieces and nephews. The baby gurgles, which might have been more at the tickle of her mother's breath than delight at relatives.

Isabelle continues to count but Ruth doesn't mind about the exact numbers, or the terminology of seconds and once removed; she will never become interested in the genealogy of faded certificates—it's the stories she wants, stories that create the larger world of family and history and the smaller one of identity. Which is exactly what Tante Marie-Josette collects. Isabelle is family peacemaker, busybody and occasionally what her great-niece Jane will learn to call stirrer, but Marie-Josette, similarly spinster but a generation older, has inherited tales of fortune and mis-, luck and courage. The English daughter-in-law of an estranged nephew is not the link to posterity that she had anticipated, but when the rapprochement is complete she accepts it eagerly.

So, every few months from now until the old lady dies in 1961, Ruth drives down to the French shore, a long hour if Bill drives and considerably less if she does herself. She takes Jane, and then Mike and then Rick, and then they are all in school and she goes alone; she will stop on the way home for scallops in Digby or blueberries at a roadside stall, and often for a walk at Port Royal, peopling the empty fort with the stories she's heard.

In between she reads history and studies French, the same assiduity that she threw into learning to fly at university now concentrated on gleaning all that she can of her children's heritage. (Bill, aware of his wife's sharp mind and the limited stimulus that a farm and rural community provide for it, watches without comment and some relief. When she's learning, she's happy, will be his motto throughout the next forty-nine years.)

Brought up to be amused by regional dialects in Britain, determined to keep her own accent and avoid idiosyncratic Valley phrasings in English, she is equally determined to lose her expensively acquired French accent and learn every nuance of St Mary's Bay Acadian. And although her proper English inflection never quite loses itself in the rapid French, she becomes fluent enough to follow the stories—because stories, Marie-Josette says, must be told in French, English being a language for facts and business, not the subtleties of hearts and history.

Marie-Josette tells the stories as if they are from her own time, as if she herself has seen the smoke of her sacked home in the Deportation of 1755 or knows the two Guillaumes, a generation apart, who were navigators—'On boats, you understand...'

Accounts of old sailing voyages are added to Ruth's list of reading and become one thing in which Bill will join her, intrigue in the details of direction overcoming the lack of interest in cold water.

But the family started with Bernard, Marie-Josette explains, just a boy in 1604 when he sailed with his carpenter father on Champlain's expedition to build Port Royal...

Ruth begins with a search for these snippets of past lives, family tales for her children to cherish, but her abiding passion is the pattern that a story makes as it wends its way through time and space. Tragic or fortuitous coincidence; the ragged edges of war and the hard lines of peace jostle and shape the soft flesh of human destiny. Cause and effect stretch back through history; entanglements ripple across oceans.

Impossible, she thinks, applying the Oxford-trained brain that she believes is commonsense, to speculate on why Bernard returned with his own family to this uncharted wilderness without first studying the French wars of religion. She speculates on whether the Edict of Nantes and subsequent horrors were the reasons for steadfast Acadian pacifism through a century of conflict, but decides that the recently finished war, so soon after the one to end all wars, disproves any theory of peace born of blood.

However, unlike the classics she's been brought up to study, family tales do not have neat endings; legends can quickly unravel when small holes are picked at with the veracity of history texts.

Bernard's son Louis, who is said to have been born in Port Royal, married a Mi'kmaq woman and became a fur trader. 'But tragically,' the old lady sighs, 'Louis was cut off from his father during the war of the fur trade.'

Ruth, wondering whether the name Dubois comes from this life in the woods, goes back to read the history: dates of colonisation, the land grant for the first Acadian-born French child, the internecine fur wars.

Louis could not have been born in the New World.

However, for nearly three hundred years, this story has been part of his family, shaping the family as the family shapes the story. After the terror of the Deportation, would the sixty-five year old Bernard-le-Jeune have returned to Grand Pré from his twenty years in Cherbourg if he hadn't been descended from one of the very first Acadians?

Ruth is never sure whether Marie-Josette has come to the conclusion that the story is more important than the truth, or whether, having little interest in reading more official histories, she has simply never added up the dates.

*

Jane has always been struck more by the divergence in what is known about different ancestors. She knows that her own story, sandwiched between her charismatic mother and daughter, will be one of the invisibles.

Perhaps this feeling was behind the project she began in her second year at Narling Primary and briefly imagined as a paper: 'Children's Own Stories: A Novel Approach to the Social Sciences'. They would look at not only their own brief lives but the context they'd been inserted into: family, history and society. Jane pictured it as a social snapshot, especially in schools with a less homogenous racial mix than her class's one Italian child, one half-Dutch, one Koori and twenty-two Anglo–Celts. For many of the latter, her own accent was the most foreign they knew.

The Koori girl's mother came to see her at lunch. Her people were worried, she said, although she did not word it so bluntly or directly, that Jane wanted to appropriate their stories. The children's family stories belonged to them and their kin, not to a teacher to put in a book. 'We've had enough stolen,' she did not say, but Jane—discussing, explaining, finally convincing that it was empowerment not confiscation she was aiming at—heard it and felt the weight of a history she hadn't known she shared.

Ruth has always told herself that her study of family history is purely for her children's benefit, and her sense of betrayal when they all leave the province is deep.

I've used you as a journal for nearly thirty years, she writes to Mary after Rick's departure, *so perhaps you won't question my sanity now. The last thing one would wish for one's children is a life of un- or underemployment in an increasingly impoverished province. (I'm sure you'll have noted the irony in the only one interested in farming having followed her husband to the opposite end of the world to do so.) They've each done the best, or the only thing they could do—so why do I feel so angry?*

I suppose it's not pure anger. It's more the feeling of going to infinite trouble to present the perfect gift and being slapped in the face for one's pains. Rejection.

The worst of expressing an emotion on paper is the way in which it exaggerates into melodrama. One feels quite ashamed. (Though not enough, I note, to cross it out.)

Which will make Jane, sitting in her childhood bedroom another twenty years later, wonder whether her mother's emails, written with the facility of delete keys, have always been as spontaneous as they've seemed.

A yet more humiliating thought has just struck me. Is it possible that I'm simply experiencing the despondency all mothers feel when their children grow up and leave home? Perhaps I could take up reading women's magazines on 'How to Keep Cheerful in the Empty Nest'.

I think I'd rather go on being cross.

'Oh, Mom!' Jane thinks despairingly. She doesn't wonder, though, at Ruth sharing this with an unseen cousin rather than a husband. Her mother, who never enjoyed allowing sentiment to defeat logic, preferred Bill to see her in the light she had chosen to paint herself.

✺

In Ruth's personal mythology, her first Canadian Christmas is not the one that occurred a few days after she arrived, a clumsily bulging parcel fussed over by strangers. She prefers to forget the nights of lying wide-eyed in the cold bedroom, her body with its restless passenger as alien as the husband on the other side of the world, as unknown as his friendly parents and embittered sister asleep just down the hall. She has remoulded the story, obliterating the loneliness that drove her to open the curtains on the night skies, braving the chill air for the familiarity of sidereal patterns and sometimes, during the baby's quiet spells, losing herself in a projection of flight. There is nothing shamanic about Ruth's imagination; she visualises a Spitfire on the runway, feels the weight of the cockpit cover as she lowers it over her head and the throbbing of the Merlin engines readying for take-off. Once in the air, she dips and soars through the blackness, guided only by the constant stars.

She will forget completely that on some nights, when the baby or other discomforts of pregnancy make her flight dream impossible, the stars seem a cold comfort and the absence of any friendly light below them makes her wonder if any place on earth is as isolated as this.

She will deny that on Christmas Day itself the unaccustomed quantity and richness of the food leave her queasy and uncomfortable, and the strain of being merry with these intimate strangers, knowing that the unfamiliar routine is the one that will be hers for life, has her crying in her room before supper.

She will simply count the first Christmas as the one that came twelve months later.

The house at Evelyn's Pond has been theirs since the spring; it is part of her now, its corners and gables as familiar as a childhood friend. She has blossomed into it; only her room at home (inspected by Nanny, even when she returned at the start of the war) and at St Hilda's in the Oxford years have ever been her own. To place a chair in the parlour the way she wants it, to decide on the colour of the new paint for the kitchen, seems an extraordinary freedom.

And her husband is hers. Oh so hers. And her body is her own—for although Ruth copes well with pregnancy she doesn't enjoy it, and now the baby is weaned she is as strong, as fit as she's ever been, sometimes as full with brimming life as that strange night in the soft Swiss snow. And Jane, who sleeps through the night and laughs more than she cries, who crawls strongly but is not yet into the roaming disaster-area of toddlerhood, is still hers, and melts her heart with joy and pride.

The snow comes on the Saturday before Christmas, a gentle, solid fall, showing off for an English bride with its draping of barn roof, frosting of fir trees and mounding of fenceposts.

'Should have cut the tree yesterday,' says Bill, 'so we wouldn't have to tramp through all that snow.' He has one eye on his wife as he says it—he'd promised her white Christmases, that first doodlebug June evening, and he knows how her eyes will spark at the thought of that adventure now. The day is so mild, sunny and bright that he feels almost smug, as if he's arranged it specially—which he would have, if he could.

George and Myrtle arrive; Myrtle has brought mince tarts and shortbread. 'Leave Jane with me,' she begs when she sees that Ruth is determined to tramp with the men, but—'It's her first Christmas!' exclaims the baby's mother. 'She should start it properly.'

So Jane is well bundled, in snow suit and mitts, with her

red tuque on top, and tied by a scarf onto the toboggan. The adults pull on boots, coats, hats and mitts; Bill gets the axe and they all head into the woods. It is not deep enough for snowshoes—'You'll get a chance yet!' Bill assures his wife.

The snow is just deep and sticky enough for the men's feet to make neat holes, which the toboggan smudges before Ruth reprints them. There is a different atmosphere as they enter the woods, a primordial stillness, 'lovely, dark and deep,' thinks Ruth, though she is not yet familiar enough with American poetry to be sure where the line has sprung from.

She breaks a fir twig and inhales the sharp scent, imagines herself as a tracker, partner to an intrepid *courier du bois*. Her face is fresh with cold, as invigorating as an elixir of youth. She scoops a snowball, clapping it firm between her mittens, but afraid that she might hit George or spatter Jane, changes her aim from Bill to a distant tree. A pheasant flies up in shock, showering snow behind him.

They tramp on through the maples, skeletal storers of sweetness, and on to a patch of young firs. 'You choose,' says Bill, scooping Jane up from her toboggan.

Ruth feels the two men enjoying her delight, the bond between them so close in this moment that it nearly glows, and she is stabbed by a sliver of pure happiness, framing this scene in her mind as one of those rare moments in life that can be taken out later like a snapshot to be cherished.

The Christmas tree candidates are dwarfed by the parent trees; Ruth is surprised to find her first choice towering over her. 'I wasn't intending to cut a hole in the ceiling,' says Bill, 'but if that's what you want!'

She darts between smaller ones, not over ten feet; some have grown too close to their neighbours and are squashed on one side; one has a broken branch and several have bent heads, but finally she finds it, Jane's first Christmas tree. It's only nine feet tall, eight when it's felled, perfectly symmetrical, and the tips of its branches are so fresh and surprising that she can hardly bear to have it cut, but Bill says it would have begun to crowd next year, and either it or its neighbours would have to go soon.

She holds Jane, who is surprised by the thumps of the axe and amused by its swinging glint, and then they return home in triumphant procession. Like Peter and the Wolf, Ruth thinks, although the tree had not been not such a formidable opponent.

This is the first year, too, that Bill, remembering six lonely Christmases, begins the tradition of posting an invitation on a bulletin board at Greenwood Air Force Base. He has only just reached the mess door when he meets Hank McBain coming out.

Hank, first met in training for their pioneering flight in that cold Hudson over the North Atlantic, last heard of missing over France—which was not, it appears, the end of his story.

They retire to the mess to fill in the gaps. It's less than a year since Bill's been in an officer's mess; the atmosphere is familiar but he no longer belongs. But Hank is still in—'I'd never have picked you for a mug who'd sign on again!'

Hank hadn't known what else to do; could no longer imagine civilian life. The girl he'd been engaged to had met someone else while he was recuperating from a broken ankle in a French barn; married while he was in Colditz. He's glad he hadn't known it at the time.

He stares moodily into his beer; his story is not yet easy to tell. 'I was on bombers—Lancs. Good crew; the pilot was as green as the rest of us, a lanky kid from Moose Jaw who looked like he should be cutting the corn or whatever they do in Moose Jaw, but he grew up fast. Top pilot; top captain. The rest of the crew was English except for a South African rear gunner.

'You know the saying about the first mission and the last being the most dangerous? I don't know if it was that or not; sometimes your time is up. They'd changed the number of missions so often none of us really believed it was the last one. We thought we'd just go on flying till we died.'

He laughs without humour. 'We were right, too, except for me.

'It was one of those big raids—a thousand planes to Berlin. You wouldn't believe what it was like!'

Bill realises that Hank didn't see D-day or Arnhem, and is quiet.

'I don't know what it did; should have smashed the bejesus out of Berlin and got us on the road to winning the war. I sure as hell hope so because we took some flak when we were nearly out of Germany; the gunner...' He pauses again, swallows. 'Poor bastard didn't have a chance. And the navigator had a big hole in his thigh. We put a tourniquet on, but—. I spent too long with the gunner, that's the thing. If I'd got the tourniquet on West first, he might have made it.'

Bill is silent. That night, lying snug against Ruth, he will think of the things he could have said, and though he knows they wouldn't have made any difference, feels a sense of failure in his silence.

'Moose gave us the order to evacuate. I heard the copilot arguing for him to get out too, but he wanted to hold her steady for us. In the end the copilot didn't get out in time either; I was the last to jump and by the time I'd opened my parachute the Lanc had gone into a spin. You feel sick when you see any plane crash and burn, but when it's your own crew...'

He gulps the rest of his beer, wipes his mouth with the back of his hand. Bill will not be able to think of anything he could have said to that.

'I landed not far from Westie, but it was no good; he must have come down on the bad leg—I had a lot of time to think it out later—and twisted it so badly the tourniquet had come off. Funny thing was, I didn't realise I'd broken my own ankle till I saw that the poor bastard was dead, but when I looked down then my foot was sitting at a funny kind of angle and swelling like a football inside my flying boot. Hurt like hell once I noticed. We'd landed on the edge of a wood—I heard later that the flight engineer landed in a tree. The official line on him was shot trying to evade capture; I always wondered if he ever got out of the tree.

'Anyways, I was in a field, and it was light enough by then I could see a haystack, so I got myself there quick as I could and buried my parachute in the bottom. Still didn't know if I was in Germany or France, but I figured that the best I could do was turn my back to the sunrise and keep on going. Problem was, even with a stick I was bloody slow. After two days a French girl saw me creeping out from my next haystack. I thought I'd had it, but she was more worried about getting me out of there—I was still way too close to where the Lanc had come down. She set my ankle and her brother drove me past a patrol in a load of manure to a Resistance safe house till I was fit to travel. I got nearly to Marseilles before I was arrested. Didn't like prison much; I kept getting out and they kept putting me back and finally they sent me to Colditz. Bloody awful way to sit out the war. But that's enough of me, how've you been?'

'Come out home for Christmas,' says Bill.

By Jane's first Australian Christmas, ten months after stepping onto the hot tarmac of Tullamarine, she was starting to believe that home could be the Goulburn, not the Annapolis, Valley. Winter had been a shock; no snow, she discovered, did not mean warm and in a dark and draughty house the heat of the wood stove did not reach the clammy bedroom.

But as the temperatures began to climb she felt herself thrive: *Think of me sunbaking on Christmas Day*, she wrote to Patsy and Gail, *while you shovel snow!*

That was late October, last sea mail before Christmas, but

it stayed true all the way to the day she went Christmas shopping. She didn't have much on her list—the glossy *This is Australia* had left for Evelyn's Pond long ago; a classical record for Ian and something for his parents' new house, pottery coffee mugs maybe—but it would still be Christmas shopping. Still the anticipation of pleasure, the buzz of excitement in the tinselled stores, the old ladies in queues who smile approvingly at some gift intended for mother or father.

It was a hot day, furnace hot. Maybe that's all it was. Maybe it was just that stepping out of oven heat into the shops' chilly blast is not as comforting as coming into overheated buildings from outside frigidity. The Christmas lights were dim against the glare of the sun, the Santa Clauses sweltered in their fur-trimmed suits, the pine trees stacked outside the greengrocers drooped limp and pathetic, and the canned carols of dark winter evenings sang surreal and alien. Relentlessly the day continued to point out that some customs are not transplantable, and if not customs, why people?

Maybe it was just that childhood Christmases can never be regained, or that a latent xenophobia makes our earliest traditions the one true standard against which all else will be compared. Whatever it was, when the woman ahead of her in the queue at the music shop said conspiratorially, 'Won't you be glad when it's over?' Jane was mortifyingly afraid that she was going to burst into tears.

And did, when she got home to find the red candles in her cleverly adapted bottlebrush arrangement on the windowsill melted into sad, recumbent curves, which was not supposed to happen at Christmas, because Christmas was supposed to be in the winter. Christmas was the butterfly anticipation of hanging stockings on the mantelpiece and the four a.m. waking to wiggle toes to the end of the bed and feel for that same stuffed stocking with the lumps and bumps all the way down to the tangerine in the toe, and going downstairs to the magic of the lit tree and the presents heaped under it, and only crumbs and a rimmed glass left from Santa's milk and cookies and the carrot for his reindeer gone too.

The memory of that part of Christmas is subsumed with the loss of childhood and reborn with the advent of children, and Jane was at that stage in between where the magic had been lost and not yet rediscovered. But that part was not all. If she closed her eyes and said 'Christmas,' she could smell the freshness of fir and feel the cold on her red cheeks and the comforting warmth of a kitchen; Christmas was darkness and houses outlined with lights; it was looking out her window to the smoothness of snow and moonlight on the white; it was neighbours stopping by for eggnog and stamping snow off boots and buttoning coats up warmly to go back out to the cold. Christmas was so enmeshed with winter that if she went back far enough into childhood she could taste the wool of her scarf wrapped over her face and the texture of ice chewed from frozen mittens and feel the rhythm of Ruth sweeping snow off her snow suit before the unwrapping in the kitchen. It was church, like the houses, redolent with pine and fir; it was breath frosting in the air when they came out afterwards and the silence of the night at the welcoming lit house. It was watching her grandfather and then her father harnessing a horse to the sleigh that went for the doctor the night she was born, and the sound of the sleigh bells, and the whoosh of the sleigh in the night. It was the playing of Ruth's carol records, the taste of tourtiere and turkey and cranberries; the primitive contrast of warmth and cold, darkness and light, and over it all was the red glow of inner happiness and knowing that everyone in her world shared that joy and that knowledge.

For the first time Jane understood that, same language and loving husband notwithstanding, she was a migrant, and if she was going to survive in a foreign country she would have to bend, lose parts of her identity and heritage.

Understood that no matter how much she grew to love gum trees and wattles, she would never quite lose the longing for spruce trees and maples; that a part of her heart might always turn over at the sound of a soft, flat accent that was not quite American and the distinctive Canadian sound of house and about. That sometimes there would be a physical ache of loneliness for someone who could understand the references of her childhood—although luckily, having not yet experienced either childbirth or parents' aging, she didn't realise just how searing that particular longing could be.

So Jane decided that the way to combat homesickness was to make new traditions, something that belonged fresh to Ian and herself. That they would have dinner, at noon, with Ian's parents, was understood, though Jane did not realise at the time that even at fifty, when she will be cooking turkeys at home and transporting them, she will not be allowed to host the meal herself. There were several things in which Fred and Dulcie's sense of rightness was immutable, and responsibilities of the older generation were the mainstay.

'You can bring the pudding,' Dulcie said, that first Christmas. 'Do you need a recipe?'

With a flash of inspiration, Jane saw the answer for a perfect meld of tradition and place, and could have hugged herself, childlike, with the secret of surprise. 'I've got one,' she said, which was true: Ruth, love of tradition overcoming dislike of cooking, had sent a starting-your-new-life in-Australia gift of a looseleaf binder with family recipes copied out in her most formal script. Some were from her war brides' cookbook, some were Acadian—most of which Jane had no recollection of Ruth ever making—and there was Mrs Beeton's plum pudding. But that was not the one she intended to use.

Something old, something new—though she should have remembered that was for weddings—glacéd fruit and liqueur for tradition, ice cream for the climate, the recipe cut from a review of a new Italian restaurant in the food section of the *Age*.

'If you can't find focaccia, sponge cake will do...' As it would be twenty years before she could find the former, Jane attempted the latter. '...Preferably, a rather dense sponge'— which was still the way most of hers turned out, luckily enough.

In the absence of a churn, the ice cream was less success-ful, although Ian's dog, in secret collusion, seemed well satisfied, but the chocolate and strawberry layers were very nearly home-made, their grated or crushed ingredients mixed into the bought vanilla ice cream by hand. Then 'mould and freeze' the instructions said blithely, not mentioning that it might take two days to successfully complete the manoeuvre; there seemed to be a very fine gap between the ice cream being soft enough to mould and firm enough not to slide down into the bottom of the bowl.

'Why do you need the esky?' Ian asked as they climbed into the ute after morning milking, showered, Sunday-dressed and gift-laden.

'For the pudding.'

'It's not going to go off that quickly!'

'It might,' Jane said, and Ian realised that she was as excited as a kid about Christmas and her contribution to it, and smiled with only a trace of condescension at her northern fear of heat.

'We'll put it on now,' said Dulcie when esky and present box had been brought in from the ute and Merry Christmas kisses exchanged. 'Three hours to steam?'

Feeling like a conjurer, Jane pulled out her cassata. Years later, it would amaze her that she'd been so intent on this surprise and the forging of her own new traditions, that she'd never once thought of consulting anyone about how they felt about changing theirs.

The answer was obvious. The tableau was as frozen as the dessert.

'Good thing we didn't drop that in the pot!' Dulcie said,

recovering herself quickly and opening the freezer. 'That *would* have been a mess.'

Ian surreptitiously checked the esky to see if his wife might have brought a proper pudding as well and worried about what his father might say. Jane had been uncharacteristically touchy the last few days; he had no idea why but suspected it wouldn't take much for her to burst into tears. 'I'll be Father Christmas!' he announced. 'Who wants a present?'

That afternoon, when they had worked their way through roast chicken, lamb, beef and vegetables, and dessert had been salvaged by spooning cassata onto fruit cake and smothering it with custard and cream, Jane and Dulcie washed the dishes as the men dozed in preparation for afternoon tea. Hands busy in the soapy water, her mother-in-law asked the question that had been bothering her all day. 'Do you have Christmas in Canada?'

Ruth and Bill's first family Christmas, the Christmas of '46, is also the start of Bill telling his sister, 'Don't ever say I didn't bring you anything home from the war.'

Or so the family story goes. In fact Bill wouldn't have said that on Christmas Day, because it would have been cruel, unlucky and destructive; but he did say it eventually, and even Louise smiles when he says it at her wedding, although she does not find it funny for nearly as long or as often as Bill and Hank do.

In fact the only hint of the future, when Louise and Hank meet on Christmas morning, is not Louise's smiling or Hank's gallantry but the baby. Jane is frightened at first and then, when he lets her reach and twist it, fascinated by Hank's handlebar moustache; Hank clowns energetically and patiently, and Louise, who unless she thinks herself unobserved, normally treats Jane as if she were about as fascinating as a pet geranium, coos, peekaboos and even does a capable aunt act, whisking the baby off the visitor's knee at the first whiff of trouble and returning her clean and fresh a few minutes later. Naturally she also listens and laughs at Hank's stories, but there's no particular surprise in that, because to listen to Bill and Hank, the war had been one long jolly boys' own prank.

Ruth watches the others and wonders how much they believe. Not that the stories are untrue, not that Hank hadn't lit a fire with the back of his sentry box one cold night of guard duty, breaking off a bit more and a bit more until there was nothing left but the frame, or that Bill hadn't mastered the mess game of running up a wall and adding to the score of footprints on the ceiling, 'long before I met Ruth, of course!'—but there is so much they can't mention that these snippets give a lie to the whole.

'Landing at Prestwick, you remember that? Fools that we were, we thought there'd be some r and r, a day anyways, my God, we'd flown right across the Atlantic and it wasn't that long since you'd get a hero's welcome and your name in the papers. But for us it was "Jump on the train, boys, and get going."'

'Straight to Bournemouth.'

'Funniest little trains you ever saw,' Hank adds, forgetting that his hostess may have seen them, may not even consider them funny. 'And it was the heck of a long way to sit up all night.'

'You were lucky to get a seat!' Ruth says tartly.

'Lucky? Bill was the lucky one, that's for sure. Lucky he ever got out of Bournemouth.'

'And lucky to've had this delicious dinner tonight,' says Bill gallantly—desperately, thinks Ruth—but Hank will not be detoured around Bournemouth.

'The hotel I got sent to was okay, but Bill being an officer, his was really top class.'

'Everyone went to Bournemouth when they got to England,'

Bill explains pedantically, 'to wait for their posting. It would've been a pretty place if the beaches hadn't been full of barbed wire. Then I went to Scotland.'

'You're so boring, Bill!' snaps Louise. 'Let Hank tell the story.'

Ruth pats her husband's hand, raising an eyebrow at his sister, who doesn't notice, having eyes only for the narrator.

'Anyways, I saw Bill go off to his hotel and I went to mine. All you had to do was turn up for parade twice a day and if your name wasn't called you went off again, played tennis, whatever you liked. So that first afternoon, I was back at the hotel playing pool with some of the fellows when we heard a Messerchmidt coming in low. We dived under a table but the plane was so close I could see its bomb bay open and it looked to me like it was right over Bill's hotel. I saw that bomb drop and there was just nothing I could do except think this wasn't supposed to happen, it was our first day and I don't know if I thought the war would wait for us to settle in or what, but I couldn't believe it. Then the bomb hit, and you had to believe it then. Thing is, Bill had said all he wanted to do that day was sleep, and I knew he'd have to be in his room.'

'But I wasn't,' says Bill. 'I'd just got unpacked, even took a picture of the garden from my window, which I guess would be the last picture anyone ever took from that hotel, when word came that Group Captain Somebody wanted five Canadian officers, and so me and four others were sent to his hotel, and five minutes later we heard the bang. Funny thing was I never did meet that group captain, which is a shame, because I'd sure have liked to shake his hand!' He grins apologetically at his wife—this is not a story he'd intended to share with her—but Ruth is not going to allow herself to think about bombs and their consequences on Christmas Day. She is watching her sister-in-law, who is gazing at Hank with the sort of awe appropriate for a hero who has defused a bomb or shot down a raiding craft with his air pistol.

Louise, thinks Ruth, has no idea whatsoever of the randomness of fate, the tenuous nature of the threads that spin our lives. But you cannot protect yourself with intellectualism forever, and when Hank quotes Lord Haw-Haw's broadcast from Berlin, 'How did you like that, you Canadians? We'll be back to see you again soon!', Ruth feels venom rising in her like bile and is afraid of what could vomit out if she opens her mouth. She's aware that of all the evil things that happened in the war, the supercilious sneers and misinformation of a traitor are not even on the list; she knew people at the time who could listen to him and laugh. However forgiveness is not high on Ruth's list of virtues—she will never forget his broadcast on the night Miles died, and to think of his mocking Bill's intended death as well is more than she can bear in polite company.

It may be, too, that when you have seen rescue workers picking their way through your childhood home and can do nothing but hope they don't bring out any bits of your parents' bodies while you're watching, bomb stories will never make for easy listening.

'Time for Jane to be in bed,' she announces, her voice surprisingly level. She can guess from the almost imperceptible way in which Louise is leaning towards her guest that Hank is about to hear of the bombing death of his hostess's parents, and perhaps of her sister-in-law's role as comforter. Which is fair enough, but is part of the reason why Louise will never hear all the layers of that tragedy. The loss of one set of parents is quite enough for an after-dinner story; two would be melodrama.

Myrtle heats the baby's bottle in the kitchen, but Bill interrupts her at the stairs and follows his wife to what Ruth still calls the nursery. His mother is relieved; much as she loves Ruth, she has never met anyone so difficult to console, or even to know whether consolation is required.

Ruth herself isn't sure what her emotions are. She's been

euphoric all day in her various Christmas roles, been briefly engulfed by the old rages and hatreds of the war, the desolation of loss and the relief of love. It's a heady mix and when Bill slips his arms around her as she straightens up from the crib, she twists against him with the fierceness he'd fantasised about during their long separation, but never dreamed of tonight, putting their daughter to bed at the end of a long day. He finds Ruth beautiful naked or clothed, but never more exciting than in high heels, making her nearly as tall as he, and under her best dress the stockings ending in garters. His hands are already at her skirt when she pulls away—'Your mother might want to say goodnight to Jane'—but he feels the slight quiver of her flesh as his hand slips upwards between her thighs.

Bill thinks of himself as enslaved by his passion for Ruth but the realisation of the power his touch holds for her is the most potent aphrodisiac he knows. 'Mother thinks you're upset. She'll leave us alone.' He kicks the laundry basket against the door just in case, and hears the shudder of her breath as his fingers tease through the parachute silk of her knickers to feel her warm and moist and opening to him.

And so, in whispered passion and later bemusement, against the wall and discreetly out of sight of the crib where Jane is falling asleep with her bottle against her lips, Michael is conceived.

Which is why even the Bournemouth bomb story is transformed in Ruth's memory to a golden Christmas glow.

✆

If Ruth sees stories, no matter how tangled their web, as essentially linear, and Megan understands the universe as an intricate dance of synchronicities past and future, Jane views the world in strata. History to her is associated with place; in one of the parallel universes her daughter talks about, perhaps she is an archaeologist, patiently sorting through layers of earth to discover the stories stacked in dust.

She had played with her brothers on the grass of Port Royal and stood with her husband on the sand of Gallipoli, but it came as an epiphany to her that each blade and grain of the world's less bloodied corners holds as much history as those wept-over sites. When her EcoFarm group was asked to research the history of the Gundanna Lagoon, not five hundred metres from her own farm gate, she realised she'd found a new metier in life.

The lagoon was a small muddy waterhole straddling the riparian state forest and the old-money Chathams' end paddock. ('Isn't it a billabong?' Ruth asked, and though Jane explained the difference, her mother was not to be denied the use of such a unique word.) One bend was choked by a fallen river gum and in recent times it had often been scummed with blue-green algae in the summer, but when Megan was small it had been a favourite expedition for mother and daughter, close enough to walk, exotic enough for adventure, and peopled, in Megan's mind at least, with shadowy presences: 'They live there but we can't see them,' she explained. Jane and Ian added lagoon people to the list of their daughter's imaginary friends, but as an adult Megan continued to feel the quiet ghosts. Not threatening or creepy, she said, just there, which Jane found creepy enough, and now wondered whether even this project was another affront to these spirits.

She didn't have to believe in them to know who they were, but it shocked her to realise that after twenty-eight years in this country, she did not know one Aborigine with whom she could discuss their history. And although in the end she found phone numbers for two Koori community groups, neither was able to provide much information beyond a map with scattered dots showing the region's former meeting places, shell middens and the startling granite domes that rose out of the plains like the backs of breaching whales, an evidently sacred place now quarried and abandoned. Gundanna Lagoon, where water from wet winters would have remained trapped and fertile until the height of summer evaporation, was not marked and the life of its earliest inhabitants remained conjecture. A first-hand lesson in the irrevocability of the loss of history.

The rest of the project proceeded more satisfactorily. Working for the best part of a year, Jane identified the encroaching noxious weeds and, with more difficulty, the true indigenous species, from cumbungi and knot weed to ubiquitous river red gum, recorded the vulnerable status of the Superb Parrot and other wildlife, and finally, in a satisfyingly thick, ring-backed publication, outlined management strategies for control, replanting and protection. The history was relegated to a page of anecdotes from older residents, some in nursing homes and some Ian's contemporaries, who corroborated his memories of the days when muddy waters were clear enough to drink, when Murray cod could be caught in the bend, eagles soared overhead, goannas scurried underfoot and baby turtles hatched on the banks. If some of the stories were touched with childhood sunshine, the details remained too consistent for them not to be broadly true, and she included them as not only a record of the past, but a hope for the future.

Chapter
TEN

*J*ane hasn't returned to the sorting of Ruth's room since the shock of the dream-presaged photograph, but it must be done, time will run short and there's no point in putting it off. Etc. However, she continues to procrastinate until the day before she is due to fly, when the piles of belongings can no longer be ignored, and it's then that she finds the packet of cigarettes under the *Poldark* on the bedside table. Not deliberately hidden, simply laid down as a heavy smoker might, in easy reach for next morning's succouring drag, the book dropped haphazardly on top when the lamp was turned off for the night.

This time Jane does not wait to compose herself before facing Mary, marching down the stairs as enraged as if the endangered respiratory system belonged to an adolescent daughter rather than a dead mother.

'Didn't you know she'd started again? She was so lonely after your father died; she said a cigarette in the evenings gave her a sense of companionship.' (*A false sense*, Ruth had said, but Mary modifies. There is enough hysteria in the air already.)

Lonely. A widow with nothing but a cigarette as companion. Jane knows she should feel guilty, knows she is overreacting, but bad daughter Jane is furious, as if her mother had wilfully, spitefully, clogged up those arteries to avoid saying goodbye. How much longer would she have had without tar and nicotine? Another month, a year, a decade, a day? Nonsmokers die too, even of strokes and even at times inconvenient to their offspring, but at the moment Jane doesn't believe it. Besides, she's still stuck on the end of Mary's first sentence.

'*Again*? Mom didn't used to smoke.'

'Like the proverbial chimney before she went to Canada! She stopped on the ship. I don't know if she was seasick herself, but one of the women in her cabin was so ill she vomited whenever your mother lit up. She said after a few days the smell invaded the taste until she couldn't bear it.'

This is not at all how Ruth had described the war brides' ship to her daughter. White bread and orange juice, the awesome expanse of ocean, neat anecdotes of her mothercraft lessons.

'She smoked the whole time she was pregnant with me!'

A more satisfying, self-righteous focus of rage, stripped of guilt though not of futility; no wonder she never grew tall like Mommy. No wonder she, unlike her later-born, nicotine-free brothers, is a direct throwback to the short and stocky Dubois, without a modifying inch from mother or father.

On the bumpy bus back to civilisation Megan's mind is split between fear for her grandmother and the more selfish but immediate desolation of leaving Adam. What will be will be, but there comes a time when being takes acting and the thought of being without him is so grey that she cannot see through it. The bodies that had touched so gingerly, so apparently haphazardly, on the outgoing bus, seven days, a lifetime ago, now rub companionably, tenderly, though with some apprehension; legs waiting to walk away touch differently than legs anticipating the continuance of leisurely entwining.

They have talked about everything but this. Everything except what happens now. Distant futures, maybe futures, but not the right here and now of what we'll do when we get off the ferry in Tsawwassen and is it over, this week that seemed like love, like something that could never end, was it just the sea air and the ancient trees and the sense of freedom? And if one of us doesn't say something soon, thinks Megan, then the ferry will be bumping against the dock and we'll be strapping on backpacks and am I crazy thinking he wants me in his everyday life. So I'll simply say it, 'Can I stay at your place tonight?'

But she doesn't, because Adam is saying why doesn't she call her grandmother as soon as they get home, he's sure that everything will be alright but it will put her mind at ease, and it stabs her to see how she would have hurt him with that moment's doubt. The future can be delayed till morning; till she leaves Vancouver.

It's too late to phone Nova Scotia when they get home; Megan has a feeling that Ruth may be a late-night person, but she also knows that old people go to bed early and Ruth, after all, is old. 'Phone your parents,' says Adam, but no one is home. 'I'll call back,' Megan tells the machine, because parents are parents no matter how old you are and they mightn't understand about her staying with Adam. Or they might understand too well.

Then they have baths, separately because it's a small tub and they are really extraordinarily grimy and their hair is greasy but stiff with salt. Adam orders Thai takeaway because even noodles seem too much effort to cook, but by the time the delivery boy comes they have thought of something much more urgent than food, and the gang dang and the phad Thai phuk have to wait to be microwaved for breakfast the next morning. And making love in a bed in an apartment is not the same as loving in a small tent with the waves breaking on the beach, but there is something to be said for a good mattress and fresh sheets, so that sometimes it is much, much nicer.

There is also the feeling of waking with the body of someone you love still wrapped close around you, and lazy morning loving. 'Whatever we do today,' says Adam, smug at having used up their entire supply of condoms, 'I'll have to get to a drugstore,' which Megan says sounds as if he needs a quick hit of heroin; but making love to her, Adam says, is more addictive than any drug. None of which is terribly original, but is part of the process of laying down their own private mythology, as well making them both feel infinitely desirable and sexy, which isn't such a bad thing either.

They're still languidly replete from this last fix when she asks, 'What are we going to do?'

Because it's now obvious that the magic is not just to do with holiday hedonism and is everything to do with life that goes on and is beginning to seem as if it cannot go on without the other. And they both know that Megan means after the holiday but Adam believes in plans and logic and is not quite ready to speak the future out loud, when it will become real. When you stop to think about love, it seems amazing that anyone could do it, could take the risk, could say no to a life which is spinning along quite nicely on its own and jump headfirst into someone else's, as if the writer had changed the plot midway through the story.

'You'll phone your grandmother,' he says, procrastinating, 'while I make some coffee. And when you hear that she's fine we'll decide.'

There is, of course, no answer. 'Out shopping?' Adam suggests, and Megan tries again, after coffee, after breakfast, after shower, until finally it's late enough for her mother to be awake in Australia.

Her mother is not in either. 'She must be in the dairy already,' says Megan, but is not convinced and this time she leaves Adam's number. Her father phones back: 'I'm afraid Nan died last week. Your mother's gone to England to get her.'

Megan had forgotten about her grandmother's bus tour, which was to have been over long before her own arrival at the farm; and although she'd thought she was sure Ruth was dead, she realises now that she hadn't been, not at all. She feels surprisingly lost before anxiety about her own mother overtakes her. The bleakness of the trip is not easy to imagine.

'Bloody awful,' Ian agrees. 'But she's having a few days with Mary before she takes the ashes back to Evelyn's Pond. Your uncles are flying out to meet her there.'

Adam holds Megan close as she hangs up and the back of her mind thinks how nice it is to be held like this, just for comfort, and maybe that's why men were made bigger and stronger, for feeling safe in times of need. Even strong women are allowed to think like this when tragedy falls hard on the heels of love.

'Poor Mum,' she says at last. Her own trip is thrown into confusion too, but she doesn't mind that, any more than she sees the shadow of exiled daughters and mothers over her own life. She phones Mary's. 'I'm okay,' Jane says. 'But you know the boys'—forgetting that Megan doesn't—'they're getting there Saturday morning and they'll go home again Sunday night. We're not going to be able to organise everything in one weekend. And I can't leave your father for too long this time of year!'

She finishes by telling her daughter not to worry; she feels better for having a whinge; the important thing is that Megan should have this holiday she's planned for so long.

'I think I should meet her there,' Megan says, staring at the phone and wondering whether it's possible to become addicted to being held comfortingly. 'She sounds like she's going to need some help.'

'I'll drive you,' says Adam quixotically. Which would be a sensible idea if Canada were the size of Luxembourg, or if trains, planes and Greyhound buses were all on strike. Or if he were in love, that song of poets now reduced by treacherous Italian scientists to a chemical imbalance with the properties of an obsessive-compulsive disorder. Luckily Megan and Adam have not yet read this research, so they consider the idea as if it were the product of a rational mind.

'You'll see more that way; we can stop where we like.'

'Do you still have that much leave? Don't you have any plans?'

'I was just going to visit my parents. They won't mind.'

Maybe they won't. They might be thrilled to hear that their son has been overwhelmed by love and will welcome Megan with open arms if they meet her one day. Or this could be the first step of a long-held grudge, a bitter family story about the time Adam promised to help them fix up the cottage or go down to the time-share in Mexico, and dropped them at a moment's notice. Either way, it won't make any difference to Megan and Adam's decision now.

And so practical, pragmatic Adam finds himself packing again; they pick up Megan's suitcase from the Y, picnic supplies from the supermarket, maps and accommodation guides from the British Columbia Autoclub. Two hours later they are on the road out of Vancouver, heading towards the Rockies, and ultimately, a continent later, the Annapolis Valley.

❧

There's something comforting about maps, Jane thinks. Maps are defined, with clear starting points, routes and destinations; north is north no matter where you are in the world,

even in upside-down hemispheres where cold is unaccount-
ably to the south (except that it is not unaccountable at all,
logic being the other pure pleasure of geography).

She's never worried that the possession of a sense of direction seems to be considered unfeminine by some psychologists
and a majority of men—Ian is not one of them, and neither
was her father. And she is impatient with the theory that
women are inherently unable to navigate, oestrogen defeating spatial skills on the challenge of heading south without
turning a map upside-down. This atavistic line never explains
why cave women, wandering further than usual in a quest
for berries or straying child, would not have needed to find
their way home, or why stories handed on from one generation of gatherers to the next wouldn't have included some
useful geographical data: the clear-water spring on the sunrise side of the hill; the magic mushrooms on the cold side of
the fallen tree.

In any case, whether her forebears had or not, Jane finds
navigation, real or virtual, a reassuring activity.

She just sometimes wishes that life could be as easily followed. If only destinations were known; if missed turn-offs
and wrong ways were quickly obvious. Not that she's sure
what fresh starts she'd make, but that's the point: with a map
she'd know.

If navigation is something that comes naturally to Jane, she
is intrigued on the other hand by the amount of housekeeping lore that Sue, that most women of her generation, know
as self-evident truth but that she must discover by trial and
error. A pinch of salt to stop colours running in the wash,
pegging clothes on the line inside out to prevent fading—this
is not the type of knowledge that interested Ruth, and no
matter how frustrated Jane becomes when she learns that her
sheets might not have pilled so badly if she hadn't washed

them with the towels, she's always been slightly smug about a mother who'd sooner discuss Lawrence than laundry. Which is perhaps why, when Megan left home and Jane passed on her own few Heloise hints, she felt as diffident as if attempting some last-minute birds-and-bees session.

◌

The role of housewife sits lightly on Ruth, as if it's one she's trying on for size and is likely to discard at any moment. It has nothing to do with loving Bill, or her happiness at choosing this life, or how much a part of her the house, the farm and the region have come to be. She often says that she doesn't know how her Mama could have shared her house for so many years with the cook and the daily, or the garden with the gardener, let alone accepted the strictly limited role Nanny had allowed in childcare. In fact she is surprisingly good at what she does, determinedly learning everything that a good farm wife needs to know. Myrtle is fond of telling anyone who will listen that, although her daughter-in-law arrived with barely the nous to boil water for tea, after a year she could have won prizes in the exhibition, if only she could have been persuaded to enter.

Myrtle exaggerates slightly on both ends. Ruth becomes a competent everyday cook, working her way through her war brides' recipe book, but the hands that could throttle back a twin-engined fighter plane produce heavy pastry and chewy cakes, and she quickly loses interest in this particular skill. And her love–hate relationship with the wood stove lasts for ten years, until the day that Simpson Sears delivers a glossy white electric stove, with elements regulated by precise dials and an oven that not only goes from cold to hot in twenty minutes but stays there without a constant vigil. The monster itself, relegated to baking potatoes or simmering soups as it warms the winter kitchen, becomes purely traditional and once again lovable.

The garden holds her longer. Myrtle's interest in flowers had not extended beyond a narrow bed of peonies and columbines beside the front porch, and Ruth will leave it like this for years, until her children leaving home throws her into a new frenzy of creativity and planting: pansies, petunias, crocuses, daffodils and roses to throw bright colours against darkly manured beds. However, from the very beginning she finds something innately satisfying about nourishing her family with vegetables she's grown and fruit she's picked, so that Myrtle's vegetable garden is continued and expanded as soon as the snow thaws in Ruth's first Canadian spring.

As a teenager Jane will ride her bike in the summers down the hill, past Evelyn's Pond to the corner of the road to Applevale, where she will board an old pick-up truck to Gordie Grimard's strawberry farm. It's standing room only by the time she joins, clinging to the jolting wooden cage while the bravest take turns waving at passing cars from the back bumper. She will never earn as much as she hopes, never as much as the Chase twins, who were born with strawberry-seeking fingers that turn their summers to gold, but enough to buy a new bridle, a heavy German snaffle bit to go in it, and mascara from Zellers. She will enjoy, for the first mornings at least, the sense of camaraderie and honest exchange of hard labour for earnings, and by the afternoons she will lose any doubt that her mother is right about school leading to university rather than work. And although the berries will regain their sweetness with time, the smell of hot strawberry leaves will nauseate her for the rest of her life.

Ruth's picking is not on a similar scale. Her berries ripen in short rows, at first barely enough for dessert—'pudding', Ruth calls it, even when it's fresh fruit with cream; carrots wave feathery tops, begging to be pulled; beans dangle from their vines; tomatoes plump and redden. Eventually there is more than enough for a meal, for a week of meals, and Ruth discovers the one household task that will bring her a true sense of satisfaction.

It's not just the food, though after the long rationed war years, when even if one rarely went truly hungry, appetite was seldom tempted and rarely sated, food will never be underrated again. It's not just because it requires one intense, though prolonged, burst of energy or because it's a clear-cut, slightly technical job at which she quickly feels competent. It's all of these, haloed with a ring of tradition and continuity which she is never able to feel when icing brownies or ironing Bill's good shirt.

She cans tomatoes and beans, strawberries, raspberries and blueberries, plums, pears and peaches; makes apple sauce, pickles (both dill and bread and butter), tomato ketchup and relish, and jams and jellies from anything that could possibly be smeared on bread. 'Don't stand still in the kitchen,' Bill tells the children every summer, 'or you'll wind up in a bottle and be served up for Christmas.' In the weeks beforehand she rewashes bottles, inspects for chips and cracks, replenishes her supply of lids and sealing wax. For a month the big canning kettle is never off the stove; the compost bucket overflows with kernels, pips and peels, and the kitchen could be mistaken for a peculiarly redolent sauna. From an up-ended chair on the corner bench, a linen udder drips apple juice into a bowl; boxes of fruit wait their turn along the walls, there is a constant rapping of bottles on counters to knock out spoiling air. Boiled jars are stacked in precise pyramids to cool, jellies catching the light like cathedral windows, the jams deeply red or warmly apricot, and the peaches golden and perfect.

Finally the kettle is moved back to the shed to collect dust and spiders for another year, and the bottles are moved to the pantry: satisfyingly generous, orderly rows of bounty, and sometimes surprising Ruth during the dark days of winter with their promise that spring will come again.

Of all the jams, the jellies and preserves, the blueberries remain her favourite. She doesn't particularly like their taste, but she loves the picking. It is an excuse to ramble away from the house in the sun on the cow path down to the low pasture, or if the midday heat has risen past pleasure, detouring through the woods; the secret joy of stumbling across the first ripe clusters, the powdery sheen of their deep blue against the green.

One year, when the children are in school and Ruth is still on her Acadian study quest, quizzing Marie-Josette on folklore, she begins collecting herbs and wild plants, dandelions for salad, teaberry and tansy for tea. It is essentially similar to what she might have learned from any British countrywoman but, as Bill points out, it would not have been so interesting in her own language and environment.

To her family's relief, the canning season brings her back to more conventional foods, and that August Myrtle, having nagged for years about the exhibition, slyly enters a gift bottle of blueberry preserve. It comes home with a blue rosette. 'What did I tell you?' asks Myrtle, and Ruth, though mocking her own reaction, is amazed at how pleased she is to have tangible proof of being a proper farm wife.

Not that Bill, who considers blueberry preserves the least of them, has ever doubted her wifely attributes. He has never got over his wonder that she should be his, this lovely, clever woman who turns to him in the night with her eyes soft, placing his hand warmly between her legs or tracing her fingers across him when he's on the verge of sleep. He wonders if this is how it is in all marriages, but he looks at his friends' wives, seeing them homely and plain beside Ruth, and cannot imagine it. Then flushes with painful, shameful rage at the thought of any of his friends wondering the same of her.

He can't imagine what his life would have been like with any of the girls he knew before the war, with the women his friends have married. That is, he can see exactly what his life would have been like, but can't picture himself in the scene. It's easy enough to imagine the porch better swept and a bed-side table clear of books; what is beyond understanding is that there could ever be that leap of desire at watching another woman undressing each night, or the pure pleasure at her wit and conversation.

The neighbours are not all equally convinced, although—except for the ones who have entered blueberry preserves themselves—the little victory doesn't hurt. Many of the older members of the community and some of the younger will die without ever being sure what to make of Ruth. Her accent and bearing immediately labelled her as stuck-up, but opin-ion is later divided; she's not lazy, though her house is not as apple-pie as some people would like; she is generous at bake sales and browses happily for white elephants. But she doesn't fit in; even her friends admit that. She quotes poetry, con-fusingly and unself-consciously; ask her if she misses England and she's more likely to reply, 'And is there honey still for tea?' than answer the question. At a time when women rarely drive at all, she drives fast and far, insists on learning to use the tractor—and the rumour persists that she was a pilot during the war. Yet she remains the most elegant woman this side of Wolfville.

It's the reading, the gossips decide. Can't be good for anyone, all that book-reading.

If you drop in for a cup of tea, there'll be a book open on the kitchen table, if you stay too long her eyes will stray back to it; in fact the books in that house seem to wander unaided from their proper place in the parlour bookcase to chairs, win-dowsills or wherever Ruth happens to be. They continue to roam even when the storage problem is solved shortly after her thirtieth birthday, when her inheritance begins to trickle through. There is a surprising amount of it, although she can't have it all at once.

'Do you want a trip back to England?' Bill suggests.

But Ruth knows exactly what she wants, and it's not a long trip with two tiny children, back to a country where her friends are scattered and Cousin Mary the only relative not dead or estranged. Practicalities first: a proper bathroom, with a good deep bath, sink and matching toilet, is built into the laundry off the kitchen. That takes most of the first instalment, but what's more important is that she now has an allowance. Her own money.

Ruth had known it would be difficult to give up flying, but it's a shock to find how much she misses the pay. She hadn't realised she was so acquisitive. It takes another generation's perspective to see that the money itself is not the point. It doesn't matter how generous, how trusting Bill is, the habit of financial independence proves a difficult one to break. And no matter how grateful she is for the selection of English magazines, newspapers and books that Mary sends twice a year, it's not the same as choosing herself. Now she writes to Foyles, and when it's confirmed that books can be shipped direct from Charing Cross Road to her door, spends a week of dreamy evenings compiling her list.

Two months later the crate arrives: a complete set of Jane Austen, most of Dickens (Bill already has *Great Expectations* and *David Copperfield*); *Kim* and *Puck of Pook's Hill,* Rupert Brooke's *Poems 1911*, and two newer books: Nancy Mitford's *Pursuit of Love* and Evelyn Waugh's *Brideshead Revisited* (both of which she enjoys, but far from making her homesick, they make her new life more real in comparison). For Jane and Mike she's chosen a thick selection of nursery rhymes, *Tom Kitten, The Tale of Peter Rabbit, The Tailor of Gloucester* and a picture book of Jack and Jill whose drawings seem disappointingly twee compared to the ones of her memory.

'You'll need a library next,' Bill says, coming into the parlour as she swims through her sea of books.

'The trunk room,' says Ruth. 'We don't ever use it.'

The trunk room is a gabled cubbyhole at the top of the

stairs. The ceilings slope wildly; it's papered with the odds and ends of wallpaper from every other room in the house, some many paperings ago; the window is of leaded glass, bubbled with imperfections.

'That'll never make a library!'

'It's exactly what I want.' She strips off the old wallpaper and chooses one bright with yellow flowers, papering it herself despite Bill's advice and the toddlers' help. Bill planes shelves from seasoned maple; she sands and oils, and by the time Rick is born, early the following November, has a room entirely her own.

✑

Louise's two sons were born in Germany, where Hank had been posted soon after their marriage. They bought a large black Mercedes to see the Europe Hank had missed in Colditz; postcards arrived from Towers Eiffel to Leaning, cathedrals and castles.

But eventually Hank decided he'd had enough of air force life, found a job with a mining company and moved back to Cape Breton. The August after the iceberg visit, which years later will inspire Jane's trip to the Corso del Palio, Ruth took the children to visit again. It was the time of the pit ponies' annual holiday: long days of sunshine and fresh air, bucking, frisking and freedom.

'They shouldn't have to go back down the mines!' Jane protested. 'It's not fair!'

'It's their job,' explained Ruth, who could not think of a worse nightmare than subterranean darkness and had to remind herself that it wasn't so long since children younger than Rick had worked in worse conditions than these ponies.

Jane was twelve years old and not interested in comparisons of history. Carefully noting a map to work out the route, she simply plotted to steal the friendliest pony and ride it home to freedom. Once it was safely established on the farm, her parents could not be cruel enough to send it back to slavery. The only flaw she could see, presuming that the miners wouldn't object to the well-intentioned theft, was why Ruth wouldn't notice her missing on the day's tour of Louisbourg. Eventually she had to admit that even the attraction of ruined ramparts made this unlikely.

The pit ponies went back to work; Ruth and the children went back to the Valley, and in December Bold Brennan arrived.

There'd been horses on the farm all Jane's life: Lady, the unimaginatively named big bay mare that had been Bill's before he went to war, over twenty now but still willing to amble passively with a small child or unseat experienced riders who mistook her gentleness for docility. Merry Legs, a dapple grey Shetland with the appealing face and appalling nature of her breed, had arrived when Jane was six, her foal unexpectedly on a misty June morning shortly after. Misdemeanour—father unknown, known as Miss D—grew taller and sweeter than her mother, but Jane had outgrown her by twelve, and the pony was gentle enough for Rick. Mike, who was not particularly interested in riding, preferred the battle with Merry when he did.

There hadn't been a horse for the sleigh for several years, not since George's black gelding that had fetched the doctor for Jane, but that was not why she chose Brennan. He became hers because he was a challenge (and she was, after all, her mother's daughter), and because she often felt so small and insignificant that there was something powerfully appealing about being mounted on a tall horse's back. But the main reason was simply that he was the first horse she looked at, and rejecting him would have meant remaining horseless another day.

Bold Brennan was about five years old; seventeen hands of raw-boned roan; the carefully clipped feathers which grew silkily and quickly around his fetlocks suggested Clydesdale, but he'd managed to inherit a full degree of artistic temperament from some hotter blooded ancestor. 'If he were a woman,' Ruth always claimed, 'you could see him wringing his hands.'

The first sight of him, forlorn and muddy in a dealer's corral, was unprepossessing. 'He's awful ugly,' said Bill, 'and the size of him—you'd be better off with something neater you could use for pony club.' But the promise had been made: the decision was Jane's.

The dealer had no saddle; Bill hoisted himself across the prominent backbone to see that the horse did not object to his weight, and the animal moved freely around the corral with no obvious vices. Then Jane, her eyes shining, was given a leg-up. Twice around the ring and she headed out the gate and up the hill, where the horse, on being urged to speed up from a trot, simply lengthened his stride, his body settling lower as the legs flashed long, straight and smooth as a canter, the most extraordinary ride Jane had ever had. At the top of the hill she turned him, intending to descend slowly as Bill had drilled her, but the horse promptly bolted, raising his Roman nose so high that it was impossible for a small twelve year old to rein it down or in. In the end there was nothing to do but clamp knees to his sides and arms to his neck. At the entrance to the corral he swerved and they continued to gallop around the flat lands at the foot of the hill until suddenly he had run himself out and Jane was able to rein him in with a semblance of control.

Ruth's face was white, Bill's grim. The dealer looked depressed.

'Cool!' Jane breathed, sliding off the sweat-streaked animal and offering him a sugarlump from her pocket. Which Brennan may or may not have known he did not deserve but accepted anyway.

'At least our parents, ' Ruth said later to Bill, 'never saw us learning to fly!'

Forty years later, sorting out the collection of coats in the shed, Jane will find a sugarlump in the pocket of her farm parka. Brennan had stepped happily into the horse trailer that took him to his new home, the second winter of teachers' college; he hadn't needed sugar to coax him, and she'd kissed him on the nose and fled without remembering to give it to him. Another small betrayal, she thinks; life seems to be full of them once you start remembering.

Ruth's horse, Lochinvar, is a gift from Bill in the spring after Brennan's arrival: an elegant, mostly standardbred chestnut. Ruth isn't a proficient rider, but Bill thinks she needs a challenge now that Rick has started school, and a horse is easier to provide than an aeroplane. Absorbed by the challenges of farming, he doesn't miss flying the way she does, and the memories of a navigator on a hulking great flying boat or transport are not of the same freedom as a pilot of smaller craft.

'I *mind* not flying,' Ruth said once, out of the blue, or maybe because of the clarity of the blue that day, when Jane was chasing butterflies and Mike was asleep in the baby carriage in the shade. 'I wouldn't change anything, but wouldn't it be lovely just to fly again?' He'd thought of a horse then, but if Ruth does something she has to do it well, and he's waited for the time to be right.

'You've been planning this for that long, for eight years?' Ruth asks, as overwhelmed by this as by the totally unexpected gift. And if she's had any doubts about learning to ride, they evaporate into that same bright sky.

Lochie was as perfect for Ruth as Brennan was unsuitable for Jane (leaving Ruth and Bill with another twist of parental guilt as well as a change of heart about free choice of gifts);

he was lively but beautifully schooled and totally without vice. Ruth suggested that Jane might use him as well, but Jane was loyal, and stubborn. She and Brennan started pony club that summer and by the time he'd trotted the nine miles there, he was generally quite well behaved, bolting only rarely on the way home.

However, as Bill had predicted, he was never a pony club horse. In addition to the usual startles at loud noises or unexpected movements, he was terrified of running water, the smell of pigs, the sound of frogs and the sight of small fences. His awkward frame was not made for bucking, but he occasionally reared and was a consummate shier—like a sideways Superman, he could have leapt wide buildings in a single bound. This ability stood him in good stead when confronted with the miniature fences of their first gymkhana. 'You could *step* over them,' Jane whispered in a burst of realism. 'You don't even have to jump.'

Brennan jumped. Sideways. A refusal that would have more than cleared the eighteen-inch post and rail if it had been placed in that direction, and then, beautifully, classically, right out of the ring, over the four-foot fence and the six-foot spectators. 'Duck!' screamed the instructor, and Jane, in that frozen instant of time while her horse seemed suspended in midair, looked down at the white faces and realised she'd been disqualified.

She didn't rejoin pony club the next summer. Instead she turned to long-distance trail riding, endurance tests with negligible audiences, much better suited to a rangy, skittish horse.

In the winter between, she dragged out the sleigh and discovered another of Brennan's fears. The first time they tried to harness him he reared in such terror that he nearly pierced himself on a shaft. Thinking of that deep-dropping trot, Jane decided that he'd started as a harness racer and been injured or frightened in an accident, which would have been a logical assumption in a horse with a less lengthy list of phobias.

This one, however, was something that Bill could deal with; together he and Jane worked on getting the horse to accept the sight of the sleigh, the feel of the harness, to stand quietly in the shafts, until finally, in one of the last snow-covered days of winter, Brennan pulled the sleigh and two proud passengers down to Evelyn's Pond and back without mishap. 'Next year,' Bill promised, 'when he's settled down, I'll teach you to drive.'

Unlike his wife, Bill was a patient teacher: Brennan settled so well to the sleigh that once the snow fell he began to object to being saddled instead of harnessed, and Jane became one of the few North Americans of her generation to experience dashing through the snow with jingling bells rather than roaring skidoo. Which is why, although she's never particularly enjoyed horse racing or gambling, she now sometimes persuades Ian to go to the trots in Yarralong, where the drivers in their light-wheeled sulkies hold hands on reins behind that same long flashing stride.

Chapter
ELEVEN

*E*very year around Anzac or Remembrance Days, when the papers publish stories of other fathers' lives and wars, Ian planned to ask Fred more about his.

'You'll regret it if you don't,' Jane would agree.

Fred, scrawny as ever, frequently out of breath or caught by sudden spasms of pain, was ageing rapidly, as if years older than Dulcie, a generation older than Jane's own parents.

But it's easier to wonder than query. Like most of us, Fred preferred sharing humorous moments rather than tales of degradation and despair; facing slow, grim death is not something to be reduced to anecdote, or even, when that grip on survival is our own, to see as heroic.

When Ian did gather up his nerve to ask, his very desire to understand left him sounding formal and stilted, a junior reporter interviewing a stranger: 'How long did you work on the railway? What was the jungle like?' He couldn't ask what he most wanted to know: the terrible details—were you beaten, were you tortured, is that why there were no babies after me, after the war? How did you survive? was the core. Would I be as strong?

Luckily Megan was too young for such niceties. 'Poppie,' she asked, at a Sunday lunch not long before her tenth Anzac Day, 'were you in the war they're talking about?'

'One of them,' said Fred.

'Which side were you on?'

Fred laughed, Dulcie and Ian answered sharp and shocked; Jane wondered if the school ought to rethink its history program.

'But you've never told us much about the war,' Ian said later.

'Not much to tell.'

'Not much!' For nearly forty years Dulcie had suffered through Fred's nightmares, awake and asleep, but it wasn't her story.

'You wouldn't want to know,' said Fred.

Three months later, on Megan's birthday, when cake had been eaten and presents unwrapped—rollerskates from her parents, a large doll from one set of grandparents, *Anne of Green Gables* from the other—Fred presented her with another gift. Dulcie caught Jane's eye with an 'absolutely no idea!' shrug, and Megan unwrapped a notebook: *Poppie in the Army*.

'I'm not much of a writer,' Fred said gruffly, 'so I did it with cartoons.'

Small figures—'me', 'Jack', 'Corporal Butler'—parade outside their tents in the training camp at Trawool (where, twelve years later, Megan will attend a luxurious wedding and wonder why she knows the name); the *Ile de France* wends its way to the Middle East; a flea hops across the desert from a camel to the unsuspecting 'me', who on the following page is standing on a rock in front of a Red Cross hut—*in the nuddy*, the caption says—while a medico lances his flea boils and small girls giggle. 'I closed my eyes so they couldn't see me,' Fred told Megan, and she giggled too.

There are battles with the French Foreign Legion, glamorous pyramids, mosques, and another ship, the *Orestes*, pointing towards Fremantle, with a question mark thought bubble of Dulcie and two babies, one pink, one blue. 'That's your dad,' Fred explained. 'The last letter I'd had from Gran said the baby would be coming soon. I reckoned soon was past and the baby must be there, but blow me if I could work out if it was a boy or a girl!'

'If Daddy was a girl,' Megan began, starting her next month's agonising 'what if' series, 'he'd be my mum...' She looked at Jane and changed tack. 'Then you found out he was a boy!'

'And my word, what a day when I got that letter! But it was some time coming, and I thought a bloke could go crazy wondering if the baby was born yet and what it was. So I made up his birthday—4 February, I said, but I was three days early, that was the day your Gran wished he'd been born. Then I thought, A bloke's got to get to know his kid somehow! So every night when I lay down on my mat I said to myself, "Now I'm in Coburg again," and I said goodnight to your Gran, and goodnight to a boy baby called Ian and a girl baby called Sandra. Every 4 February I wished them happy birthday, and in between I talked to the men who had kids and some of the doctors. "What do you reckon," I'd ask, "about what a kid can do when it's six months old, or one year old?" "Oh, it'll be crawling," they'd say, "and laughing, or starting to walk," or whatever it was, and I'd think about Ian laughing, or Sandra learning to walk.'

'What happened to Sandra?'

'She never got born—I had to wait a long time for my little girl! It was queer when I found out, not saying goodnight to her any more, or happy birthday next time February came around.'

Megan clambered onto his lap, giving the others a chance to blink or surreptitiously wipe eyes.

'But you should have seen your Poppie smile when that letter came! I still know it by heart: *Ian is walking well now; he is a lively little chap and everyone says quite big for eighteen months.* I carried the letter around with me all the time, till it was all holes from being folded and opened again; you have no idea how I read it! It's a poor lookout when a bloke's son is two and a half years old before he even knows it's a boy, but that's how it was.'

Megan, growing up on weekly letters from her other grandmother, stared accusingly at Dulcie. 'Why didn't you write before?'

'Don't you blame your poor Gran! Prisoners didn't get much mail, it wasn't her fault.'

'You weren't in prison!' Megan squealed, but calmed on seeing the adults' faces. 'Were you very bad, Poppie?'

'Must of been!' said Fred. 'Now let's get on with this story or your dad's cows will never get milked tonight.'

The 'me' is now on another ship, waving goodbye to his machine gun on the pier; mortars explode in jungle; friend Jack has shrapnel pulled 'out of his *bum*,' said Fred, with a wicked look at his grand-daughter, but though Megan knew he'd like her to giggle again, she'd caught her parents' mood and was still. The pages Ian and Jane would study later—a prison camp in Java, a railway built through rock and jungle, a hospital hut with skeleton patients and staff, the dark tunnel of a mine—Fred turned as one, saying Megan was too young for that now but he'd thought he might as well put it all in while he was at it.

That was the year Bill and Ruth came out for Christmas. The mothers now had Megan in common, and the fathers, as Grandpère would have said, *'s'entendaient tres bien'*. Their discussions diffused outwards from farming to geography, the differences in the night skies and on to astral navigation, although Ian wondered where on earth his father could have picked up his knowledge of the latter.

'It was at the first POW camp in Java, Bandoeng. We had lectures from Laurens van der Post—you've heard of him?—and a bloke who talked about Odysseus and ancient Troy, marvellous stories he told, and a navigation school. I went along and learned about the pole star and rhumb lines and all sorts.'

'On a long flight over the sea at night,' Bill offered, 'sometimes it was hard to believe that there was anything beneath you. I always thought I was luckier than the other fellows, because at least I had the stars.'

Fred nodded. 'That's exactly right. Not that I'd have fancied your job—solid ground below my feet, that's my motto—but when things were bad in the camps, a bloke could see the stars and know that something somewhere made sense, even if nothing on earth did.'

'Remember that day in Gallipoli?' Ian asked in bed that night. 'When I wondered where Dad had learned the *Iliad* and the *Odyssey*?'

'And you didn't guess at a prison school in the jungle!'

She was nearly asleep when he added, 'They're about men being away at war a long time and not getting home, aren't they?'

'They kept offending the gods, and those gods didn't give second chances.'

☙

Whether it was the book or Bill's visit or a combination of the two, over the next few years something opened, not a floodgate, but a trickle of memories that Fred was finally ready to share: snapshot snippets of an unimaginable life.

'The night before the Japanese invaded Batavia,' he'd say, 'Jack and me were billeted in this native hut, made of bamboo. It was fairly pissing down outside, pardon the French, and we were sleeping in muddy straw and duck manure. Jack woke me up and said, "You know, Fred, I have a feeling we mightn't get out of this." Then he pulled out his whisky flask: "We'd better have a drink; it could be the last chance we get." He was right, too; it was the last drink we had for a bloody long time. Which reminds me, how about a cold one?'

Washing dishes after one Sunday lunch, while the men watched football and Megan read upside down on the sofa, Dulcie confided that Fred rarely went to bed at all now, the pain of lying flat so great that he preferred to pace the night away and doze in the recliner when he could. 'I thought about one of those hospital beds you see on the telly, that fold up and down, but he said a bloke would look like an invalid with something like that in the house.'

He died the following day, a bright autumn afternoon not long before his seventy-third birthday. He was digging out a camellia that hadn't survived the summer heat; the heart attack was quick and thorough, and they were all more than ordinarily grateful that he'd been spared the pain and indignities of further illness.

Ian, however, continued to wish that he'd asked more: 'Dad told us all he wanted,' Dulcie said. 'You can't talk about something without remembering it, and those nightmares... fair enough if he didn't want them in the day too.'

Which was little consolation to his son, now that no more questions could be answered. Over the next few years he threw himself into an orgy of war reading: biographies of Weary Dunlop to Montgomery; anything at all on prisoners of war, from Patsy Adam Smith's massive volume of interviews— feeling oddly cheated not to find his father included—to meticulously prepared self-published diaries, often with heart-rending drawings, and fiction, which sometimes, he felt, must be closer to the inner truth than the dryly factual accounts. But it was not until he read the *Odyssey*, reaching past enchanted pigs and supernatural tempests, that Ian felt he might have touched something of what his own father had survived in the alien jungle, pitting his wits and puny strength against its vengeful gods.

❧

Dulcie had never got used to living at Kooring. She didn't like the house, didn't like looking out on dry, dusty pad-docks, didn't like being so far from a neighbour. She was a Victorian, and irritated that she had become a part of New South Wales simply by crossing a rickety bridge. When she started paying bills after Fred died, sorting out the intricacies of chequebooks and bank accounts with an ease that astounded her son, and discovered just how much extra her new side of the bridge cost in car registration, she put the farm on the market and found herself a neat new house in the centre of Narling.

It was 1988. Wool was singing a siren's song of record prices; Dulcie auctioned off the Herefords Fred had spent nearly twenty years breeding, and sold the entire five hun-dred acres to a dairy farmer looking for sheep and an easier life.

'She didn't even ask me!' Ian spluttered. 'Just said she'd found a buyer and that was it. *I* might have wanted to try sheep too.'

'She tried to discuss it with you,' Jane protested mildly. 'You said you'd spent too long building up your herd to sell it now.'

'I thought that would make her stop and think about sell-ing Dad's! Anyway, that was a crazy idea, selling this farm to buy his. I could have used Kooring as an outpaddock and run sheep as well.'

Jane didn't ask where, since it was only two years since they'd bought the farm next door, he'd find the money or the time. 'She couldn't stay there without your dad; she misses him too much.'

Privately she suspected that the true cause of Ian's annoyance was that his mother didn't seem to be missing Fred enough. Despite frequent tears and constant, emotional references to him, it was obvious that Dulcie had burst forth from her subservient, protected role into sudden competence. Ian's memory didn't stretch back to the time when his mother—possibly widowed, possibly deserted, she couldn't know which—had combined raising a child with munitions factory work, boarding with her mother to save against an uncertain future. If it had, he might have guessed that Fred's determination to insulate his wife against financial worries was an attempt to make up for those years, or maybe to regain some power and control in his own life. Jane didn't think Dulcie had ever tried to tease out the reasons; it had been enough for her that Fred needed to be a benevolent dictator, and for over forty years she'd protected him from the knowledge that she'd never needed to be cocooned.

'It just seems a shame,' Jane told Sue, 'that she had to wait for Fred to die before she could be herself.'

'How did she put up with it? I know he was a nice old bloke, but you wouldn't catch me keeping quiet all that time!'

Jane didn't find it particularly difficult to imagine, but the new Dulcie was a shock to her son. The haste with which she upgraded her weekly social bowls to competitive pennant, joined a Probus club where she learned to speak in public without more than average terror, and climbed onto widows' bus tours of gardens and wineries ('She's never home!' Ian complained) seemed positively indecent in the first year After Fred.

Within three years, when he'd become accustomed to Dulcie's new persona, annoyance and dreams of sheep farming would both be obliterated from Ian's memory. By then wool and lambs were equally worthless; hobby farmers were inundated with offers of lawn-mowing sheep, and family farms were going bankrupt. The new owner of Kooring would shoot

his flock ram by ram and ewe by ewe, taking the government's incentive a step further with the final addition of his
own body to the freshly dug pit.

❧

The wallpaper in Jane's bedroom is Sears Victorian, a delicate blue-flowered pattern she chose in grade 11, a lifetime
ago. In fact, apart from the addition of a folding bed in the
corner for Mike's visiting children, very little has changed at
all. Except her.

She wonders if this is how her mother felt when she walked
into the unchanged clubroom at the air base. Had she needed
to look around at the clues—the changed fashions, the mobile
phones, the digital watches—to convince herself that she hadn't
slipped back in a time warp?

It's not long since your last visit, Jane tells herself sternly;
four years from the last time she slept in this bed. There's no
particular excuse for this disorientation.

The day had started well enough: and though the morning seems a lifetime ago, now, it's no more than the usual
illusion caused by rapid geographical shift. There'd been a
last long walk in Burnham Beeches with galumphing dogs,
a last attempt at persuading Mary to visit Australia and knowing that she wouldn't, not while the world had stray dogs
and hedgehogs left to adopt. The packing wasn't difficult—
yesterday, when her cigarette rage had settled, she'd finally
sorted through Ruth's case: a cardigan to the smaller and
stouter Mary, a blouse and a scarf for herself, the rest of the
clothes to Oxfam. There was something irrevocable about
bundling good clothes for an op shop, as if until then she
hadn't been quite sure whether Ruth might need them again.

The books were sorted similarly—battered bus trip *Poldark*
and *Barchester Towers* to Oxfam; a new, beautifully dust-
jacketed James Herriot an obvious and presumably intended
gift for Mary. *Britain from the Air* and a few products of her

mother's literary tour, Jane packaged and sent to herself, sea mail. There will be enough, she thought, probing the thought for avarice, to carry when she eventually returns home. Her now home, the one where Ian is, in Australia. The word is not always exclusive.

She took the *Poldark* back out of the Oxfam sack for the flight, then repacked her things into her own shabby suitcase and her mother's new one, Ruth's jewellery—the pearls from her twenty-first birthday, the cameo brooch from her thirtieth, wedding and engagement ring—safely in her handbag. The box of letters, still unread, fitted into her mother's wheeled, stewardess-type bag. As did Ruth herself. Mother-in-a-handbag, Jane thought, as if she might suddenly be required to market it. Take her anywhere; travels free! Also the funeral director's form, easily accessible for the more likely question of what's in the box: heroin or heroine? (No one asked. She was almost disappointed, she'd rehearsed for so long.)

It was more difficult than she'd expected to say goodbye to Mary. She's ashamed that it wasn't until the last minute that she'd realised just how much Mary meant to her, in her own right, not simply as a repository of memories or a last link to her mother; humbled, too, to realise just how much she means to Mary. They hugged for a long moment, Jane reassured by the older woman's solid bulk, though her cheek, when kissed, had the softness of age.

'Keep in touch,' Mary said, eyes welling, and neither needed to finish the sentence, 'now that Ruth's no longer an intermediary.' Jane wondered if last night's dinner was an adequate thank you for all Mary had done, and knew that nothing could be. 'I'll phone every month or so,' she said.

In the departure lounge she wiped away tears that hadn't fallen on that nightmare trip ten days earlier; settled herself by checking that passport and ticket were safely stowed, boarding pass bookmarking the unstarted *Poldark*. The seat number was surprisingly low: Jane had always been convinced, on no particular evidence except the general rule of life, that only attractive women get flight upgrades, but found herself ridiculously excited with hope. And although she claims not to be superstitious, when the flight attendant did in fact wave her to a plush seat in front of the curtains, she couldn't help seeing it as a sort of omen: the gods were smiling.

If they were, it was cynicism rather than kindliness. Spacious seat, freer air and flowers in the bathroom notwithstanding, it's still a long time to sit in one place, and although Halifax Airport seemed a friendly, manageable size after Heathrow, the conversation about her passport had taken a little time and a lot of emotional energy, so that it was well after eight, or well after two a.m. in London, by the time she'd retrieved her mother's car from the long-term carpark. It might have been more sensible to have gone to a motel for the night, but she was quite unable to visualise finding one and sleeping there alone. She could picture herself driving, so that's what she did.

It had been such a long, special-occasions-only drive when she was young, nearly ninety miles from the farm to Halifax, but in the world she lives in now, a hundred and fifty kilometres had shrunk. Except for tonight. Tonight, driving an unfamiliar car on what was now the wrong side of the road, windscreen wipers waving to signal every turn, the farm with its empty house kept receding into the distance, further than the longest childhood drive.

The eventual turn-offs were, however, faithfully familiar: Applevale and then Evelyn's Pond, the road to the farm and there was the house, appropriately ghostly in the headlights. She parked in the shed and sat long enough that the sensor light, new since her last visit, switched itself off and she had to get out and stumble towards the boot before she could see. The suitcases weren't heavy but combined with the hand-luggage to be momentarily a burden too great to bear. The wheels jerked on the unevenness of the shed's wooden floor.

She thought this was probably the first time she'd ever unlocked the kitchen door herself, and the first time she'd ever been entirely alone in the house—without people occasionally but never without a dog or a cat to share the echoes.

Through the house quickly, pulling curtains shut in every room against the odd chance of neighbours or a passing car spotting the light. Only local cars would pass and locals would know that Ruth had been away. Jane is not ready for visitors. She leaves her unchanged, unsettling bedroom and returns to the kitchen where the thin, dulling layer of dust suits her mood. She badly needs a cup of coffee. Chamomile tea, Megan would have said, or chrysanthemum to calm the nerves, but Jane wants coffee and wouldn't mind it laced. Switching on the kettle, she drags the suitcases up the stairs and down the hall to her room, places her mother's casket on her mother's bed, makes the coffee and takes it to the armchair by the kitchen phone. There's a chance Ian will be having coffee too, breakfast type.

'I'm here,' she tells her disembodied voice. 'Call me in the morning; I'm going to bed now.' She can't tell him on the answering machine, would avoid telling him at all if it were avoidable.

She takes her coffee to bed but can't sleep. 'Not surprising!' Megan would say.

The immigration official had seemed so casual as she flicked through the passport, pointing out that Jane hadn't filled out the permanent address details.

'Sorry,' Jane said. 'I live in Australia.' As if to prove that she did have some sort of permanent abode, even if she hadn't thought it worth registering. The woman flicked further to discover there was no Australian visa.

'But I live there,' Jane repeated, not panicking yet, 'I don't need one.'

'You do,' said the woman, and Jane remembered at the same instant that it was true. She's always had a passport, organised against future emergencies and wholly justified by the present one; but the previous re-entry visas had been organised at the same time as tickets.

'There's a fast-tracking system for tourist visas, because of the Olympics. But you want to stay there?'

Jane did.

And still does, but lies in the darkness besieged by monster stories; one of them an elusive clue, a tale so terrible that the only thing not blocked from her memory is a feeling that she ought to have paid attention, like the realisation as one is sucked down into the waters that a half-glimpsed sign had read *Dangerous Rip*. She does remember, however, the Australian war brides who'd wanted to return from the States when their husbands died, ten years or so ago, and found that they were no longer Australian and no longer welcome. Then there was the old man who'd emigrated as a boy, fought for Australia in two wars, and made the mistake of returning to the old country once before he died: a quick visit indefinitely extended by his lack of re-entry visa. Who wants an eighty year old migrant? the government had asked, or so the current affairs programs reported.

The problem with news stories is that you don't always hear the ending. And if you don't hear, you're free to make up your own, depending on your state of mind at the moment.

'Phone the Australian High Commission in the morning,' the official had said, in a soothing tone that suggested Jane's face was more distressed than her brain had registered. 'It should just be a formality.'

'Phone the Australian High Commission in the morning,' Jane repeats to herself now, as if this is something she is likely to forget. It sounds Gilbert and Sullivanish, or was that the Lord High Executioner? It also sounds like the start of a list: go through papers; notify social security, insurance, lawyer, the myriad of relatives, whoever else she's supposed to notify; find the will; talk to Gillespies next door.

On the scale of jobs she does not want to, which the list is composed of exclusively, visiting Gillespies is only one step down from telling Ian she doesn't have a re-entry permit. No matter how much they liked her mother, the neighbours have been leasing the farm since before Bill died and their primary interest will be details of property sale or lease—decisions, legalities and more indications of the irrevocability of death and the end of a family farm. Seventeen eighty-seven when Richard Leighton had been granted the land, a generation later when his youngest son Timothy had built this house on his quarter inheritance. Our genes all stretch back equal distances into history, but there's something intriguing about knowing that the bearers of those genes walked the same fields, climbed the same stairs to bed, that you do. Their stories won't change if Jane no longer has the right to walk these fields or climb these stairs, but hers will.

However, it's not just her history, it's Mike's and Rick's too, so meeting Gillespies can be legitimately shelved until they're here and the will's read. Which still leaves plenty on her list.

So much, in fact, that she gives up the attempt to sleep and gets out of bed to pull on socks and the dressing gown from the wardrobe. It's her own, the baby-blue cosy one she'd bought in her first year of teaching, and as familiar against her skin as if it had only been slipped off for this morning's shower.

Down the hall to the old trunk room, Ruth's little library. She's forgotten that it's been altered since she was last saw it; the tiny alcove at the entrance is now a powder room, just enough space for a toilet, the smallest handbasin and a sliding door. Luxury, thinks Jane, who has often spent an hour debating how badly she needs to leave the warmth of the house in the middle of the night.

The library itself, except for the addition of computer and printer, is unchanged from her childhood: bookcases from

Austen to Woolf, flowered yellow wallpaper on the fraction of bare walls, wooden desk in front of the bubbled lead-glass window. If the ghost of Ruth is anywhere, it should be here, rising from the old maple armchair.

Envy for the comfort of an inside toilet is swamped by a much stronger, almost primeval longing for a room of her own. I'd give anything, Jane thinks, though she knows that's an exaggeration, for a room that is hers as this room is Ruth's. A place that expresses her own personality—because although it's difficult to believe at the moment, when it's not the middle of the night after a transatlantic flight she does have some idea of who she is—but it's not the decorating, not the paint colour or the furniture, it's the freedom to choose whatever she might desire without worrying what anyone else would want or think.

'But you use Megan's room,' Ian would say if he could hear her thoughts, which he can't; it's one of life's lessons Jane needs to learn, that he can't hear her unless she speaks.

And Jane would answer, if she were assertive enough, which she isn't, that's why the conversation is inside her head on the other side of the world, 'But that's just it. It's still Megan's room. Just like your office is your office, and our bedroom is ours, and the living room is still your parents'.' Because Fred and Dulcie had very sensibly abandoned their old green vinyl armchairs when they left the farm, and Jane and Ian are using them still. They've swung right around into fashion but not into comfort, and the room is still Fred and Dulcie's lounge with no sign of Jane except more frequent dust.

'If we don't move,' she says now, 'we'll renovate. We're not *that* poor.' What she can't say yet, even to herself and especially in this room, is that she has presumably just inherited a substantial amount of money, a renovation lump of cash, possibly even a new house.

Yet her mother had taken over her parents-in-law's house, her husband's childhood home, just as Jane had, but not even the added weight of ancestors had prevented Ruth from making the house her own. Without major renovation—so the only answer seems to be the force of a personality that knew what she wanted and never felt the need to ask for permission to be herself. Just as she would, in the same situation as Jane, have bought that Royal Worcester.

However, Jane is here to sort out physical rather than psychological items: 'Just start,' she tells herself, and the desk is the obvious place, but it's not that easy. In the end she switches on the computer; the operating program is the same as hers and connecting for email is automatic.

She doesn't know what she's expecting: her own letters and her brothers perhaps, a few references to the bus tour. *Retrieving 1 of 64 messages*, says the box on the screen.

Why should privacy be more invaded because her mother has never read these notes? Maybe it's sadness for the writers not knowing that Ruth was already dead.

The spam mail is easy. Even if alive, it's unlikely that Ruth would have wanted to assemble woodwork in her own home, gamble for a Caribbean holiday or call the hot girls waiting to speak to her now, 'Live!' the ad insists, which is ironic since Ruth isn't, though it would be odder if the girls weren't.

Thirty-two messages are from a Literary Calendar, snippets of esoteric information—on this day, so many years ago, a poet was born, a novelist died, someone else wrote a libellous review of an enemy.

Jane laughs aloud. Her mother's literary knowledge had been vast, her references almost untraceable for the average reader. 'Unlike Lady Peabury,' Ruth would say, looking up from a book at the breakfast table, 'I've never considered novels before luncheon to be a sin.'

Into a letter, apropos of nothing, she would drop a snippet: 'When Robert Frost was asked why he didn't write free verse, he replied, "I'd just as soon play tennis with the net down."'

Then there were the anniversaries. Jane has always known that she was born on Jules Verne's birthday, and of the tenuous connection her mother had managed to trace between the writer and Acadia, while Megan shares Emily Bronte's. But over the past year or two this knowledge had increased exponentially, so that no matter whose birthday Jane mentioned, Ruth would reply, 'Tell her that she shares it with Edmund Spenser', or 'The day that *Vanity Fair* was published.'

An innocent vanity, but Jane feels a less than innocent prick of pleasure at having caught her mother out. Closely followed by a stab of guilt.

The remainder are personal letters; some from people Jane has never heard of. Several seem to have a common theme, and now the guilt is different and strong enough to nauseate, because she'd believed her mother's claim that her adoption held no more grief. Had she in fact been searching all these years?

If not, she'd been extremely interested in the process. The letters all refer to the writers' own searches. Two of them Jane guesses to be from Ruth's own era. Depression children, informally adopted, one advertised in the *Daily Standard* like a puppy to a good home; one taken off the hands of impecunious neighbours by a wealthier but childless couple. Another had discovered that there was no particular mystery: being the fourth girl, her parents had simply swapped her for a boy cousin. *If we'd only been told!* the woman rages. *Did they not think that it might be relevant to us to know the truth of our stories?*

It is the sort of thing Ruth could have said herself, though never to her daughter.

The fourth, Jane would guess as much younger, less educated, an unlikely penpal for Ruth.

Your letter made me brave enough to start searching for my natural mother. I don't want to be as old as you and start wishing I'd done it when she's already dead. So I've filled in the forms today. My mom didn't want me to but I showed her your letter and she said maybe that was right and she hoped I wouldn't get my feelings hurt. Cross your fingers for me.

What letter? wonders Jane.

The last is from Australia, a Barnado boy sent out for a better life. His earliest memory is the feeling of bewildered abandonment as his mother left him at the orphanage.

'Be good,' she said, 'and when you come home you'll have a new baby to play with.' I'll never forget that, and I'll never forget knowing the lady was lying when she told me my mum had died. Now with all this publicity about other kids who came out with me, I wonder if I was right all along, and if my poor mum got a story about me dropping dead while she was having her baby. She's not likely to still be alive now, whatever happened, but that brother or sister might be. I'll tell you how I go.

Jane is unmoved. 'And Mom obviously told you how she went!' she snaps, sending the letters to the oblivion of *Delete*. 'But she sure never told me!'

She needs more coffee; this is hard. This is hurtful.

But the obligation to do the right thing is strong too, so she reopens all the messages in the *Deleted* folder and pastes in: *Ruth died on the 16th of August*. She does not feel a better person for doing so.

She doesn't want to read any more of her mother's mail, but it's compulsive now she's started, and it can hardly get worse, though she does have to make the coffee before she can go on, and allows herself to fantasise briefly that one of the unread notes will be for her from Ian. He would never write a love letter, which is what she longs for, but she'd settle for calving news or even a quick hi from Sue.

The person she does not expect to hear from is Winston. Although of course the letter isn't to her, and is a continuation of a conversation which she knows nothing about. *Are you back and unjetlagged, O Wise One? I've thought some more about your comments on the paragraphs I sent you and have to admit you're right after all. The extended metaphor doesn't work in that context. Okay, it doesn't work at all—satisfied?*

My mother the editor, she thinks bitterly, although for the moment she's too numb to work out exactly what she's bitter about. Mothers are not supposed to go on writing to daughter's boyfriends once they become ex, but even that doesn't touch the surface of the hurt, the old fear that Winston had always been more infatuated by her mother's mind than her own body. Her own self. She deletes the letter, admits that it does deserve a reply at some stage, drags it back to the *Inbox* and switches the computer off.

Her head aches and her eyes itch; she should go to bed. Instead she tries again to phone Ian, who's still not in or is out again, and starts on the top desk drawer. Pens, pencils, a spare ink cartridge for the printer, envelopes and stamps; nothing significant. She shuts the drawer and opens it again: it all has to be sorted, significant or not. She throws a pencil stub and ink-marked eraser into the wastepaper basket, lines the pens up in a row and shuts the drawer again. Inheritance is supposed to be about sentiment or money—jewellery and mementoes, land and shares—but pens and paperclips don't seem much easier to decide on.

As if in answer to her thoughts, the envelope on the top of the second drawer is neatly labelled *Will*.

She knows the contents, or pretty well. Ruth and Bill had discussed their plans with all of them, some time after Rick moved to Toronto, but there's still a sneaky feeling about opening this now, on her own, no family lawyer, no brothers, just Jane in an old dressing gown and socks in the middle of the night. Though she's not quite sure where the old family lawyer vision comes from; they were a family who'd had remarkably few uses for a lawyer over the years, and whoever had drawn this up would have long since retired or died.

In fact it's a newer one, from after Bill's death, and in Ruth's own handwriting, which is a shock but makes the document instantly more real—her mother had known she would die one day and that the world would carry on. Jane is not as ready to believe this, about her mother or herself or anyone she loves. But then she hasn't had the experience with death that her parents had.

A few bequests: the jewellery is hers, Bill's desk goes to Rick and the family Bible to Mike; ten thousand dollars to a fund to trace families of the children sent to Canada and Australia during the war; furniture and personal belongings to be divided 'as equitably as possible', and the estate equally into three portions, although:

in the event that one of my children or grandchildren should wish to occupy the house or the house and land, they may lease or buy the desired property from the other beneficiaries at a fair market price. Deposit and conditions to be negotiated in a proper commercial manner, but any interest payable on the amount owed to other beneficiaries to be at 2 per cent below current home lending rates. Failing purchase or lease by these direct descendants, the property to be offered to my nephews Howard and Ronald McBain, then to Leighton descendants and finally to all other family members, with any necessary loans at interest 1 per cent below current rates.

'I could stay here myself,' says a voice in Jane's head, just fleetingly, the same sort of crazy voice that suggests jumping off high buildings or shrieking at pompous bores.

She leaves the will out on the desk for when Mike and Rick arrive.

Next is a small stack of last year's Christmas letters, for

the few people that Ruth writes to only once a year; other letters, like her emails, seem to have been trashed as answered and presumably replied to before she left for England. Was her mother always this organised, or was there some presentiment of the need for affairs to be tidied, like the nesting urge before birth?

Jane considers, too, how lonely Ruth must have been these last few years; letters and emails might be more tempting to answer if they're your major human contact. More guilt, though it's difficult to know what she could have done about it.

A photograph under the letters, and it's strange she hasn't seen it because it's taken before her last visit. Bill is in it, alive and well, proud and happy. With good reason as his wife, with the embarrassed smile that could so easily look supercilious, is in graduation gown and cap, holding a rolled certificate.

'What the hell!' Jane is nearly as angry as she'd been at the cigarettes. Weekly letters of life's daily trivia: plants in the garden, books from the library, a blouse from Sears, and yet her mother had failed to mention something as significant as a university graduation—a second one, as if a degree from Oxford wasn't enough. She'd mentioned some courses from Acadia University, hobby study she'd implied or Jane had presumed, keeping the brain alive. It was much the same time that Jane had finally commenced on that Bachelor of Education Ruth had so wanted her to do twenty years earlier; making heavy weather, she suspects now, of struggling away at her books after a day of teaching, as if she were the only one with the perseverance to submit herself to the uncertainty, the occasional despair and the joy of late-life study. Meanwhile her mother, her proud, sharp-tongued mother, had not only never said 'I told you so,' but had refused to steal her thunder by admitting she was quietly, secretly, driving off to Wolfville however many times a week. Jane is scrabbling through the rest of the drawer now to find the degree at the bottom, unframed but not necessarily unvalued: Bachelor of Canadian Studies, 1989. Six months before Jane received hers.

'I'm not that weak!' she shouts. 'You could have told me! Did you think I'd be jealous?'

Which is exactly what she is. Jealous and humiliated, her achievement subtly belittled by her mother once again out-doing her, though even that isn't as crushing as being protected from it. 'I had to find out eventually! You didn't think of that, or did you think you'd done everything else so much better, you'd outlive me too?'

She can't believe what she's just said; hitting below the belt, or whatever the equivalent is on a ghost. 'But, Jesus, Mom, give me a break!' (Sounding even to her own ears like a petulant teenager.) 'What else have you got up your sleeve? Any more little surprises I should know about?'

She yanks open the other desk drawers, dumps contents on the floor: Christmas cards, computer paper, coupons for free photo enlargements. 'No,' her mother could have said, 'no more surprises. Now have you quite finished with this tantrum?'

Jane isn't sure. The room is small and the mess fills it, over-whelms her; she has to squat on the floor to pick it up again, sorting into piles and drawers, weeping noisily and messily like a chastened five year old, not even a teenager now.

'And I'm so tired!' she wails, at which she hears herself and orders herself back into bed. It is so late now, or so nearly morning, and she is so desperate for sleep, that she takes the phone off the hook first.

It makes no difference. 'Overwrought,' the mother in her says, which is not much help. She needs something to read, something soothing, but instead of the *Poldark* she decides it's finally time to start on the box Mary has given her, and reads the letter announcing her own birth.

It's the way she felt when Megan was born, or would have if she hadn't been stitched and sedated; it's all the feelings of motherhood that her generation thought they'd invented with Leboyer births and bonding. She cannot imagine her mother feeling the same sort of ecstasy for a baby—for her, for Jane—but it's here, it's true, and she is still angry that her mother didn't trust her with her secrets and had so little faith in her strength, and she's still absolutely furious about the smoking, because without that maybe they would have had time to sort this out before Ruth died instead of her muddling through on her own; but she feels bathed in love, it's the only way to express it, though she would have never said it out loud: her mother loved her the way she loves Megan. Because whatever secrets Jane doesn't share with Megan—and there are some, if she's honest, which she hasn't been these past few hours—the ultimate bond, the mother–daughterness, she knows to be stronger than any doubts or misunderstandings that could ever come between them.

Snug in this glow, the phone still safely off the hook, her body relaxes. Though it's strange lying in her narrow childhood bed; in Mary's spare room she'd lain neatly on the right-hand side, never taking more than her fair share of the empty double bed, but here she lies right in the middle. There is no room for Ian.

Finally she sleeps. And wakes, heart pounding, from a dream of the consul's office, the red-faced, jacket-ripping official of 1969. 'How can you qualify for family reunion,' he shouts, 'when your husband's dead?'

A nightmare, not a portent. She's not psychic.

Though there was the Ruth's-eye-view of Hamble.

And death's so easy. People do it all the time. Just look at Mom. And the opportunities on a farm are endless. Gored by a bull...

The cows are calving—the bulls aren't with them.

No, they're sitting celibate in their paddock, getting cranky as the testosterone builds up, waiting for an opportunity— rape or rampage, it's all the same to them. And then there's the tractor, the bale feeder, the grain auger, waiting for that moment's inattention to run amok, their sleepy operator jumping down without turning the engine off, a foot slipping under a wheel or arm under a pulley.

Ian's careful. He knows about machines.

He's never had to do it all on his own before; it's too much for one man at this time of year, when dairy families and even the vets and technicians who work with them look pale and haggard and begin to make foolish mistakes. Then there's watering, the drought adding an out-of-season chore to this time of year—bore pumps and motors to be caught in, channels to be drowned in. Or just a falling gum branch, a widowmaker they used to be called.

The logical Jane, failing a little against this onslaught, picks up the phone but is not comforted by hearing her own message once again. 'I'll try later,' she tells it. Working out that it's now five-thirty, afternoon milking, doesn't negate the possibility of Ian lying dead in a paddock. She dials Sue's number but she must be milking too and Jane doesn't leave a message.

She gets up properly now, defeating incipient widowhood with open curtains, boiling kettle. But what would you do? she asks herself. If he were. It would be a new start wherever you chose. Where do you belong?

In this grey light of early morning her imagination cannot stretch as far as Australia and the self who lives there. Images of husband and daughter elude her in the slippery manner of well-loved faces; easier to picture cows, paddocks, the lagoon. Easy enough, too, to visualise daily routine, what-would-I-be-doing-now, early morning ballet between the narrow kitchen benches—fill the kettle, turn to bread maker, turn again to thump out the bread, back to last night's dishes in the draining rack, stoop or stretch to put them away.

Like watching a TV ad, too familiar to notice; nothing to do with her, with Jane. Whoever Jane is. Wherever Jane belongs.

Because right now there is no life that feels like her own, and the future seems as unreal but not nearly as exciting as when she was in grade 12 and trying to imagine life after school. Because it's one thing to mention retirement in passing but another to try to imagine it, and she thinks that maybe this time Ian is serious about selling the farm, it's not just the rigours of the calving season or the despair of the drought that sees farms yo-yo on and off the market, every place in the district for sale if someone would only offer the right price. Fifty-six is getting old for dairying, never mind that the average age of farmers gets higher every year; Ian a young farmer when he started and still younger than some, but he's ageing before her eyes, stiff and sore in the mornings and asleep at the dinner table at night. He's starting to talk about wanting some other sort of life, travelling again before they're too old, simply having the leisure to lie in bed on a Sunday morning or go away for a weekend.

Except that fifty-six, even fifty-seven or fifty-eight, is too young to retire. He'll have to do something, and they have discussed it round the table and the bed, but nothing is right. He loves that farm, can't imagine living anywhere else, and the thought of anyone else working it hurts him like a physical pain; but to finish milking and simply live there to raise beef or other people's heifers would be to waste that huge shed, the twenty-four stall gates, the milk vat that cost the price of a small house, the automatic cup-removers, in-line cleaners, pumps and motors and all the other things that go into a two hundred cow dairy. And the cold hard fact is that the money they've sunk into it means they simply can't afford to retire without getting it back.

'I'll work for EcoFarm with you,' he says occasionally, and how can she be selfish enough to say no, that's mine; I need that part of my life where I'm Jane, not just your wife. People respect me there for who I am, what I know and what I've done, and if you come in, with your strong arms planting two trees to my one, and above all your masculinity, they'll look to you, and even what I've done will be changed in time to Ian. It's not your fault; it's the way it is. But it doesn't make it any easier to picture the future.

In fact, at the moment, swamped by the artifacts of generations and her own childhood, it's difficult to picture anything at all. And if this sorting out of the past seems unbearable, sorting out the bureaucracy of the present seems impossible. It can't be true that she'll have to go to Otttawa. There must be an easier, closer way of sorting it out. It should be simple. As if bureaucracy is known for simplicity. Or logic or humanity. What if she has to go through the whole immigration procedure again? It took months the first time. She was young then, at the beginning of her earning life, teachers were in short supply and migrants, especially English speaking, were being actively pursued. Policies have changed, times have changed, she's changed—she is no longer an attractive proposition.

You own half a business, says the logical part of her mind. You have a husband and daughter. On family reunion grounds only, you'd have to be admitted.

But remember? says the panicker, and now she does remember the story too close for comfort, told by the South African physio at the Bayswater hotel about the woman from Australia. You didn't pay attention because the country was no more than a name to you then. Her mother had broken her hip, was dying in a North London hospital, and the daughter had dashed back—sound familiar?—to see her. And when she got there the mother didn't die, but the daughter couldn't go back because she hadn't got a re-entry visa before she left, and how could you forget that, that warning story? Was there something at the back of your mind that made you want to get stuck here one day?

The physio had left before the end of the story, so Jane never knew whether that woman, who'd lived in Australia for twenty years, thirty years, had a husband, two sons and a farm—or maybe she's made the farm up, the coincidence is too great—ever got home again.

Of course she did, says the voice of reason. She's not still wandering around North London trying to find her way to Australia.

Because she's probably dead now anyway, died trying. She was as old as Ruth, a war bride too, quite likely; the strain would have been too great. Husband and kids gave up on her; forgot her, their wife/mother on the other side of the world.

Now the voice of reason, the mother voice, says that she is getting hysterical and points out she hasn't eaten since yesterday's airline supper. There will be bread in the freezer, crackers in the cupboard, but Jane wants something comforting and doesn't know what that might be. She roams the pantry like a teenager home from school and finds a jar of dried dulse.

What she's asking for is Proustian magic: childhood relived through salty pungency. What she gets is tough bitter seaweed.

She tries another piece and spits it out. One more, tentatively, and then there's no doubt—it's not the dulse that's off, it's her. There are no crackers in the pantry after all, so she has another coffee to wipe out the taste, crying softly at the symbolism: if she can't eat dulse any more or vegemite yet, then where does she belong?

She feels jittery; her skin is too tight for her body. She wonders how much coffee she's drunk. She takes the phone off the hook again, goes back to bed and tries desperately to relax. Megan would lecture her about coffee depleting chi, but Jane would have put up with the lecture if Megan had been there to insinuate silver needles into relevant points; 'Window to the sky,' she might explain, treating her mother in a strange, caring reversal of roles, and Jane would feel herself drifting through clouds, dreamy and peaceful. Megan sees the colours of the meridians on the body she is working with—the liver meridian yellow, gall bladder green; not all corresponding to their official colours on Chinese medicine charts but useful to her—and the points that she will choose to needle once she has taken the pulses and examined the tongue are often darker or even red, like an angry spot on the line of colour. She is dreamy herself as she inserts the needles, concentrating on what no one else can see, and Jane doesn't view her then as Megan her daughter but as some priestess of the body communing with its soul.

How will I bear it, she thinks, if Megan falls in love and stays in Canada, and I'm back in Australia?

As promised, Megan does see a lot on this Trans-Canada drive. Barns of the lush Fraser Valley, so different from the concrete dairies and irrigated paddocks of her childhood; over Rogers Pass with a stop at Hell's Gate, a few more photo stops and a wander on a Rockies trail for picnic lunch. She has a brief turn at driving, enjoying the racy gear changes of steep curving roads, but has trouble remembering that a left-hand turn involves crossing a lane of traffic. At the first sinister scenic stop, despite the excellent brakes of the bus hurtling down the mountain towards them, a white-faced Adam says he'll take over.

'You navigate,' he suggests, as if the Trans-Canada is a maze of alternative routes, because they don't know each other well enough to risk hurting feelings.

Despite her heritage, Megan has no sense of direction and little interest in maps. She is an utterly unreliable navigator. On the few occasions decisions need to be made, Adam follows highway signs and politely ignores her directions. 'It's being in the wrong hemisphere,' she explains next morning, surprised at where the sun rises in Kamloops; but in fact her internal compass is no better in Melbourne. She accepts being lost as one of life's experiences, but would have liked to be sufficiently in harmony with nature to instinctively face the sunrise.

Now, map on knee, she is pleased to match the litany of names with the green highway signs: Coquitlam and Chilliwack; Medicine Hat and Moose Jaw; Qu'Appelle and Portage La Prairie; and the ones that are the same as home: Sorrento and Rutherglen, Port Arthur of grisly fame. They blend with snapshot impressions and sensory imprints—a smell of pines, soughing of wind through prairie cottonwoods, gophers popping up by quiet holes.

Lake Louise is more beautiful than she'd expected, Banff more touristy; she'd have been grateful for her West Coast hike even without what came with it. The prairies are not as flat as home or as featureless as advertised, but even so, between Calgary and Lake Superior it begins to blur: endless sunsets and wheatfields; red silos and small country towns. Picnicking near the turn-off to Rivers, loving in a motel in Winnipeg, she is unaware of any connection with the places where her grandfather studied sextant and astrotables to plot that first, heart-in-mouth blind flight. And yet her very existence has been created from those twists of fate; another course, another week, a mark lower or higher, and Ruth, landing on that air-field three years later, would have been met by some other airman. It doesn't take much to change a life, or make it.

For once, however, Megan is not interested in the links of fate. And when, much later, she looks through photograph albums, she will be surprised at how clear her memory is of the places they have visited, because at the time, whether they are in the car or out of it, her world consists of a small enclosed bubble in which nothing is real but Adam and her own emotions.

Blurring again through the expanses of rural Quebec and New Brunswick, not so much the fault of the forests as near-ness to journey's end. But it is not till Moncton, the last night

and by unspoken agreement an almost luxurious motel, that
Adam wakes and says, continuing Megan's 'What are we going
to do?' of a week earlier, 'Where are we going to live?'

This is not a question that Megan's grandfather or father
could, or did, ask. This is a question of their generation, but
momentous enough at any time.

'Compromise halfway,' she says, twirling the hairs on his
chest into tiny ringlets, 'Tahiti.'

He pictures her in grass skirt and lei. 'I'd never get to
work.' But adds, so as not to seem sexist or domineering,
'And your patients would forget why they came,' which also
sounds more sexist, or at least more about sex, than he'd
intended.

'We could spend a year in each place and then decide.'
Megan is glowing; more than happiness, she feels the chi of
her body coursing through its meridians like a palpable force.
If she'd been alone she would have bounced on the bed or
turned cartwheels, though if she'd been alone there wouldn't
have been the reason for it. The decision itself does not seem
particularly daunting to her—if the universe has seen fit to
bring them together, there will be a solution for the minor
technicalities of continents.

'We'll have to find out about qualifications and things,' says
Adam, more practised in bureaucracy than synchronicity and
fate. He knows that whichever direction they travel, there will
be interviews, medicals, police checks, work permits, visas,
possible problems with degrees and careers. The mud and ladders of their first week will be easy in comparison.

'Have I ever shown you this?' Megan asks, though of course
she hasn't, neither Canadian motels nor falling in love requiring proof of identity. 'Mum thought dual nationality might
come in handy one day. It's my Canadian citizenship card.
I must have been about seven.'

Since Adam does not look for omens, he doesn't see this
small, laminated photo-ID as anything more than a solution

to one possible, although extremely significant problem. Instead, as he studies the picture of a dark-haired, bright-eyed child, he's simply overwhelmed by his conviction. This, he thinks, is what our daughter will look like.

Chapter
TWELVE

*T*he number of objects in a house is finite; it's a law of physics, or ought to be. But if the house has been a family home for nearly two hundred years and includes a shed for storage, the sum total of the accumulation is so close to infinity that it doesn't much matter. And if the person trying to sort the accumulation into piles keeps stopping to read fifty-two years worth of letters, the task becomes exponentially greater. For by now, as well as Ruth's letters to Mary, Jane has found the drawer containing her own letters to her parents, the story of her life from age twenty-three to the present in weekly instalments.

By midnight Thursday she has cleared Ruth's bedroom and bathroom; she leaves Bill's coats for Mike and Rick to check. She has gone through her own bedroom, which takes longer even though there seems no point in packing till she knows when she's going. She's done a preliminary hunt through the bookcases and has found the signed copy of Winston's first novel, *Black Shadows in Acadia*, with his picture on the back. He's a better looking man than boy, but she's not sure if the emotion she feels is manufactured or real. She puts the book onto her private stack.

The bags for the Salvation Army have been dragged down to the shed, but she's kept away from windows and garden because she's still not ready to face the neighbours. But she's read most of her mother's letters and samples of her own, and maybe that's why she's forgotten to phone the Australian High Commission, and forgotten to try Ian in the hours when he could be in and awake. And perhaps it's the letters, and perhaps it's having three hours of sleep in forty-eight, or being in this home where Ian's never been and so can't be imagined, or forgetting that the phone is still off the hook and deciding that Ian's silence makes his death increasingly likely, but she's cried more than in all the years since her last miscarriage. A dead baby is a logical thing to cry for and so is a dead mother, but she's not sure that she's crying for Ruth.

This wouldn't be so hard, she thinks, if I'd visited more often! Which may or may not be true, but definitely leaves her feeling unfairly treated so that she's angry enough to make lists of demands to be resolved if she goes home—and she realises *if* has become a possibility—a dog, the EcoFarm job, her own spending money. Later still, as she's dumping plastic containers into yet another bag for the Salvos, it strikes her that it's twenty-eight years since she's tried to negotiate any of these things, and maybe Ian would have bent a little more with time if she hadn't surrendered unconditionally back then. Not a comfortable thought, and she bursts into tears again and wonders if this is what a nervous breakdown is like.

'Or maybe this *is* a nervous breakdown,' she thinks, and decides that if so she'd better get some sleep so she can get over it before her brothers arrive.

The night is cool and Jane, half waking to snuggle against Ian's warmth, is momentarily bereft at finding him not there.

I miss him, she thinks and the revelation stirs her; she wants to make love. What do people do for sex when they don't have husbands? By people she means middle-aged women, and specifically fifty-two year old, long-married women who aren't sure which continent they belong in. She doesn't find the answers appealing, and thinks instead about being in bed with Ian, and the way his hands can still obliterate everything except the sense of touch, as if her body is nothing but a collection of nerve ends to be stroked and sated. So many years since their games on the bus; control games, she thinks now, but no less erotic for that. She wonders if he'd play those games now, or if she would, and falls asleep wondering.

And wakes, early as the sun, still with a sense of altered reality and possibilities, so that when the horse appears through the morning mist in the old apple orchard behind the house, she lets herself believe that it belongs to Ruth. There are so many things her mother hadn't mentioned, a horse is minor in comparison. There is still a bridle in the shed, and a saddle, which is just as well because a last flicker of realism tells her that she is past the age for bareback riding, no matter how romantic and in keeping with her mood it might be. Perhaps most importantly, there's the sugar cube from her old riding coat and although this horse is probably too modern to have been given sugar, he recognises the outstretched palm with gift and the coaxing *tsk*, and after a quick canter around the field to demonstrate his independence sidles up to accept both bribe and bridle. Lochinvar's saddle fits him well though he's taller than Lockie had been. Fifteen two, Jane decides, stepping easily into her old way of measuring horses against her own height and absurdly smug that she remembers.

Gingerly around the apple orchard and he's a lovely boy, a dream horse, but the orchard is not a place for riding, with low branches and rough ground, and the horse's own paddock, as Jane calls it now, is his place for relaxing not work. She dismounts for the gate and then heads to the road, that long gravel road winding the rest of the way up to the top of the mountain before starting down towards Spa Springs, safely anonymous past the farms on this side, past the curve in the dark woods where Brennan used to shy and once bolted three miles before she could turn him for home, but this lovely boy trots on without a flicker. Where the road runs straight and sandy for a good kilometre along the crest of the mountain, they canter and it's as if she's always ridden him, has had years to accustom herself to his movement lively and smooth beneath her, his warm bulk between her legs. Her body doesn't know that it's been thirty years since she rode; it has no idea of age or gravity or tomorrow's stiffness and Jane follows its lead and feels nothing but this pure and simple joy of being astride the best horse she's ever ridden, on a soft fall morning past the forest and fields that are her soul's standard of beauty, in the land where she belongs.

That's it, she thinks, that's my answer. This is where I come from, this is where I should stay.

There's a group of new houses ahead where Lightfoots' farm used to be, houses too close to the road and she is no longer confident of remaining anonymous, or at least of the horse remaining so, so she turns, her golden boy responding to the gentlest touch of the reins, and they canter back to where the Dubois woods start, her woods. The path is still there where she used to ride Brennan, clearer even than the last time she used it as if the forest has opened its heart to her; face-slapping branches trimmed and the ground cleared of horse-tripping sticks. The blueberry clearing too is more open than she remembers, a secret meadow, large enough to canter in circles and figure eights, and then there is the log in the middle, a wind-toppled fir, a metre diameter—not high as jumps go, but as substantial as inevitable. She is leaning over the horse's neck, rising in her seat, knees gripping so firmly she could lose her stirrups and not falter, riding better than she's ever ridden, more alive than she's ever been.

The lovely boy gathers his haunches and springs, an effort-less float like a metaphor of freedom, and then fluidly to ground, Jane still with him and settling back into the saddle. She rubs his neck, 'Good boy, good horse,' and he's hot and sweating with that wonderful pungent horse smell, and they turn for home.

In the apple orchard again, her legs are jelly and not just from exercise. She finds brush and curry comb in the tack room and guiltily smooths away all traces of sweat and saddle marks; wipes saddle and bridle with a dish towel from the kitchen and shakes out the saddle blanket, all the while standing back, watching herself and wondering.

The horse belongs to Natalie Gillespie and they won something at the Halifax Royal last year—Jane doesn't remem-ber, may never have known exactly what—but she does most definitely know that this horse does not belong to her mother, was kept here because of the convenience of the good stable; a valuable, beloved horse that a deranged middle-aged woman had set at a great thick log which could have snapped one of its delicate legs. Or her own, because not falling off must have been a miracle after all this time, and if sorting out visas was not going to be much fun, doing it with a broken limb would have been a special kind of hell.

Twinges of pain are already creeping into her legs and bottom and even shoulders; when the muscles stop being jelly they will set stiff and sore. The puritan in her is glad, or would be if she didn't have to face the Gillespies so soon. She needs a hot shower but the phone call is more urgent still.

'Don't let it be the answering machine,' she prays, but it's Ian at the first ring as if he's been poised over the receiver, and then her own relief and a rush of love, overwhelming, reducing her jellied leg muscles to total surrender. Not that there isn't also a flippant flicker of relief, now she knows the nightmare's not true, at not having to sort out and pack up two farms in one week.

Ian's voice is irritable with anxiety; if she hadn't known better she'd have thought he was near tears. 'Has the phone been out of order? Every time I try it's engaged.'

It would be easier to say yes. 'I took it off the hook.'

Ian doesn't know that he's just been reprieved. He's still angry, but he does ask: 'Are you okay?'

'I'm okay.'

'You don't sound it.'

Neither does he, but one thing at a time. 'There's a problem with my visa. I need a re-entry permit for Australia.'

He explodes, which isn't like Ian, not on the phone. 'Fucking dickheads!'

'It'll be just a formality.'

'There shouldn't be any bloody formality, for Christ's sake! How long have you lived here? How many years have you paid taxes? And now you've got this new job; do they think just anyone could come along and do that?'

'I'm taping this!'

Ian's too angry to laugh.

'I'm not legally Australian.'

'But you're my *wife*!'

'It'll be okay,' she repeats. 'I'll start organising the visa and my ticket right away, and by the time I've sorted out the house with the boys it should be ready. Are you managing okay there?'

'It's not me; it's Mum. She bought herself a puppy, and of course the bloody thing tripped her up when she was going to bed last night and broke her hip. A friend found her this morning when she didn't turn up for some excursion. She'd been on the floor the whole night.'

Now he *is* crying. So's Jane. She doesn't want Dulcie to die, not now, not yet; it's all too much.

'Is she going to be alright?'

'I don't know; the doctor says so. She looks bloody awful. You want the good news?'

'There is some?'

'You've got a dog. Mum doesn't want it put down—all she cared about when I got to the hospital was what was going to happen to the puppy, stupid thing, like a fluffy white rat.'

'So who's looking after it now?'

'I am; he's just gone to sleep on my lap. Little bugger was crying so much about being on the floor, you'd never have been able to hear me.'

Jane's been married for a long time, she doesn't laugh, though she might tease later. 'Never mind, I'll be home soon. He'll probably settle once he gets into a routine.'

'He better.'

'Your mum's going to want him back when she's strong enough. But I've been thinking that I really want a dog of my own. This might be the best time to get one. They'll be company for each other, and I'll train them so hers will be well behaved enough for her to handle.'

An instant's silence, barely more than the echo gap of the satellite connection. 'A little dog, you mean, like this?'

'Maybe a bit bigger. Something big enough to follow a horse and small enough to be in the house.'

Another instant's gap. 'It's up to you. They'd keep you busy, but you might be right, they mightn't whinge as much with two. And don't forget to get rid of that email before your brothers get there.'

Winston's? she wonders. The adoptees'?

'The one I sent last night.'

'I haven't checked yet.'

'Doesn't matter. You don't have to bother reading it.'

She nearly doesn't. He sounds just embarrassed enough that she knows it will be description of some problem with machinery or cows, petty now compared to his mother's real disaster. He'll have told her to hurry up and get home, make sure her brothers do their fair share because he can't run this farm on his own, which will also seem petty now that getting home has become so complicated. Right this moment she doesn't want to know about farm dramas she can do nothing about, and she doesn't want to feel irritated with Ian while she sorts out her own problems.

But it's impossible to delete without reading.

I've been trying to phone you but it's always engaged. I got your message so I know you got there okay, but call me right away, even if it wakes me up, because I know you're alone out there and I hope everything's alright.

It's lonely here without you. Standing at the airport window watching your plane leave was such a lonely feeling I didn't think it could get worse, but tonight it has. It's strange to think that even though you've left England you're still not on your way home.

Sue asked me over for tea tonight but I didn't go; one of the heifers broke a feeder in the dairy, and by the time I fixed that I didn't feel like talking to anyone except you, so I stayed home in case your phone started working again and you called. It's nearly midnight now and I'm absolutely dead but I can't sleep. I miss you even more than the last time you went away, or maybe I've forgotten how bad that was too. You'll think I'm a sentimental old fool but I got out the photograph album of the bus trip. It was a long time ago but you haven't changed that much. I was thinking about the first day, and seeing you there at the bus stop in that blue blouse just the same colour as your eyes, and when you smiled at me I knew the bus trip was going to be alright, and I wanted to get to know you. That's what I've always told you but what I really wanted was to sleep with you and it was all I could think about the whole time we were in Paris and everywhere until it finally happened.

Tonight when I couldn't sleep and the bed was so cold and empty without you curled up beside me, I started thinking about it, which probably wasn't a great idea but for some reason I thought of how awkward it was getting undressed in that little tent, and that started me remembering that night in Gallipoli when I first saw you naked, and it was too dark to see much but I could imagine the rest and in the morning it was just as good as I thought. I think I can remember everything we did that night, every touch and taste and how it felt, and then I thought about other times that have been special, like when you came home from Canada when Megan was a baby and I thought you'd be too tired to have sex but you weren't, and last month the first day the cows went out and we stayed in bed all morning. And I thought about how lucky we are to still have that. That's why I was writing to you except I wasn't going to say all that about sex, but I thought maybe you were lonely too in your mum's house and I wanted to tell you how much I miss you, and not just in bed and not just in the dairy but just talking and being together. I really love you, Jane.

She would have called the Australian High Commission anyway; thinks now that she's always known, somewhere deep at the back of her mind, what her decision would be. Certainly since she heard his voice on the phone. But the letter makes a difference; such a difference between uncertainty and clarity, between duty and desire.

The call will be lengthy, complicated and undoubtedly frustrating; she goes first to her purse for the other kind of Visa and the card from the antique shop in Chelsea.

'That Royal Worcester tea setting—I'd like it shipped to Australia.'

She is at the window seat of her parents' bedroom with a pile of photograph albums, small black and white pictures subtitled in her mother's handwriting. A young Ruth in this same window seat with newborn babe: *Jane at two days*, says the caption, and the next: *Bill's first day home*, both her parents standing at the fireplace in the parlour, her father holding the bundled baby. They are gazing at each other over the baby's head, as if they could not bear to glance away even for the photographer, but it's the way they lean into each other, an indefinable intimacy, that makes Jane's eyes mist until she has to blink and look away.

A car is coming down the road, slowing and turning into the driveway; it's smaller than she'd expect farming neighbours to own and dustier than the rental car her brothers will arrive in. Jane puts the album down without the feeling of panic she might have had yesterday: she's had some sleep and she's ready for whoever it might be. The perspective from her window transforms the scene to a tableau of homecoming, and is perhaps also the reason for the strong sensation of déjà vu. A young man gets out, stretching with arms extended while a young woman steps from the passenger seat, her face obscured as she gazes over the fields and orchard, until she turns to put her hand on the young man's arm in the same gesture Ruth has in the photograph, and her face in that moment is Ruth's as well.

And Jane is completely and utterly disoriented, because she knows that Ruth is dead, and knows that even if it were some other woman's ashes sitting in the box on the bed, the Ruth outside the window is half a century younger than the Ruth that was Jane's mother—and yet her heart leaps in recognition to say, Look! It's all right. Here she is after all. There is no thought that this could be a ghost, because even through the window the woman's corporeal state—and the man's and the dusty little blue car's—are all too plain, but it seems quite feasible that time has become confused so that past and present and very possibly future have all been seamlessly blended. Which might become distressing if dwelt on for long, but in this frozen moment is a deeply satisfying realisation.

Then the young woman turns to face the house and Jane

sees that her heart's recognition had not been mistaken, only her head's, and the blending of past and future not as bizarre as it had at first seemed, because it is now clear that the woman is Megan and that the young man is her lover. They are united by the same, though still indefinable, link she's just observed in the photograph—she recognises the way they turn to each other as the way Ruth and Bill did, as the way she and Ian do, an intimate reassurance before facing outsiders. She sees, too, as Megan tucks her hair behind her ears in what Jane knows is her own mannerism, that although Megan is not a reincarnation of Ruth, parts of Ruth will live on in her, as they do in Jane, and that Jane herself will live on in Megan and in any children Megan may have.

In the end we're nothing but the stories that other people remember, her mother had written not very long ago, but Jane sees now that the truth is more, and greater. The line extends back further than we can remember, and is less of a line than a web as genes overlap with myth and memory. Ruth's unknown parents will continue to exhibit their secret heritage in colour of eye, wave of hair and quirk of wit, but the Townsends who loved and raised her will also live on, in the passion for books and learning that their great-grand-daughter shares, and in the heritage that will be passed on, story by story, until Megan's own great-grand-daughter may not know exactly who it was that learned to fly or moved to Australia, but understand that these snippets are part of the past that make her who she is.

Jane sees, too, that the same web gives strength to the present, and is the reason that she will be strong enough to live at the opposite end of the world from her daughter if she must, just as she has from her mother, because the links that bind them are as intangible and as real as the earth's meridians that divide them.

Then Megan glances up, sees her and waves, laughing with excitement, and the scene is no longer a tableau of new generations reflecting the past or a potential of new histories —it is her own dear daughter and perhaps a new son, who have driven right across Canada to be with her, and Jane runs down the stairs to meet them.

NOTES ON SOURCES

Chapter 1

GIRL FLIER'S FIGHT FOR LIFE; SIX FEET ABOVE SHARK-INFESTED SEAS: 'Highlights of the Century: 1930–1932' *Knowledge*, no. 201, vol. 17, Purnell & Sons Lit, Paulton, Nr Bristol, 1964, p. 3217.

'poor little typist': Grey, Elizabeth 1966 *Winged Victory: The Story of Amy Johnson*, Constable Young Books, London.

'The hand that rocks the cradle wrecks the kite': Fahie, Michael 1995 *A Harvest of Memories: The Life of Pauline Gower MBE*, GMS Enterprises, Petersborough, UK.

Chapter 2

'He was in logic a great critic
Profoundly skilled in analytic
He could distinguish, and divide
A hair 'twixt south and south-west side': Butler, Samuel 'Hudibras', quoted in the Literary Calendar of 8.2.2000, edited by Timothy Ervin of Yasuda Women's University, Hiroshima, Japan, http://litcal.yasuda-u.ac.jp

Chapter 3

'My ebb is come, his life was my spring tide': Dyer, Edward 1593 'Elegy on the Death of Sir Philip Sidney', *Oxford Dictionary of Quotations*, Fifth Edition, Oxford University Press, Oxford, p. 286.

'the moon on the breast of the new-fallen snow': Moore, Clement C 1823 'A Visit From St Nicholas', *Random House Book of Poetry for Children*, 1983, Random House, New York, p. 50.

Chapter 4

'The female of the species is more deadly than the male': Kipling, Rudyard, 1911, 'The Female of the Species', *Kipling: A Selection of his Stories and Poems*, vol. II, Doubleday & Co, Garden City New York, 1956, p. 453.

Chapter 6

'You blocks, you stones, you worse then senseless things!
Oh you hard hearts, you cruel men of Rome, knew you not Pompey?': Shakespeare, William 1599 *Julius Caesar*, in *Tragedies, Everyman's Library*, vol. 155, 1906, J M Dent & Sons, London.

Chapter 7

'Oh woman-country, wooed not wed,
Loved all the more by earth's male lands
Laid to their hearts instead!': Browning, Robert, 'By the Fireside', *Sean Miller's Book Page*, http//denmead.cc/books/browning_fireside.htm

'green and pleasant land'; 'dark satanic mills': Blake, William, 1804–10 *Milton* (Preface), Shambala Publications, 1978, Boulder, Colorado, in association with Random House, New York, p. 62.

Chapter 9

'lovely, dark and deep': Robert Frost, 'Stopping by Woods on a Snowy Evening', Frost, Robert 1923 *Selected Poems*, 1973, Penguin, London, p. 130.

Chapter 10

'And is there honey still for tea?': Brooke, Rupert 1912 'The Old Vicarage, Grantchester', *1914 and Other Poems*, 1999, Penguin, London, p. 53.

Chapter 11

'When Robert Frost was asked why he didn't write free verse, he replied, "I'd just as soon play tennis with the net down."': *Newsweek*, 30.1.56, quoted in the Literary Calendar, edited by P. Timothy Ervin, Yasuda Women's University Hiroshima, Japan, http://litcal.yasuda-u.ac.jp